About the Author

I was born in Northern Ireland, moving to New Zealand with my husband and son in 1999. I had trained as a teacher, and thoroughly enjoyed my profession until resigning to write the book that had been rumbling around in my head for so long. Teaching was my ambition, but writing is my dream. Aged six, I told my Mum I would write a book some day, not knowing it would take this long. Writing is a passion I can indulge in a beautiful and safe part of the world.

Feb

Aleata Fullerton

Feb

Olympia Publishers
London

www.olympiapublishers.com
OLYMPIA PAPERBACK EDITION

A CIP catalogue record for this title is
available from the British Library.

ISBN: 978-1-80074-599-5

First Published in 2022

**Olympia Publishers
Tallis House
2 Tallis Street
London
EC4Y 0AB**

Printed in Great Britain

Dedication

I dedicate this book to the men in my life. My husband Cameron, my son John and his partner Glenn and my grandson Sean

Acknowledgements

I acknowledge the encouragement and unfailing support of my wonderful husband Cameron without whom this book may never have been finished. Also Ilone Hanne , for her wonderful advice and guidance.

Month	Known as	
January	Jan	Second to last month to be created. Was last in calendar, but now first. Market gardener and brewer of dark beer favoured by the Irish. Plays the piano.
February	February (Feb)	Sculptor and catcher of rabbits. Great musician playing guitar, banjo and ukulele. Last month to be created with fewer days than anyone else.
March	March	Healer maker of potions. Sings beautifully. Was originally the first month as named after Mars the chief Roman god.
April	Ari (Aristophanes)	Entertainer. Playwriter and practical joker. Can play any instrument, current favourite is the saxophone.
May	May	Baker and cook. Good friend to February. Good listener to anyone in trouble. Plays the drums.
June	June	Accountant and financial advisor. Enjoys the company of Ari and February. Plays the cello.
July	July (Jules)	Librarian and maker of scented candles, and soaps. Her lover, Paulinus died in battle, he was a centurion.
August	Gust	Ostman (Viking). Worker in metal and catcher of rabbits. Plays the

		flute and clarinet.
September	Ember	Cares for the river and catches fish for food. Lived in Ireland and brews the dark beer favoured there. Loves to sing.
October	Tober	Works on the farm, enjoys working with horses. Plays the violin.
November	Vem	Unofficial leader of the Months. Looks after the animals and grows the crops.
December	Dec	Builder and worker in wood. Friend of Gust.

Watcher

Watcher	Planet under their care	
Stolesc	Mercury	Votes by whistling to show approval. Large being who is afraid of no one, but cautious in his dealings with Hiemal.
Neja	Venus	From the Fire World on the other side of the Milky Way Galaxy. Natural enemy of Uclairians.
t'Hura	Earth	From Efriston – money lenders to the galaxy.
Thades	Hernian	Has mottled skin which glows to show approval. Only makes one friend in a

		lifetime. Brews Pestiar wine.
Verna	Jupiter	From Rofetsd- a world of interacting vegetation. A kind and gentle soul.
Dynak	Saturn	The last of her kind. She can communicate directly into the mind of those she chooses. A wise woman.
Balack	Uranus	A large, insecure person who has a good heart but often makes mistakes. Enjoys Pestiar wine brewed by Thades.
Kalend	Neptune	Presidion of this System Watch. Becomes Watcher of the Months. A clever and honest person.
Hiemal	Pluto	From the house of Uclair. An arrogant, and angry person who resents his position within this Watch
Tir Dhuchais	Land where the System watch live and meet.	
Sen Thorien	Head of the Senaten	Uncle of Hiemal. Careful to put the needs of his House of Uclair before the needs of the Senaten.
Sen Glarte	Member of the Senaten	Sponsor of Kalend as Presidion. An honest person who resents the deceit found

		in his political world.
Rogue	Creature of Tir Dhuchais	Friend of Kalend who enjoys going fishing with him. He has an important part to play in the unfolding story.
Quaan	Creatures from an unknown world	The Quaan collect and store the memories from beings across the universe. The Months are among their favourite sources.

"I am Presidion Kalend"

"No, Feb, you can't."

"If you have a better idea, Gust, let me have it. If not, it's the only way. I have to try."

Tober, July, Ember and Dec joined them. Looking at the missing part of the path and the raging torrent below the cliff face, they agreed with Gust. Ember had been silent as the others begged Feb not to try to cross it, but now spoke.

"Feb is right. We can't go back and we can't stay here. I know you have to try Feb, but if you can't make it, come back and we will find another way. Just be careful, please."

"I have no more desire to fall into that whirlpool than you have. I intend to be careful."

Turning the knot on the rope around so it was behind him – letting him get closer to the rockface – Feb began his climb. The first part was relatively easy with both hand and foot holds within reach, but then he reached a section where it looked like a slice of the rockface had been washed away. The remaining surface was smooth as glass. He had no choice but to climb higher. The trailing rope became heavier making a difficult climb impossible.

"Gust, hold the rope up off the ground. It's dragging me down."

Gust, Dec and Tober rushed to help, holding the rope above their heads and feeding it out as he climbed. Feb was now well above the water, but the rockface was wet and slippery. Both feet slipped from crumbling projections, leaving him dangling by his fingertips several metres above the swirling water. With no food for over a day, he was exhausted and feared he would fall. The shouted encouragement of the others could no longer sustain him; his strength was gone. All this for an extra day. If he fell, the Quest would fail, and their destruction was assured. Desperately trying to lift himself just a little higher, his searching feet found only air. His fingers began to slip.

Back in the Chamber of Watchers, Kalend stared, silently helpless as Feb's strength failed him. All in the Chamber held their breath. Kalend wished he had never gone to see Glarte, never found out the truth about the Senaten. It was his wounded pride that had orchestrated the arrival of Feb and his friends. Perhaps if things had been done differently…

Kalend recalled with great clarity how he had felt as a newly appointed Presidion so long ago. In the System under his care, nine planets orbited a star on the edge of the Milky Way galaxy. He was confident and optimistic as he visited the Carina Nebula to prepare a home where he and eight Watchers would live. Tir Dhuchais, meaning homeland in his native tongue, was within easy reach of their new worlds. A Watcher was appointed to encourage and oversee each world's development and had been selected from across the universe. While Kalend had been given their names, he knew nothing more of them.

On the day appointed for the Watch to meet, Kalend waited in the Chamber he had prepared; all System Watch business would be conducted here. He stood beside the large, central table surveying his handiwork. He had wrestled enormous stone slabs from what had been barren land. They now formed the walls of the Chamber with inner surfaces like polished glass. Outside the stone was still rough and textured. Tall Hrutnim trees grew between them; their distinctive red branches finding every crack and crevice as they stretched out to tightly embrace each stone. Their topmost branches reached overhead to hold the clear dome that filled the central expanse. Through this, a shimmering star-studded sky could be seen. Despite the darkness of the night sky, the Chamber was filled with a soft, clear light that cast no shadows, filling Kalend with hope that this would be a place of harmony and collaboration.

Dressed in his favourite dun coloured tunic and trousers, and without his staff or cloak of office, Kalend should have looked unimpressive, but no one could deny his air of authority. A Presidion's leadership should never be questioned by those in his Watch, but Kalend believed in equality, truth, and justice; he would seek and expect the best from his Watchers and would give his best in return.

A slender, dark-haired woman was first to arrive. Kalend felt a rush of warmth envelop him, while words whispered in his mind.

"Presidion, there are few who can correctly say my name in the language of my world, so here I will be known as Dynak."

The warmth flowed from him, leaving an unexpected sense of emptiness. Before he could reply, a man entered, dressed entirely in black with the distinctive grey and cream mottled skin indicating he was Hernian. Renowned for their reticence and solitary preferences, Hernians seldom associated with others, but if a friendship were to be made, it would last forever. Raising both bent arms to shoulder height, he bowed his head in the Hernian gesture of respect.

"I am Thades."

"I am Kalend and this is Dynak. Welcome to my Watch."

Sounds of laughter from outside alerted them to the arrival of others. Into the chamber strode a group of three with a tall, well-muscled man escorting a woman on either arm. The man's golden hair reached almost to the ground behind him, while his smile radiated warmth and a cheerful disposition. On his left was a generously proportioned woman with a cheery, motherly face, while the other was short with a boyish figure, vibrant red hair, and the startling red eyes of the Fire World in a distant galaxy.

All three bowed to Kalend, but it was the man who spoke.

"Presidion, we are glad to be here. I am Stolesc. Let me introduce my fellow companions. On my left is the delightful t'Hura and on my right the equally wonderful Neja."

They stood around the refreshment table sharing a little of who they were. Kalend observed that while Thades smiled at the often witty conversation of the red haired Neja, he listened rather than speaking.

When Dynak saw Kalend watching her speaking aloud to the others, she sent a feeling of warmth over him again.

"I can speak openly, or just to those I wish to hear."

It was obvious no one else heard her words and seeing his bemused expression, her laugh whispered in his mind.

Neja commented on the mirrored surface of the inner walls and with all turning to admire Kalend's work, they failed to notice the next arrival, hearing only the sound of an autocratic voice.

"We are Hiemal of Uclair."

A striking figure with white hair gathered at the nape of his neck and the blue cloak of Uclair draped around his shoulders stood in the entrance. Neja turned to face Hiemal, dislike clearly on her face. For many aeons of time, a feud existed between the hot and passionate Fire World people and the cool, detached House of Uclair.

t'Hura was confused by the 'we' and asked Thades if there

was a companion of Hiemal that was yet to arrive.

"It is a characteristic of Uclairian men to refer to themselves in the plural, nothing more." Dynak spoke to Kalend's mind.

"I have never heard of an Uclairian being appointed as a Watcher."

Kalend glanced at her but made no reply. Fear and respect would be felt by many throughout the Galaxy by just a glimpse of a blue cloak; the wearer could, and did, expect obedience from any they considered to be inferior, and there were few they considered equals.

Hiemal let his gaze fall briefly on each of them. Icy-blue eyes now stared directly at Kalend who greeted him.

"Welcome Hiemal, I am Presidion Kalend."

Kalend hadn't felt the need to introduce himself as Presidion to anyone else and silently rebuked himself for being unnerved by Hiemal's arrival. He had been unaware that one of his Watchers would be from Uclair and felt the first stirring of unease. The slight, upward tilt of Hiemal's chin together with the tone of his voice, spoke of an arrogance designed to be intimidating.

Following Hiemal's arrival, there was a noticeable change in what had been a cheerful, relaxed atmosphere in the Chamber. The only time anyone knew of an Uclairan being a Watch member was if he were Presidion. A time of cautious exchanges passed before a large man with a halo of brown hair and a petulant expression arrived. His flamboyant clothing billowed around his rotund figure. He looked around briefly before bowing to Hiemal.

"Presidion, I am Balack. It is an honour to have a member of Uclair as Presidion of this System."

Hiemal smirked, making no attempt to conceal his

amusement. He inclined his head and pointed towards Kalend.

"Welcome Balack, I am Presidion Kalend."

An embarrassed Balack, bowed even more deeply to Kalend.

"Forgive my mistake, Presidion. Oh dear, oh dear, just weary after the journey."

"Do not concern yourself. Please greet your fellow Watchers."

Balack moved quickly to join the others where Hiemal continued to dominate the conversation. He regarded Stolesc for a short time before addressing him directly.

"Stolesc, my uncle has often visited your home world in his capacity as leader of the Senaten."

The Senaten was the governing body for System Watches and was made up of twenty-five Sen from the most powerful Houses in the universe. Their primary function was to assess those wishing to be Watchers, and then pairing those chosen with the needs of the planets. All Presidions had to spend time as a Watcher until selected to join the Hoameta, or lower tier of government, answerable to the Senaten.

Stolesc was unimpressed by Hiemal's blatant name dropping.

"Sen Thorien has often been a guest in our home but I have never heard him mention you."

Kalend watched but would not intervene in this jostling for position unless it became unpleasant or aggressive.

Going outside to wait for the arrival of the last Watcher, Kalend saw a slight, disheveled figure hurrying towards him and went to meet her.

"You must be Verna. Please do not hurry, I am Kalend and the meeting cannot start without me."

Verna had sparkling, silver hair which had been tastefully

arranged before commencing her journey, but several strands now fell loosely around her smiling face.

"Presidion, forgive my lateness, but the growing plants are so unusual; I am afraid I stopped to admire every one of them."

Kalend smiled warmly.

"I am pleased you approve of your new home and know already that other Watchers share your interest."

As they walked, he noticed a dirty hem and a tear in the edge of her cloak; his face showed his concern.

"Have you suffered harm?"

"No, no. I am fine. Some green creatures came out of the forest and surrounded me. In my haste to get away, one of their tusks became tangled in my clothing, but I am unhurt."

"Aah, those would be the Neutsche. They look fearsome but are harmless. They simply came to you in the hope you would feed them, which would be most unwise unless you plan to adopt them on a permanent basis."

Verna laughed and it seemed the trees around them rustled in accompaniment. As she spoke, the trees fell silent.

"Should we not go to the Chamber? I have kept you waiting too long."

Kalend felt an affinity with this gentle woman and would have given her time to tidy herself, but insisting she was fine, they entered the Chamber arm in arm.

Neja and Dynak noticing Verna's appearance, came to ask if she was in need of care. Verna smiled widely in response and embraced the two women, assuring them she was splendid.

Kalend was glad Verna was among them. Her warm and gentle nature was in sharp contrast to the solitude of Thades, the cold superiority of Hiemal, and the fiery temperament of Neja.

"Fellow Watchers, welcome Verna. She has spent some

unplanned time in the company of the local wildlife, but I assure her and you all, there is nothing here that is harmful to you."

Introductions made, Kalend sat in the Presidion's seat of office and the other Watchers joined him, reclining their chairs to watch the sky above. Hiemal took the chair directly opposite Kalend and invited t'Hura to sit on his right. He had learned she was from Efriston, a house responsible for financing many ventures in the galaxy. An Uclairian would not normally associate with money lenders, but it was never too early to form a useful alliance.

Silence fell and Kalend began.

"The inaugural meeting of a System Watch is a time of excitement and responsibility. The planets in this system are greatly varied in size and composition, but all are equally valued and in need of committed Watchers."

The stars above them began to move faster before slowing as one star shone brightly, surrounded by nine orbiting worlds. All watchers could see immediately why Kalend had spoken as he had. Each planet in turn came close so it could be observed. Some were giants, while others were small, but one stood out from the others.

The third planet from the sun was like no world anyone had seen. It was blue, shining like a precious gem. As it rotated before them, each could see something from their home world.

Balack saw mighty mountains reminding him of similar features from the land around his home. Neja's face shone as she watched fire and molten rock spew from mountains – like the fire mountains on her home world.

t'Hura, Stolesc, and Verna were entranced by the proliferation and variety of green growing life; all three felt an affinity for the blue and green world above them.

Verna's eyes swept from growing plants, to flying creatures, and felt a pang of homesickness for the joyful movement of life she had left behind in her home world of Rofetsd.

Dynak's face showed little emotion as she watched creatures of differing shapes and sizes, while an expanse of red dirt brought a fleeting memory to Thades of hunting with his father as a youngling.

Hiemal's normally expressionless face was bathed in delight as he observed water covering huge parts of the surface. He had been introduced to water almost from birth and could move through and under it with ease. There was no doubt this blue world was to be his.

As the blue planet moved from their gaze to be replaced by the next world, an audible sigh escaped the lips of those gathered below; the desire to be Watcher of this world was strong.

The planet closest to the Star would normally be considered the most favoured, but the blue planet was undoubtedly the prize of this system. Stolesc, like many others, wished for the blue planet, but was certain such a treasure would be allocated to a person of importance. If not to be Presidion, then why else would Hiemal be here?

All worlds having passed before them, Kalend took a pouch from his belt tossing nine equally sized, clear spheres into the air.

Seeing the desire for the blue planet on each face, Kalend spoke clearly. He wanted to leave no room for misunderstanding.

"The allocation of these worlds has been determined by the Senaten. The qualities you each possess have determined the world with which you have been paired."

Watchers were mesmerised as the spheres began to circle one another, some growing, others diminishing or changing colour, until they resembled the nine worlds above them. They waited expectantly as one by one the spheres emitted a soft glow before gently dropping in front of their paired Watcher. As each Watcher touched their sphere, an unbreakable bond filled them with a sense of belonging and acceptance.

Verna was to be Watcher of the largest world, Dynak the one with the vibrant rings. Stolesc was paired with the smallest world, the one closest to the Sun. Balack with the seventh, Thades the fourth, Kalend the eighth and Neja the second.

Just two remained. The blue one and the small grey one on the outer edge of the system. t'Hura and Hiemal waited, both sure Hiemal would be Watcher of the blue planet.

The spheres now rotated above where they sat. As the blue sphere began to drop, Hiemal reached out his hand for it, but it spun away from him before dropping beside t'Hura.

Hiemal's outstretched hand fell back to his side as the small grey world fell softly beside him. Refusing to touch it, he pushed his chair back and jumped to his feet. Seeing everyone's eyes on him, he strode to the refreshment table. His world remained alone on the table and lost the glow which should have formed the bond with its Watcher.

Hiemal cleared a platter and put nine glasses on it. His hands were shaking. Was it not enough he had been sent to an insignificant system without the humiliation of this paltry world? He poured the golden drink into each glass unaware Verna had come to join him. She saw and felt his pain and disappointment before touching his arm in the gesture of friendship of her people and spoke softly.

"I am sure there must be something wonderful in your world for it to have you as its Watcher.'

Hiemal shook her hand free and hissed his response. "How dare you presume to touch us? We do not want or need your pity."

The outrage in his voice and anger on his face made Verna recoil. She hurried back to the table where t'Hura lovingly gazed at her blue sphere. She could not believe this world was to be hers. Becoming a Watcher was a surprise, but this world filled her with a sense of pride in herself; t'Hura resolved to be the best Watcher she could be.

A sense of grateful contentment filled each Watcher, with only Hiemal feeling he had been unfairly judged. Composing his features, he returned with the tray of drinks which he passed around, then raised his glass.

"The allocation of worlds is complete. Let us hope each world will thrive as it should under the care of the Watcher selected to be paired with it."

As they raised their glasses, only Balack could see Hiemal's clenched fist and the blood that seeped from the cuts his fingernails made in his palm. He was concerned Hiemal hadn't touched his sphere before it lost its ability to bond with him. This was a proud and angry man who would find no comfort here without the contentment given by his world.

Before leaving the Chamber to explore their new home, Kalend explained that time in Tir Dhuchais had been aligned with the orbit of the blue planet. Normally this would have been done using the world closest to the sun, but the blue world had been selected by the Senaten, reinforcing its importance but with no explanation of its significance being given.

Opening a box containing nine rings, Kalend gave one to each Watcher. Each had a large crystal in the centre. These were always to be worn and served two purposes. The first purpose was as a communication and location device, the second as an indicator of the motivation of the wearer.

Hiemal objected. "All Watchers make a solemn vow to

respect the Chamber in which they serve. Why do you feel it necessary to challenge our integrity?"

Balack added his voice to Hiemal's objection and a foul smell filled the chamber. Neja and Dynak covered their noses, both unaware this was how someone from Balack's world showed displeasure.

Kalend spoke firmly.

"The wearing of rings is not a matter for debate. They are used throughout the universe. The rings communicate through contact with the skin of the wearer. Only when a Watcher is speaking in the Chamber will the crystal show colour. A clear crystal will indicate a calm indifference. Gold is for love, silver for truth, blue for compassion, yellow for fear, green for envy or contempt, orange for sorrow, red for anger, purple for a lie and black for hate."

Kalend waited to give everyone time to absorb all he had said before continuing.

"A purple crystal for a lie will mean the removal of the Watcher for a time determined by the Watch. Anyone causing a black crystal will face serious disciplinary procedures and possible removal from the Watch. A black crystal has never been seen, and I am sure this will not happen here."

After a pause when mutterings could be heard, Balack replaced his smell with the gentle aroma of approval. Kalend called for silence once more.

"The first task of a Watcher is to name the planet they have been given. You will visit your world, returning for the important Naming Ceremony. Your world will be known to itself and throughout the galaxy by the name you choose. Choose carefully."

Upon hearing these words, Verna couldn't wait and vanished

from sight as she travelled by thought to her new world. Stolesc smiled at her sudden departure.

"It seems Verna is more impetuous than I would have anticipated."

The Chamber quickly emptied, only Kalend remained, looking at his ring. Appearing to be identical to the ones given to the Watchers, his was subject to his will allowing him to choose whether to allow or to prevent the crystal revealing his emotions. As Presidion, he would be privy to information from the Senaten which may not be for the Watch to hear. If asked about certain matters, it would be important for him to withhold facts without discovery. This deception did not sit easily with him.

Hiemal visited his small world, staring with mortification and chagrin at a barren landscape devoid of water or a single growing plant. Returning to Tir Dhuchais almost immediately, he began changing the humble dwelling he had been given into a grand home resembling the great house of his parents. His position as a person of importance would never be doubted here.

"The Naming of Worlds"

Kalend called the Naming of Worlds meeting but t'Hura was late, hurrying back when she learned everyone was waiting.

As Watchers began to take their seats, Kalend stopped them.

"From now, Watchers will sit around this table in the order their worlds are from the sun. Stolesc will begin by taking the first seat on my left."

t'Hura was glad not to be seated next to Hiemal, who was furious his key position opposite Kalend was now occupied by Verna. With no reasonable grounds to object, Hiemal found himself seated on Kalend's right.

With chairs reclined, each world would appear so its Watcher could give it a name. Watchers would show their approval in the manner used by their species. Kalend would begin with his world, then Stolesc with the others following in turn.

The eight-planet appeared above them as Kalend began.

"My world is the smallest of the gas planets, with storms raging in its thick atmosphere. It has a mantle of super compacted warm ice made of water, ammonia and methane. It has rings, dark in colour so not evident from a distance. It has fourteen moons so I name it in honour of the fourteenth ruler of my home world. I name my world Neptune."

Neptune, Neptune, Neptune was chanted by those around the table while each showed their approval. Dynak was relieved when Balack emitted a pleasant aroma declaring his liking for the name.

Stolesc stood to speak. "My world is the smallest but is

nevertheless beautiful. It has a core of metal with a mantle of rock; its mantle is somewhat smaller than originally intended, but a collision with a large asteroid smashed a large part of it away. What remains is bone dry and as smooth as glass. If this were to happen again, I would probably be able to put my world in my pocket and bring it here to show you."

This caused a ripple of laughter around the table.

"The smooth surface reminds me of the field of play in a challenge faced by the strongest and fittest young people on my home world. This challenge is known as Mercur and I name my world Mercury."

Watchers chanted Mercury, Mercury, Mercury, while Neja opened her mouth to emit a small flame of approval. Balack was startled, and glad he was not sitting opposite her.

Neja was next. "Like Mercury, my world has a metal core and a mantle of rock, but it's different in one respect from any of the others in this system. All your worlds spin around their axis in the same direction, but my world spins extremely slowly in the other. One rotation takes longer than one orbit of the star. It's indescribably hot on my world and there is a fire mountain on its surface. A favourite food for my family is a hot, slow cooked dish prepared in a vessel called a Vena. I name my hot, slow turning world – Venus."

Venus, Venus, Venus.

Glancing across the table, Stolesc was surprised to discover the warm glow felt by everyone came from Dynak. She was pushing the warmth towards them from a hand held in front of her.

t'Hura rose slowly and then turned to Kalend. "Presidion, I am still undecided about the name for my world, so could I name it after the others?"

29

Before Kalend could reply, Hiemal snorted.

"Oh, for goodness sake, just think of something. It's not as if it really matters anyway."

"Hiemal, your comment is uncalled for. The naming of worlds is of great importance; perhaps you need to consider your position here if you fail to appreciate that."

Kalend stared at him until he stood, gave a small bow, and apologized to t'Hura.

Kalend continued. "t'Hura, all worlds must receive a name today, but I will come back to you for your decision."

While Kalend had agreed to the extra time, his tone showed an irritation that despite the amount of time she had spent time on her world, she hadn't yet made her choice.

Thades stood, stretching out his arms at shoulder height then spreading them to the side while bowing his head to show respect not just to Kalend, but to all.

"My world is also metal based with a rocky mantle. It is larger than Mercury and Venus but smaller than the Blue planet. The surface is covered in a red dust, but the core has a lake of ice. Hernian males learn to hunt a small evasive creature called an Egiotj on the red sand hills of Hernia. I learned to hunt with my father and name my world in his honour. My world is Mars."

Balack liked how Verna raised both arms, entwining and turning them slowly as if in a dance to show her approval.

Mars. Mars. Mars.

Verna spoke of her world in excited, glowing terms. "This is a huge gas giant, more than ten times the size of the Blue planet. It has a large red spot that can easily be seen from a great distance; it's rings are dark in colour and it has sixty-five moons. I don't intend to give them all names, but I have called one with a liquid surface Europa. I spent my time listening to the sounds of my world and it told me it already has a name. That name is Jupiter."

The cream patches on Thades' skin glowed softly in appreciation.

Jupiter. Jupiter. Jupiter.

Dynak stood. "My world is also an enormous place, with a violent, constantly moving atmosphere. Yet it is a gas, so light it could float in a pool of water, were a pool big enough to be found. My world's many coloured rings can be seen from great distances in the system. On my home world, a multi-coloured skin, filled with a weightless liquid, is a toy for children. It is called a Sat Urn, so I name my world Saturn."

Neja was finding it difficult not to laugh as Stolesc tossed his head back and howled in approval but considered t'Hura's nodding head rather dull.

Saturn. Saturn. Saturn.

Balack was a little nervous and cleared his throat. "Aahem. My world is also one of those gas planets, and has a ring of dust, rubble and lumps of ice around it. I have named one of its moons Miranda after my sister, as it has steep ice cliffs as cold as her personality. Neja, Venus may rotate in the opposite way from the rest of our worlds, but mine has its axis so tilted it is almost on its side and it spins around the sun in this manner. I name my world Uranus which means to recline."

Kalend, seeing his nervousness slapped his hand on the table while Hiemal's eyes shone, filling the space around him with a blue light. Approval from the others followed and a relieved Balack sat down.

Uranus. Uranus. Uranus.

Hiemal's world spun above them. Verna, noticing the clarity of its surface considered it beautiful.

31

Hiemal stood, looked around and spoke curtly before sitting down. "My world is small, rocky and cold. I name it Pluto in honour of the founder of Uclair."

Balack immediately smelled sweet but a less enthusiastic approval was given by the others.

Pluto. Pluto. Pluto.

Kalend considered asking Hiemal to speak more of his world but a warmth containing the words "let him be," changed his mind. He gave a small smile in Dynak's direction before nodding at t'Hura who cleared her throat nervously before beginning.

With the blue planet rotating above them, t'Hura was certain others would see her world as she did.

"The first time I saw my world I could not help but love and cherish it. Its finished form is greater than I could have dreamed. There are mighty forests, rivers, lakes, vegetation and creatures in such profusion it takes my breath away. All living things on my world breathe. Plants breathe out what creatures need to breathe in and the creatures breathe out what the plants need. This good breath gives life, harmony and goodness to all. There is only one name that can fit my world; a name that means the breath of life. That name is HEART."

Balack guffawed so violently he almost rolled from his seat. "Good breath! Heart is no name for a planet".

Hiemal added his support of Balack in a tone laced with contempt. "We must agree with Balack. Heart is not a suitable name and we are dismayed that a Watcher would suggest it."

Hiemal may have been lounging in his chair but had placed his hand under the table as he spoke. He would not have chosen such a name if the blue planet had been his. His ring glowed an acid green, betraying his feelings of contempt for t'Hura's decision. He was sitting next to Kalend and only he could see the crystal in Hiemal's ring.

Kalend faced him. "I will not tolerate a further personal attack on t'Hura. You will apologise immediately."

"Oh, it's alright Kalend, I…" began t'Hura, but Kalend silenced her with a look before returning his gaze to Hiemal whose ice-cold eyes glared his dislike. Kalend quietly reminded Hiemal he must always show his crystal when speaking. Hiemal was no fool and knew which battles were worth fighting. This was not one of them. Using the time to compose himself, he strode across the Chamber to kneel at t'Hura's feet and took her hand.

"My dearest t'Hura, I do not know what possessed me. You know I hold you in the highest esteem and would not hurt your feelings intentionally. Please accept my most abject apology."

t'Hura's crystal showed traces of yellow, reflecting her fear of him; Hiemal saw it too and smirked – t'Hura should fear him, for the blue planet would be his. The yellow in her crystal changed to the red of anger as she snatched her hand away from him. "My most esteemed Hiemal, I accept your apology in the same spirit as it was given."

Many in the Chamber laughed at her fitting reply and Hiemal hid his flash of anger. Kalend sighed in relief.

"Now, if we could return to the purpose of this meeting. t'Hura, please continue."

Strengthened by Kalend's show of support, t'Hura stood and spoke strongly. "My planet is more beautiful than I can find words to express. All things work together in harmony. I say again, the name for my world is Heart."

Silence filled the Chamber and t'Hura flicked her eyes around the others looking for even one to give their approval. Kalend was silent; the blue planet was the most desirable in the system and t'Hura must show why she was most suited to be its Watcher. Her eyes settled on Stolesc. His clear indifference to Hiemal's status or the wealth of his house would make him immune to any attempt by Hiemal to intimidate him. He saw the plea in t'Hura's eyes and did indeed come to her rescue.

"t'Hura, may I make a suggestion?"

She nodded, glad of the chance to collect her thoughts and her courage.

Writing the word HEART in shining letters in the air, Stolesc casually flicked the H so it tumbled backwards several times before coming to rest at the end of the word. t'Hura looked at it and then her eyes flicked from face to face trying to gauge the response. There were smiles and murmurs of approval from around the chamber and her mind argued that an anagram of heart would still let her world thrive. Even to her, her voice sounded thin and weak as she replied, "I will accept the suggestion made by Stolesc and name my world Earth."

Kalend spoke before any response could be made. "t'Hura, may I remind you that the choice of name for your world is your decision and yours alone. If you believe Heart is the name in accordance with the standards you, and you alone have set, then Heart it shall be."

For just a moment she considered choosing Heart but having the support of her fellow watchers was important to her, so made a cowardly decision, one she would come to regret.

"Thank you, Presidion, but I name my world Earth."

Earth, Earth, Earth.

As the meeting ended, Kalend was surprised when Hiemal remained seated.

"Presidion, I feel something is wrong here."

Kalend turned to face him as Hiemal carefully composed his

features to show only concern.

"The Senaten decide which Watcher is to be paired with each world. The blue planet is clearly the most favoured so why was it not paired with you? t'Hura is weak, unable even to fight for the silly name she chose. I doubt her ability to fulfill her role as Watcher."

Kalend wasn't fooled by Hiemal's flattery but knew he wasn't the only one to be curious.

"I appreciate your concerns Hiemal, and there may be others who question the world they have been given. The Senaten will have good reasons for all their choices. If you wish, I can ask for a transcript of their decisions."

Hiemal left without replying but Kalend remained for a time. He then visited the Senaten world seeking Sen Glarte, a long-held friend.

Glarte's wide smile of welcome faded at the worried expression on Kalend's face.

"Kalend, welcome. I am pleased by your visit. Please come into my sanctum where we will not be disturbed."

Kalend's unease deepened. On his many previous visits he would always have greeted Glarte's companion and children on arrival, but there was an urgency in Glarte's invitation. The two friends faced each other across Glarte's desk.

"My friend, tell me what troubles you and I will help if I can."

Kalend wasted no time in coming to the reason for his visit. "The blue planet in my system is unlike any world I have seen. I expected it to be mine but when an Uclairian arrived, I thought it would be his. t'Hura, the unexpected Watcher of the blue planet is a pleasant person, but I struggle to find the intellect, experience or strength that will be required of her. I am at a loss to understand why this appointment has been made."

Glarte sat in silence for a moment before asking, "What do you know of t'Hura?"

"She is from the House of Efriston."

Glarte thought highly of Kalend and trusted him. He would tell the truth even though it would break the rules of silence sworn by all Sen.

"You need to know that when I nominated you as Presidion, I was unaware of what would happen in your System. If I had known I would not have put you in this position. I will speak of t'Hura first. Efriston is a financial house, the largest in the Galaxy. Several important members of the Senaten owed a great debt to them. Those debts were cancelled in exchange for the daughter of the head of the House of Efriston being appointed Watcher of the blue planet."

Kalend stood in disbelief. "What else did they ask for in return?"

"Nothing. Efristonal are a strange people. The blue planet is different to any other world in the Galaxy and that is enough to make them desire it. They simply wanted something no one else would have."

"You say the Senaten agreed to this?"

Glarte took a piece of paper and wrote on it. The amount was staggering and Kalend sat again, staring in disbelief. Glarte waited until Kalend raised his head before continuing.

"t'Hura is unaware of the deal made by her father. She was not assessed to discover what abilities she had to be a Watcher and may well be totally unsuited for her position. It is the Uclairian that concerns me. Hiemal has been a disgrace to his family since a young age, but something happened before the last Senaten meeting; something serious enough for his uncle, Sen Thorien, to put pressure on the Senaten to send him to your new system. A punishment that is essentially exile is reserved for acts of extreme violence."

Glarte hesitated. "There was much rumour and speculation but I could find no evidence. If Hiemal's crime is one of violence he should have been sent to the prison world of Hatrion. The House of Uclair has many faults, but violence in anathema to them."

Kalend was furious that his system was being used as a depository for those the Senaten considered a problem but did not doubt the truth of what he had been told. Glarte wished Kalend to remain for a short time with him and his family, but he needed time to consider the implications of the information he had been given. Thanking Glarte, he went to leave but his friend stopped him with a warning.

"The Senaten appointed you as Presidion because they believe your inexperience will mean you present no threat to them. Do not make yourself one. There is nothing you can do about the deals that have been made. You are the most intelligent and honourable man I know. Act as if you are unaware of the Senaten actions. As for t'Hura', offer her guidance and support. Hiemal is arrogant and ambitious. His exile is not likely to improve his legendary bad temper. Never turn your back on him, my friend."

Kalend took his leave of Glarte, returning to his dwelling in Tir Dhuchais.

From a child, Kalend had aspired to become a Sen. His respect and admiration for the Senaten was now diminished and he felt its loss. Because of their self-serving deals, he had not one, but two Watchers unsuited to the worlds entrusted to their care. Angered by their actions, he vowed Senaten corruption would not touch his System again.

"Will we get to play with them?"

Ten orbits passed as the Watchers made Tir Dhuchais their home. All but one spent time on their world to watch. At Watch meetings, a change in orbit, a collision with a meteor and most importantly, any sign of life would be reported and then watched for any development.

In Tir Dhuchais, many changes were being made. Dynak was a collector of coloured pigments which she used to create vivid illustrations on the walls of her dwelling. She invited Kalend to see her work.

The wall at the back of her dwelling seemed to no longer exist. Plants and creatures created a landscape that removed the dwelling completely. They were so real Kalend had to reach out to assure himself the wall did in fact remain.

Dynak, pleased with his response had a request. "If you like the work of my hands, may I create such as these on the outside walls of the Chamber?"

"Dynak, this is beautiful beyond my ability to express, but the time taken to do this to the vastness of the Chamber is incalculable."

"I have time to spare and this would please me, but if you do not wish it, I…"

"No, no. You couldn't be more wrong. To have a Chamber like this would make it the most magnificent in the Galaxy. However, the Chamber belongs to the Watch, so their approval must be sought."

"I am happy to do so."

"I will summon them to come here now to see the work of your hands for themselves."

A surprised Watch gathered at the dwelling of Dynak. Only the Chamber had been used for previous meetings. Kalend invited Dynak to speak.

"I have a request to make, but first you need to come to the back of my dwelling."

Curiosity aroused, even Hiemal went to see what Dynak wanted. They were as stunned as Kalend. Balack was so impressed he emitted an aroma so strong it was almost overpowering. Hiemal couldn't resist touching a creature which looked as if it was about to move.

A huge smile on his face made him look pleasant as he spoke. "Dynak, we would be honoured to have our dwelling covered in this way."

Kalend did not want Dynak, or any of his Watchers to spend time alone in the company of Hiemal, so gave Dynak no time to reply.

"I called this meeting as Dynak wants to use the walls of the Chamber for her work and needs your permission to do so."

Hiemal was angered to be dismissed so curtly but joined an enthusiastic approval. A joyful Dynak gave her thanks.

Balack's pastime was more self-indulgent. He visited many worlds sampling their cuisines and his waistline gradually increased.

Thades was a connoisseur of fine beverages and upon finding Pestiar berries growing wild in Tir Dhuchais, he experimented with producing a beverage of his own. His first attempts were undrinkable and later efforts rendered Hiemal, Stolesc and Balack incapable of either speech or movement for several days. Determined to succeed, he continued with his attempts.

t'Hura began planting her garden with the help of Stolesc and Verna. Seedlings from Earth grew into plants many times the height of Stolesc. The garden begun around t'Hura's dwelling grew quickly so a new garden was planted beside the lake with the specimens Stolesc and t'Hura collected from across the galaxy. The friendship with Stolesc and Verna was a great comfort to t'Hura, whose natural disposition of friendliness and good cheer became apparent to all.

t'Hura had been so excited by her world and its beauty that all Watchers had been invited to accompany her to see the wonders of Earth. They saw the Niagara Falls long before man set foot on that continent. They visited the expanse of desert in the land that would become Africa. They were amazed by great forests filled with exotic creatures and high mountains covered with a white substance that t'Hura called snow. Stolesc had been shocked to find this snow was cold; a similar substance on his home world was warm and children would wrap themselves in it.

Hiemal never accepted t'Hura's invitation as he refused to let others see his longing for the blue planet and his disappointment with his own. Most watchers went to Earth a few times. Stolesc and Verna went more often but even their presence was now a rare event.

Kalend was a regular visitor, each time asking t'Hura's permission to visit alone but she always insisted it would be her pleasure to escort him.

Despite the passage of time, t'Hura's failure to have her preferred name for her blue planet caused her many restless nights. Early one morning, t'Hura woke and hid her face in her hands. Earth should have been called Heart; she knew this in every bone of her body. The good breath should have filled the hearts and minds of all creatures – especially Man.

Man became the dominant species with t'Hura at first delighting to report on his creativity and ingenuity. Later describing the great Pyramids, the Colossus of Rhodes, the Hanging gardens of Babylon, but was careful never to mention the slave labour involved in their building. She watched with anguish as the destruction of villages wiped out the women and children, while the men were dragged off in chains.

As Watcher, she should have known what to do. She was responsible for the welfare of all her creatures but could only watch with horror as tusks were savagely torn from the heads of great beasts and huge holes were dug in the earth to remove precious stones. She desperately breathed words of love, tolerance and peace into the ears of sleeping kings, but her words were either unheard or ignored.

Powerful, ambitious men warred for wealth and land. They took without thought or care for the creatures or people in lands they conquered. Pleasure was the determining factor in their lives; their minds were dominated by basic, materialistic… earthly desires. Great buildings were erected to glorify rulers, ritual killings were made to satisfy their gods, gladiatorial combat was popular, where men would fight to the death for the entertainment of their owners. Women were treated as subservient, inferior beings to be used by men in any way they chose.

On her early travels to Earth, t'Hura had been in awe of the life that flourished there, but not now. Now she hid the truth, ashamed of her world and ashamed of her failure as its Watcher. Now Man had committed another atrocity, one which couldn't be ignored.

She dressed and headed towards Kalend's home.

Kalend stirred, moaning softly in his throat, he raised his arms in a slow stretch while yawning. Swinging his legs over the side of the bed, he dressed for the day. As he pulled back the curtains, a small far away movement caught his eye. Someone was coming to visit. He sighed, an early morning call could mean trouble and he had planned to go fishing.

Moving into the next room, he picked up a thick glass disc. Fastening it inside a stout leather tube, he raised it to his eye, easily recognising the ample figure of t'Hura and set about preparing food. Arkolin fruit was a rare delicacy, mainly because of the sharp thorns which surrounded it. Longer than Kalend's middle finger, they formed a spiny flower to protect each fruit from would-be harvesters. The restorative and healing properties of Arkolin were valued more than its sweetness. Kalend had planted almost fifty of these great trees on the shore surrounding the lake that covered a third of Tir Dhuchais, but only six had grown. Each seed was precious. Having selected one fruit from the tree in his garden, he took it inside to slit the skin and allow the golden juice to flow, carefully picking out the delicate seed and placing it on his table to dry.

He filled a glass with water to which he added just two drops of the potent juice, pouring the remainder into a small jug. t'Hura must have begun her journey long before dawn so would greatly appreciate the Arkolin drink. He placed the jug on the courtyard table laden with fresh querbana, fish and fruits from his garden. He opened the gates in the stout fence that surrounded three sides of his property, the fourth side being the river which eventually flowed into the lake.

A chirruping sound heralded the arrival of Rogue. Kalend had found the wounded Flugh as a youngster and having cared for him, he was now a firm friend. Covered in iridescent feathers, Rogue reached Kalend's knee in height and was an excellent fisherman. Sitting upright in the water and paddling with feet on the end of short, stout legs, he steered with his tail. This allowed him to use the talons on the end of his upper limbs to snatch any fish that came within range. He waddled in, sniffing the air and Kalend rushed to the table.

"Oh no you don't!" he scolded, as Rogue headed straight for the Arkolin juice. Arkolin affected Flughs more strongly than any other creature; the tiniest amount would cause Rogue to sleep for many days, making him easy prey for the Neutsche in the forest. Neutsche ate anything they found and had once eaten everything in Kalend's garden. The fence around his property was the only way to keep them out.

t'Hura was glad when the open gates came into view and quickened her stride.

Despite the unease he felt about t'Hura's visit, Kalend hurried to meet her, smiling warmly.

He could see circles under her eyes and strain on her face; something was very wrong. t'Hura greeted Kalend formally and patted Rogue on the head, smiling when she saw the glass on the table. Rogue whimpered beside her as she sipped the reviving drink until Kalend shooed him away. After giving t'Hura time to recover, he asked what had brought her here.

She mentioned Man, making it clear the problem wasn't with man, but rather with an unexpected creation of his. Man had unknowingly created beings with human immortality.

Kalend listened with growing alarm as t'Hura talked. She was so agitated she couldn't sit still, constantly getting up and pacing around the courtyard before sitting again. Kalend insisted he would accompany t'Hura to Earth to see these beings for

43

himself. Trying to avoid places where Man's violent and cruel excesses were most evident, Kalend still saw enough to fill him with anger and something close to despair. How could she have allowed this to happen and then kept it secret from him?

t'Hura slept peacefully on their return now her problem was shared, but sleep eluded Kalend. While it was clear the existence of these beings must be brought before the Watch, the nature of Man was a different issue. t'Hura must take some responsibility for the odious, dishonourable behaviour manifested by the worst of their kind, but many showed kindness and a willingness to put others before themselves. If he held t'Hura responsible for one, he must also recognise her contribution to the other. The chaos on Earth was a result of t'Hura's inability to oversee its peaceful development. If discovered, Hiemal would use her failure to insist she was unfit to be Watcher of Earth. Kalend felt he could be right.

He forced his thoughts to return to the beings Man called Months. They were unremarkable in appearance but exhibited all the best qualities of Man and none of their worst.

Before his talk with Glarte, he wouldn't have hesitated to approach the Senaten, but not now. They would visit Earth and see the ravages of Man. The deal securing t'Hura's appointment would mean she would be judged blameless. The responsibility for Earth would be securely fixed around his shoulders, resulting in not only his removal, but possibly the removal of any Watchers who had visited Earth. A Watcher, once removed, would never be appointed Watcher or Presidion again. The problem of the Months must be resolved within the Watch, no matter what the cost. With daylight approaching, he woke t'Hura, telling her it was time.

An emergency meeting was a rare event and the watchers

were quick to gather. Kalend opened the meeting with these words of caution.

"A matter of great seriousness has arisen on one of our worlds. It would be easy to attribute blame within this Chamber but I will not tolerate any such judgements at this time. I ask for your compassion and understanding. It is essential a solution to this matter is found here and quickly."

Kalend asked t'Hura to make her report.

The Watch listened with increasing disbelief as a nervous t'Hura spoke.

"I have often spoken of the ingenuity of Man, but to allow him to plan for his future and organize his life, he has divided time into portions. The planting of crops, harvesting and celebrating his many religious festivals needed measurements of time. A full rotation of the seasons – an orbit – man calls a year, and he has divided this into periods of the moon called months."

"While I find his arrogance unpalatable, I don't see this as doing any harm."

This comment from Neja showed her puzzlement as to why this should have necessitated an emergency meeting.

t'Hura's palms were sweating and her voice quavered. "At first there were ten Months with Man allocating festivals and celebration days in each. By giving them names and being unaware of what they were doing, they changed ten beings, born human, into beings who now have human immortality."

All watchers were now on their feet demanding answers.

Kalend stood and banged repeatedly on the table.

"Shouting at one another is not helping. I will allow everyone to ask questions and ensure they are answered. Stolesc, ask your question."

"What is human immortality? Surely they can only be

45

human or immortal."

t'Hura explained, "Human immortality means they will not grow old and die, but may still be killed in battle, through illness or an accident."

"What are these Months called?"

This question came from Dynak. She was equally concerned by the events revealed by t'Hura but seeing the strain on her face wished to provide a distraction from the angry questions filling the Chamber.

"I am curious to know how man has named them."

t'Hura happily supplied the names, explaining that July and August were named after two of their rulers, Julius Caesar and Caesar Augustus. September, October, November and December were named after the words used for seven, eight, nine and ten. March, April, May and June, were named after their gods with March being first in their calendar. Recently January, named after the two-headed Janus the god of beginnings and endings, had been added at the end of the year with the remaining days simply called winter.

Murmurs of approval were heard around the chamber but not from Balack.

"We are all born immortal. Immortality is not something to be bestowed upon inferior beings by other inferior beings. There are now eleven of these Months. They must be destroyed and mankind stripped of the ability to create more."

t'Hura felt her unworthiness like a heavy blanket around her shoulders. Already feeling guilty, she responded aggressively.

"When asked to be Watchers, we all took a solemn vow to protect our worlds. That vow includes *all* creatures of my world. I will hear no talk of destroying them."

Thades asked Kalend if the months could be taken to another

46

one of their worlds.

"Earth is the only world in this system that can sustain the human part of them. Only the Senaten has the power to move them to another system."

Kalend hesitated. He must convince the Watch to find a solution.

"If the Senaten believe we have failed to act in the best interests of one of our worlds, it would not be uncommon for an entire Watch to be removed. It could prove difficult, if not impossible to gain another position as Watcher if we were considered unfit here."

Kalend shivered as a cold breeze wafted by him.

A heated and lengthy debate followed which divided the Watch into two opposing camps. Those who wished the Months destroyed and those who felt they should be saved. Neja wanted to know more about them.

"Are they fearsome, misshapen beings? Surely Man could not have created perfect creatures."

"You saw Man when we visited Earth. The Months look just like them."

Stolesc was confused.

"Why can't they just stay on Earth. If they don't look different, I don't see the problem."

This was the question t'Hura and Kalend had feared. Man must not discover he had created immortal beings. His desire for power could result in the creation of more such beings, using them for evil purposes.

Despite the Arkolin drink Kalend had given t'Hura to calm her, she looked nervously at him before speaking. A look immediately noticed by Hiemal who jumped to his feet.

"Am I correct in thinking our Presidion has more

information than he has disclosed?"

Kalend remained seated before casually replying, "t'Hura followed the correct procedure by speaking to me first. As Presidion, it is what I would have expected."

Despite his relaxed appearance, Kalend knew he would have to reveal more of t'Hura's visit.

"t'Hura asked for my advice as the Months had made friends with Man who naturally noticed they did not age. Questions were being asked and she was unsure what to do. Which is why we are having this meeting."

Dynak, trying to understand why this was such a problem asked, "What would man do if he became aware of the nature of these Months?"

T'Hura was desperately struggling to retain her composure.

"Some men already know there is something different about the Months but have no idea they are responsible for their existence. So far the Months have managed to avoid falling into the clutches of such men."

Thades did not speak much in the Chamber, but his sharp intellect missed nothing.

"You said 'falling into their clutches'. Is the nature of man violent?"

Kalend answered this question.

"It is natural among all species, on Earth and even our home worlds, for violence to show itself in certain circumstances. Man has long shown a desire for immortality. The removal of the Months would prevent his search being successful."

The usually quiet Verna intervened.

"t'Hura you have told us nothing of their nature. What are they like?"

Glad to speak of the positive nature of the Months, t'Hura

explained.

"These Months exemplify all that is good in Man, his kindness, compassion, creativity and generosity. They all work to provide for themselves and for those less fortunate. They share with the poor and hungry, care for the sick, and provide comfort wherever they can."

Kalend could see many were impressed but this did not bring a solution any nearer.

After his earlier concern, Hiemal was the only watcher who wasn't expressing an opinion. The possibility of removing t'Hura as watcher of Earth stirred his intense longing for the blue planet; he must show her unfitness.

He stood to speak, addressing his question to t'Hura.

"How long have these months been in existence?"

"I'm not sure, I had no idea they were there until I saw one disappear before my eyes."

"Disappear, what do you mean?

"When they wish to travel from one place to another, they can do so by thought, as we do."

Hiemal was determined to discredit t'Hura.

"How long before you brought this matter to us?"

t'Hura hesitated, aware she should have acted sooner.

"As Watcher of Earth, it was my duty to uncover the extent of the problem before presenting it to our Presidion."

"We ask again. How long has it been?"

Kalend could see where this was going.

"The issue before us is what we do about them now; any other considerations are irrelevant at this time."

"With all due respect, Presidion, we disagree. It would appear t'Hura has failed in her duty of care for her world. Now may be the time to put someone else in her place."

Neja was indignant, her red hair standing straight upright as she glared at Hiemal.

"And I suppose you think you should be that someone? t'Hura has always acted with the utmost integrity."

"We appear to have a different understanding of 'integrity'. She allowed an atrocity of huge proportions to go unchecked and neither she nor Kalend will disclose how long they have kept it secret."

Kalend called the meeting to order.

"Sit down both of you. Neja, t'Hura does not need you to speak for her. Hiemal, I do not answer to you. No action against t'Hura will be taken."

Hiemal was furious his protest had been dismissed and would have argued further, but Kalend's stony face brooked no further discussion. No further solutions having been suggested, Kalend stated the situation as clearly as he could.

He explained the three options open to them.

The months would stay on Earth in a remote, secret location but t'Hura felt this wouldn't be possible as man was an intrepid explorer, and no place would remain hidden for long.

The matter could be taken to the Senaten, but this could mean the removal of them all.

The Months could be destroyed, but t'Hura had the right to refuse to allow her creatures to be harmed in any way.

"If they can't stay on Earth, they will have to come here."

Verna's idea took everyone by surprise. Balack loved it.

"Live here, with us. Would we get to play with them?"

Hiemal told Balack not to be stupid, so he sulked. His folded arms and pouting lips were followed by the stench of his disapproval which he knew could not be ignored. He enjoyed a moment of satisfaction before Hiemal hissed at him.

"Curtail your stench or leave the Chamber."

Having made his feelings clear, Balack emitted a pleasant aroma which removed all trace of the odour which had offended those seated closest to him.

Dynak supported Verna's idea, saying the finer details could be sorted once the decision was made to bring them here, but Neja disagreed.

"We can't make that decision without knowing exactly what would be involved. It is not only their welfare that has to be considered."

Stolesc had no answers, only questions.

"Where would they live? It has always been the policy of Watchers to keep our existence secret from our worlds. Would the Months come and go as they please? Would they know of us and what we do here? How would our lives be affected by their presence? These are issues we must address. It is disturbing to think of these beings living so close to us. I do, however, recognise that their existence is not of their making, and we should not punish them for a crime of which they are completely innocent."

Verna agreed that may be so, but after some thought offered a solution.

"The untouched Valley of Stone behind the mountains on the far side of Tir Dhuchais could be made into a home for the Months."

Dynak was quick to add a further idea.

"It's separated from us by high mountains which would keep our two communities separate."

Hiemal was incensed but waited until he was calm before speaking.

"t'Hura has told us these perversions of creation can travel

51

by thought. What if they thought to travel over the mountains and come here? We will not tolerate such abhorrent beings living close to us."

Hiemal could feel his anger rising but knowing his crystal would betray him, fell silent. Verna answered him.

"We would have to build some form of temporal bridge to allow the Months to travel back and forth to Earth. A screening device in it could strip them of their powers here but allow them to use them on Earth."

Hiemal had seen these human immortals as an opportunity for him to become Watcher of the blue planet, but his protest had been denied. When Kalend mentioned the Senaten, Hiemal feared their involvement. It was possible the Senaten would remove the Watch putting the blue planet beyond his reach and his future in jeopardy. The Watch had to solve the problem, but how? He was shaken out of his reverie by t'Hura and Thades both on their feet, one in frustration, the other displaying a calm indifference.

Thades' practical way of thinking was evident as he continued.

"The Months don't have to go anywhere. Verna spoke of stripping them of their powers to come here, so why don't we just do that on Earth. If we remove their immortality they will just fade into insignificance, end of problem."

With great patience, t'Hura once again reminded him of her vow.

"These Months are creatures of my planet and I have a duty to care for them. Let us have no more talk of 'ending'."

Thades was indifferent to t'Hura's anger.

"If we are to discuss all options, then this is an option as valid as any other. If we bring the Months here we don't know what kind of trouble we may be making for ourselves. I am only pointing out that we do have an alternative."

Verna had not spoken again and Kalend asked her for her thoughts.

"The Months are good and deserve to live. t'Hura fears their immortality will be discovered if they remain on Earth, so the only solution is to bring them here and put safeguards in place to protect them and us."

Stolesc added his approval for Verna's suggestion and asked for the proposal to be put to a vote.

A silence fell on the Chamber while Kalend considered the implications of Verna's suggestion.

"This is a matter of such magnitude I feel it shouldn't be decided by a majority. It's obvious we are divided. If the months are to come here it should be with the complete approval of all. To those opposed to the proposal, what safeguards would need to be put in place to let you agree to it? To those who are in favour, what compromises would you make to accommodate those with reservations?"

t'Hura was asked to make herself available to answer any question the Watchers may have and Kalend stood to close the meeting until a suggestion or plan could be prepared.

As Dynak went to leave, Kalend asked her to stay as he valued her insights. As she turned to face him, a blast of icy air pierced his flesh rendering him unable to breathe. Struggling for air, he reached for the back of a chair before stumbling into a half sitting position. A warmth gradually replaced the cold as his frozen joints were able to move again and the pain in them lessened. Sitting up, he saw Dynak on her knees before him and he felt her remorse as he heard her sobs.

"Forgive me, Presidion. I did not know the Scler of my kind would inflict such suffering on you. I will leave Tir Dhuchais and ask the Senaten to replace me."

Kalend stood a little shakily and held out a hand to help

Dynak to her feet. Gesturing to a chair, he indicated she should sit next to him.

"We have been friends too long for you to address me as Presidion when we are alone. I can think of nothing I want less than to have you leave. Please tell me what just happened and why."

"The Scler is the opposite of the warmth you experience when I speak to your mind. It is a weapon designed to prevent thought or deed in an enemy. When you said the Senaten could remove us from this Watch, I felt a great fear."

Kalend gently held her hands, her description of him as her enemy wounding him.

"What is it you fear so much you call me an enemy?"

Dynak hesitated, her usually serene face reflecting the conflicting emotions within her.

"I am the last of my kind. If I leave here, I have nowhere to go. Tir Dhuchais has become my home and my fellow watchers my family. Even Hiemal is like an unruly brother. You appear to place greater value on the lives of these unknown months than you do on us. The Scler came unbidden. I do not consider you my enemy and ask your forgiveness."

"Forgiveness is given on the condition there is no more talk of leaving. I have good reasons for the directions I give but cannot share those, even with you. All I can do is ask you to trust me as a friend."

"After the Scler, you consider me a friend?"

"Our friendship is based on mutual respect but there are matters known to me as Presidion that I cannot share. Can you consider me a friend if I keep secrets from you?"

"Your friendship means a great deal to me, and I trust the things you say."

"Charter of the Months"

Over the following days, two groups emerged. Both had concerns as well as some points in favour of Verna's suggestion to bring the Months there. Having beings from one of their worlds living close to them was in contravention of everything they had been told on becoming Watchers. The inherent goodness of the Months championed by t'Hura influenced many in favour of the proposal. Dynak, moved by t'Hura's report and her own fears, believed their unselfishness and kindness made them worthy of being saved; Stolesc simply trusted Kalend to make the right decision.

Thades, Hiemal and Balack felt there should be no pollution of their lives by the introduction of inferior beings. Balack, after his initial delight at the suggestion to bring the Months to Tir Dhuchais had been confused by the differing opinions. If he was to have no contact with them, then Balack was firmly in the opposition camp.

Kalend had to remain impartial, but when asked by those in favour, pointed out that Hiemal was likely to come back saying there was nothing that would change their minds and the stalemate would be resumed. If saving the Months was what they decided to do, it would be crucial to agree with those opposed if they did make a proposal.

Hiemal was convinced t'Hura and Kalend were keeping something secret from the Watch and determined to discover what it was. He risked visiting Earth even though t'Hura hadn't given him permission to do so. If there was anything he could use to his advantage, he needed to find it.

Having listened to t'Hura's reports on the beauty of Earth he thought he knew what to expect, but nothing prepared him for the bombardment to his senses. The colours and perfumes of flowering plants, the size and variety of the trees, the sounds of animals and flying creatures. More than these was water. From trickling streams to mighty waterfalls, tranquil lakes and storm lashed oceans. He swam in the warm waters surrounding an idyllic island, communicating with creatures he found there. Carried on the back of a great creature t'Hura called a whale, he felt its giant heartbeat and thought how much his parents would be bonded to this world. His desire for Earth filled every part of him and he vowed to do whatever it took to make it his.

Moved by the natural beauty of Earth, he moved on to survey the cities inhabited by Man. Great ingenuity had been needed to construct the most impressive buildings, but he was surprised by how little human life was valued. Men in chains were forced to carry heavy burdens, while other men hurt them with weapons which cut the flesh on their naked backs.

He was familiar with greed and the politics of power, but the cruelty, poverty and slavery on Earth was like nothing he had seen. Uclair would never condone such extreme savagery. If he presented this world to them it would not gain him the respect and reputation he desired. His plan to present Earth as the new Uclair would only succeed if Man was eradicated. t'Hura had been right to keep this secret from the Watch, but why would Kalend support her? Hiemal disliked the Presidion but considered him to be a person of integrity. His alliance with t'Hura made no sense.

Throughout the time of darkness, Hiemal sat in his dwelling. Even if he were Watcher of Earth he wouldn't have the authority to destroy an entire species. He would need power and authority from the Senaten, but the reasons surrounding his appointment as a mere Watcher meant it unlikely he would even be permitted to ask. A Presidion had power. By morning he had begun to formulate a plan.

Thades and Balack were surprised when Hiemal invited them to his dwelling to tell them of his desire to find a way to bring the Months here. Thades was suspicious.

"Why?"

"Kalend made it clear the Watch could be disbanded if the Senaten were to become involved. I know many of our Watchers want to remain. Can you imagine t'Hura or Verna or even Balack finding a new position?"

Balack nodded his head in acceptance that Hiemal's words were true but Thades was not convinced.

"It is heart-warming to see how you care for your fellow watchers. The Hiemal I spoke to after the meeting did not care about them. What has happened to change you?"

Irritated with Thades, Hiemal went to another room. Balack watched the receding back of an angry Hiemal.

"Thades, I know a Hernian will only make one friendship but I don't understand why you would choose Hiemal to be that friend."

Thades looked sadly at Balack.

"You misunderstand the Hernian way. I did not choose Hiemal, he chose me."

Balack was devastated.

"If I had known that I would have chosen you on the first day."

Thades smiled fondly.

"We still meet to spend time together. The nature of our relationship is different but no less important to me."

Hiemal returned to the room with a conciliatory expression on his face.

"Forgive me if I failed to make my reasons clear. Thades, you were right to question my motives. We must ensure the conditions surrounding the arrival of the Months safeguard us as we were initially opposed to their coming here. If there were to be unforeseeable consequences the responsibility must rest with t'Hura and Kalend. We three must be protected."

Thades could see the sense in these words and Hiemal's desire to protect himself fitted with Thades' knowledge of him.

Together they worked to draw up a Charter for the Months, although Balack was often more of a hindrance than a help. There was discussion and disagreement over one particular part but Hiemal used his argument about protecting themselves to win their support.

With the Charter complete, Hiemal went to see Kalend, delighted with the startled look on Kalend's face when he said he would present a Charter for the Months at the meeting.

After Hiemal's' visit, Kalend invited Stolesc, Neja, Verna and Dynak to come to his dwelling, an unusual event.

"This is the dwelling of Kalend, Watcher of Neptune."

Stolesc was quick to grasp the meaning behind this specific greeting.

"You are not speaking to us as Presidion, but as a fellow Watcher?"

"Thank you Stolesc for your understanding. I have visited Earth with t'Hura and have her permission to share this information with you. She wishes to prepare for the meeting so sends her fondest wishes to you all."

Verna had wondered why t'Hura was not present, but since the emergency meeting she had rarely been seen despite Verna visiting her dwelling many times.

Kalend continued.

"All t'Hura said of the Months is true, they are good, kind and compassionate. Unfortunately, Man has other characteristics. The worst of their kind are increasingly cruel, violent and greedy. Earth is a dangerous place for the poor and disadvantaged. Man however, are t'Hura's responsibility. We can only concern ourselves with the Months. Their good works are needed as they show Man there is a better way to live. Helping others is a way to help themselves." He paused briefly.

"Perhaps the survival of the Months could help with the survival of mankind."

Verna shed tears of compassion.

"t'Hura is a gentle and loving person. It must grieve her to see her world in this way."

"If she hadn't been so gentle perhaps her world wouldn't be in this way."

Stolesc disliked Neja's negative attitude to many things and spoke in t'Hura's defence.

"Neja, it is easy to judge when you are not the one who has to make the decisions."

Stolesc was concerned by Kalend's words about Man but a sense of fairness prompted his defence of t'Hura; however, he did consider she had failed Earth.

Neja was critical of what she perceived to be t'Hura's weakness and lack of self-belief. No one could believe she was most suited to be paired with Earth when it was obvious Earth should have been the world of Kalend. t'Hura had not fitted in since the naming ceremony, with Verna and Stolesc the only ones to befriend her.

Neja went on to point out that if Hiemal voted against the

59

Months, all this wouldn't matter. Kalend looked steadily around the room.

"Hiemal came to see me today. He, Thades and Balack have drawn up a Charter which would allow the Months to be brought here. Agreement with this charter would be essential if we wish the Months to come here."

"Why? He must have an ulterior motive, something to benefit himself."

Neja always sought the worst of motives in all Hiemal did but this time others shared her distrust.

Kalend, aware he must not force his opinion upon them, knew Hiemal's Charter may be the only hope of saving not only the Months, but the Watch.

"I am sure he will have an ulterior motive but if we can find a way to agree with him we could save the Months. I hope the information I have given you in favour of the Months is helpful when making your decision."

As Stolesc stood to take his leave, Kalend spoke again.

"t'Hura is finding all of this difficult and any support you feel you can give her would be an act of great kindness."

As Stolesc, Verna and Neja left, Dynak whispered to Kalend's mind.

"May I have a moment of your time?"

Once alone, she came to the point.

"I have often wondered why an Uclairian would be sent to a system on the edge of the Galaxy, not as Presidion, but as Watcher to the least world in it."

She waited, but Kalend said nothing.

"While in attendance at the Senaten have you not asked why this might be?"

Senaten business was confidential but Kalend trusted her

enough to share just a little of the information he knew.

"I did ask for clarification at my first Senaten meeting but it was made clear by Sen Turien that this was a question I didn't need to have answered. Turien is Hiemal's uncle and it would make sense he would protect one of his own House if protection were to be needed."

Dynak could understand this reasoning but feared anyone who could put her future at risk.

"He is an angry and ambitious man; this makes him dangerous. We would be better off without him."

"What would you have me do? Challenge the entire Senaten and the House of Uclair too?"

"Forgive me, I don't mean to suggest you could have done more."

Dynak turned to leave but stopped in the doorway.

"My fear is what Hiemal may ask in return for his Charter."

She was gone before Kalend could reply.

Everyone was on time for the meeting the next morning. Kalend started by thanking them for their willingness to find a solution.

"All will have a chance to speak, but Hiemal, Thades and Balack have produced a Charter to allow the Months to come here. Does anyone object if I ask Hiemal to begin?"

Those in favour of Verna's idea were curious about Hiemal's apparent change of heart, agreeing to let him speak first. Hiemal unrolled several sheets of writing material, working hard not to show his satisfaction.

"Moved by t'Hura's description of the character of the Months, we have a balanced and just Charter for your approval. It has five sections, and all five must be agreed if we are to welcome them to share this land with us."

Kalend asked him to read out the sections, each to be discussed before moving to the next.

1. The valley of stone on the other side of the mountain to be changed to look like some secret and hidden place on Earth. The mountains to have a sheer cliff face on all sides, plus a curtain of protection to prevent any accidental discovery of Tir Dhuchais.

As Hiemal read out this point, there were words of agreement throughout the chamber.

2. The temporal bridge to Earth would contain an invisible curtain to strip the Months of their ability to travel by thought when they were in their valley. Another curtain would render them unable to father or bear children. The Months would be unaware of these curtains or their purpose.

Dynak was unhappy with the removal of these abilities without the knowledge of the Months, but Hiemal pointed out the valley was of limited size and would only support a fixed population. Dynak had to agree Hiemal did have a valid point and mindful that support for Hiemal's charter must be given if possible, made no further protest.

3. The existence of the Watch to be kept secret from the Months. One Watcher to be appointed to supervise and accept full responsibility for them. This Watcher will travel to Earth, meet the Months and then live in The Valley with them. All decisions regarding the Months and The Valley will be made by this person.

Before anyone could volunteer, Thades stood to speak.

"Such a position must be held by a person with the authority to make decisions and we would all have to report back to the Presidion for answers. I therefore nominate Kalend to be Watcher of the Months."

Kalend suspected Thades made the nomination at Hiemal's prompting and wanted these proceedings to be fair.

"Does anyone else wish to be considered for this post?"

No one spoke as all could see Thades' reasoning was valid. Balack had tried to persuade Hiemal he would be perfect for the job, but Hiemal insisted the Watcher had to be Kalend. It was essential to his plan, a plan he did not share with either Thades or Balack.

"Presidion, will you accept the post of Watcher of the Months?"

Kalend would have liked time to work out what Hiemal was up to. If the position of Watcher of the Months was desirable, then why didn't Hiemal put himself forward? The Chamber was silent, waiting for his reply. Kalend thought it best he should have close scrutiny over the Months so accepted.

Dynak's warning still clear in his mind, Kalend's unease grew. He waited for the point upon which he was certain the decision would ultimately hang.

4. The Months must have a set of rules to live by:

a) Each month will only leave The Valley when it is their calendar time.

b) Each month will return by sunset on the last day of their time.

c) Each month will use their talents to provide for themselves and others.

d) The Months must treat with respect The Valley they have been given.

All agreed this was necessary if the idea were to work and supported this point.

5. A contract, covering the matters listed in point four, would be drawn up between the Months and their Watcher before

coming to the valley.

a) If the contract were broken by one Month, then all Months would be destroyed immediately.

b) No Month was to be told the consequences of breaking the contract.

c) The Watcher for the Months would be responsible for their removal.

There was an immediate feeling of unfairness. Stolesc voiced his concern.

"To ask Kalend to destroy beings he would have lived in close contact with is harsh. What reason is there for not telling them what would happen if they broke the rules?"

Hiemal appeared hurt by this comment.

"Stolesc, we did not intend harshness but you previously stated you had concerns about the Months living in such close proximity. We have tried to address those concerns. We believe it would be cruel to ask the Months to live in constant fear of destruction when all they have to do is follow a few simple rules."

Without allowing any further response, Hiemal smiled as he reached the pivotal part of his plan.

"There is a part which can be included now the Watcher of the Months has been appointed. His primary purpose is to ensure the rules are followed. If they are not, then someone must take responsibility for their failure.

d) If a breach of the rules were to occur, immediately following the Months destruction, Kalend would be stripped of his position as Presidion and Hiemal would be named as his successor."

Dynak, Stolesc and Neja all immediately objected and began speaking at once. Kalend reeled with shock. He knew Hiemal was acting out of self-interest, but this was quite simply brilliant!

He began to smile and then to laugh, quietly at first and then more loudly. Everyone fell silent and stared at him. He regained control and spoke.

"Hiemal, I must congratulate you. In one short point you have the means to destroy the Months, remove me, and achieve what you have always wanted."

Hiemal was at pains to appear as the protector of his fellow watchers.

"To bring beings from a world under our care to live with us is something never before seen in the Galaxy. The whole system of governance is being put at risk, as is everyone in this Chamber. You urged us to keep this matter secret but if discovered someone must accept responsibility and protect the Watch from the judgement of the Senaten. That someone must be the Watcher for the Months."

There was truth and reason in Hiemal's words and reluctant agreement was murmured, but Hiemal was determined to justify his reasoning…

"A new Presidion must be acceptable to the Senaten and we have been persuaded that person should be us. We did make it clear all sections of the Charter must be approved, but of course you are free to reject it."

Thades wryly remembered Hiemal was the one doing the persuading.

Dynak spoke in a calm and reasoned way that belied the outrage she felt.

"Of course we will not accept it. Innocent Months cannot be held responsible for the behaviour of one, especially when they would be unaware of the consequences. Secondly, you cannot nominate Kalend for a post that you then intend to use to take his role as Presidion."

Before Hiemal could reply, Kalend raised his hand for silence.

"As the final part of this section applies only to me, I will decide if I accept it or not. The other parts do seem unfair. If I accept my part will you remove them?"

Hiemal's tone was silky smooth as he replied.

"Have you so little faith in these creatures you think they will be unable to follow four simple instructions? If so, they are certainly unfit to come here and live alongside us."

Despite a long and heated debate, Hiemal would not move on this point. Kalend closed the meeting to allow feelings to cool before resuming the next morning.

At the close of meeting, Dynak invited everyone to share refreshments at her dwelling. Hiemal, Thades and Balack declined. Stolesc, Neja, Dynak and Verna had made up their minds to reject the Charter, but Kalend needed to persuade them otherwise.

He hesitated, unsure how much of his thoughts he should share. He could not reveal what he knew of t'Hura or Hiemal and as Presidion, he could not show bias. Knowing it was the threat to his Presidionship that angered them, he spoke only of that.

"When Thades nominated me to be their Watcher, I thought it was at Hiemal's prompting, but Thades is a fair man. I suspect he agreed knowing I would do all possible to protect the Months and ensure the rules were followed."

Neja interrupted.

"He is Hiemal's lackey, doing what Hiemal tells him."

Neja's aggression towards Thades was uncalled for and Kalend spoke sharply.

"Do not misjudge his friendship with Hiemal for subservience. Thades is his own man and no one's lackey."

All felt the Months would need protecting from Hiemal but Neja didn't trust Thades or Balack either.

t'Hura remembered the pride on her father's face when he told of her selection as a Watcher. The acclaim she had received from her House when the blue planet was paired with her was a memory she treasured. Fearing the response of her family if she were removed as Watcher of Earth, she kept silent. She would do what was necessary to remain a Watcher in this system.

Next morning, the Chamber was filled with a strong sense of expectancy as Kalend called the meeting to order.

"Is there an alternative solution to be brought before this meeting?"

Silence. Watchers looked to each other but no response was forthcoming.

"The Charter of the Months has been drawn up and all have been given the opportunity to speak. All must support it if the Months are to come here. Declare now if you are in favour."

Hiemal, Thades and Balack were quick to approve. Hiemal's eyes shone, Thades' skin glowed and Balack filled the Chamber with a pleasant aroma. Neja, Dynak and Stolesc had been persuaded by Kalend's words; fire, warmth and whistling showed their approval, while t'Hura hesitated before giving the briefest of nods. Verna was overjoyed her idea to save the Months was possible and danced her hands in approval. Kalend didn't need to declare but slapped the table in relief, and so it was done.

"She never danced in the woods again"

After the meeting, Verna went over to Hiemal who was standing with Balack and Thades. Forgetting his response at the allocation of worlds, she placed a hand on his arm.

"I wanted to thank you for finding a way to let the months come here. I know it was not something you wanted, but I'm sure it is a decision you'll not regret."

Thades saw the look on Hiemal's face and quickly intervened. He was grateful for the kindness always shown by Verna and bowed to her.

"Verna, thank you for your kind words. You are the only one to acknowledge the effort we have made and it is appreciated."

Hiemal strode away without speaking and Verna returned to the others. Neja was surprised by what she'd just seen.

"What did you do that for? This Charter wasn't done for the good of the Months, it was all for the good of Hiemal."

"I know, but it's done now and we have to work together without rancor or bitterness. Someone needed to make the first move and Thades was most gracious and appreciative."

Neja was not convinced.

"Hiemal was his usual rude self and he's the problem."

Despite his victory, Hiemal went home angry. The first part of his plan was complete but an old resentment consumed him after Verna placed her hand on his arm. Memories and feelings he had tried to keep hidden resurfaced.

Uclairian parents from the top rank of society would only have two children. One to become part of the family business, while the other would go into politics. Hiemal was a third, unplanned child. This was so unacceptable that Perfosa, his mother, was snubbed by those she had considered friends. She spent little time with her new son and as he grew, he acted in ever more unsociable and undesirable ways to gain her attention, even when this was to vent her anger and scorn upon him. His behaviour did not improve as he became a young man. After his latest outrageous behaviour her distaste for him reached new heights. Learning he had stolen from the business and wasted it on illicit pleasures, she sent for him.

"We wish you had never been born. You have brought shame on this family for the last time. Leave our presence and this house and never return."

He did leave, but only to sit on a seat overlooking the area where food for the house was produced. Thinking himself alone, tears trickled down his face.

He felt a hand touch his arm and a voice call him 'Hraetic,' a term of endearment used among the lowest serving class. He turned to see a woman with what he perceived as pity on her face. She was a servant on his parent's estate and had known Hiemal since he was a child. Unaware of moving, just feeling pleasure and a release of his pain as he wrapped his hands around her throat, Hiemal squeezed. As her struggles ceased he released her and strode away without a backward glance. Fortunately for the woman, she survived and after receiving care, named Hiemal as her attacker.

When his House learned of Hiemal's crime they wanted to enforce the rule of exile. If Hiemal had attacked anyone from his own class, the prison world of Hatrion would have been his destination. Due to the influence and wealth of the House of Uclair, it was eventually agreed by the Senaten to send Hiemal to an insignificant System on the edge of the Milky Way where he was to be paired with the least planet. If he committed another crime, he would be immediately sent to Hatrion.

Hiemal had spoken no word in his defense. How dare he be judged on the word of a servant. The look on the face of that woman was imprinted on Hiemal's memory. It was the same expression he had seen on Verna's face and anger at Verna engulfed him. She was constantly in his head. Everything that had gone wrong since he arrived was Verna's fault.

On the first day she had dared to touch him and show pity… pity for him! She was worse than nothing. Arriving late with dirty, torn clothing and hair awry, she had been given the largest planet, while he had been given a degrading little nothing on the edge of the system.

Verna was the friend of t'Hura, that fat, ugly, useless woman who had been given the world that should have been his.

The final insult was Verna coming over to touch and thank him, believing he would want or need her approval. Wisely keeping his hands by his side, he had walked away, for now.

Sitting with clenched fists Hiemal could still hear the words of his uncle as his fate was revealed.

"You have been given a chance to redeem yourself and save the reputation of this noble house. Disappoint us again and your name will be permanently removed from the family record."

Hiemal remembered the look of disappointment on his father's face, but his mother's refusal to bid him farewell hurt the most.

When he'd seen the blue planet, he knew he had to have it. He would name it Uclair and both his reputation and his relationship with his mother would be redeemed.

Dynak and t'Hura had prepared a celebratory meal in the Chamber but once again Hiemal declined. Feeling they should look for him, Thades and Balack thanked Dynak but also declined.

Despite the resolution of the problem, there was an undercurrent of unease among those who remained. There was no way of knowing how the bringing of these beings to their world would change their future. Kalend tried to reassure them and himself.

"First I have to convince the Months to come here. If they do, I'm sure they will do nothing to give cause for concern. I will report on their life in The Valley at our regular meetings. They are good people and I look forward to spending time with them."

The celebration did not last long as Kalend, Stolesc and t'Hura left to begin preparing The Valley for the arrival of the Months.

Thades and Balack decided to have a celebration on their own as Hiemal refused to join them. The latest brew of Pestiar wine had proved to be barely adequate but improved with the quantity consumed. They drained two bottles each and slept where they sat until morning.

All night Hiemal thought of Verna, allowing his anger to run hot. In the early morning, knowing where she liked to walk, he went to the woods behind her dwelling. He must find a release for his anger but an attack on anyone would mean his removal to Hatrion. He believed Verna was weak and could be intimidated without harm to her or to himself.

Verna had woken early as was her custom. She loved this time of day when she would dance naked among the trees in the manner of her people; her spirit would be refreshed and renewed. She whirled and moved to a rhythm she could hear in her head, lost in the wonder of the moment. The trees around her moved to the same rhythm and Verna was filled with a pleasure too deep for words. She shrieked when she saw Hiemal watching her and reaching for her robe, held it in front of her.

"What are you doing here?"

"We like these woods. We may walk here more often now we have seen their beauty."

While his words appeared complimentary, they belied his twisted smile and eyes glowing with anger.

"Please don't let me stop you dancing."

Hiemal found a nearby rock and sat on it. His gaze intently running over her body, unaware of the increasing strength of the moving branches above him. They recognised his evil intention and would protect Verna if he moved to harm her.

In one swift movement Verna turned the gown so she could put it on, fastening it tightly before raising one hand in a gesture that stilled the trees.

"On my world, the customs of my people are respected. No one would invade the privacy of a dancer."

"Aah. We are not on your world. We are in Tir Dhuchais and here we can walk where we please, and it pleases us to walk in these woods. Surely you would not deny us the peace and beauty you find here?"

Turning to go back to her dwelling, Verna forced herself to walk. Hearing his following footsteps, her resolve broke and she fled with his laughter pursuing her. Back in her dwelling she closed every door and window. Hiemal hadn't physically harmed her but she felt as violated as if his hands had wounded her. His words could be described as harmless, even complimentary, making it difficult to use his words against him, but the expression on his face terrified her.

Many times in the following days Verna saw Hiemal close to her home, walking or watching her. She tried going to other places to dance but he would suddenly appear, making light-hearted conversation while his face was stiff with anger. Even if she told someone what he was doing, his words could easily be explained as flirtation. Verna would have told t'Hura but she was with Kalend, so she kept silent.

Verna never dared to dance in the woods again, spending time wandering by the lake or occasionally in the garden she was planting with t'Hura and Stolesc. Something inside her shriveled and almost died. To save herself she returned to her home world, vowing to spend only a short time before and after Watch meetings in Tir Dhuchais. She used her ring to send Kalend, t'Hura and Stolesc a message saying family illness necessitated her time away.

"There is no 'we'. There is you and there is us"

Their knowledge and skill with growing things made Stolesc and t'Hura the obvious choice to accompany Kalend to The Valley of Stone to make a suitable home for the Months. Both were avid gardeners, combing the universe for exotic plants for the garden beside the lake. Some of their choices had proved to be challenging as the unique environment could mean a hardy plant could die, or a small flower on another world could become an enormous one in Tir Dhuchais. To contain such specimens, a strong fence had been built around the garden. They were keen to help Kalend prepare for the coming of the Months and happily went with him.

The valley was twice as long as it was wide, taking Kalend a full day to walk its length. There wasn't a single growing thing there and t'Hura stared at it in shock.

"Was Tir Dhuchais like this when you first came here?"

Kalend grimaced as he remembered how hard he had worked.

"The lake was there, but the rest was stone with just a few stunted trees along the shore."

He asked t'Hura and Stolesc to travel to Earth to study and select the plant life and domesticated animals needed to provide food and shelter for the Months. Variety and beauty were all very well, but everything they brought must contribute to the well-being of all that would live there. It was essential the Months would never question that this was part of Earth.

While they were gone, Kalend began the work of creating

the structure and form of the valley. Removing the stone from the valley floor, stacking it along the sides and then smoothing it to make an impenetrable barrier of sheer cliffs took time and effort. Creating a waterfall at one end to make a river supplying the needs of Months, plants and animals was more complex. Nothing lived or grew here before Kalend made the changes, but he scoured The Valley to ensure there was no trace of anything that would not be found on Earth.

The river would divide the valley into two parts. The smaller part with a concealed entrance to Tir Dhuchais would be Kalend's domain, leaving the much larger part for the Months. Kalend felt physical separation from them would be essential for his sanity and peace of mind, and for their sense of independence.

The cave and temporal bridge to Earth were hewn out of the foot of the mountain, and their walls carefully screened to look and feel like the solid rock of Earth. The curtain of recognition and those to strip them of their powers and fertility wouldn't be formed or put in place until everything else was complete.

Stolesc and t'Hura brought soil, flowering plants and edible crops creating a beautiful place that closely resembled Earth. A forest of Oak, Beech, Ash and Pine was planted at the waterfall end of the valley, with weeping willows along the riverbank. Fruit trees, berries and vegetables were planted in a garden. Fields with fences were prepared for the animals that would come. The only difference between this and Earth was the lack of vermin, wild animals and anything harmful to human life.

When it was complete, domesticated animals were brought – cattle, sheep, horses, pigs, ducks, chickens and deer. Stolesc found a creature on earth called a rabbit and liked it so much he was sure Kalend would like it too, selecting two of them. He was surprised when the time came to transport all they had collected, that there were now six small rabbits too. His gentle nature could not separate the young from their parents so he brought them all. Bees and other insects were brought for pollination and as food for the many varieties of birds that would fill the trees. Despite some misgivings, Kalend knew he could be content here. All he had to do now was to find and convince the Months to come; if not, this work would have been for nothing.

Travelling to Earth, Kalend knew he must be careful in his choice of words. He had to convince the Months of the urgent need to come with him, while reassuring them he did not pose any threat to them. Rehearsing in his mind what he would say he remained unsure he would be listened to. April was easiest to find and had just finished performing one of his songs for a small crowd in a marketplace. Kalend congratulated him warmly asking if he could speak to him about his work. Hoping to receive a commission, April readily agreed but insisted they remain in the marketplace. Moving to a less conspicuous spot, Kalend placed a friendly hand on April's arm.

"You and I have something in common. Both of us can simply wish to be somewhere else and it happens."

April's face showed fear and he tried to leave but Kalend tightened his grip. Aware of people around them he smiled disarmingly at April.

"I mean you no harm, quite the contrary. You are in danger and I've come to help you."

"Who, or what are you? What danger are you talking about?"

"I am Kalend and like you, an immortal. Your friendships with people put you and them at risk. I would prefer to explain all this just once to the others of your kind. If I let go of your arm, will you help me?"

April was suspicious, demanding some proof.

Kalend looked around and saw a tree on a nearby hill. He pointed it out to April and asked him to watch it.

In an instant Kalend appeared on the hill, waving to April before returning.

A shaken April asked what Kalend wanted.

t'Hura had told Kalend that October, November and December spent most of their time together working in the countryside in the northern part of the province. Kalend asked April if he knew any of them and when he said he had met November once, it was agreed he would find them and bring them to a meeting on the 14th day of October in a villa t'Hura had rented on the outskirts of Rome. If April could find any others, he was to bring them too.

Kalend was going to search for the female Months as they were more widely scattered. Before leaving, he begged April to believe he was a friend, but April had misgivings. He would talk to the others before deciding about going to any meeting.

Finding the female Months proved difficult despite the information given by t'Hura. July was in Rome and he noticed her first. His ability as Presidion meant he could see a glow around her that was unseen by those close to her. She had met and fallen in love with a dashing centurion in the Roman army and was adamant she wanted nothing to do with whatever Kalend was up to. Her radiant smile and lightness of movement showed her contentment with her life. Kalend feared she would be left behind but was hopeful of the others.

Searching distant lands suggested by t'Hura, he found March who worked as a healer. She was from Africa, a member of the Samburu people in a place that would later be known as Kenya. Kalend was stunned by the landscape and the magnificent animals. Massive grey beasts with huge flapping ears and a long facial protuberance March called a trunk both frightened and enthralled him, but was grateful Stolesc hadn't brought any of those to The Valley. Ungainly creatures with long spotted legs and equally long necks made him smile and then laugh as they stopped by a waterhole to drink, splaying their legs so they could reach the water.

March listened to Kalend but was already aware of the danger. Chieftains in the villages she visited began to demand the potion that would keep them youthful as she was. Her visits became more secretive, meeting women from the villages in marketplaces and helping them when she could.

Kalend travelled to a land in the east to find June. Kalend suspected she was in hiding but when he found her she showed no fear, her face remaining impassive throughout his visit. It took a long time to persuade her to come to the meeting.

May and September were easier to find as each preferred to remain in one place whenever possible. May lived in a croft beside a loch north of the great wall that had been built by the Roman ruler Hadrian. September had found her place in a land called Ireland, filled with rolling hills and a people who loved music and stories. Living in isolated places, both found the thought of company appealing.

If April found October, November and December that would just leave August and the newly formed January to contact. t'Hura had told him August came from a sea-faring background and could be anywhere, but January was most likely to be found wherever good wine was plentiful. The day before the meeting, Kalend found him in a vineyard and bribed him with several bottles of wine to accompany him.

On the morning of the meeting Kalend waited. January was sleeping off the large quantity of wine he had drunk the night before. As mid-morning approached with no sign of anyone, Kalend went outside the villa gates to look for them. He was surprised to find a group talking earnestly together. They stopped, turning to look when April pointed to Kalend. Among this group he was delighted to see July but something had happened to her, the warmth and joy which had been so evident in her had gone. April went to shake Kalend's hand but with distrust still in his eyes.

"Salve, Kalend. I have found all you asked and one you didn't."

Kalend quickly counted them and was delighted to find there were ten, with January asleep inside he had them all.

April's welcome cheered Kalend. He smiled warmly, inviting them to come in.

"For many of your years I was unaware of your existence, believing I was alone. My given name is Kalend. I would be honoured if you would address me as such."

Waking January, he asked each Month to identify themselves. A man, taller even than Stolesc, with long, flaming red hair and beard spoke in a guttural and stilted manner.

"Heill ok saell. My calendar name is August but I am Gust. I am Ostmen."

He wore a woollen tunic over leather leg coverings and across his back hung a large disc which Kalend later learned was called a shield and used to offer protection in battle. A stout leather belt around his waist held a long blade which was obviously a weapon. Kalend noticed the others stood at a distance from him.

An older but strong looking man stepped forward.

"Salve, I am October known as Tober."

He was a quiet man, preferring the company of horses to

people, his broad shoulders and muscled chest speaking of his physical work in the fields.

November – Vem – a slighter version of Tober, simply stated his name and watched Kalend through suspicious, even antagonistic eyes.

"I am April, known as Ari in tribute to Aristophanes, the greatest writer in all of Greece. I am a citizen of Rome and entertainer to the rich and famous."

A smiling Jan pointed to Ari's well-worn footwear and almost threadbare tunic.

"Doesn't look like they pay well."

December, or Dec as he preferred, offered information about his homeland in the centre of the then Roman Empire where he was a worker in wood.

September was known as Ember. Behind her smile Kalend could see she was guarded in what she said. Like Vem and Ari, she was suspicious. She said she was a fisherwoman, caring for the life of rivers and the creatures living there.

March was looked at with interest by the other women. She was tall and beautiful. Her dark skin different to the fair skins they were familiar with. Her voice was rich and deep and Ember especially wished to know her well, suspecting she would sing beautifully.

May was the oldest of the group with white curling hair and a warm, motherly expression. When she said she was a baker, cheers and words of welcome flowed around her.

June said her name and that she was from the East.

July whispered her name and nothing more.

Kalend thanked them for coming, offering refreshments but Vem stood.

"I've been asked to speak for us all. We've not come here

for a feast. Tell us what you meant when you spoke to Ari about being in danger."

The warmth of his smile and the genuine concern in Kalend's voice did nothing to change the suspicion he could see on every face.

"Of course. You all know you are not like the people around you. We are immortal, with the gift of travelling by thought. We…"

Vem interrupted. "There is no 'we'. There is you and there is us."

Kalend was surprised by the resistance he saw on his face and took a moment to gather his thoughts before continuing.

"This is the first time you have all been gathered together in one place. Some of you are friends, but most of you have friendships with the people around you. Those friends grow old and die, but you will not."

July jumped to her feet.

"Not all of them will grow old. My Paulinus is dead, killed in battle in a strange land, far from his home and me."

Kalend understood now the reason for July's changed demeanour and wishing to show his concern reached out a hand to touch her but she pulled away. March put a comforting arm around her shoulders as Kalend went on.

"I'm truly sorry Paulinus is dead, but death awaits all people of Earth, except you. Your friends and their families will notice you are not growing older and will begin to question you."

Ari spoke a little shamefacedly, all his cheerfulness gone.

"Just a few weeks ago, a man in the crowd shouted out that I didn't look a day older than when he first saw me when he was a boy. I joked it was beautiful women and good wine that kept me young, but I could see he and others weren't convinced. Later a group of men took hold of me and taking me to an empty building, demanded I give them the potion that keeps me young. I told them I had no potion but they tied me to a chair and the oldest of them put on a leather glove with studs in it. I knew they would keep on beating me for something I couldn't give. I have never disappeared in front of anyone before but I did so then, fearing for my life."

Following Ari's lead most had a similar experience to tell, even the women. March, Ember and June all saying their seemingly endless youth made women friends increasingly jealous.

Kalend was aghast at the violence shown to them and sighed.

"This is the danger I spoke of. Word of your long life will spread to the ears of ambitious and cruel men who will desire above all else to know your secret. They will seek tirelessly for you."

Gust spoke.

"They can look for us but we can just go somewhere else."

"You can, but your friends can't. Ruthless men will take them prisoner to force them to disclose where you are and the secret of your long life. A secret they don't know. They would pay the price for your friendship. You must leave and go to a place of safety where these men will never find you; you must go now, while your friends are still safe."

"And where is this miraculous place?" asked July.

Reaching into a leather tube beside him, Kalend took out a rolled piece of fabric. It looked dirty, stained with blobs of colour. Unrolling and spreading it over part of the table, he touched one corner. The dark stains around the outside rose up to form a ring of mountains. A blue stripe began to ripple and flow while trees and all manner of plants grew up from the surface. Magic was unknown to the Months and they stepped back from the table. Kalend spoke reassuringly.

"There is nothing to fear. This is The Valley. It is my secret and hidden estate in a remote island in the South Seas and I invite all of you to share it with me."

Gust overcame his feelings and pushed forward to study the map.

"I have sailed many seas. I have never seen this land you speak off."

"There are many islands in the great seas to the south. Even your people have not yet reached them."

Kalend pointed to a dark shape.

"In this corner of the valley is a cave. In it is a tunnel which leads to the land beyond. When you leave The Valley, you can travel by thought anywhere in the world you wish. In the valley the high mountains prevent me from travelling by thought and it may well be true for you too. You may have to walk."

"Walk," exclaimed May.

Kalend smiled.

"It is quite a pleasant, even enjoyable activity. Man uses the calendar to plan his life. When it is your 'calendar time' each of you would pass through the cave and tunnel, returning when your time is up and the next month would leave."

Vem had been studying the 'map' carefully.

"What would we do with the rest of our time? You say this is your estate, so does that mean we would be your servants, or your slaves?"

Kalend was horrified by this question.

"There would be no slaves or masters in The Valley. You wouldn't even be my guests. The larger part of The Valley would belong to you. You would work to grow crops, tend animals, care for the land, using the skills you have to provide for yourself and for each other. No one will take what you work for. The Valley and all it contains will be yours. There is nothing to fear. I can take you there and if you decide to leave you will be free to go. I give you my promise."

July spoke again.

"Would we really be safe there? What about wild animals or invading soldiers? Would we have shelter and food, for I have known what it is like to be unbearably hungry and alone."

Kalend was touched by the longing on July's face and in her words. The beautiful, laughing girl was gone. In The Valley she would have a chance to regain her love of life.

"There are no wild animals or soldiers and none can come through the tunnel as I would put a protective curtain across it. Only you would be able to pass through it. When a Month leaves the valley, the curtain would recognize him or her and only that Month would be able to pass back through on their return. No other Month would be able to leave until the previous one returned."

"All this sounds wonderful. A beautiful place of plenty where we can do as we please if we are your prisoners. Have I got that right?"

Like Vem, Dec was suspicious. Sighing inwardly, Kalend tried to sound convincing.

"You wouldn't be prisoners, but the price you would pay for your safety and the safety of your friends is that you would remain in the valley when it's not your time."

Murmurs about 'the truth coming out now', and how it was 'too good to be true' could be heard. Kalend's map became flat once more and taking a rolled scroll from the tube, placed it on the table. He explained it was a contract between them and each must sign if they wished to come to The Valley.

"The Contract protects you and The Valley, guaranteeing certain rights.

Your right to live there when it's not your calendar time.

Your right to return when that time is over.

Your right to use what you produce to meet your needs.

It reassures me that you will faithfully maintain the use of your calendar time. Man is much less likely to find you if there is only one of you there at a time. I cannot risk men learning of what would be our home. It also assures me that you will not harm or damage the land that I freely give to you."

On the scroll were the simple rules Hiemal had written. Kalend read out each one.

Each month will only leave The Valley when it is their calendar time.

Each month will return by sunset on the last day of their allotted time.

In The Valley, each month will use their talents to provide for themselves and for others.

Each must treat with respect The Valley they have been given.

There was silence while each month scrutinized the scroll. Vem spoke again.

"We need some time to discuss this by ourselves. Will you wait outside until we ask you to return?"

Kalend, knowing he'd said all he could, left them.

He stood outside the gates where the months had gathered earlier. He was no longer amused by the cleverness of Hiemal's charter, he was trapped by it.

If the Months refused to come to The Valley, they would be destroyed. If only some came, those who remained on Earth would be destroyed. The Valley Months would blame him for their death making any kind of relationship between them impossible. In any of these scenarios, Hiemal could claim Kalend had failed in his responsibility and force him to step down. The only way to survive was if all agreed to come with him, and that didn't look likely.

Inside the villa there was silence before Vem asked what they thought. Tober was first to speak.

"We all know it is becoming more difficult to escape the suspicions of those around us, even our friends are asking questions."

"That may be so," said Ember. "But leaving our homes and those we love is a lot to ask. Kalend may appear genuine but I feel he is keeping things from us."

June had been thinking quietly since the meeting began. "He is using this claim that we are in danger to hide who, or what he really is. Like some of you, I too have fears of what the future may hold for me. The question we must ask is this. Is the future Kalend is offering better than the one we face if we remain here?"

Vem was impressed with June's insight.

"June is right. Is going with Kalend better than not going with him?"

July suddenly stood and spoke in a shrill voice.

"I want to go with him. I am afraid to stay."

May was filled with such longing, tears flowed as she spoke.

"I have been so lonely. Friends grow old and die. Children I helped be born are now dead. I want to belong to a family that will not grow old and die. A family we could all have if we go with him."

A silence filled the room as each felt the strength of May's argument. Each was filled with the same desire to no longer have to leave a place suddenly. Not to leave friends when they became suspicious. Not to look over their shoulder constantly to see if they were being watched or followed. The longing for a permanent home was strong in each of them.

Kalend saw Vem coming out of the villa and moved towards him, but Vem put up his hand to stop him.

"The others may believe what they will. I don't know who or what you are, but I believe you have your own reasons for the offer you make."

Kalend tried to reassure him but Vem spoke angrily.

"Don't waste your breath denying it. All I need to know is the answer to one question. Is taking us to your Valley to save us or to imprison us?"

Kalend held Vem's gaze as he answered fervently.

"I came to save you, and I'm the only chance you've got."

Vem stared at him for a long moment, he could see the truth in Kalend's eyes and nodded before gesturing to return to the villa.

When they entered the room, silence fell, all eyes fixed on them.

"I believe we should go with him." Vem turned to Kalend. "Where do I sign?"

One by one they signed as the parchment was passed around the table, until it came to July.

"No harm will come to us there?"

"No, you will be safe."

July held out her hand. "I will sign."

After sharing the meal Kalend had prepared it was a simple matter to get everyone to gather their belongings as no one kept more than they could carry. June had a wooden box that Gust offered to carry for her, surprised by its weight.

They travelled with Kalend to a remote wilderness. The tunnel entrance was hidden in a patch of trees with a simple but spacious hut in front of it. When they left The Valley, the hut would give them time to decide where they would go. It would also serve as a holding place for any items they needed to bring back with them.

As they stood at its door, Kalend hesitated. He already liked these Months and would live in close contact with them, but it would all be based on deception. The Valley wasn't on Earth, the consequences of breaking the rules hadn't been told, the existence of the Watch was a secret. But if he didn't do this, they would die. He had no choice.

Led by Vem, the Months entered the hut, passing through the unseen curtains to walk down the tunnel into the cave. They saw The Valley for the first time. Their faces showed relief that it was as they had been shown, and delight at how beautiful it was. Two buildings had been placed beside the river containing tools, clothing and food until crops were ready for harvesting. Eleven cabins had been built for the Months to live in until they could build homes in a style of their choosing. Kalend was aware he must allow the Months to feel in charge of their own destiny, not one he decided for them.

No one asked to leave The Valley and a relieved Kalend crossed the river, saying he would be there if they needed him. Two small boats had been made, one on each side of the river. A pulley system meant as one boat crossed, the other would return to take its place.

From his cabin across the river he could hear talking and laughter. Kalend slept more soundly than he had since t'Hura had come to him with her problem. He believed it was a problem no more.

Left alone the Months began to organize themselves and explore their new home. It was agreed they would all meet again in the morning to discuss how life here would be. Vem suggested Tober should be present for that meeting, leaving afterwards. He would return on the 31st of October and Vem would leave.

Next morning they met again, surprised to find May had been up early and prepared breakfast for them.

Vem stood and the group fell silent, before Gust spoke.

"Who decided Vem should be in charge? I do not disagree but should it not be agreed by all?"

Vem was first to support Gust's question but others were angry. Dec had hurtful memories of Viking raids and felt no love for the big man.

"I suppose you think you should be in charge. If we don't agree, will you take that sword of yours and strike us down?"

Gust bowed his head in sorrow. He knew only too well the reputation of his people.

"Ostmen take what they need from those who cannot defend themselves."

He looked around the table at many antagonistic faces.

"I am Ostmen no longer. I am a man of The Valley."

He spoke with conviction but Dec was still not ready to accept him. Vem could see it would take some time for the 'family' May wanted to become a reality.

Ember suggested The Valley didn't need a leader. All should have equal rights to speak, to ask questions and make suggestions. March, June and Jan were in agreement, but March added Vem should probably start the meeting, or the day would soon pass. Murmurs of agreement were heard and Vem began.

"How will we live here? We are accustomed to caring for ourselves and now we are a family."

"I am a farmer and care for animals. I can provide food for our tables. Any extra can be taken to market."

Jan was willing to do his share.

"Salve everyone, I work with the earth, growing fruit and vegetables. Like Vem I can provide food for our tables and extra for trade."

March's face was expressionless as she looked around the table.

"I care for the sick, making potions and salves to heal wounds. I trade some of these for food and shelter but seldom have coin."

"I am an entertainer," said an enthusiastic Ari. "I make music and sing songs in villas and markets. I usually get paid in food and lodgings but not often in coin. I would be happy to work for whichever Month is away and to provide entertainment for you."

May was glad she had prepared food for them.

"I bake bread for the marketplace, but often small items of trade are my only payment."

July took a man's garment from a bag and spread it on the table.

"I make garments for those who can afford to pay for them. My work is not always in demand and often earn barely enough to survive."

Ember and May studied the garment and expressed wonder at the quality of the cloth and the stitching. July was grateful for their appreciation of her work.

"I made this for Paulinus, but he never returned to wear it. I can make clothing for all of us and sell others in the markets."

Gust stood, taking his sword and blade from his belt and placing them on the table.

"I work in metal, I can make shoes for the horses, nails for building and blades like these to sell."

Ember was silent for a moment.

"I am a fisherwoman and can provide food for our tables. I can work with Vem and Jan when I am here and take any trade goods they have to sell."

Dec was next.

"I work in wood. I can make huts and dwellings for us, but I also like to carve wooden toys for children. These I can sell at market."

The quiet June knocked a spoon on the table and all eyes turned to her.

"We have a chance here to make a new beginning."

She opened the wooden box Gust had left on the table the night before. She took out a wooden frame with coloured beads in rows along it.

"I use this to count faster than any man. I have been paid well for my skill."

She removed a cloth to reveal the box was filled with coin.

"Can you teach me to do that?" asked a wide-eyed Ari. June ignored him.

"This is no longer mine. It is ours. When each of you leave, I will give you enough coin to purchase the things we need but cannot provide. When you return, all the coin you have earned will be given to me. I will keep an account of what each has brought. For the first year we will spend more coin than we earn, but soon we will be able to produce more and our funds will grow."

Gust said what others were thinking.

"Why do you keep the coin if we all work to earn it?"

She looked around the room.

"Do any of you have coin to give?"

Silence greeted her question.

"Good. I am happy for Vem to keep this box, but I will decide how best to use its contents."

Closing the lid, June sat down.

"Kalend, how nice of you to call"

Curiosity about the Months led to many conversations among the Watchers, but all knew they must not interfere or interact with them and life returned to its usual routine, except for Verna. t'Hura and Stolesc were concerned by how little time Verna was spending in Tir Dhuchais and spoke to Kalend about it. He had been aware of her absence but hadn't questioned the family issues that prompted it. Verna's attendance at Watch meetings was all that was required by System law, the remainder of her time she could spend as she chose. He was, however, concerned to think something was wrong and at the close of the next Watch meeting, went to visit her. After a rather restrained greeting from a normally warm and outgoing Verna, Kalend came to the reason for his visit.

"Stolesc and t'Hura are worried about you. If there is a problem on your home world it is of no concern to me, but if there is a problem here I must know of it."

Faced with his direct question she could not lie. Speaking softly, she began.

"It is the custom of my people to dance naked among the trees to renew our contact with the act of creation. The morning after the Charter of the Months was accepted, I was happy the problem faced by t'Hura had been solved without the destruction of the Months."

She stopped as memories of that day brought her to tears. She told Kalend what Hiemal had done, sobbing as she described the hate and anger on his face, while his words were complimentary.

"Please do not tell anyone as I am ashamed of my weakness. I will perform my duties as Watcher but spend no other time here."

Kalend held Verna's hand while anger at Hiemal flooded through him. Verna was the sweetest, gentlest and kindest member of the Watch. The fact that Hiemal would do this to her was unforgiveable.

"You are not the one who has done wrong. I consider you the most valued member of my Watch. Your nature is one of calmness among a horde of noise. Your presence here is a joy to me and to others. I will speak to Hiemal and you will have no need to fear him again. Promise me you will stay."

Verna looked into the beseeching eyes of Kalend and managed a smile.

"Very well, I will stay. Will you keep this matter between us?"

"It is up to you who you share with, but Stolesc and t'Hura came to me out of concern for you. Perhaps telling Stolesc is not a good idea. He is likely to knock Hiemal down."

Verna laughed and Kalend saw a genuine twinkle in her eyes.

Stolesc and t'Hura were delighted when Verna said she was staying, happily agreeing when asked if they would help with her garden as it was overgrown. She didn't mention Kalend and they accepted her word that her family were now well and didn't need her.

Kalend decided to walk to see Hiemal, taking time to plan what he would say. On his way, he met Balack.

"Kalend, you must come with me to try some of Thades' wine. The last lot made me unwell for some time and I fear the consequences of going alone."

"You could just not go. That would be sensible."

"Yes it would, but while I am not Thades' friend, our relationship is important to him. He told me so. It would be unkind to refuse his invitation."

"Balack, you are a good person. You could perhaps choose other friends more carefully."

Kalend left a bewildered Balack looking after him. It was obvious Kalend was referring to Hiemal but such an outspoken comment was out of character. He wondered what Hiemal had done to upset him.

"Kalend, how nice of you to call. We have never seen you in our home." Kalend went inside but refused the drink Hiemal offered him, preferring to stand. "Please allow us to show you the beauty of our dwelling."

As they walked from room-to-room Kalend saw exquisite furniture, soft fabrics that warmed under his touch and intricate design work on doors and wall panels. "This is a very elaborate dwelling. You are obviously used to a high standard of life. This makes me wonder why you agreed to accept a position as Watcher of an insignificant world. In fact, I asked that very question at a Senaten meeting."

Hiemal noticeably paled, swallowing nervously but forcing a laugh. "You know what political bodies are like, you can never trust a word they say." Hiemal turned his back, walking towards a window. His uncle had assured him Kalend would never know why he had been sent to his system. "Politicians are not to be trusted. What half-truths did they shower upon me?"

"I think we both know the answer to that." The look on Hiemal's face as he turned confirmed the rumours of violence Kalend had heard, but without any details of Hiemal's previous crime, he could only speak of Verna. "That is not what brings me here today. I have just come from Verna. I cannot believe someone who pretends to be honourable would treat a gentle soul like Verna in the way you have. She has returned and you will never again go near her, or speak to her, except in the Chamber." Hiemal felt a rush of relief as Kalend mentioned Verna but confused by his talk of the Senaten. Did Kalend know something, or only suspect?

"How dare you presume to accept her word without asking for our statement of the facts. We will not tolerate such lack of respect in our own dwelling." Hiemal knew he must keep control of this situation. Kalend could not be allowed to continue his attempts to intimidate him. Face suffused with anger, Hiemal continued his angry tirade. "The Senaten would not tolerate an insignificant Presidion speaking to them on the word of a nothing from an obscure world of no importance in the Galaxy."

Angered by Hiemal's arrogance, Kalend forced himself to remain calm. Meeting Hiemal's gaze he waited a few moments before responding. "We can speak of this in a Watch meeting in the Chamber where your crystal will show truth or a lie. If I then speak to the Senaten about your attack on a member of my Watch, you may face consequences you do not like."

Hiemal was trapped and both he and Kalend knew it, but Hiemal refused to show fear or contrition.

"The Senaten has better things to do than deal with a petty complaint against a member of the House of Uclair. Very well, I will never go near Verna again. Who would want to?"

Angered by Hiemal's lack of remorse and his flagrant contempt for Verna, Kalend moved to within inches of Hiemal, his anger flaring in her defence.

"Your days here will be few if I hear you speak of Verna with such a lack of respect again."

Faced with Kalend's unexpected anger, Hiemal stepped back, tripping over the chair behind him and sprawling on the floor. Leaving him lying there Kalend returned to his dwelling to calm his outrage.

Hiemal picked himself up, consumed with anger, fear and hate.

His anger directed at Verna who had dared to make a complaint against him.

His fear was for himself and the danger he would be in if Kalend reported him to the Senaten.

His dislike for Kalend turned to hate for the humiliation he had endured. How dare Kalend come into his dwelling and threaten him. It was obvious Kalend had spoken to someone, but who? Had someone from the Senaten broken their vow of silence? How much did Kalend know? Whatever it was, he had used it to trick him, Hiemal of Uclair, into letting his fear show.

Filled with hate, Hiemal travelled to Pluto, howling his rage where no-one could hear. Realising his hatred for Kalend would turn his crystal black if he spoke in the Chamber, he knew a way must be found to fix his ring.

Travelling from one remote world to another he searched for something to negate his crystal. Many laughed at him saying he wasn't the first to seek such a thing. With no other option open to him, he sent a message to his Uncle Turien asking for a meeting. Hiemal spoke of his remorse for his behaviour and asked if Turien knew of anyone who could help him control his anger. Turien was surprised but pleased at Hiemal's apparent willingness to change; however, he knew him well enough to be suspicious.

"Wise men on a remote part of the Uclairian home world practice self-discipline. They could help if you are truly desirous to change. Your mother would be pleased to learn of your willingness to restore your honour."

The mention of his mother stirred emotions he had long strived to control.

"We give our word that we will do whatever is necessary."

As Hiemal took his leave, Turien wondered what had happened to bring about this change.

Kalend was fishing with Rogue when Turien paid him a visit.

"Sen Turien, it is a surprise to have you visit our System. Please allow me to call a meeting so my Watchers can pay their respects."

"Thank you, but that is not why we are here. May we sit?"

Kalend poured two glasses of Thades' Pestiar wine, which had proved very palatable despite Balack's misgivings. Both men sat in silence, neither wanting to be the first to speak. Turien regarded Kalend for some moments then began.

"We are here as we have been told you are an honourable man. My nephew is Hiemal of Uclair."

Kalend made no response and Turien was irritated. "He came to see us to ask for help to curtail his emotions. We have made arrangements for him to do this."

Kalend still made no reply and Turien's irritation grew. Forcing himself to appear calm, he continued.

"We would be grateful for your counsel if there was anything you can offer which could prove useful to those helping him?"

Kalend was unsure what Sen Turien had been told, so was cautious in his reply.

"Hiemal is a passionate young man and being so far from his home world is difficult for him. The pairing with the smallest world was, I feel, a disappointment for him. If there is anything you would have me know, I will be happy to help."

Turien knew Kalend was fishing for a reason for Hiemal's appointment but would not be drawn. If Kalend would or could not shed any light on Hiemal's changed demeanour, there was nothing he could do. The information he had been given about Kalend's shrewdness appeared to be true.

"Hiemal will be absent for one orbit of your blue planet. We would appreciate you informing the Watch that urgent family business necessitates Hiemal's assistance. There is no need to tell of our visit here."

"If that is your wish, but it is disappointing you will not have time to explore the home we have made here."

"Perhaps another time."

Without a word of farewell, Turien left.

Kalend sat for a long time breathing deeply. He had feared Hiemal had told his uncle about the Months or his last, heated conversation with him. A feeling of relief washed over him followed by the realisation that Hiemal's crime must have been a serious one to bring Turien here. He needed to prepare for what he would do if Hiemal's violence showed itself in Tir Dhuchais. For now, Hiemal's absence of one orbit would provide a welcome break for everyone, especially Verna. The smile and laughter that greeted the news when he told her, made him smile too.

Hiemal spent time with the wise men of Uclair, learning how to use physical activity and long periods submerged in ice to slow and cool his emotions. Cold emotions were much harder for the crystal to recognise than hot ones.

Anger was easy to manage when you knew how. Hate was a different matter; Hiemal's hatred for Kalend burned deep within him. With practice and discipline, it could be controlled but not erased.

Hiemal was absent so long he missed the next three Watch meetings but Kalend's explanation satisfied any curiosity. When he did return, he appeared to be calmer than the old Hiemal. Thades asked what had happened to him but he refused to discuss it, saying it was a private matter.

Every morning Hiemal would run to Stolesc's fenced garden and back. Physically tired he was able to control his emotions, making them burn cold. As he ran, he thought of only one thing; it would take time, but he would get his revenge on all who had conspired against him.

"You are in my way, remove yourself"

Time passed and four hundred orbits of Earth brought many changes to the life of the Months. The family May wanted so badly was now a reality.

Gust and Dec, after an initial hostility, were great friends, building a workshop where Gust would use his forge and Dec would do his carpentry. Their original cabins were now storerooms with new houses on either side of the workshop.

Ember used all her powers of persuasion, which were considerable, to convince Dec to build her a house on stilts over the edge of the river. She would sit inside on a rocking chair with a fishing pole dangling out of the window, while drinking beer with Jan. June formed an unlikely friendship with the outgoing and mischievous Ari and their laughter could often be heard by Kalend from across the river. Relationships had been forged, sometimes with difficulty, but all in all the family of Months worked well. Individual houses had replaced most of the original cabins, with trees and flowers blooming in gardens. Animals grazed in fields and Kalend was proud of all he and the Months had achieved.

Kalend's only concern was July. She had never recovered from her grief of losing Paulinus and had become increasingly solitary. Her only friend was March but she seldom joined in any of the social activities that Ari arranged.

Kalend was summoned to a meeting of the Senaten but knew Vem could deal with any issues that may arise in his absence.

As he entered Tir Dhuchais to take his leave of the Watch,

he was waylaid by t'Hura.

"Kalend, I must speak with you, it's about Earth."

"It will have to be quick. I'm about to leave for an important meeting."

"Man has made another change to the Calendar. They realised the days they called winter were insufficient for the length of the season and gathered the remaining days to form the last month, calling it February. I last saw February in a small fishing village in the south of a country called Hispania, but I'm not sure the Watch will give their approval to bring him here."

"I don't need their approval. I have complete authority over the Months and that will include this new one. There won't be any more, will there?"

"No, all the days have been allocated now."

"t'Hura, I have to leave. You must find this February and send me word as to where he is now. Ari is on Earth and I will call with him after I hear from you. He can befriend February and bring him back with him. DO NOT tell anyone else about his existence, please. I have enough to deal with without this being a problem."

t'Hura gave her promise.

Ari was delighted at the prospect of another young man joining the Months and happily agreed to meet with him. Kalend hoped he might be back in time to meet them on Earth but made it clear to Ari that if not, it was imperative that on his return to The Valley, HE must go through the tunnel first, opening the curtain of recognition. Only then could February follow so the curtain could recognize him and then May could leave. Ari assured Kalend he would do exactly as he asked.

Kalend's meeting lasted much longer than he thought and Ari had already brought February to The Valley before he returned.

It was in the early hours of the first day of the month of August when Kalend returned. As he was about to go to bed, he saw something strange across the river. A green light was shining somewhere in the meeting house area, a green light that had no place there.

Travelling across the river, he saw the light was coming from July's house. It dimmed then disappeared but he could just make out several creatures leaving her cabin. They were very tall, greyish in colour and when they turned sideways, they seemed to disappear, being no thicker than a blade of grass. Kalend had never seen anything like them and fearing for July's safety, entered her cabin, only to find her sleeping peacefully. With her hair loose and spread over the pillow she looked younger, more like the July he had first seen in Rome.

Leaving July, Kalend tried to follow the creatures. Their long legs meant they could travel amazingly fast and he lost them in the forest. He spent several hours trying to find some trace of them, or a place where they might have gone, but there was nothing. He had never seen or heard of creatures like these and briefly considered asking his fellow Presidions on the Hoameta but realising any questions could reveal the existence of the Months, he knew he would have to keep his own counsel.

It was already daylight as he rushed back, only to meet Ari, June and a dark-haired young man. Ari smiled and then winked lasciviously.

"Hi Kalend, where have you been? We thought you'd found some beautiful woman and couldn't bear to leave her. Oh, this is Feb, we've sorted him out with Tober's old house as he's living at the farm now. We've told him all he needs to know about the rules and how things work."

February scowled.

"Hola. My name is February, not Feb. I'm pleased to meet you, Kalend."

Kalend briefly smiled.

"Welcome February. Have any of you seen July this morning?"

June was surprised by Kalend's lack of interest in February.

"Is something wrong?"

Without replying, Kalend hurried towards July's house. Even though he'd checked July was sleeping soundly before leaving her, he needed to make sure she was unhurt and unchanged by whatever had happened the night before. Ari and June were surprised by Kalend's dismissal of them.

"What's got into him? He's usually happy to talk; in fact, sometimes you can't get him to stop."

February had heard a lot about Kalend and took his lack of interest in him as a personal affront. He was quiet for the rest of the day, believing Kalend ignored him because he considered him to be of lesser importance than the other Months.

As Kalend left them he saw a figure leave March's home, heading towards the meeting house. It was July. A sigh escaped him as he hurried after her.

"July, wait please."

She turned when she heard him shout.

"July, how are you. Are you well?"

"Yes, thank you."

Kalend searched her face for any signs of stress or change. There must have been a reason for the creatures to be in her cabin. And what was the green mist? Realizing he was staring, he smiled and asked July about her calendar time.

"I did as I always do, visited places, gathered the items on my list and then returned."

There was no outward sign of change but Kalend needed to ask one more question.

"Did you sleep well last night? It must be nice to be back in your own bed."

"How or where I sleep is none of your concern. Now if you have finished with your questions, I will get on with my day."

She certainly seemed to be her usual, unfriendly self with no awareness of a disturbed night. While there was no evidence of harm, he would monitor her over the coming days.

Kalend, realizing he had not slept or eaten for some time called in with May who happily supplied him with a few of the cheese filled rolls he liked. She also gave him cold meats, salad and apple crumble left over from the shared meal of the night before. Kalend asked May if she had seen July that morning.

"Of course, regular as clockwork that one. But I just saw you talking to her, so why ask me?"

Kalend had no idea what to say and May put a hand on his forehead.

"You look exhausted and you have a temperature. You should go and see March. She'll fix you up. As to July, she likes her own company. Best leave her be."

Kalend didn't go to see March. He went home. He ate a little before lying on his bed to think, but tiredness overcame him and he slept. He was unaware of March entering his cabin, resting a cool hand gently on his forehead before rubbing a salve on his brow. She watched as he muttered and tossed in his sleep, waiting until he slept calmly before leaving.

Unaware of his visitor, only of having slept well, Kalend sat at a table to relive the events of the night and day. Sites chosen as bases for System Watches were always checked for indigenous life, so it was unlikely the creatures were from Tir Dhuchais. This would leave only two questions:

1. Who or what were they and how had they found their way here?

2. What did the creatures want with July? What was so special about her? Or perhaps she wasn't special at all, perhaps these creatures visited all the Months?

Kalend decided to keep watch that night in case they came back. He roamed through The Valley peering through the windows of each house in turn, but all was quiet.

Vem saw him but was caring for an ailing calf born that day; he didn't have time to speak. The next day he went over to Kalend's side of the river. When Kalend saw him coming he hoped to discover if Vem knew something about the creatures. As usual, Vem came straight to the point.

"Hello Kalend. It's nice to have you back among us. I saw you last night, wandering about on our side of the river, peering in through windows. Ari, June and May said you were acting strangely when they saw you earlier. What's going on?"

Not for the first time, Kalend would have liked to confide in Vem but knew his loyalty would always be to the Months. He couldn't be sure Vem would keep any information he gave him to himself and didn't want to start a panic. He'd promised July they would be safe here and until he knew otherwise, he would keep his own counsel.

"I had returned late the night before and then slept during the day. Not needing sleep I just went for a walk. If I'd seen you, I would have stopped to speak. Was something wrong that had you up so late?"

Vem spoke of the animal he had been tending, not completely sure Kalend was telling the whole truth. Ari had told him Kalend had hardly acknowledged February, asking only about July and was suspicious.

"If there is something I should know, you would tell me, wouldn't you?"

Kalend knew he must allay Vem's fears and put an end to speculation now.

"If there is a problem, I wouldn't keep it from you, I give you my word. If you would like me to speak to Ari, June and February, I'm happy to do so."

Vem considered for the briefest of moments.

"That won't be necessary; no need to alarm anyone if there is no cause."

"There is no cause, but thank you for bringing your concerns to me, my door is always open. Would you like some tea before you leave?"

Despite, or perhaps because of Vem's suspicions, Kalend felt his relationship with him was more honest than with any of the others and was pleased when Vem sat down and stayed to talk. Tea had been brought to The Valley by June and having sampled it on a visit to her home, Kalend had become a firm fan. June now supplied him with it on a regular basis. Vem was still suspicious Kalend kept secrets from them.

"Why were you in such a hurry to find July?"

Kalend expressed his concern for her increasing solitude, explaining he would normally make time to speak to her during the shared meal on her return. He said his constant hope was that her Calendar time would bring her some happiness.

"Don't we all." was Vem's heartfelt reply. As he returned to the farm, Vem's suspicions about Kalend were raised one more notch. He liked him, time spent fishing with him was always pleasant but something unspoken lurked beneath the surface, he was sure of it.

After Vem had gone, Kalend decided any more late-night visits to the other side of the river would have to be postponed for the time being, but he would keep watch from this side.

Kalend again searched the woodland where the creatures had vanished but there was not so much as a footprint. Only the Watch knew about the Months, so how had these beings learned of them? How had they been able to penetrate the barriers he had put in place? July may have been unharmed but he needed to know how and why these creatures had come to The Valley. Perhaps other Months had been visited too.

Throughout the days of August, Kalend managed to have a conversation with each Month, talking about their calendar time, their work in The Valley, anything general. Everyone seemed just as they had always been, no signs of harm or awareness of the creatures.

Kalend's thoughts were plagued with unanswered questions. Who were they? How did they get here? Would they harm those they visited?

The only idea that occurred to him was that they had come to July on the night she had returned from her Calendar time. Was this a coincidence?

As the last day of the month of August approached, Kalend determined to spend the night outside Gust's house to watch and guard. He always joined the Months for the shared meal and did so when Gust returned. Afterwards he took his leave, returning as soon as it was dark and hiding among the trees until the light in Gust's room went out. He then moved to stand in front of his door through which he could hear snoring.

Several hours passed and Kalend was beginning to think he was wrong when he saw them.

There were seven of the creatures. As they came closer Kalend could see their skin was rough and mottled. Their heads were as wide as their shoulders with what looked like ears lying flat on either side of a round twitching nose. What Kalend supposed to be a mouth was nothing more than a slit; large, rectangular, unblinking eyes dominated the face.

The creature in front had a series of decorative symbols on the skin around his throat – Kalend assumed he was their leader. Warily, he stood in front of the door and waited for the creature to approach. It was taller than the roof of Gust's house and suddenly leaned forward, his face just inches away from Kalend.

"You are in our way. Remove yourself."

"I am Kalend and the care of this Valley is in my hands. What is your business here?"

"I know who you are. Our business is not your concern. You are in our way. Remove yourself."

"Tell me what your business is."

Kalend folded his arms and met the gaze of the creature. The leader turned back to the others and Kalend could hear strange hissing noises which appeared to be their form of communication. The leader turned back to Kalend.

"We are Quaan, gatherers and custodians of memories throughout the universe. We collect the memories of the Months and keep them safe for all time. We do not harm them, for they are possessors of the knowledge we desire. It is getting late and we must gather the memories of August before this night is over."

Kalend had never heard of such a species and was angry at their assumption they could come without any consultation.

"What do you mean you gather them? I have certainly never heard any Month speak of you. If they don't know what you do, they can't have given you permission. If I am to consider this, you will answer my questions."

The leader hissed strongly and leaned closer to Kalend.

"I am Y Quaan, and you do not tell me what I can or can't do."

"If you want to go through this door you will do. I can spend every night standing in front of this door if I have to."

Kalend posed his questions. There was lots of hissing and glaring looks as the Quaan deliberated. The Y Quaan faced Kalend and spoke again, amazing Kalend with the information he gave.

The Quaan were from another galaxy; memories of the lives of others provided the nourishment that allowed them to exist. They had been visitors to the planet called Earth for many centuries but the discovery of the Months was a great treasure. They were able to travel through the tunnel, as Y Quaan modified Kalend's curtain to allow free passage to them. To be able to collect memories from the same beings for all time gave a life force like none ever experienced before. To lose the collecting of memories from The Valley would be a huge loss to them.

Kalend listened in disbelief which turned to anger when they spoke of altering the curtain in the tunnel. Finally, he was filled with wonderment. Y Quaan spoke again.

"We have answered your impertinent questions. For this night only, you may accompany us to gather and then see the memories of August. No one who is not Quaan has ever been permitted to do this. You are in our way. Remove yourself."

"When you say, 'see the memories' what do you mean?"

"You will come with us to where the memories are stored, see what we see and then you will be permitted to leave, unharmed as your Months are, for we are not a cruel race."

With some trepidation, Kalend stepped aside and opened the

door. Despite Gust's doors being taller than anyone else's, the Quaan still had to bend almost double to enter. Kalend followed them inside. They sat on the floor around Gust's bed and the Y Quaan gestured Kalend to a chair.

Two small bottles of clear liquid were taken out of a pouch around Y Quaan's waist and mixed. Immediately the liquid turned green and began to pour out of the bottle until the room was filled with a green mist. The Y Quaan turned to look at Kalend, surprised and amused to see he was now as soundly asleep as Gust and wouldn't interfere with the gathering.

The first Quaan lifted the bedding from Gust's feet and placed a thick pad of cloth under them. He took hold of one foot, threw back his head and a low humming sound came from his throat. The mind holds the memories, but it is the feet that make the journey, and they remember. The index finger on the right hand of the Quaan had a long, very pointed tip and if the Quaan wasn't happy with the memory or wanted more information, he used this to jab into the sole of Gust's foot, but even this did not awaken him. The pad under the feet soaked up the blood that was spilled, quickly becoming red.

When the first Quaan had recovered all the memories he could, his place was taken by the second, then third, until all six recovery Quaan had been filled. The bottles were opened to allow the green mist to return to them and once again become clear liquid. A thick ointment was wiped over Gust's bleeding feet and the wounds healed, all trace of them disappearing under perfectly healthy skin. Gust would sleep soundly, waking totally refreshed in the morning.

When all was as it had been, two Quaan carried Kalend back through the forest. When they came to the cliff wall, Y Quaan placed his hand in a thin crack in the rock and a doorway opened to allow Kalend to be taken inside where he was placed on the ground. Y Quaan used his pointed finger to draw a symbol gently on Kalend's forehead, waking him instantly. He stared around him and jumped to his feet

"What trickery is this, you said I could witness the gathering?"

"It's not our fault if you are susceptible to the green mist. We have carried you here to witness the 'telling.'"

"Where is here? Where am I?"

"You are under the mountains that surround your Valley. This is where we have our Repository for the memories we collect. Come with us to see for I grow tired of you."

They followed a walkway which was lit by flaming torches placed at regular intervals along the walls. Their dancing light played on carvings which depicted momentous moments in history. Kalend recognised some places from t'Hura's reports to the Watch.

The walkway ended in an amphitheatre so large the top row of torches were pinpoints of light that looked like stars. Tiers of seats adorned the walls and every seat was filled with Quaan as the telling of Gust was eagerly anticipated. At intervals around the cavern were doorways that opened into smaller caves. Above the entrance to each were carved the names of the Month whose memories were kept there. The extent of the caves indicated that this practice had been going on for a long time. A new cave was being prepared for February.

Y Quaan stood on a stage in the centre of the amphitheatre and the crowd fell silent. The six Quaan who had visited Gust sat around the stage, each with their eyes fixed firmly on Y Quaan's face. Out of deference to Kalend, he spoke in words, not the hissing sound he'd used earlier. When he began to speak, every word could be heard in the furthest reaches of the cavern. He gave no introduction to Kalend, welcoming the gathering to the telling of Gust. He nodded to the first Quaan and then took his seat.

The six who had visited Gust did not speak. They recalled in their minds all they had gathered. Words, music and pictures of Earth that could be viewed from any seat in the cavern were replayed on the stage.

Gust loved the sea, and his memories were always full of great ships crossing storm lashed oceans, bringing supplies to people in far flung corners of the Roman world. Kalend could hear the roar of the sea and looking around, saw the Quaan bending and swaying as if they too were on the ship.

On land, Gust visited a village in the northern part of the known Earth. It was clear to see this was his homeland, for he was welcomed as one of them. There was one scene showing him playing with the children of the village. A horde of small boys overwhelmed him, forcing him to the ground where they clambered over him as he roared with laughter and joy. A great swell of whispered pleasure filled the cavern, embracing Kalend with the same joy.

Gust's visit turned sorrowful as he visited a grave site and knelt, shedding tears for those he had lost. Kalend was almost overwhelmed at the depth of empathy felt by these strange creatures which was now touching him.

Now Gust was part of a happy crowd, singing, drinking, dancing, and filling the stage with their friendship; an appreciative sound came from the throats of those watching and from the sound of feet moving and stamping in time with the music.

No one would leave until the Telling was over, so great was the thirst for the memories of Gust.

Kalend realised he knew little of this man. On Earth, Gust was filled with sorrow, joy and laughter and Kalend saw the extent of the sacrifice he and the others had made to leave Earth. He determined to know each one better.

With the Telling over, Kalend was swiftly escorted back to the entrance, the doorway opened, and he was told to leave.

"How can you store a memory?"

"The memories are available for us to share many times. How we do this is not your concern."

Y Quaan went to push Kalend out the door.

"Wait. One more question. Do you remain here all the time, or only come when it is time to gather memories?"

"We travel the universe. We are only here to collect and then store the memories when each Month returns."

The doorway closed in front of him and the solid wall of rock once again confronted him with no sign of a way in. As he walked back through the forest in the morning light, Kalend mused on the night's events. He was unhappy not to have seen the 'Gathering' but would call on Gust to see if he, like July, was unharmed and unknowing. The Telling of the story of Gust was impressive and had affected him deeply. He would have liked to see more of these, but Y Quaan made it clear that would not be happening.

Gust was busy in his workshop, cheerfully singing as he worked and Kalend recognised the song as one of those sung when he was away. He welcomed Kalend and offered him refreshment, which he gladly accepted. As they chatted it was clear Gust was not affected in any way by his night-time visitors.

Back home Kalend considered his options. If he told the Watch of the Quaan they were unlikely to allow their presence to continue but it would need the enforcement of the Senaten to remove them. All he had done to ensure the Senaten didn't learn of the Months would be exposed.

He had two choices, tell the Watch and risk everything, or do nothing and let continue a practice which had been in existence for centuries without harm. Keeping such a secret from both Watchers and Months was a huge responsibility and Kalend already felt the burden of secrets he kept.

As he was preparing an evening meal, he had a sudden, horrifying thought. The green mist had rendered him unaware of anything for hours. What if the Quaan came back for his memories? Knowledge of the Watch and Senaten would be exposed, and he had no idea what the Quaan would do with such information.

He hurried outside and peered into the growing darkness. The entrance to Tir Dhuchais was protected with a curtain extending high above the cliffs, keeping it safe from discovery, but he was unprotected. He quickly formed a temporary barrier curtain to surround his house, including the roof and felt a little more secure. Surprised by his lack of tiredness, he resolved not to go to bed. He stood in the darkened room by the window, watching.

A few hours later he saw Y Quaan. He must have crossed by the waterfall and made his way down his side of the river. Surprised to find his way barred by something he couldn't see, he moved around the house, searching for a break in the barrier. When he found none, he returned to the front of his cabin hissing and in a state of great agitation. Turning to leave, Y Quann stopped, looking back at the window directly into the eyes of Kalend who felt himself shiver but still believed the decision to keep their existence secret was the right one. He no longer trusted the Senaten so all decisions about the safety and protection of

The Valley and the Watch were his responsibility.

He would make a more substantial barrier around his home the next day and then return to Tir Dhuchais for a short time so he wouldn't be at any risk until he was sure the Quaan left. The barrier above the mountains that kept the Months from discovering Tir Dhuchais should keep out the Quaan too. It was important they never learned of its existence or the Watch.

Dynak noticed his strained appearance and asked him if she could help with anything, but he assured her he was fine. Some days spent with the Watchers helped to restore his resolve about the Quaan, but after each shared meal with the Months, he left The Valley, returning only when he felt sure the Quaan had moved on.

"You will just have to accept it"

Two millennia had passed since the Months had first come to The Valley and life had adapted to changes on Earth.

July seldom made clothing for the others now as they brought back whatever they needed. She didn't approve of the shorts and skimpy tops favoured by June and most definitely not the lycra sports gear worn by February. When not helping March with her herbs and potions, July made perfumes, scented soaps and candles. Her garden was full of aromatic plants and flowers, especially roses. When making soaps the aromas would waft their way from her cabin all the way to Ember's house by the river. Behind July's cabin a large bush of rosemary grew, it was her favourite plant and she spent long hours sitting beside it. She was the only Month still living in her original cabin. Most used them now for storage or work rooms.

July also maintained a library. She first became interested in words when Paulinus would receive written orders. She found it fascinating he could make words out of the squiggles on the paper. Seeing her delight, he taught her to read and a passion was born. When printed books became plentiful, July began to bring some back to The Valley asking Dec to make her a library. The smaller of the two original buildings had fallen into disrepair but she'd persuaded Dec to fix it and install shelves along each side.

Ari was a keen reader of plays but none of the others could read. Gust was first to ask July to teach him, followed by Ember then May. Now all could read but not everyone shared July's passion.

The library had proved its worth during shared meal at the beginning of a second millennium when Jan had returned with an abandoned kitten. When asked what it was called, he replied.

"I thought I'd call it cat."

There was a roar of protest, but Jan said if someone else wanted to give it a name that was fine with him.

Many suggestions were made and discarded until July said a decision had to be made or they would be there until breakfast. She made a typical July suggestion.

"Everyone should think of the name of their favourite author or book character and we'll choose from those. Ari, you can't choose Aristophanes as it's too long and one Ari is enough."

Ember loved Anna Karenina, but Vem had discovered the kitten was male.

Banned from choosing Aristophanes, Ari was determined a Greek playwright should be considered.

"Sophocles wrote Antigone, I think either of these would be a great name for a cat."

This suggestion was greeted with good humoured boos and jeers.

Jan wasn't a great reader and could only think of one name.

"My favourite character is Noddy."

Roars of laughter greeted this but a good-natured Jan joined the merriment.

"He is a character, so is as valid a suggestion as Ari's Greek guy."

Aldous Huxley was suggested by June with March and Gust both liking Huxley.

When Tober asked July for her thoughts she had difficulty choosing, eventually saying.

"In my opinion, Glass Menagerie by Tennessee Williams is

the best book ever written and Tennessee would be a good name."

Every Christmas Eve May would bake Christmas cake and mince pies; everyone would gather to hear A Christmas Carol by Charles Dickens so no one was surprised by her suggestion.

"I think he looks like a Dickens."

Not sure what a 'dickens' looked like, everyone none the less liked the name.

The advances in the use of tools and machines also affected The Valley. Ari had brought back a two-wheeled object called a bicycle which proved extremely popular with February and June. Ember had tried one but was a constant 'wobbler'.

Gust made anything metal that was required but no longer needed to make nails as he could obtain these in large packets from a great undercover market called B and Q. Gust would spend many hours there inspecting the nails and screws and sighing over power tools that wouldn't work in The Valley. When battery powered tools became available, he found it difficult to choose which one he would use first before settling on a drill plus an extra battery. He was bitterly disappointed when the battery life was short, but each leaving Month would take one back and recharge it for him. Gust also helped Ember to brew a dark beer favoured by the Irish which was drunk in large quantities on the Irish celebration of St Patrick's day. Ember would dress in green, and an all-night party would follow. As this was held in March, plentiful supplies of potions for headaches would be collected in advance for the sore heads which inevitably followed.

Ember's close friendship with Gust emboldened her to offer to cut his long, tangled hair and beard. He may say he was no longer Ostmen but he certainly looked like one. He resisted her attempts for several hundred years but finally agreed when short hair for men became the fashion, and his appearance made some people reluctant to approach his stall in markets. When he emerged several hours later his closely trimmed beard and short hair stopped others in their tracks. Vem said he looked so pretty the men would want to kiss him as well as the women.

February worked with Gust to contain a rabbit problem, trapping and transporting them back through the tunnel. Despite their best efforts, rabbit was on the menu of most Months at least once each week, much to the disgust of March who was a vegetarian long before the word existed.

For Kalend, the greatest joy from having the Months in The Valley was his discovery of music. This was unknown on his home world and he had been transfixed by it from the moment he first heard it. Jan started it by bringing back a piano, though fitting it through the tunnel and down to the meeting hall had been something of a challenge.

June played the cello and Ember the harp which had been almost as difficult to get through the tunnel as the piano had been. Gust played the flute and clarinet while Tober could bring tears to everyone's eyes when he played the violin.

May surprised everyone when she brought back an entire drum kit. It took Tober, Feb, Dec and Vem to carry it to the meeting hall as her own cabin was too small to house it. Everyone was glad the meeting hall wasn't close to their cabins as it took her some time to become the accomplished player she was now.

February played the guitar, banjo and ukulele. Ari was able to play almost any instrument he picked up, recently discovering the saxophone. March did not play but had a beautiful singing voice and would accompany the musicians. Kalend always attended musical evenings but despite many attempts did not appear to have any talent for it. Ari was determined to find something he could play, bringing back a variety of instruments, including a Jewish harp, a harmonica, and a didgeridoo, but a triangle was the best Kalend could manage.

February came from a time six hundred years after Kalend brought the others to The Valley. Society, tools, clothing and expected behaviours were all quite different. Fitting in was difficult for February as firm friendships had already been established. It wasn't helped by his belief Kalend considered him to be inferior to the others. Ari and June became his closest companions, often asking him to accompany them on mischief making expeditions or rehearsing Ari's latest play. When not trapping rabbits or standing in for whichever Month was away, February created sculptures, some of wood, but others from any rock he found on the valley floor. He was a very skilled artist, often selling his work to bijou art galleries in Paris and Madrid. A large rock found in his garden had been transformed into an intricate curved and intertwined sculpture with a small, detached piece to one side. This was his depiction of the relationships in The Valley, all connected, except for him. Despite his skill and hard work, he believed he was considered to be less important because of his fewer days.

Many years ago, he had appealed to Kalend to reconsider his time allocation. Time had been changed before, so why not now? If one day was taken from January and March, they would each be left with thirty days and so would he, keeping the total to three hundred and sixty-five days. He would happily let either of them have his leap year if they wanted it.

Kalend spoke gently but firmly in response to his impassioned plea.

"February, the calendar was devised by man and any changes would have to be made by them, not by me. I understand your frustration, I truly do. Even if I could make changes it would

121

cause unbelievable chaos. You must understand you are the only Month to have any variation in the number of days allocated to you. Only February has a Leap Year – don't you see that this makes you special?"

February was too angry to understand, turning his back and walking out, slamming the door behind him. Kalend sat for a few minutes before getting wearily to his feet. He hoped February would calm down and accept what could not be changed but fearing his temper might make him do something foolish, resolved to keep a close eye on him.

February went to see May, telling her what Kalend had said. She sympathised.

"I know you are disappointed but there is no point in getting upset over something you can do nothing about. You will just have to accept it."

February stopped mentioning his lack of days but his resentment festered making him moody and sullen. Matters came to a head when he came back from his last calendar time.

During the shared meal he told them where he'd been, who he'd seen and how the world was managing without them. Then it was time for the accounting.

June always monitored spending and when banks became used for financial transactions, she first opened one bank account, then several. She would deposit funds, transferring money from place to place as the value of stocks rose or fell. The wealth of the Months grew steadily because of June's astuteness.

When cash and credit cards became the norm, June applied for one of each in all of the countries in which she had opened bank accounts. The returning Month passing these to the one leaving. Money raised while away would be deposited on the last day and the deposit slip given to June.

When February returned he was wearing a designer tracksuit and expensive trainers. When he gave his deposit slip to June she accepted it without comment but Tober asked to see it, grabbing it from June's hand. His scowl as he flung it back on the table reflected his anger that his suspicions had been justified.

"Why is it that you contribute less than anyone else? You always have money to spend on fancy clothes and shoes instead of being careful like the rest of us."

"How do you expect me to earn money when I have three less days than you do?"

"Oh not this again, we all know how you feel about having less days, but it's not an excuse to spend our money."

June however spoke fairly.

"February is correct when he says he cannot earn as much as you. In the time since he came here, he has had thirteen years less time than you, and that is a significant figure."

February stayed to eat the shared meal, his straight back and dour expression clearly expressing his resentment at Tober's accusation. He returned home and while preparing for bed an idea came to him. It was so simple he couldn't believe he hadn't thought of it before. He mulled the idea over in his head for several days but could find no flaw in his plan.

Ari had told him he was supposed to return after his allocated days, but what if he just didn't? What if he stayed an extra day? Unsure of what would happen, he went to see Ember who always knew everything. He bumped into her while out for his morning run and stopped for a chat. Ember was a bit surprised as February wasn't usually the chatty type. They talked about her last trip and he managed to bring the subject around to the system of justice on Earth. After some chat about a recent, highly publicised trial there, he innocently asked.

"What would happen to someone here who committed a crime?"

Ember was immediately suspicious. February and Ari were friends and Ari was known for playing tricks on the others.

"Is Ari up to some mischief again? If he is, he won't get off so lightly this time."

February smiled as it occurred to him that letting Ember think Ari was the one plotting would suit his purpose.

"Ari is my friend. I wouldn't dream of saying he was up to anything. What do you mean about him not getting off so lightly this time? What could you do to him; it's not as if we have a prison or anything?"

"Well, I know that, but I'm certain Gust or Vem could come up with something. He was lucky May forgave him for putting that bird's nest in her chimney. Her house stank for weeks afterwards. You tell Ari to think very carefully, and it had better not be me he is plotting against."

Satisfied with his conversation with Ember, February finished his run.

In the months before his calendar time he refined his plan. As part of his preparations, he told May he would like steak and salad followed by fresh fruit salad and cream. None of this required much preparation and could be kept until the next night when he returned. He was careful not to do anything to arouse suspicion, especially when Kalend was around but did think about the consequences of his plan. Perhaps Kalend would have a punishment for him. He said the cave was the only way in and out of The Valley, but it was possible another cave was hidden by one of those curtains, somewhere he could be locked away.

Now the time to leave had finally come, other fears occurred to him. What if something happened to him if he stayed another day? Maybe he would just fade away or even die. Would Kalend come after him and drag him back as some kind of criminal? He forced these thoughts from his mind. It was ridiculous to think spending one extra day would be taken that seriously. A smack on the wrist was much more likely.

He was prepared for whatever his punishment would be. It would be worth it to make his point, one Kalend could not dismiss so easily.

In the last days of January, February slept little. He had been planning for a year, working out where he would spend his extra time and what he would do when he returned to face the music. While his plan had been a theoretical proposition it was fine, but now that it was about to become a reality, he was anxious and constantly fidgeting. June noticed his nervousness.

"What's the matter with you? Are you unwell? You had better go to see March. You don't want to be ill when you are away."

"No, I'm fine, really. Just excited. Nothing to be worried about."

June wasn't satisfied with his answer and spoke to Ari.

"Oh, don't worry about him. He has been a bit funny all week and I asked him about it. It turns out he met a girl last trip and he's hoping to see her again. I think our February is in love."

The last day of each month was always busy for May as she would cook the shared meal that evening in addition to making the daily bread. As always she was first up. A wisp of smoke was soon rising from her chimney. Still in her dressing gown, she stoked the fire in preparation for baking the bread. She checked her order once more before putting the bread into the large oven.

She muttered to herself as she ran her finger down the list.

'Multi-grain rolls for the health-conscious February, March, Ari and July.

Crusty cottage loaves for the hard-working Gust, Vem and Dec.

Pita bread for Tober and June who shared a love of spicy food.

A ciabatta for July.

Spiced fruit buns for January and herself.'

May smiled as she thought of Jan's return tonight. The two of them were great friends and shared a passion for poker, wine and good food, but not necessarily in that order. May baked an extra cottage loaf and several spicy buns to satisfy Jan's enormous appetite.

Bread in the oven, she went to get dressed. She returned to the kitchen to make tea and toast for breakfast while thinking about the evening's meal. Life was so much simpler now that she had established and firmly enforced ground rules for the shared meal.

A few decades ago, July had asked her to make a simple omelette for her as her stomach was upset and she didn't want to eat a heavy meal late in the evening. After that first one, another Month had come and asked for something different. When Gust came and asked for a special pudding, May had had enough. She called a meeting and told the Months she would only cook one meal and one dessert. If anyone wanted something different, they could bring it themselves.

As a concession, it was agreed that the returning Month could choose the menu before leaving, and the system worked extremely well. Jan was easy to cook for — he opted for quantity rather than quality. Cottage pie, green beans, pumpkin, lots of gravy, followed by Apricot Cobbler and custard was on the menu for tonight.

Vem had promised to bring the meat down early so she could let it cook slowly throughout the day.

May guarded the recipe for her rich meat sauce jealously, even now she checked out of the window to make sure no-one was coming. In the bottom of her wardrobe was a hat box but it didn't have a hat in it. May brought out a bottle of sauce she had discovered on one of her many trips to England. The sauce, in its distinctive bottle with the words 'by appointment to her Majesty the Queen' proudly emblazoned on it was enjoyed by millions. She mixed this with chopped tomatoes, basil, lemon juice and just a pinch of ginger. This made a rich and tasty sauce with a flavour that was somehow familiar to many, yet no one could name the 'special ingredient' May used.

On each of her travels May would hide the empty bottles in the bottom of her backpack ready to deposit in a rubbish bin. New bottles would be brought back the same way; she was determined no one would discover her secret.

May had no sooner finished baking the bread when there was a knock at the door, it was June. She worked in the orchard and market garden when Jan was away. She took his bread as well as her own, putting them in the basket on the front of her bicycle. She would be back later with the needed vegetables.

Throughout the morning, each Month came to collect their bread, all except February. May knew he would be busy preparing to leave, but he always called in for his bread on the way back from his run. She decided that if he hadn't called by lunch time, she would take it round to him.

February lay in bed thinking about the days ahead and hadn't realised how late it was until he heard June shouting to Ari as she cycled past on her way to Jans. He scrambled out of bed, stretched, ran his fingers through his short, curly, black hair and yawned. He was proud of his lean and toned body, but a frown crossed his handsome face – short of days and short of stature, especially when standing next to Gust who towered half a metre over him.

February pulled on a T- shirt and Lycra shorts and went for his run. He followed the path along the river to Gust's forge, before heading up the hill behind the farm. From here he could see the whole valley; the forest at one end, the mountain with the tunnel to the rest of Earth at the other. The tidy fields and gardens were a patchwork of colour spread out below him. Already late, he returned home to weed the border and mow his lawn. June would look after the garden while he was away, but he liked to leave it tidy. As he worked she cycled past, rang her bell and shouted.

"Hi Feb."

"It's February, not Feb."

A shortened name was just one more complaint to add to his list. Scowling he went to his workshop to finish carving a beautifully veined rock he had found on his run a few weeks ago. This was for May. She liked February, one of the few Months who genuinely did, and he appreciated the friendship she freely offered him.

Gust constantly told him one day the wind would change and February's face would be stuck with a scowl forever. May believed his rare but lovely smile could only come from a good heart – no matter how hard he tried to hide it.

He took time to smooth and polish the carving, enjoying the feel of it under his hands and as he worked, his scowl disappeared and a feeling of satisfaction and accomplishment filled him. He wrapped the delicate knot he had carved in a piece of cloth and headed to May's house.

May was delighted with her gift and insisted February stay for afternoon tea. As they ate crusty bread, tomatoes fresh from Jan's market garden, and some of Tober's cheese, they talked about February's forthcoming calendar time. He was full of all the things he would do – lots of sport, catching up with people he met each year on the ski fields. He also planned to revisit art galleries around the world, sitting for hours just gazing at paintings and sculptures. This was a side of February not many in The Valley knew.

"I have to rush everything because I only have twenty-eight days and it's not fair."

He always said that. May sympathised but repeated there was no point in fretting over something he could do nothing about.

As he walked home, February thought about the coming evening and smiled. Once he left The Valley, his extra day would be a beacon of life waiting for him.

As the afternoon sun dropped lower in the sky, February headed to the meeting hall. He reminded himself not to appear cheerful or the wily Kalend would be suspicious, but inside he was churning with excitement.

When everyone was there, they formed an orderly line, each in their place with February at their head and Kalend beside him. Kalend enjoyed his time spent with the Months but he also came to ensure the changeover went smoothly, especially where February was concerned.

As they left the hall each Month picked up a large, heavy-duty torch from a shelf inside the door. Centuries ago, long poles with fabric dipped in pitch and lit from the fire would have lighted their path. When Ember brought back one of these torches, the Months liked them so much they each brought one back. Batteries were a constant on each Month's shopping list!

It was a beautiful clear evening, perfect for a gentle stroll along the path and up the hillside to the cave, but February set off at a brisk walk. May complained she could not keep up as her bunion was too painful and February's regard for her made him slow the pace. Kalend asked February if he had any special plans and was surprised when February glanced sharply at him before launching into a detailed explanation of snowboarding – his latest craze. Kalend was clever and would be quick to suspect any reticent behaviour, and as he'd known he would have to walk with Kalend, his snowboarding talk was all part of his plan.

As the sun set the temperature chilled. The cave was cool and dark but as each Month slotted their torches into the sconces hollowed into the wall, it filled with light. At the rear of the cave, the door guarded the entrance to the tunnel. It was old and on its face there was no handle of any kind.

February tried to hide his impatience as he waited for Jan to return. He made small movements to and fro, wiping his sweating hands on his jeans. Kalend watched him, there was definitely something different about February tonight. Ari had told him about February being in love and Kalend leaned towards him.

"You seem impatient tonight. Do you have an appointment to keep?"

February made a non-committal grunt and was relieved when Jan could be heard singing. The door was flung open and Jan entered the cave, pulling the cart with the supplies. His red nose indicated he had celebrated the New Year with his usual enthusiasm. February stepped forward and Jan hugged him tightly, stepping back to place his hands on February's shoulders.

"*Heus amice*. Have fun, my little friend and bring me back something nice."

"I think you have already had more than enough of your something nice."

February almost pushed Jan aside in his haste to leave and the door closed after him with a soft click.

The others gathered around Jan to welcome him home before returning to the meeting hall for the meal. Gust and Dec carried the sacks of flour and sugar over to May's bakery, while others collected what they had asked for. As well as the shopping list items there were packets of seeds and a new pair of extra strong secateurs for Jan. Chocolate and nail polish were considered essentials by June, as were new baking trays for May and soused herrings for Gust.

In the coming weeks March was extra busy preparing for her time away. She wanted to take with her as many of her medical supplies as possible. Her potions were in great need in the many small villages throughout the vastness of Africa where famine and disease killed thousands of children every year. Her medical talents were matched by her fluency in many languages and local dialects. This allowed her to move freely with few questions asked about her origins. She was careful to avoid areas of conflict which were an almost daily threat now, concentrating on helping those with the best chance of recovery.

All too soon it was the last day of February and time for March to begin her Calendar time. She was tall and straight, balancing a large basket of her wares on her head as she joined Kalend at the head of the line. It had been a lovely day, but the evening had turned cold and there was a hint of rain. March sang a beautiful song of Africa in her husky voice as they walked. Reaching the cave, they put their torches in the wall sconces and waited.

There was silence. No footsteps in the tunnel, no opening door, no exchange of greetings. The first sign of March's impatience was the tapping of one foot. Five minutes passed and still no February. It was rare for a Month to be late, but it did sometimes happen. One year Ari had been late as he had arrived early and fallen asleep, but March was not as patient as May. Kalend began to worry.

After another few minutes March began to pace backwards and forwards before whirling to face Kalend.

"He is late and I have important work to do."

March's soft and low tones belied her increasing anger. Minutes could mean the death of a child who could have been saved. A mother could be dying in childbirth while February tarried. May tried to calm things.

"I'm sure he'll be here any minute now, he's never been late before."

But the minutes stretched out with no sign of February.

"Perhaps he thinks it is a Leap Year," suggested Gust.

March's low tones were now replaced with a raised voice.

"Stop making excuses for him. February knows time as well as any of us."

Gust turned to Kalend, who was standing to one side of the cave looking extremely worried. He alone knew the danger they all faced if February didn't return.

"What if he has had an accident and is unable to get back tonight?"

But before Kalend could answer Gust, March whirled to face him.

"He has to return tonight, the Contract demands it."

Ari suspected February was still with his girl.

"Look, February is in love with some girl, he is probably taking his time to say goodbye, that's all."

More suggestions were made but everyone avoided the reason they were all thinking. February was taking the extra time he felt he deserved.

It was Tober who eventually voiced his thoughts.

"We all know he wants extra days. What if he is just taking them? What happens then?"

Kalend answered.

"February and I have discussed this matter several times. I am sure he is just late because of a girl as Ari suggests."

Vem suggested the Months return to their homes but March refused to go.

"When he returns I must be here to leave."

Kalend agreed she should stay but could see no reason for the others to wait. He said he had things to do if February didn't return and followed the other Months outside, only to be hit by an angry blast of wind.

"A storm is coming. We'd better hurry," urged Vem.

May insisted they all go to the meeting hall to share the meal as the food was already prepared. There was much speculation about where February could be. An accident on one of his dangerous sporting events perhaps. If he were unconscious he wouldn't be able to travel back, but July refused to consider this.

"You all know how much he resented having fewer days than the rest of us. I agree with Ari that he's just taken some extra time and is partying the night away somewhere."

Most were frustrated by July's willingness to see the bad in February and still hoped he would return before midnight when March would begin.

February had told Gust of his feelings many times as they

worked together; he felt guilty about his easy dismissal of them and spoke in his defence.

"We don't know that's why he isn't back. But if it is, it's not his fault he got fewer days than us. We all knew how he felt but never supported him."

Vem turned to Ari.

"What about you, he must have told you what he was planning. When is he coming back?"

Ari was most indignant at the accusation but equally angry February hadn't confided in him.

"I knew nothing of his plans. Do you really think I would have let him do this if I'd known?"

June couldn't see why everyone was so worried.

"Surely he will be back when he's had an extra day and made his point."

Gust wasn't so sure.

"How many times has he complained he'd had years less time than the rest of us? He could decide to stay for a week, a month or even a year? We've no way of knowing."

Vem hoped Gust was wrong but like June had fears of his own. He had seen the look of concern on Kalend's face before leaving the cave. While Kalend had always appeared to be a friend, having felt it necessary to have a contract, he was unlikely to dismiss February for breaking it. He was annoyed with himself for agreeing to sign it without asking what would happen if it was broken. For the first time Vem considered that Kalend may not be the autonomous figure everyone thought. Why would Kalend worry if he was the one to decide what would happen next? As midnight approached with no sign of February or Kalend, Vem's unease grew but he kept his thoughts to himself.

Unseen by the Months, a figure stood outside a window

listening. A tall figure with white hair whose face was alive with interest as he listened to their conversation. A Month hadn't returned. The contract was broken. Kalend would step down in his favour and all he had waited for was about to be his. As he was about to leave, he saw one of the Months use a clear substance to tightly wrap leftover food. This substance stuck to the food and to itself and he was, albeit unwillingly, struck by the ingenuity of these beings and the creatures who had created them.

As midnight passed Vem said they could do nothing tonight and should get some sleep.

The Quaan came to collect February's memories, but his cabin was empty. They waited until it was almost light before returning under the mountain where his news was received with great distress by the assembled Quaan.

'Very well, Kalend, I will do as you ask.'

Kalend blamed himself for not realising the depth and strength of February's feelings, but instead of hurrying back to Tir Dhuchais he returned to his cabin. Filled with worry he paced back and forth. The Months may feel irritated by February's tardiness and a delayed meal but the consequences of his actions were dire for all of them. Before he met the Months they had been faceless beings to be removed if necessary. Now they were his friends. He respected and admired them, and the thought of them being destroyed filled him with heartache. All Watchers had agreed to Hiemal's Charter. Now the contract was broken the Charter would have to be enforced.

To save them he would have to do one of two things.

1. Find a new home for them – but there was no place for them in this system.

2. Convince Hiemal to change his mind – but Hiemal would do anything to thwart any proposal Kalend might make.

As much as he wanted to go in search of February, he knew he must report to the Watch first. This was not something he could keep from them. He forced himself to sit down and think logically about what was and was not possible. There were only two places the Months could survive – The Valley and Earth. Neither of them appeared to be an option. The Charter had been passed as law by all in the Watch. Only the Senaten could repeal it but that would mean telling them about the Months. Discovery of the secret they had kept would mean the Senaten would certainly destroy the Months and dismiss the Watchers.

As Presidion he had the right to propose an amendment if all who agreed to the original law would support it. Why would the Watchers help the Months? If they could only know them as he did … A possible solution came to him, spurring him to return to Tir Dhuchais.

Kalend wasn't the only one to return to Tir Dhuchais in a great hurry. Hiemal, after listening to the Months in the meeting hall went immediately to visit Thades.

"We have been vindicated. The months have broken the contract and will be destroyed. We will be Presidion and make this Watch the one other Watches will aspire to emulate. We have waited with great patience and now is the time for that to be rewarded."

Thades was bemused to see him laughing and dancing with glee as he told all he had seen but uttered a word of caution.

"You say Kalend left The Valley before you did, so where is he now? You know he'll try to save them."

Hiemal turned in dismay.

"Are you saying he will go back on his word, refuse to enforce the Charter?"

Thades was quick to make his words plain.

"Kalend is an honourable man, but he is also a very clever one. If there is a way to save them, he will find it and convince others to support him."

"Everyone accepted the Charter and can't go back on their word."

Despite Hiemal's confident manner Thades' words concerned him and he voiced his belief, to himself as much as to Thades.

"t'Hura won't have the Months back on her world. We will

go and see her now to ensure she will keep her word. You must go to Stolesc and do the same. With their support, plus Balack, we can ensure the Charter is enforced."

To Hiemal's surprise, Thades calmly but firmly replied.

"I will not. Stolesc can make his own decision as can I. The Charter is law and all you have to do is wait for it to be enforced. If you try to influence others it is more likely they will support Kalend in any plan he may have."

Hiemal left without replying.

Kalend needed to talk to t'Hura but as he approached her dwelling, he could hear voices and stepped behind a tree to wait. He was surprised when the door opened and Hiemal stormed out. Why would Hiemal be there? He couldn't possibly know February hadn't returned, could he?

After waiting to make sure Hiemal was gone, he knocked on t'Hura's door. When she opened it, the irritated look on her face showed she was in ill humour.

"Kalend. Why am I not surprised? If you are here to bully me into breaking the Charter, you are mistaken!"

Hiemal did know February was missing. This was a problem he had not anticipated. Kalend quickly gathered his thoughts and assured t'Hura he had no intention of doing anything of the kind. However, he did need her help.

"Please listen to what I have to say, if you decline my suggestion I will leave without further words."

They spoke for a long time, with t'Hura asking questions, eventually getting up and pacing around the room. Kalend's revelation as to how she had become Watcher of Earth deeply disturbed her. She recalled in great detail the celebration that was held for family and business associates when she became

Watcher of the blue planet. Her father spoke of the great honour she had brought by securing it for the House of Efriston. She had been given the seat of honour at the favoured table, something she had only dreamed about. Now the truth was out. She was not valued; she was simply payment of a debt. She cried bitter tears and Kalend wished he had not needed to tell her.

Recovering, t'Hura was angry her father did not consider her worthy to be a Watcher, but also felt a sense of relief. If she was not the best pairing for Earth it explained why she had been unable to guide it to be the world of peace and harmony she had desired. Her unsuitability to be Watcher of Earth was the reason Man was a creature of greed and cruelty. Realising she no longer owed loyalty to a House that used her without her knowledge or consent, she dried her tears and faced Kalend waiting for his request.

"If you will give Earth to Hiemal in return for his support for my amendment to allow the Months to remain in The Valley, you would be free from the stress of Earth and become the Watcher of Pluto."

t'Hura may have felt relief that she was not the chosen Watcher of Earth but had reservations.

"Hiemal is not a good or kindly person. What damage could he do to Earth?"

"Hiemal may think he could do as he wishes with Earth but is unaware of something of great importance. Think back to the allocation of worlds. Hiemal was so convinced he would be Watcher of the blue planet that when he wasn't, he left the table without touching his sphere."

t'Hura gasped in disbelief.

"But if he didn't touch it, he could not have bonded with it."

She looked at Kalend with dawning understanding.

"He doesn't know that when he bonds with his world, he feels acceptance and joy. These feelings ensure we can do nothing to harm our world or its creatures."

"If Hiemal agrees to support the amendment, a new allocation will take place, just for you and Hiemal. As soon as he touches the sphere of the blue planet, he will only want what is best for it. He will not be able to harm it."

t'Hura smiled with relief.

"My bond with Earth would be broken allowing me to bond with Pluto. I would nurture it so it will evolve as it was meant to do."

Kalend could see relief flood t'Hura's face. The burden of Earth was one she would be pleased to set down. She was never meant to be paired with it. She looked down at her clasped hands and spoke softly.

"When we met for the very first time, everyone assumed the blue planet would be given to Hiemal. Perhaps Earth would be a better place and Hiemal a better man if it had. Very well, Kalend, I will do as you ask."

Kalend stood to take his leave.

"Thank you."

He hesitated until t'Hura raised her head.

"When the Senaten chose you to be a Watcher, they failed to recognise the rightness of the decision they made. I salute you and offer thanks for your willingness to help your people."

Kalend's genuine approval meant more to t'Hura than the falsity of the approval given by her own father.

Thades waited. His displeasure that Hiemal thought he could command him to speak to Stolesc evaporated. Even though he felt sorry for the Months the Charter must be upheld. As he sat his crystal called him to a meeting.

t'Hura was deep in thought as she walked and didn't hear Thades until he was at her elbow. She hadn't enjoyed her meeting with Hiemal and fearing he had sent Thades to put further pressure on her was displeased to see him. Her agreement with Kalend gave t'Hura a sense of peace and she had no intention of discussing the matter of the missing Month with anyone. Thades didn't mention it at all, chatting about the weather and asking how her garden was. He hoped he might learn if Hiemal had convinced her but as they neared the Chamber t'Hura stopped and turned to face him.

"I have had enough of this, please wait here. I don't want to be seen arriving with you. I would not want anyone getting the wrong idea."

Thades laughed softly.

"Of course. I understand you would not want to be seen in the company of such a reprehensible character."

t'Hura could not resist a smile, he really could be most charming. He waited until he was sure she must be at the chamber before moving on. Neither had any idea Dynak had seen the whole encounter although she was too far away to hear their conversation. Not knowing the reason for the meeting that had been called, Dynak wondered why t'Hura and Thades would act in what appeared to be furtive circumstances. She called out to t'Hura but was too far away to be heard. She quickly headed to the Chamber being the last to arrive. The loud buzz of conversation which had filled the Chamber ceased as Kalend called for silence.

"Tonight I visited The Valley to share a meal with the Months on the return of February, but he has not returned from Earth at his appointed time. He may be injured and unable to return. I will go to Earth to find him."

141

Hiemal objected.

"The Charter states that if the contract is broken the Months are to be destroyed."

Kalend tried to sound calm as he explained.

"Breaking the contract implies a deliberate act but until we know what has happened, we must wait."

Hiemal was furious at the obvious attempt to stall enforcing his Charter. Remembering his crystal he worked hard to control his outrage as Kalend continued.

"I give all here my word that I will find February and bring him back. If the contract has been deliberately broken the law will be enforced."

Worried looks passed around the Chamber as most felt Hiemal had some right to accuse Kalend of using delaying tactics. Kalend saw their faces and knew he had to act quickly; he put his and t'Hura's plan into action.

Before he could do so. Hiemal jumped to his feet and stared with undisguised venom at Kalend, his crystal turning a dark red. Hiemal saw the danger and working hard yet again to control his temper, lowered his eyes and sat down. Thades rose and Kalend nodded his permission.

"Presidion, I don't recall the name of February from the list t'Hura gave to us. Or am I mistaken?"

"You are quite correct Thades, February was not one of the original Months, but I was given, at this Watch's insistence, full responsibility for them. The Charter didn't state how many Months or name them. When Man completed his calendar, February was brought to The Valley at my instigation."

Thades had to concede the Charter had given Kalend that authority.

Hiemal stood once more and Kalend let him speak.

"When it was first suggested the Months came here, we spoke against it. Kalend stated quite clearly that any decision must have unanimous support and against our better judgment, we were party to the Charter that was drawn up. That Charter does not say the Months will be destroyed unless this or that has happened. This attempt to confuse us as to whether this is or is not a deliberate act shows Kalend's duplicity. Either he supports the Charter or he does not. The Month has not returned, our support is revoked and we demand their immediate eradication."

Kalend knew Hiemal had support in the Chamber and rose to his feet. "I will go to Earth, find February, send March on her way and then bring all the other Months here. They have the right to face their accusers and we must look them in the eye as we pass sentence."

Hiemal knew instinctively Thades had been right. Kalend had a plan to thwart all he had planned for. Kalend must destroy the Months and step down so he could be Presidion. How dare he ignore the law that had been passed in this Chamber. His rage began to grow unchecked and he stood to face the Watch

"Kalend knows this Chamber is for Watchers only. We cannot allow those deviant, dissolute creatures from Earth here. The Charter allowed them to live in their Valley. It was made plain they would know nothing of us or Tir Dhuchais. Is there not one Watcher who will act with the integrity required by us all?"

Hiemal was so close to achieving all he had waited so patiently for but in his fury and frustration, could not control his emotions and his crystal flared red. Kalend was denying him his rightful place as Presidion and his hidden hatred broke free and filled him, turning his crystal black. Neja stared at it in horror and gave a cry of alarm. All eyes became fixed on the black orb that was now filling the Chamber with darkness. Too late Hiemal realised his mistake and cried out.

"Forgive our outburst, but you must see how passionate we are about preserving the sanctity of this place."

Not even Kalend had seen a black crystal but spoke out of the darkness, his voice trembling with horror.

"Hatred is the manifestation of evil that our Galaxy is sworn to eradicate. Hiemal, you must leave us now so we can decide what to do."

A cowed and dismayed Hiemal left, feeling not only the Watch but the Galaxy was against him. As he left the blackness went with him.

For a moment no one spoke. Kalend was frustrated by this turn of events but also felt responsible. He could not deny the veracity of Hiemal's words but a black crystal could not be tolerated. With February's non-appearance he didn't have time to deal with Hiemal now.

"Fellow Watchers, please allow me a few moments to consider what has just happened."

Kalend went outside but there was no sign of Hiemal. The black crystal was a serious matter but more importantly, it could destroy his plan. He was confident Stolesc, Neja, Verna and Dynak would support t'Hura and himself once they met the Months. Thades was a fair man and may be persuaded. t'Hura would offer Earth to Hiemal in return for his support for the amendment to allow the Months to remain in The Valley

Kalend had believed Hiemal's greatest desire was to be Watcher of Earth. It could restore his status on his home world, but why did he feel such hatred for the Months and was that hatred strong enough to make him refuse t'Hura's offer?

If he threatened to report the black crystal to the Senaten he could force Hiemal to give his support but was reluctant to take such a drastic step. Wanting to take the heat out of the situation, he knew he could not antagonize Hiemal further as he could see several other Watchers show alarm at his intention to bring the Months here. How could he assert his authority as Presidion while showing his fairness and commitment to the Months? He believed Balack would support Hiemal, doing whatever he was told to do and Kalend had no way to prevent him from voting against the amendment. A sudden, bizarre thought made him smile. He would do something completely unexpected. He returned to the Chamber and retook his seat.

"There are two matters facing this Watch. A black crystal would normally be reported to the Senaten for their consideration but as Presidion, and with your support, I have the right to deal with this in the Chamber. Some of you may feel Hiemal's hate is justified but we all saw how it polluted the Chamber. A hearing will take place in which the thoughts, views and suggestions of you all will be heard and considered. Hiemal will have the right to speak in his defence."

Thades stood.

"Presidion, would any Watcher who wished to, be permitted to speak in defence of Hiemal, or are you suggesting we have the right to sit in judgement on him?"

"My wish is not to condemn Hiemal. Rather that a way may be found to put this matter behind us and return to the Watch we were before. The Watch will decide on a fair and just punishment, but until then Hiemal will remain excluded from this Chamber."

Kalend knew time was short and moved on.

"First we must deal with the Months."

Kalend hesitated, his next step would alarm some and cause amazement in others.

"I have spent over two thousand of their years with them. I

have come to know and to care for them. As Watcher of the Months I find it impossible to remain impartial in this matter. I appoint a Judicial Watcher to be in charge of all Watch matters until the problem of the Months is resolved. I will remain Presidion, but my primary role will be as Watcher of the Months. I appoint Balack as Judicial Watcher."

As expected, his appointment caused an uproar. Kalend needed to be free to act in defence of the Months, but Hiemal would certainly have used his influence to assure Balack would vote as he told him. Balack being Judicial Watcher removed that possibility.

"Me, really? I accept. What do I do now?"

Kalend gestured to the Presidion's chair and Balack quickly took his seat.

"This seat is yours until I retake it for the black crystal hearing. I take my leave now and will return with the Months."

Kalend left the chamber and headed towards his cabin in The Valley.

The Chamber was silent. Balack looked from one watcher to another to see if anyone would speak. He cleared his throat.

"It is late and I think we should retire and wait for Kalend's return. When the matter of the Months is sorted, Kalend will resume his duties as Presidion and this unfortunate matter will be resolved."

Before Balack could declare the meeting closed, Thades spoke in Hiemal's defence.

"Everyone has been equally horrified by Hiemal's outburst but I can understand his feelings. Hiemal has acted irrationally but Kalend is acting in a way that is hard to justify in the eyes of many. It would be unjust to exclude Hiemal without considering the provocation he faced."

146

Thades looked around the Chamber.

"Judicial Watcher Balack. Kalend has said you are in charge. I ask you to consider this. In all his years of service to this Watch has Hiemal ever acted in a way that he did not believe was best for us and the planets under our care?"

As he spoke his eyes roamed the room looking for anyone who could say otherwise, but no one spoke and Thades continued.

"He has never made any secret that he feels the Months are an insult to creation, and all he has done has been in support of that belief. He never wanted them here but gave in to pressure from Kalend and others here. The thought of them being here, in this special place, was just too much for him. I ask you to forgive his outburst and let him retake his rightful place among us."

Neja, always quick to condemn Hiemal, declared they should do as Kalend said and deny Hiemal access to meetings until this matter was settled. Thades strongly disagreed.

"Hiemal has spoken most ardently against the Months. If you exclude him from further discussion it may appear you have an undisclosed motive for doing so. This could make any decision open to challenge."

Stolesc could see the problem this could cause and feared the consequences.

"Let us not forget that Hiemal is of the House of Uclair. If he feels we have treated him unfairly he could take this matter to the Senaten. The existence of the Months would be revealed and the Senaten could decide to remove this Watch entirely and replace it with another."

Verna had been sitting quietly, observing all that was unfolding, but now stood.

"How we would feel if it had been someone other than

147

Hiemal who acted in this way. Can everyone here say they do not have beliefs or feelings about Hiemal which colour their judgement? We are the Watch for this system. Hiemal is part of us. I do not wish him to be excluded at a time when he is surely regretting what has happened. Should we not be offering him our support?"

Worried looks were exchanged within the chamber and Neja felt a rush of colour to her cheeks. Her dislike of Hiemal was well known. Thades smiled in gratitude at Verna.

"Your fairness reminds us we must all act with integrity."

Despite Kalend's instructions, Balack could see Hiemal must be part of the process and there was always the possibility he would be more moderate in his views given his present situation. Unsure of how he should proceed, he was glad when Dynak spoke.

"Presidion Kalend has made it clear what is to happen in relation to the black crystal hearing. This cannot happen until he returns, the matter of the Months is resolved and the Watch is once again complete. I proposal Hiemal be readmitted to the Chamber until such a hearing can take place."

Balack sat until he realised everyone was looking at him.

"Oh, sorry, Still a bit new at this. Is there anyone who wishes to speak before a vote is taken?"

With no more comments and Verna's words fresh in their minds, even Neja voted in favour. Hiemal's return was unanimously agreed. Thades left to fetch him, telling him how Verna had spoken in his defence but the flash of distaste on Hiemal's face showed a response different to the one Thades hoped for. He could not understand Hiemal's irrational dislike of Verna.

Hiemal had almost laughed when he learned the Watch

thought his hatred was for the Months. Using the Months to become Presidion was all that mattered so Hiemal returned, bowing deeply. "We do most humbly apologise. We love this Chamber and it pains us that we defiled it with our emotion." The apology was accepted and the meeting closed.

As he left the chamber Hiemal was still angry events had not gone as planned, but a solution to one problem was firmly in his mind. He returned to The Valley, going into the meeting hall to find the container which had the clear substance in it. When he tried to remove it, he found it was wrapped around a cylinder. He pulled a strip and used a small piece to wrap tightly around his crystal so when he replaced his ring, the substance formed a barrier between it and his skin. He kept the rest of the piece he'd torn for future use and returned to the empty Chamber. He recalled his anger and frustration from earlier in the day but no matter how strongly he shouted, his crystal remained clear and he cursed himself for not having done this sooner.

He visited Thades, asking him to accompany him to meet the Months as he needed to act. He was too anxious to wait.

"We need to see these Months for ourselves, who knows what we could learn from them before they reach the Chamber. We will leave first thing in the morning and wait for them by the entrance to Tir Dhuchais. You will come too." Thades protested, but Hiemal was determined to discover what Kalend was planning before they returned to the Chamber. Seeing Hiemal was in an unpredictable, even dangerous mood, Thades decided it was best to accompany him.

As soon as she was alone, t'Hura used her crystal to ask Kalend if the plan they had discussed was still possible after what had happened. He reassured her that appointing Balack as Judicial Watcher could actually make the plan better. He would now be free to act and speak in a way he couldn't have done if he was in charge. He asked her to speak to the others as they had previously agreed.

Despite the late hour, t'Hura asked Dynak, Neja, Verna and Stolesc to meet with her as she had important news. Dynak's dwelling was closest so they went there.

'No, t'Hura, you can't.'

Kalend had left the Chamber and gone swiftly to The Valley to see if February had returned, but a quick visit to the cave showed March still pacing. He returned to his cabin and was surprised to hear a thudding noise on his roof. Y Quaan stood outside, throwing pebbles onto the curtain of protection. He was holding a scroll in his outstretched hand. Kalend passed through the curtain and waited.

"We were saddened you felt it necessary to hide behind this barrier when we came to offer reassurance to you. We could have passed through it if we chose but respected your wish to remain separate. We have come now as we know February has not returned. On this scroll are the places he most liked to visit. It will aid you in your search. You will notice that at the end of his time he almost always goes to a remote place on the coast of a land called Ireland."

"Thank you, this will be most helpful. Why are you doing this?"

"We can't recover his memories until he returns. That is our only motivation."

"Thank you for your assistance."

Y Quaan was already disappearing from sight. Kalend looked at the scroll and began his search.

t'Hura knew she had to tell all she and Kalend had discussed but determined not to reveal the deal her family has made.

"Kalend has asked me to made it clear February has not been found guilty of any crime, yet."

Neja was completely baffled by Kalend's actions.

"Why did he make Balack the Judicial Watcher? I didn't know there was such a thing. And Balack? It makes no sense to me."

t'Hura sighed.

"Neja please, let me finish. Kalend thinks if he brings the Months back, they can convince all of us, except Hiemal, that they are worth saving. He plans to make an amendment to the Charter Law but wouldn't presume to ask us to vote in favour of it without giving us the opportunity to know the Months as he does."

Stolesc believed in enforcing the law in all matters.

"If this February acted deliberately he is guilty and should face the punishment we all agreed to. Kalend said he would enforce the Charter, so did he lie?"

"Let me explain the legality of this as Kalend explained it to me. The Charter is Law and must be enforced. It cannot be rescinded by any except the Senaten, but an amendment can be made by a Presidion."

Neja almost exploded with frustration.

"How can you amend a death sentence, either you die or you don't?"

"The Presidion amendment would allow the Months to remain in The Valley. February would face a trial for his reckless act, with fellow Months sitting in judgement. For the amendment to pass, all who voted in favour of the original law must support it."

Verna and Dynak were pleased with the possibilities outlined by t'Hura but Neja was still confused.

"Why would Hiemal vote in favour? The Charter gives him all he wants, the Months gone and he gets to be Presidion."

t'Hura hesitated.

"There is something Hiemal wants even more than enforcing the Charter."

Dynak rose, her face saddened.

"No, t'Hura you mustn't"

"She mustn't what." Stolesc was finding this meeting more and more perplexing.

Verna quietly whispered.

"He wants Earth."

" It's the only way to save them. If I give Earth to Hiemal, he must vote for the amendment."

Stolesc stared in disbelief.

"Why would you do that? It's the most ridiculous thing I have heard all day and it has been a very bizarre day. Have you all forgotten what just happened? Hiemal hates the Months so much he caused a Black Crystal. There is no way he is going to let them live. Giving him Earth is no guarantee he will feel any differently about them."

Dynak called for quiet as Neja and t'Hura joined in the quarrel with voices raised.

"It has been a long day and we are all tired. Go home and rest. We can meet again in the morning when everyone has calmed down."

Feelings were still running high when they gathered again. Neja couldn't believe t'Hura's willingness to give up Earth.

"Is it legal for t'Hura to just give Earth to Hiemal?" she asked.

t'Hura tried to remember all Kalend had told her.

"The Senaten would have to approve the change unless all

153

the Watchers in our system approve."

Neja was still angry and confused.

"I will never give my approval to this. What do you think he would do with Earth?"

"Once he has bonded with Earth there is little he can do. As Watchers we are to cherish and protect our worlds. I would never be part of this if I thought Earth would be at risk."

Stolesc knew the influence of the House of Uclair and voiced his worries.

"With the Charter, Hiemal gets to be Presidion. With the House of Uclair behind him what power would that give him over Earth?"

"Even as Presidion he would be limited by the Senaten. He would probably want to change Earth's name, but we would have to approve that as we did at the Naming Ceremony."

t'Hura hesitated, Kalend had asked her to only reveal what he had told her if it was absolutely necessary. Seeing hardened and disbelieving faces, she continued.

"Kalend has reason to believes Hiemal is in disgrace on his home world and wants Earth to impress his House. The last thing he would want is for the Senaten to learn of the Months. It's possible they could remove all of us, including him, if they learned what we have allowed here."

Neja was intrigued.

"What did Hiemal do?"

"Kalend didn't know for certain but to be sent to a system as unimportant as this, his crime must be serious."

A frustrated and angry Dynak spoke.

"The Charter, plus t'Hura's inexplicable gift gives Hiemal an Earth free of the Months and he gets to be Presidion. All this for a group of beings who shouldn't even exist. Something else is going on here, something Kalend isn't telling us. Perhaps Stolesc is right and we should just let them face the consequences instead of putting ourselves at risk."

t'Hura knew if the Senaten learned what was happening here, her position was the only one not at risk. She couldn't bear the shame of telling her friends how she came to be Watcher of Earth so remained silent.

Neja had been thinking all night and asked.

"Do any of you remember what Balack said when Verna proposed bringing the Months here?"

No one did, except Neja.

"He said, 'Would we get to play with them?' What we have to do is propose a game with the amendment as the prize."

The others looked at her in complete confusion.

"I remember t'Hura telling stories of the challenges faced by heroes on Earth to win a prize, get the girl or save their life. You must remember."

A memory flickered in Dynak's mind.

"The labours of Hercules, Jason and the golden fleece. Do you mean stuff like that?"

"Yes. Hiemal may not approve Kalend's amendment but if there was a chance the Months would fail, he might be persuaded. Look at it from his point of view. He would get Earth, be Presidion and there would still be a chance the Months would be destroyed."

Stolesc was having trouble getting his mind around all this but Neja hadn't finished.

"If we all approve Hiemal getting Earth and any name change he wishes then he must agree to the game with the amendment as the prize. If Hiemal doesn't agree then he doesn't get Earth. If Kalend's right he will give in. At least this way the

Months would have a chance."

Stolesc was still not convinced.

"Could t'Hura offer Earth in exchange for the amendment and if he won't agree, then suggest your game?"

t'Hura told them Kalend could only make one amendment proposal. If Hiemal rejected it, the Months would die. Verna was intrigued by Neja's idea.

"If he did agree what kind of game would they face? It would have to be one Hiemal would approve."

"If he is assured of Earth and becoming Presidion, Hiemal may not care."

For reasons of her own Dynak approved Neja's suggestion.

"I think we should proceed with Neja's idea and when Kalend returns, we can ask him what he thinks we should do."

Neja grinned widely, emitting a small flame of pleasure.

"t'Hura, do I have your permission to visit Earth to get some ideas for the game?"

"Of course, but I think we should call this game a Quest – to use an Earth word. These events are too serious to be called a game. Is there anything I can help you with?"

"I've been thinking about Balack, he will be absolutely clueless about what to do as Judicial Watcher. He may listen to you if you offer some ideas."

"About what? I know as little about it as he does."

"Kalend won't be back until tomorrow and we will need time to talk to him about all that has happened since he left. Try to get Balack to consider the order for things to happen. We need to delay sentencing until the next day."

t'Hura was reluctant to be used in this way; deceit of any kind was not something she wanted to be involved in.

"I will consider your suggestion."

February expected to feel elated at having more time, but instead he felt like a cheat. He'd gone to all his favourite places but didn't feel the exhilaration that was normal for his sporting prowess. Somehow his extra day seemed... thinner. Colours were less bright, food had lost its flavour, much of people's zest for life seemed diminished, as if everything was just too much bother.

He couldn't stop thinking about what was happening back in The Valley; March would be furious she couldn't leave; Kalend would be furious he hadn't returned; Ari would be furious he hadn't told him what he was planning; May would be disappointed. He could picture the sadness on her face and knew he should go back, but how could he face everyone?

When he passed through the walls of the cottage at Carrick-a -Rede he felt immediately at peace. He sank heavily into the old, padded armchair facing the window and for the first time wondered why he felt like this when he came here – especially now. He obviously liked to be alone at times, but it was more than that. Dec and Gust loved to discuss politics and Jan had easily fitted into that group, although he was also friendly with May and Ember. March and July shared a love of poetry and flowers, while Ari and June roamed The Valley looking for mischief and adventure. Gust, Vem and Tober loved to go fishing together, although Ember kept a close eye on how many fish they caught. February sometimes joined Ari and June and they didn't seem to mind, but he knew he was more of a spectator than a player. The rather depressing truth was that February didn't feel he belonged in The Valley. Here, in this isolated cottage he didn't have to pretend he was part of anything. He felt alone no matter where he was, and in his sorrow he cried. Pulling himself together, he gazed out of the window.

From his vantage point February could see the cliffs on the mainland and was temporarily lost in the beauty of his surroundings. This was an old place by human standards. Carrick-a-Rede was a small island of the north coast of Northern Ireland, although island was too grand a name for it. It was just a small slice of cliff that had broken away from the mainland and was now separated by a chasm of about one hundred metres. The leeward side of the island provided a sheltered place for the local fishermen to lower their boat and land their catch in what was an otherwise inhospitable coastline. Many huts had occupied the place where the cottage now stood, providing a safe haven in stormy times. For centuries a crude rope bridge was used to cross from the mainland; now an iron bridge with safety rails formed the umbilical cord that linked the two islands carrying the thousands of visitors who came here every summer. The cliffs of the mainland were completely visible now and February marvelled at the clarity of the water that washed their feet. Close to shore it was turquoise, gradually becoming jade then blue as it grew deeper. The cliff tops were covered in grass and heather – for even in winter, snow rarely covered them. The people of this land wrote more poems and sang more songs about their homeland than any other nation on Earth.

Kalend started with the places at the top of February's list, believing he would want to spend his extra time doing the things he loved best, but there was no sign of him. Eventually he travelled to the last place and entered the cottage unnoticed by February. He stood watching him, surprised by the look of wonder and the still reddened eyes in his usually disgruntled face. Despite his anger and worry, Kalend was touched by February's plight. He chose a chair on the other side of the room clearing his throat softly as he sat down. February, aware of his presence, didn't turn his head.

"Should I put out my arms for the handcuffs or will you take my word that I'll not disappear?"

Kalend knew he had to get February back as soon as possible but he also had to prepare him for what would await them. Perhaps here was as good a place as any to tell him about Tir Dhuchais, The Watch and the Charter. February learned about the consequences of his actions and the impact on the others. For the second time in one day February wept. Kalend put an arm around his shoulders and tried to comfort him.

"Come now, February, all is not yet lost. The Watch will listen to what you have to say. You have been foolish, but your heart is good and I believe good will triumph. I will ask them to show mercy and believe it may be given."

"But what do the others think of me? I have put them all at risk and they must surely hate me."

"I have not yet spoken to them, but they will know you didn't act out of malice or a desire to cause harm. I am partly to blame for not realising how strongly you felt, but we must return now. I have to tell the others what I've just told you. When I am done, March will go to the cave. You must wait for her there. When she has gone, come directly to the meeting hall. You will not let me down, will you February?"

There was a momentary flash of courage in February's eyes and Kalend smiled a thin, forced smile.

"You're not at risk here; you're one of them, a Watcher"

Ember lay awake listening to the silence and her unease increased. Getting up and quickly dressing, she hurried to February's house. Getting no reply from hammering on the door, she went inside as doors were never locked in The Valley. Lighting a lamp she looked around the room. With no sign of parcels or packaging which she would have expected if February had come back, she went into his bedroom just in case – but there was nothing there.

If February had come back he may have gone to see Ari who wasn't happy when Ember woke him. When she told him February was not in his house and she didn't know if he had returned or not, he offered to go up to the cave and let her know what he found on his return.

Back home, Ember tried to look at the situation logically. If Ari came back and said March had gone, then February must have returned. It would make sense that Kalend would have taken February with him to discuss what he had done. She didn't know what she would think if March was still there. Stoking the fire, she put the kettle on to boil.

It was dawn when Ari and March returned, but no sign of February. With Ember advising they should try and have some sleep, each returned to their homes.

That morning all went about their normal business, but their thoughts kept returning to February. Late in the afternoon the Meeting Hall bell was rung. Kalend stood on the steps, but he was alone. Inside they besieged him with questions, but he asked them to sit down. He was silent for a moment and then sighed as he began

"February is fine and is on his way back. I have told him what I am about to tell you. It is time for you to know about Tir Dhuchais and the Watchers."

The Months murmured to each other, looking mystified.

He began to speak.

"This Valley is not on Earth. Behind the cliffs surrounding this Valley is another world called Tir Dhuchais. Nine Watchers were appointed to supervise the planets in this Solar system, including Earth. I am one of the Watchers."

A stunned silence was followed by angry shouts and questions. Kalend asked them to be quiet so he could explain.

"This Valley is connected to Earth by a time and distance portal in the cave. The Valley was made to look like Earth so you would feel comfortable and safe here. There was nowhere else for you to go when Earth became unsafe for you."

Kalend watched their faces where anger was now replaced with fear. He hesitated, telling them about the consequences of February's actions would be as difficult for them to hear as it would be for him to tell.

"When we first learned of your existence, the Watch was divided over the plan to bring you to The Valley. Agreement was only reached when a Charter was drawn up which stipulated that you would cease to exist if the Contract was broken. When February didn't return, the contract you all signed was broken. I have spoken to the Watch and hope to convince them to reconsider."

All the Months began to talk at once. Everything they had ever believed about their home was a lie and now they were to die. It was too much to take in. Kalend called for silence and continued.

"I've been to Earth to find February and he waits now in the cave. He must return to face the Watch who will decide his fate and yours. You must be prepared to make a long journey."

Vem stood and the others fell silent.

"You have lied to us from the moment you met us. You cannot expect us to just accept your word now. We could just return to Earth and live as we did before."

The thought of going to this other world filled them with fear. Their tidy ordered lives had been turned upside down and now they were to be killed by unknown beings called Watchers. March stood to leave, but Kalend asked her to wait as there was more to hear.

Many voices tried to speak at one time, but the same fear and anger could be heard in them all. July stood up, demanding to be heard.

"Kalend has betrayed us. Everything here is a lie. Now he asks us to meekly wait for someone else to decide our future. We must decide what action we are going to take, not some hierarchical Watch that thinks it has the right to sit in judgement on us."

"Enough."

Gust's angry roar filled the room.

"Didn't you hear Kalend? This isn't Earth, we're on another world, a world ruled by this Watch. Earth will provide no refuge from the anger of the Watch if we run away and hide. We know Kalend and can only do as he says."

June was angered by the news.

"But he's been lying to us for centuries; we can't believe him. We have to act before…"

Dec felt heartache that his home was somehow not real. He stood, knocking his chair over and almost whispered.

"Kalend has been our friend and I see no reason to condemn him now."

Kalend had been so busy searching for February and wondering about the future of the Months, he had given little thought as to how they would react to him and the strange and difficult news he would give them. He could see hurt and anger at his betrayal on each of their faces. Even Ember would not meet his eyes.

"You are right to feel as you do, but matters were taken out of my hands. I will gladly tell you all that happened and why it happened at some later date, but now there is no time. We have to act or there will be no future for any of us."

March's concern showed clearly on her face.

"Any of us? You're not at risk here. You're one of them, a Watcher. I trusted your words, but now I don't know what to believe."

Kalend was hurt by the accusation in her voice. Everything he had done from the beginning had been to help them but before he could reply Gust spoke.

"We believed that this Valley was somewhere on Earth but now you say it is not. I am a simple man, if it looks like Earth and feels like Earth then I think it is Earth. To walk through the tunnel only takes twenty paces. I cannot believe those twenty paces cross time and space. The tunnel is solid rock, I have felt its walls and floor. I want to believe you, but it is a hard thing you are asking us to do."

Kalend's anger was softened by the honesty and confusion in Gust's words and he chose his words carefully.

"I know it's hard for you to believe. It's true I have kept

things secret from you, but my feelings of love and friendship for you are real."

Jan was slow to anger but he had a strong sense of fair play and what was happening now was blatantly unfair in his eyes.

"It's not our fault February broke the law. It's got nothing to do with us. We shouldn't be punished for his crime. I know February wouldn't have done this if he had known; how can you call this justice?"

Many voices spoke in agreement. Kalend banged the table for silence.

"February made a simple mistake with no idea of what would happen. We all knew how he felt about having less time but just ignored it. I have spoken to February and he is devastated. You must not blame him. We will go to Tir Dhuchais to meet the Watch. You must show your many admirable qualities. When they see you as I do, I am sure they will show mercy."

Kalend knew they must appear united. If they were squabbling among themselves it would only lend weight to Hiemal's argument they were not fit to live.

Vem was thinking about all the times he'd felt Kalend was keeping something from them and voiced his suspicions now.

"Is there anything you haven't told us, any more secrets you haven't shared?"

Kalend hesitated and Vem knew he'd been right.

"Tell us now if you want us to believe anything you say."

Kalend knew their anger would increase when he told them but had no choice.

"When you came here I told you the high mountains may prevent you from travelling by thought, but that was untrue. You passed through a 'curtain of recognition' in the tunnel so that you would be able to leave and return when it was your Calendar time. A second curtain stripped you of your power to travel by thought in The Valley and restored it each time you left."

Angry murmurs were heard around the hall and Kalend explained it was so they wouldn't accidentally find Tir Dhuchais over the mountains.

"And that's it, nothing else?"

Kalend knew this secret would cause great anger – and pain.

"There was a third curtain. The Valley was planned to provide for you and wouldn't sustain more. The third curtain removed your ability to father or bear children."

March was sitting next to July and hearing her gasp went to put her arm around her, but July savagely tossed it aside. Silence greeted this news, one filled with anger and despair. Most had thought it was their immortality which rendered them childless. July sat in stony silence for a few moments and then exploded with wrath.

"I always knew he was no good. We should just throw him out and carry on without him."

No one was quite sure if she was referring to Kalend or February. She left the hall with angry tears spilling down her face. March wanted to go after her but it was time for her to go to the cave. Kalend emphasized that February was to come straight to the hall. March was afraid.

"How will I know what happens at the meeting?"

"If February is successful you will return as usual and we will all be there to greet you. If February is unsuccessful I will find you."

"I will wait for you at sunset each day at the foot of the table shaped mountain in Africa, where we first met."

February was already standing in the tunnel doorway when

March entered the cave. He lowered his eyes and stepped to one side while holding the door for her. March could see February was as devastated and fearful about the future as Kalend had said. Passing him, she stopped to rest one hand on his shoulder. When he raised his head, she smiled briefly before hurrying down the tunnel. February was near to tears again. March had been kind to him so perhaps the others would be too, but just in case, he stepped back into the tunnel. Picking up a large stone he had brought with him he placed it against the open door. If things didn't work out at least they could escape to Earth before the Watch could destroy them.

Having answered all the questions he could, Kalend left the Months to sit in groups talking quietly while they waited for February. Learning of the third curtain had hit them all hard and not even Vem came to speak to him.. The lack of children in The Valley had been a source of sorrow to all. May left to check the food for the shared meal she had hoped would happen that night. There were no further outbursts from July when she returned, but Kalend knew many of the others felt as she did. It would take time to heal the breach between them and sadly time was one thing they didn't have.

February heard May call his name on his way to the meeting hall and stopped to speak with her. He was heartened by the strained, but nonetheless welcoming smile she gave him; however, her news about the children rendered him every bit as angry as the others. Knowing how the others felt, he took some time to sit and consider the reception he would receive.

Kalend was beginning to panic at the thought February had changed his mind, but the sound of footsteps outside calmed him. All eyes turned to the door, but nothing happened. February stood outside wishing desperately he could turn the clock back and undo all he had done, but he couldn't. He took a deep breath and went inside.

For a few moments no one spoke, and February almost turned to leave. Kalend walking up to him and taking him firmly by the arm, led him into the room.

"I was just listening to the others talking about you. We are all responsible for not recognising how strongly you felt, but now we will stand together, won't we?"

February shook free from Kalend and turned to face them.

"I know I have done a terrible thing but I'm not the only one. May told me about the children. How can we trust this man – if a man is what he is? For my part, if I could undo what I've done I would. I promise you I will do all I can to make sure everything will be alright."

February's voice trailed off into barely a whisper and his head dropped.

Kalend hadn't expected February to turn against him and stared at him until Ember spoke.

"We know exactly whose fault it is, but we will do all we can to help you fix it."

Several other voices joined in with her, but February didn't raise his head. Kalend was stunned by the depth of feelings he could feel in the room but spoke with a cheerfulness he did not feel.

"We must leave soon as the journey is a long one. Please pack a bag with food and water and those who can, bring your instruments. Music is unknown to many Watchers so they will be as entranced as I was. We will spend tonight in Tir Dhuchais and complete our journey the next day, so bring something warm for our camp. We will go straight to the river."

"No. We need time to consider all you've said. We can meet

again in the morning after a good night's sleep in our own beds."

Jan's suggestion met with the approval of the others and Kalend recognised he could not expect their obedience. No one asked him to join them for the shared meal and he returned to his house across the river. He too was tired, having had no sleep for some time.

While they ate Vem said he thought they should have their own plan to fight these Watchers.

"I don't intend to rely on Kalend to save us. When you go back to your cabins pack a bag with some of the products we make to sell. Show these Watchers we are gifted, hard-working people who deserve to live."

June voiced the fears of the others when she said.

"We know nothing of these Watchers. Do they look like us? Is Kalend like us or just pretending? He spoke of our destruction but didn't say how we would die. What if this Tir Dhuchais is simply a place of execution? I know we have to go, but am I the only one who is afraid?"

Silence followed then Gust, who was sitting next to June put a strong arm around her.

"If anyone tries to harm you, they will have me to answer to."

First Vem, then Tober started to laugh. Ember went to Gust giving him a big kiss on his cheek.

"Oh Gust, you are a marvel. I for one would not like to be your enemy."

The mood lightened and Vem's suggestion about taking their produce was approved. After cleaning up they were asked by Ember to sit down again.

"Kalend is right when he says we must present a united front if we are to have any chance of surviving. February is the cause of the dire situation we face. I do not judge or condemn him now, but he will have to face the consequences of his actions if we return."

February said nothing but July's anger wasn't directed at February.

"What about Kalend? When will he face us to pay for his lies and treachery?"

Vem pointed out they would need Kalend for the information he could give them about the Watch. Alienating him was detrimental to their cause. He told everyone to get some sleep before their journey next day.

February had gone with May but despite her best efforts, he said hardly anything except he was sorry. Exhausted by the day's events, he fell asleep in a comfy chair in front of her fire, and she gently placed a blanket over him.

In the darkness, the Quaan came once more. They visited the cottage of February and were angered to find it still empty. They would return one more night before leaving for their next gathering.

Early next morning, the Months gathered at the meeting hall with a backpack containing all they had been asked to bring. May had placed the beautiful carving February had given her into his backpack as he slept. Jan was carrying June's cello for her. Vem was last to arrive as he had taken time to open gates and stable doors to allow the animals to forage freely in case their return was delayed. As they walked towards the river, Ember hurried to the front to speak to Kalend.

"The boat will only take four people at a time so it will be lunch time before we are all across."

Kalend was about to answer but both boats now lay on the riverbank on The Valley side of the river. A large craft was now attached to the pulley system. A fluttering note was attached with just one word on it. STOLESC. Kalend explained that Stolesc was a Watcher and had helped to prepare The Valley for them.

July balked at the sight of the craft. She refused to get on board saying it was too small, would capsize and she would drown. Her mood had not improved since the meeting with Kalend yesterday, and dark circles under her reddened eyes showed she had slept little. Gust, feeling July didn't have the monopoly on fear or anger strode onto the riverbank, tossing her over his shoulder before depositing her none too gently on the raft. He could be heard to mutter.

"A good drowning would surely do you the power of good."

Once all were on-board, Gust, Dec and Vem pulled on the rope and the raft began to move. February sat alone at the front looking intently at the far side as if he could somehow see what was waiting for him. No one spoke to him, and Kalend worried.

"Her voice was coated with sarcasm and Hiemal found himself warming to her"

As the craft bumped into the opposite bank, Kalend jumped ashore tying it to a tree stump to hold it steady. July was still complaining so Gust once again picked her up and deposited her on the grassy bank. As she leaned forward to climb up the slight slope, her feet slipped and she fell face down slipping backwards into the river. Even February could not help but smile as the others roared with laughter. July fumed with rage. Kalend was responsible for all of this and if he thought she would meekly do as he asked, he was mistaken. The calm, united front Kalend wanted was to make him look good and them look weak. She would show her strength. The others could do as they pleased.

Kalend could read the expression on July's face.

"Enough, we have to hurry. July, are you injured?"

"I'm fine, thank you. It was foolish of me not to have been more careful."

As they moved towards the cliff May walked beside July and tried to calm her. Like Kalend, she was not fooled by her apparent conciliatory manner.

"Everyone is afraid of what will happen to us. The laughter at the river wasn't because of you, it was just a release of nervous tension. I hope you were not offended by it."

July snarled at her.

"If the only reason you walk with me is to plead for them, then I prefer to walk alone."

July lengthened her stride and moved away from May who

exchanged an anxious look with Jan who had come to walk beside her. She was concerned to hear July speak of 'them' as if she were no longer part of the Months.

At the base of the cliff Kalend disappeared into what looked like solid rock and the Months were stunned into silence.

"I told you he was up to no good. Here we are, condemned to death and he just vanishes."

July had spoken with such venom that even Tober was surprised at the strength of her words but before anyone could reply, Kalend reappeared.

"Come on, this way."

Gust moved towards the cliff and disappeared too, but his voice could be clearly heard.

"The cliff looks like its solid but there is a way through. It must be another curtain like the one in our tunnel."

July shouted back to him.

"What is this one going to do to us? Is this where we all get killed?"

Gust's reply showed his exasperation.

"For heaven's sake July, just get in here."

Most were reluctant, but Ari's sense of adventure was aroused, and he moved forward closely followed by June. The sides of the passage were tall and became narrower as they reached toward the sky. In some places they touched and the way became dark before it widened again.

When Kalend and Gust reached the other side, they sat down on some rocks to wait for the others. Gust looked around in amazement. The grass was green but nothing else was the same. Tall blue trees formed a forest around them and a silvery sun shone in a cloudless creamy sky. He turned a sad and dejected face to Kalend.

"Can we trust you? Is all you told us yesterday the truth?"

"Gust, it was never my idea to keep things secret from you. I am your friend and you can trust everything I tell you. When the others arrive, I will tell you about the Watchers. Some of them will support February but others didn't want you to come here. I beg of you, stay close to him. He has always admired you and your support will be important to him."

Before Kalend could say more they heard the others approaching and he invited them to sit down.

"You can see Tir Dhuchais is different from The Valley. The…"

"Kalend. Welcome home. We thought we would come to meet you and help you and your little friends get to the Chamber safely."

Hiemal smiled broadly at the Months.

"We are Hiemal, Watcher of Pluto and this is Thades, Watcher of Mars. Perhaps you would be kind enough to introduce yourselves."

Kalend was furious and amazed. Hiemal had been expelled from the Chamber yet here he was, obviously unaffected by whatever had happened. Hiemal understood his reaction and his smile widened. The Months stood and looked at one another and then at Hiemal and Thades.

"Come now don't be shy. Which one of you is February?"

February hesitantly stepped forward. He didn't know how to greet a Watcher but was afraid of offending them so bowed deeply.

"I am February, and I am delighted to make your acquaintance."

"Such beautiful manners — don't you think so Thades? We can see why Kalend is so fond of them. Who's next?"

One by one the Months stepped forward, bowing to the two Watchers, all except July. She glared with undisguised acrimony at them, much to the horror and anger of Kalend, but he could do nothing until this charade was over. Hiemal, watching Kalend's rising anger was delighted. This was better than he could have imagined.

Gust was the last to step forward and Kalend was pleased to see he looked at the newcomers with suspicion.

Introductions over, Kalend said they should move on, but Hiemal protested.

"We have brought refreshments for you. Surely you would not want them to go to waste."

"We haven't eaten since a meagre breakfast. We will eat and rest before going any further." July's voice had risen sharply as she spoke, shooting an angry glance at Kalend. "After all, it's not our fault we're here, is it?"

Hiemal could see trouble was already brewing – and it was obvious Kalend was not in control. Thades invited them to eat, placing two baskets on the ground containing white, bread like rolls, strange looking fruit and vegetables, fish wrapped in leaves and several large flagons of wine. Kalend protested that wine was not a good idea when they still had a long way to travel, but was ignored. Vem came to sit next to Kalend.

"Those two are not on our side are they? And what's with this 'we' that Hiemal keeps saying?

"Hiemal certainly is not on your side— he is your greatest threat. On his home world the males always refer to themselves in the plural, nothing more than that. Try to warn the others not to be taken in by him. Thades is a fair man and will make his decisions independently, but he has a deep friendship with Hiemal. I don't know why they've come but it is certainly not to

174

help us."

Their talk didn't go unnoticed by Hiemal who noted Vem appeared to be the dominant male in the group. He told Thades to befriend February, but Kalend cut short their conversation.

"We must go now, do not forget where we are going or why we have come."

His words were a sobering reminder to the Months and the mood which had relaxed after the wine changed to a more sombre one. Hiemal was delighted with the time they had spent and made no further protest. Thades wondered again if this interference, without the approval of Balack, would cause more problems than it would solve.

Hiemal made a show of graciously insisting Kalend should lead the way, drawing Thades to one side as he did so.

"We'll try to talk to July. She seems angry with everyone and we're sure we can use her to our advantage. You work on February. Find out why he broke the contract."

Hiemal hurried off before Thades could protest.

Vem managed to speak to Jan and Dec telling them what Kalend had said, and they agreed not to let anyone be alone with either Thades or Hiemal if they could help it.

Dec told Gust who moved forward to talk to Ember. In her 'canny' way she was already wary of Hiemal as she considered him 'too sweet to be wholesome'.

Hiemal approached July and spoke politely.

"You are July are you not? We are Hiemal, may we talk with you?"

When July didn't respond Hiemal resisted the urge to strike her. She had the same self-pitying look on her face as Verna had in the woods.

"We understand your fear, but we…"

"I don't fear you. I simply can't imagine what a powerful Watcher of the Universe would have to say to a mere Month."

Her voice was coated with sarcasm and Hiemal found himself warming to her. He used his most honeyed tone to continue.

"Being a Watcher is not easy, we have a great responsibility for the planets under our care and have made personal sacrifices in order to fulfil our duties."

The word 'sacrifice' infuriated July.

"And now you are prepared to sacrifice me because of someone else's mistake."

Certain he could manipulate her anger, he sighed as he spoke.

"It is not our wish to sacrifice anyone, but a law has been broken."

July stopped and turned to face him. She spoke passionately about the selflessness and courage of those throughout history who risked everything to fight against injustice and the rights of those who were unable to fight for themselves. As she spoke her eyes shone with the fire of her convictions. Hiemal forced himself to touch her arm.

"We can see we've been misinformed, but we must leave you and speak to the others or they will accuse us of favouritism. We would very much like to speak to you later, perhaps when we make camp for the night?"

July didn't answer. Hiemal's manner towards Kalend clearly showed there was division among the Watchers as Kalend couldn't hide his anger that he and Thades were there. As Hiemal moved away to talk to June and May, July resolved to watch him closely.

Taking the lead Kalend asked February to walk with him, but

Thades came to join them making it impossible to talk to February alone. As they walked Thades learned of February's love of something he called 'sport', with ice hockey and snowboarding his favourites. Thades never mentioned the contract. In a moment when February moved away Kalend angrily whispered to Thades.

"Why have you come and why is Hiemal looking so pleased with himself?"

"Would you rather Hiemal had come alone?"

As February returned Kalend left them, pondering what Thades' could have meant.

The quickest way to the Chamber was to follow the lake shore as far as Sentinel Rock and then to cut into the forest. Kalend had planned to get to the rock before nightfall allowing them to reach the Chamber the next day. May's complaining about her bunion made many rest stops necessary and they had still not reached the rock when they stopped to camp.

The Months had stood in amazement when they first saw the lake. It was the colour of melted butter. Hiemal explained that the lakebed was covered in a thin layer of golden rock. The water reacted with it to give this creamy yellow colour, but it was still water and quite safe to drink.

The lake shore was close to the forest where they camped. Kalend asked Gust and Dec to go with him to collect leaves from the strange, tall blue trees. The blue leaves were many metres above the ground and looked like large sails with hanging cords which rustled in the slightest breeze. Thades offered to accompany them but when Gust became nervous saying he could hear voices, Thades explained it was the trees. The gentlest of breezes would cause vibrations in the massive sails high overhead making the sounds he heard. These gatherings of trees were known as a Whispering Forest.

Kalend showed how to wrap the trailing cord from a leaf around his waist, pulling gently but steadily until the sail fell. Only one sail could be taken from each tree. As the first sail fell, Gust moved to one side to avoid being hit but it was soft as it brushed his arm before settling on the ground. Looking at them from below had given no indication that they were as thick as Gust's forearm. He reached for it, surprised by the velvet like texture and a softness that sprang back as soon as he released it. The cord was thin but incredibly strong and Gust couldn't break it.

Dec struggled to control his emotions as Kalend came to work beside him. He remembered Vem's words about not alienating Kalend, but pain at his betrayal was strong and he made no response to Kalends attempts at conversation.

"We will use these as sleeping mats tonight. They will provide comfort and warmth."

Dec continued to count in silence, ensuring there was one sail for each person before returning to the camp.

July was exhausted after the stress of the night before but felt greatly refreshed after Hiemal gave her a drink from his own water bottle. He asked her to walk with him towards the lake and curiosity aroused, went with him.

July had thought Hiemal meant him and Thades when he said 'we' but Gust told her it was just the custom of Hiemal's home world.

She made little response as Hiemal spoke of The Valley being without leadership, saying it was no surprise February flouted the law when he had obviously not received any guidance from Kalend.

Any criticism of Kalend stirred July's feelings against him

and Hiemal was astute enough to see her anger. Her voice became sharp and loud.

"Kalend has never tried to guide us. He lives on the other side of the river and visits when we have some kind of community event. Before we agreed to come to The Valley, Kalend assured us we would be free to live as we chose."

There was an incredulous tone and look of amazement on Hiemal's face.

"But who makes decisions, who is in charge?"

"We don't have anyone in charge. If a decision has to be made, we all meet, have our say and a vote is taken, but that is a rare event. We usually just do what we want."

Hiemal continued his charade, turning away from her and running his fingers through his hair. He paced back and forth for a few minutes, obviously deep in thought, July's words filling him with delight. At last he stopped, composing his features before turning to face her.

"We cannot believe Kalend has let things deteriorate this far. No wonder he didn't want any of us to visit your valley."

"Kalend kept you from visiting us. How could he do that?"
"Kalend is Presidion of the Watch and insisted on becoming your Watcher too. As such he had the right to control everything to do with you and your friends. When Kalend told us February had not returned, the Watchers were divided over your fate. The rules of the Watch mean we cannot tell you who was for and who was against you, but Kalend was sent to Earth to find February and then bring you all here."

July's anger made her willing to think ill of Kalend but she was wise enough to distrust Hiemal as he obviously had his own agenda.

"I am confused. On one hand you say Kalend is a dictator in

179

Tir Dhuchais but then say he failed to be a leader in The Valley. Which is it? Why did you really come here, and what do you hope to achieve?"

Hiemal hadn't expected July to show such perception but was saved from having to answer as he could see Ember bearing down on them

"There the two of you are, there is food left from lunch and we will share it now. Please join us."

Ember smiled at Hiemal and folded her arms, making it was clear she was not going back without them. Hiemal offered one arm to Ember and the other to July who hesitated before taking it. She had no reason to believe him any more than Kalend but her anger at Kalend clouded all other thoughts. As they neared camp, Ember looked into Hiemal's face saying

"Imeacht gan teacht ort." explaining it was an Irish blessing.

With both Hiemal and Thades out of the way, Jan and Dec sat either side of February asking him what he and Thades talked about all day.

"Why should I tell you? You didn't want to talk to me and Thades seems like a nice person. He's interested in me and what I think, which is more than either of you have ever been. Go away and leave me be."

Jan looked at Dec in dismay but realised there was no time now to try to right centuries of imagined wrongs and put a large arm around February's shoulders. Together they told February all Kalend had told Vem about their two fellow travellers. February had thought he couldn't possibly feel any worse but added to his misery he now felt a fool for not realising that Thades was like everyone else and not to be trusted.

"I won't speak to him anymore. I will walk alone."

"No, no. Don't do that. We need to know what they are up

to, and you are the only one who can find out. Keep on pretending that we are all angry with you and let Thades talk but watch what you say to him."

Jan gave February's shoulder another hug which threatened to squash him and then both moved away.

When Hiemal returned to the camp with Ember and July, he was pleased to see February sitting on his own with his back to the others. Things were going much better than he could have hoped and his contempt for the Months grew.

Hiemal went to check with Thades and July turned to Ember.

"What did you say to him? It didn't sound like a blessing to me."

"I told him what you should have done – rough translation 'Bugger off.'"

With the coming of night another surprise greeted the Months. Not one, but two moons hung in the sky, one significantly larger than the other. Kalend told them Tir Dhuchais had seven moons but only these two were visible to the naked eye. Two moons served to increase the unease of many of the Months and despite the very comfortable blue sails, all but February and July slept fitfully.

As the Months slept in Tir Dhuchais, the Quaan once again came to The Valley. They found February's cottage empty but animals normally in fields or barns were roaming freely.

Y Quaan felt disappointment rise in him. The Months were their most valued source of memories, and he would not easily give them up. Sending Quaan to each cottage to see if February was somewhere else, his unease increased when they returned to tell of empty homes with obvious signs of a hasty departure. The Quaan were confused. They knew each Month would only leave when it was their turn to go to Earth. Having searched The Valley

181

the Quaan returned to the cave. If the Months had gone to Earth they would have been able to open the door from the tunnel side, meaning there would be no need to prop open the door. Who did the Months expect to use it?

Y Quaan was angry, something was happening and he couldn't work it out. A young Quaan suggested the animals were still in The Valley so perhaps the open door was to allow them to leave and make their way to Earth. This seemed possible.

Not ready to give up his Months yet, Y Quaan told all but one Quaan to return to the mountain ready to depart for their next gathering. The remaining Quaan would watch to see if any Month returned. Y Quaan removed the stone and the door closed.

This day was getting stranger and stranger.

Next morning the Months awoke, surprised to find the blue sails were now wrapped cosily around them. When they made to stand the sails unfurled and almost immediately regained their original thickness and shape. Kalend showed them how to roll the sails, fastening them with the cord trailing from the ends. This he used to tie his ready for use the next night.

As Kalend and the months made their way to the Chamber, t'Hura was restless. Neja had asked her to see Balack and tell him what to do when the Months arrived, but she felt this was wrong. Balack was Judicial Watcher and should be treated with respect and not as a fool. Walking towards the lake deep in thought she was unaware of a figure watching and waiting for her to approach.

"Good morning t'Hura, we both had the same thought. A walk by the lake to consider what will come next. Please sit next to me."

Startled from her reverie, she spoke without thinking,

"Balack, I didn't see you there, Oh, forgive me, I meant Judicial Watcher Balack."

"You're not the only one who forgets, when I looked in the mirror, I just saw me, not a person in authority. I have decided to be simply addressed as Balack, otherwise I may forget who I am."

There was a wistfulness in his voice and t'Hura felt sorry for him as she sat down.

Balack was silent for a long minute as they both gazed over the lake.

"My family is neither rich nor important, laughing when I said I had applied to be a Watcher. Like everyone here they consider me a fool. I didn't even know there was such a thing as a Judicial Watcher."

t'Hura knew Kalend had invented the position but reassured Balack.

"I'm sure your family would be proud of you, and you are too hard on yourself. I see strength and courage in you if you just believe it."

"My family have not contacted me since I came here, their last words were 'Try not to make too big a mess of things'."

t'Hura was concerned at the sadness on his face and her voice was gentle as she continued.

"I am sure when Kalend looked around the Chamber to see who he would appoint, there was only you. Everyone was plotting to try and get what they wanted, but you weren't part of that. He made the right choice, and everyone will see that."

"Really, so what do you think I should do when Kalend returns?"

"I don't know. This is a new situation for us all."

"Well, that makes two of us for I have no idea what to do."

There was such a look of misery on his face t'Hura was silent in her guilt and then made a proposal.

"What if we put our heads together to see what we can come up with?"

A smile lit up Balack's face and she noticed for the first time that he was a very pleasant man.

"That sounds wonderful, where do we start?"

For a long time they considered, rejected and finally agreed on the best course of action. Balack's confidence had grown as they talked, and both were surprised how easy they felt in one another's company.

Balack gave a huge sigh of relief and turned to t'Hura with another of his lovely smiles.

"When all this is over and I am simply a Watcher again, I would like to visit the garden you and Stolesc have made, if you would permit it?"

"I would be pleased to do so, and future walks beside the lake might be another possibility."

Balack laughed.

"I made a poor choice spending time with Hiemal when I first arrived, I won't make that mistake again, even when he is Presidion."

t'Hura joined uneasily with his laughter but quietly wondered if a Watcher who had caused a black crystal could be Presidion. Balack pulled at the green surface they were sitting on.

"What is this stuff, it didn't use to be here, did it?"

"It's called grass and is found on Earth. The animals in The Valley eat it and Kalend thinks some of the seeds must have been brought here on his garments or footwear and started to grow, but it has gradually spread over most of Tir Dhuchais. I like it."

Balack said he did too and perhaps he could visit Earth again when all this was over to see all the other grass-like stuff. t'Hura gave a small sad smile. Would Hiemal allow her, Balack or any of them to visit Earth once he was its Watcher?

Stolesc would have liked to talk to Thades but he was not at his dwelling. Hiemal's dwelling was empty too. He wondered where they were and what they were up to. On his way back to Dynak's he saw T'Hura and Balack sitting together in what was obviously a companionable manner, smiling and even laughing together. This day was getting stranger and stranger.

By the time t'Hura had taken her leave of Balack and gone to join Dynak, Stolesc had told them of her meeting and all except Neja regarded her with curious expressions. Unaware Stolesc had seen them, t'Hura was confused by their looks.

"What's the matter? Why are you looking at me like that?"

Neja jumped in to explain her plan to get Balack to do what they wanted but t'Hura was quick to contradict her. "You asked me to do this, but I decided I wouldn't be party to anything which involved making a fool of Balack. He is a good man who didn't ask for this to happen. We must show him the respect and courtesy we would have shown to Kalend. If you can't assure me of this, I may find it difficult to play my part in your plan."

The others were surprised by the vehemence of her words. Neja had assumed t'Hura would simply fall in with whatever they told her to and wasn't happy with her new-found assertiveness.

"Did you get him to agree to what I asked?"

"What we discussed was in private. You will have to wait with everyone else until Kalend returns."

"t'Hura, it was never our intention to make a fool of Balack."

Dynak was interrupted by Neja,

"He can do that without our help."

"You misjudge him. He is determined to do the best he can, and we should support him in that, not undermine him."

Stolesc could see the situation getting out of hand and diverted their attention by telling them of the disappearance of Hiemal and Thades.

There was much discussion about where they could have gone, some believing they must have gone to Earth while others suspected they may have gone to The Valley to learn more of the Months. t'Hura left soon after, without speaking to Neja who was furious her plan could be in jeopardy. Dynak had tried to mollify her by saying t'Hura had made a good point. To alienate Balack would almost certainly push him back into Hiemal's camp, Dynak's attempts to calm her failed and Neja also left in a bad temper. Stolesc and Dynak worried that all Kalend was trying to do could be for nothing.

"Next"

The Watchers who had been at the meeting at Dynak's decided not to meet again the next morning. t'Hura had no wish to confront Neja who had decided Dynak was right about not alienating Balack but had no desire to tell t'Hura that. Stolesc just wanted Kalend to return as he considered women to be very strange and wanted no more time with them. Dynak was tired of being the peacemaker and took herself off to Saturn for a short time where the storms raging there seemed more peaceful than what was waiting in Tir Dhuchais.

The Months slept little better than the night before, except for February and July who once again had been given a drink from the flasks of Thades and Hiemal. During the night, the camp was visited by a group of fledgling Flughs who moved silently among the sleepers looking for shiny things to take away. One found silver hair clips in July's hair and gently removed several of them without disturbing her. Kalend however was awake and quickly shooed them away.

Next morning July was upset to find her hair tumbling around one shoulder and no sign of the clips which should have held it. She made do with less but on the way several strands of her hair came undone and straggled around her shoulders. Hiemal had come up to her as soon as they began to walk and July, encouraged by Vem, tried to find out what she could from him.

Hiemal had spent some time thinking about how the Months had behaved the previous day. They were not as he had imagined them to be. They showed a primitive intelligence and July's aggression appeared to be directed at Kalend, but he hadn't been able to find out why. After enquiring about how she had slept, Hiemal came to the point.

"I would like to support Kalend with his plan to save you, but without knowing what that is makes it difficult."

July knew helping Kalend was not what Hiemal intended.

"He hasn't told us what he intends but why don't you just ask him?"

"I will if the opportunity arises."

Hiemal's opinion that the Months would be dull and easily manipulated was rapidly changing. July hid a smile but changed her tactics, realizing she would learn nothing from him if she continued to belittle him. She turned to face him placing her hand on his arm.

"Forgive my sharpness. I am just worried that tomorrow I will die. Is there anything you can tell me about the Watchers that could save us?"

Irritated by her touch, he forced himself to smile. Now was the time to implement the plan he had formulated overnight but only if he was right about how July felt towards Kalend.

"The greatest concern expressed by many Watchers was that February broke the contract without any thought for the danger he was placing you in. If Kalend had shown leadership and guided the young February, then this matter could have been avoided."

July lifted her eyes to meet his and he could see this idea appealed to her.

"Are you saying that if Kalend is guilty of failing in his responsibilities, then February can't be held to blame?"

"It may be possible, but any complaint against him would have to come from you and your friends."

"Kalend has been with us for a very long time and it would be difficult to persuade Vem to stand against him."

"Why would it have to be Vem? Surely there is someone else who could demonstrate they were capable of leading. Someone with strong principles and a sense of justice who would impress the Watch, as I have been impressed."

July knew he was flattering her for his own ends but there was merit to his idea.

"If we made this complaint, what would happen to Kalend? Would he be removed as the Watcher for us?"

"He says he cares deeply for you. He thinks of you as his children and being parted from you would bring him great sorrow. However, if it is his failure that has endangered you, he must pay the price."

July was angered by the idea of Kalend considering them his children when he had removed any possibility of them having children of their own.

She told Hiemal she would think about this and talk to him later.

"Please keep this matter between us until you have made a decision. Kalend is a clever man and could find a way to prevent your complaint if he knew about it in advance."

Instead of talking to Vem, July walked alone considering how best to proceed. She knew Gust, Vem, Ari, Ember and May wanted to believe in Kalend and would oppose any suggestion of removing him, especially if they thought the suggestion came from Hiemal. She also knew she could present a good case to the Watchers which would hopefully exonerate February, but would anyone support her? She was still unsure if Hiemal was deliberately misleading her but her desire to punish Kalend was greater than her distrust of Hiemal.

Ember and Vem had watched July deep in conversation with Hiemal and hoped she was doing as had been suggested but when Ember tried to approach her, Hiemal intervened.

"Ember, perhaps you could speak to me again in the language of your people. Your words last night have proved to be a blessing indeed."

Ember could not hide her smile which Hiemal thought meant she was flattered by him, rather than amused at him.

"Slainte ne bhfear agus go maire na mna go deo'. This means 'cheers to the men and may the women live forever'. In our case, I hope both men and women will live forever."

"That is unfortunately out of my hands. February should have considered more carefully before breaking the contract."

Hiemal was determined to maintain any divisions within the Months and Ember was proving to be very annoying, having interrupted his talk with July twice now.

During lunch Ember sat next to July and asked her what she had learned. She was careful in her reply.

"The Watchers are divided about our future. We must show we are deserving of their help. Hiemal said Kalend thinks of us as his children which I find offensive, but he has said things about Kalend which contradict each other. Hiemal may not be trusted, but neither can Kalend. Don't forget how he has lied and deceived us for all of our time in The Valley."

Ember felt July was not telling her everything, but it was time to resume their journey. July approached Hiemal and said she believed his suggestion was a good one but doubted she could convince the others, as they looked to Vem as the natural leader. Hiemal took great pains to reassure her she was the only one who had shown the intelligence required to save them. They were so engrossed in conversation that July walked into a spiny bush and sharp thorns ripped the sleeve of her dress in several places. Hiemal took advantage of this.

"July, are you hurt?"

He put an arm around her, calling for someone to aid them. Ember rushed over but was surprised to find a single scratch on July's arm rather than the multiple injuries suggested by Hiemal's shout for aid.

"I think she'll live and can probably walk without your arm around her shoulders." Her sarcasm angered Hiemal but he smiled reassuringly at July.

Nearing the Chamber, Kalend used his crystal to inform Balack of their imminent arrival so he could summon the others to meet inside the Chamber. Balack was surprised to find Hiemal and Thades weren't there and asked if anyone knew where they might be, but no one did.

Following the suggestion made by t'Hura, Balack asked Dynak if the Months could use her dwelling to rest while the Watch met, and she went to prepare some food before returning. Balack instructed the others to remain in the Chamber, insisting they were not to come out when Kalend and the Months returned. They were to wait for the Watch meeting which would follow. If anyone was surprised by Balack's new show of authority, they managed to hide their feelings. t'Hura gave him a small smile of approval.

Kalend had spoken to several of the Months, describing the size and nature of the Chamber. When they saw a man standing in an open glade in a beautiful coloured forest, they were surprised not to see a building. Where was the Chamber Kalend had spoken of? Dynak had worked industriously over many centuries to transform the outer wall of the Chamber and it was now invisible to the casual observer.

As Kalend approached, Balack stepped forward, angered to see Hiemal and Thades. Aware of wanting to appear as a person of importance and justice, Balack ignored them as he spoke to the Months.

"I am Balack, Judicial Watcher for these proceedings. Welcome to our Chamber. Kalend will take you to the dwelling of Watcher Dynak where you will have time to rest before appearing before us. Kalend you will return here immediately."

Kalend asked the now subdued Months to follow him. On the way he praised the work of Dynak, explaining the Chamber was covered with the work of her hands and the inside of the Chamber would be clearly seen when they entered it.

Balack, still ignoring Hiemal and Thades, went into the Chamber and took his seat.

"Oh dear, it looks as if our friend Balack is a little peeved with us." smirked Hiemal, but Thades was not amused.

"We would do well to remember he is no longer 'our friend Balack', but Judicial Watcher Balack who is justifiably angry with us."

Hiemal snorted with derision and strode into the chamber towards his seat.

"Hiemal and Thades, you will remain standing until Kalend returns and I have spoken to you."

Hiemal was furious at being asked to remain standing, but Thades told him he had better be careful or he might find himself outside the Chamber once more, with no one to speak for him this time.

Dynak and Stolesc were surprised at the change in Balack and wondered just what he and t'Hura had talked about.

Kalend hurried back to the Chamber, gladdened to find Hiemal and Thades standing before an obviously angry Balack.

He hoped to learn why Hiemal had been readmitted to the Chamber when he had made his instructions clear before leaving.

Strengthened by the words of encouragement and support offered by t'Hura, Balack raised his eyes to look around the Chamber before coming to rest on Kalend.

"Ah, Kalend, thank you for returning so promptly. I will inform you of all developments in a moment, first I have another matter to deal with. Hiemal and Thades, you did not ask for or receive permission to join the Months on their journey here. Such a lack of respect for me and my position is intolerable."

Thades stepped forward, bowed and then knelt before him with outstretched arms. Such an attitude of submission was a sign of respect Balack had not expected.

"Judicial Watcher Balack, I acted without thought but it was not my intention to disrespect you or your position. I ask the forgiveness of you and this Watch."

Balack was stunned into silence and glanced at t'Hura who gave a slight nod to show he should accept the apology.

"Thades, I recognise that your actions were out of character and forgiveness is granted, please take your seat."

All eyes turned to Hiemal who was seething with rage. He was soon to be Presidion and would kneel to no one. He did bow his head as he spoke.

"We were concerned that Kalend had been left to bring a large group of Months here without assistance and went to see if we could help. We apologise if our actions have offended you."

"You will address me as Judicial Watcher Balack. What offends me are your words. Helping Kalend or the Months is the last thing you would do. You not only insult my position, but also my intelligence. If you were not the spokesperson for the Charter I would remove you from these proceedings, but I assure you I will do so if you give me the slightest cause. Take your seat before I change my mind."

A stunned silence filled the Chamber, not one person there would have believed Balack capable of such strength, including Balack himself. Being Judicial Watcher was proving to be a thoroughly enjoyable experience. Hiemal was enraged by Balack's treatment of him and was glad his ring was powerless.

Balack turned to address Kalend, speaking with the respect he had always shown him.

"Presidion Kalend, following your leaving of this Chamber, it was the unanimous will of the Watch that Hiemal be allowed to return. He is the speaker for those opposed to the continued existence of the Months. To exclude him could be seen as an attempt to force a solution pleasing to you. He is aware the black crystal will be dealt with after the conclusion of this matter."

Kalend was angry his instructions had not been followed but he had given Balack authority to act in his absence and could not now complain if he had done so.

"Thank you, Judicial Watcher Balack. I wish you and this Watch good fortune under your leadership."

Balack thanked Kalend for his words and asked him to take a seat.

"Judicial Watcher Balack is too long a form of address. You will simply address me as Balack, except for Hiemal who must learn respect. Now to the matter of the Months. We will spend our first meeting getting to know them. They will come to the chamber, introduce themselves and then speak of what they do in their Valley and on their calendar time. They will stay in the Chamber overnight. In the morning February will explain his actions and sentence will be passed. Stolesc, you have not had any contact with the Months, so will you please go and summon them to appear before us now."

Stolesc was happy to do so and strode briskly from the chamber.

As soon as Kalend was out of earshot, Vem had called the Months together on Dynak's porch.

"We don't know how much time we will have so we had better make the most of it. February, what did you learn from your talk with Thades?"

July couldn't help her anger at February from bubbling over now that there were no Watchers to hear her, but Vem knew he mustn't let accusations take up valuable time.

"July, no one knows better than February that he is responsible for what is happening, but perhaps you can enlighten us about Hiemal's position in all of this."

July took a deep breath to calm her anger.

"It is clear there is no love lost between him and Kalend, but Kalend has shown himself to be a liar and a deceiver. I believe Hiemal will support us."

Vem was normally placid and slow to anger, but in a rare show of emotion he raised his voice.

"Don't you know he's making a fool out of you? He is the one Watcher who wants rid of us more than any other. Kalend..."

July was really angry now and her voice became shriller.

"Don't speak to me of Kalend. For centuries he has lied and kept the other Watchers from coming to visit us. Hiemal is sure if all had been given the chance to know us, we would be safe."

All eyes were staring at her now, but it was Ember who was first to speak.

"You have spent two days in the company of Hiemal and that's enough to wipe out two thousand years of knowing Kalend?"

Hiemal had told July not to tell anyone of their plan and believing she was the only one who could save them, chose to be circumspect with the information she would share.

"I know the Watch is divided but don't know who is for and who is against us. I believe Hiemal speaks truth when he says he wants to help us."

Gust knew July was wrong but how could he reassure those who wavered?

"I trust my instincts and they tell me Kalend is our friend. Why ask us to bring our instruments so we could entertain them if he wanted us to fail? Hiemal didn't speak for any length of time to anyone but July, so we only have her word for what he said. February, did Thades say anything that would support Hiemal?"

February told how he had tried to steer the conversation towards the Watch, but Thades simply ignored his questions and focused on matters not related to the situation they were in.

A fierce argument broke out with several people shouting until Ember stood up and putting both hands over her ears, screamed loudly until everyone else was silent.

"Do you really think it matters who is on our side and who is not. The contract has been broken and there may be nothing we can do to stop them from destroying us. Even if Kalend can save us, if we can't stay here and can't go to Earth, where will we go?"

No one spoke as they knew Ember was right. February hesitated, everyone was angry and frightened, but knew he must tell them.

"There is a way out. When I came back, I jammed the door to the tunnel open with a rock. If things turn out badly tomorrow, you must all go to The Valley and escape to Earth."

Ari looked up suddenly.

"But you'll come with us, won't you? I mean, if we can get away so can you."

February thanked Ari for his concern adding

"I was the one to break the contract and you may need a diversion while you get away. It's only right I should remain here."

Tober's anger had been simmering below the surface all the way from The Valley to the Chamber.

"How very noble of you, but don't you think it's a little late to be thinking of us. If you hadn't…"

Ember interrupted him.

"As has already been said, what point is there in arguing about what should or shouldn't have been done. We have to decide what to do next. Kalend said we should present a united front – if we argue like this, they will certainly send us away. I think we should be calm and supportive of February as Kalend asked."

July was irritated February had his own plan to save them but bit her tongue; Hiemal had impressed upon her the importance of keeping their plan to herself and so kept silent. The others discussed the matter, eventually agreeing a united front was the only hope they had. As July did not speak against it, Ember hoped she would do as they had agreed.

The walk and stress of the last few days took their toll. One by one, the Months wandered around the house and garden and found quiet spots to sit and contemplate all that had befallen them since leaving The Valley. Ari wandered from room to room looking at books with strange writing in them. The illustrations in one were of beautiful, unbelievable creatures and he wondered what Watcher Dynak was like.

July didn't find a quiet spot to rest. She had never liked

February and her feelings against Kalend were even stronger since Hiemal spoke of his treachery. February's plan was ridiculous. It had taken them two days to get here and if they tried to leave, the Watchers, able to travel by thought, would simply catch them. It had no chance of success but if she told Hiemal what February was planning, he may be able to help.

She tore a page out of her diary and hurrying to the boulder where Hiemal had told her to leave any messages, tucked her quickly drawn note into a crevice at its base. As she headed back, she saw someone on the path in front of her and hid among the trees until he was out of sight and then rushed back to the others. She assumed the man with long blonde hair was a Watcher.

Stolesc walked quickly and had already gathered the others before July returned and Ember eyed her suspiciously as she appeared, red-faced, from the garden. Stolesc had told them all the Watchers were in the Chamber waiting for them. July couldn't have been with Hiemal if that had been her intent, but Ember resolved to keep a close eye on her.

Back in the Chamber the meeting had broken into groups who talked quietly together, t'Hura told Kalend she would explain everything after the meeting was over, whispering they may have a possible addition to his amendment.

The chairs had been moved closer together forming a semi-circle around the table leaving a space facing the entrance.

As they neared the Chamber Stolesc stopped and spoke gently to them.

"When you enter the Chamber, you will see the Watchers waiting for you. You will all stand before them and wait until Balack asks you to speak."

Stolesc hesitated for a moment before continuing.

"I am a friend of Kalend. The best advice I can give is to be honest and respectful – the Chamber is no place for anger or accusation."

Even as he said the words, he hoped they were true, recent events making him doubt the Chamber would ever be the same again. He stood to one side and touched the wall to show the way inside, but even Gust was reluctant to be first. July seeing her chance pushed to the front. She should show the Watchers she was the person to be reckoned with. She bravely stepped between the trees and was rendered speechless by the appearance of the Chamber. The tall, mirrored pillars seemed to reach a sky that could be seen through a flawless glass ceiling. July remembering where she was, lowered her eyes to look at the Watchers but Gust following her, almost knocked her to the floor. One by one the others entered until only May was left. After a short pause she appeared, arm in arm with a smiling Stolesc. May, fearing this may be the place they would be killed was so relieved to see the others alive and well she cried and hugged several of them before July reached for her arm and shook her.

"You forget where you are, try and behave with some dignity."

February stepped between them. "Back off, no one put you in charge."

Hiemal was delighted with the spectacle the Months had displayed so far.

Balack stood and waved them forward.

"Come into the centre where we can all see you."

He studied them properly for the first time, disappointed to find most of them looked ordinary and boring, except for an enormous man with red hair and beard who looked fearlessly back at him. When they had all assembled Balack called for silence, even though no one was speaking.

"I am Balack, Watcher of Uranus and Judicial Watcher for these proceedings. Each Watcher will introduce themselves, even though you know some of them."

Stolesc was first on his left and began. Each Watcher stated their name and the name of their planet while the Months studied each in turn. Most Watchers were pleasant and smiled as they spoke, including Hiemal, only t'Hura was solemn. Balack beamed at them.

"Now it is your turn; it would be best if you stood in a line in the same order as your Month falls on Earth. You will state your name, what you do to contribute to The Valley and the number of days you spend on Earth. When you have finished you will answer any questions I may put to you."

Dynak had to admit she was pleasantly surprised by the organized way Balack was conducting the meeting. Perhaps they had misjudged him. There was some shuffling as a rather wobbly line was formed; Jan dwarfed February who stood next to him and Kalend thought this was a good idea as it might gain some sympathy for him.

Balack nodded to Jan who stepped forward with his pack.

"I am Jan, my month is January. I grow fruits and vegetables for us to eat and to trade. I have thirty-one calendar days."

As he spoke, he placed apples, tomatoes, and asparagus on the table.

Balack reached for a piece of asparagus but after taking a bite threw the remainder away.

"Next."

When February said his name, Balack looked at him with interest. So, this was the contract breaker.

"How old are you, are you still a child?'

Hiemal could not quite stifle his laughter and February felt the familiar emotion of inadequacy fill him.

"I am a man, not a child. A child would not have acted as I have done."

His anger was obvious in his voice and Balack frowned his disapproval.

"You forget your place, February. Is this temper of yours normal behaviour?"

February, realising he may have already condemned them stuttered.

"Forgive me, my words were spoken in haste."

Trying to find the right words February paused for a moment before speaking again.

"Sir, all my life I have been short. Short of height and short of days. I'm not trying to excuse my temper, just to explain it. The last few days have been very stressful, and I ask you not to judge me too harshly."

He placed his stone carving on the table.

"I work in stone, making decorative items which I sell. I have twenty-eight or twenty-nine days."

Balack snorted but didn't ask February anything else. Neja reached for the carving, turning it over in her hands. This February was a strange mixture of man and child who had creative talent requiring patience and commitment.

"Next."

February stepped back into his place in the line furious with himself. Why could he not control his temper? He turned his head to look at Kalend and saw him sitting with his head in his hands.

Ari pointed out that March's place was between him and February and that she was the healer of The Valley. He then spoke of his own place there. Balack's face lightened considerably when he heard Ari was an entertainer. He smiled delightedly.

"What kind of entertainment? Can you do something entertaining now?"

Ari took his banjo from his pack but hesitated as Hiemal jumped to his feet.

"Bal... Judicial Watcher Balack, it is getting late and there are still seven Months to introduce themselves. Perhaps we should curtail the questioning until the morning when everyone has rested."

Balack sat up straight.

"Perhaps you wouldn't be so tired if you hadn't gone, without permission, to join Kalend with the Months. You had plenty of time to speak with them and now you would try to deny those of us who were less fortunate the opportunity to do the same. May I remind you I will decide what we will do in this Chamber."

Dynak, realizing that an angry Balack wouldn't help the Month's cause, stood to speak.

"Balack, you are right that it is important to learn as much about the Months as we can, but perhaps the entertainment can wait until the introductions have all been made."

Balack was appeased by the conciliatory tone in Dynak's voice.

"An excellent suggestion. Next!"

Balack wasn't interested in an elderly baker until she placed a large fruit cake on the table and cut a slice which she offered to him.

"Sir, I bake bread but also cakes."

"What are cakes?"

"They are sweet treats to be shared with friends."

Balack sniffed the cake and then took a bite. His face glowed with pleasure.

203

"I like cakes. Next."

June spoke her name before emptying a pouch of coins onto the table. Balack knew all about coin and handled the pieces as he ate more cake.

"Next!"

July took a deep breath before stepping forward. She bowed to Balack and then introduced herself but before she could speak, Balack demanded.

"Have you been attacked by something?"

July was confused and looked at Hiemal for some kind of signal; he smiled his encouragement.

"I do not understand the question, but if I may speak on behalf of the Months. I ..."

"No, you may not. I asked if you had been attacked, your dress is torn and your hair is a mess. Did something do this to you?"

July self-consciously touched her shoulder where the thorns had ripped her sleeve that morning.

"No, no nothing attacked me."

"So, your appearance is because you chose to look like that?"

July felt humiliated by Balack's blatant disapproving stare and mumbled something about thorns, but Balack had already lost interest in her and she stepped back after putting some scented soap on the table. Balack reached for it and after sniffing it went to take a bite.

"No please, it is soap for washing your body, not for eating."

"Next!"

"I am Gust and I work with metal."

He took two blades out of his pack and after tossing one of Jan's apples in the air, quickly sliced it as it fell. He put both blades beside the growing array of goods.

Stolesc reached for one blade, testing its sharpness on his thumb which quickly showed a line of golden blood. Balack was impressed with the blades but knew in this Chamber he could do as he wanted, and he wanted to be amused.

"A man of your physique must be a great favourite with the ladies. Do you confine your amorous activities to Earth, or do you satisfy the ladies in your Valley too?"

This time it was Kalend who jumped to his feet.

"I must object. Your question is vulgar and totally uncalled for. You know nothing of this man, yet you deliberately try to antagonize and embarrass him."

Balack had always respected Kalend and realised he had perhaps gone too far.

"August or Gust or whatever you call yourself, I am sorry if I shocked or offended you. You do not have to answer my question, at least not in public. Next!"

Ember spoke clearly and with confidence, this annoyed Balack who was enjoying being in control.

"Do you spend everyday fishing? Is that the sum total of your existence? It seems you have less to do than anyone else. Do they mind?"

Ember smiled. "I am also responsible for ensuring the health of the river and for replenishing fish stocks. As to whether anyone minds, I've never asked. I also work with Gust to brew this dark stout which is the favoured drink among my people."

Balack reached for the opened bottle she handed to him. Sniffing it he handed it to Thades. He took one small sip, followed by two much larger mouthfuls before Stolesc nudged him, holding out his hand. Stolesc finished the bottle and the two smiled at Ember in appreciation.

"Next!"

Tober spoke quietly about his work with horses and his skill making a variety of cheeses. He placed three pieces of his cheese on the table with a cheese knife.

"Aha! You care for the creatures in your Valley. I intend to visit Earth to see them when all this matter is over."

Balack looked at the strange shaped implement and cut a piece of the cheese before using the forked end to pick up the piece and ate it. He smiled in delight at the clever and useful small blade.

"I like cheese, but not as much as I like cake. Next."

Vem stood straight and looked Balack in the eye as he told of his work as a farmer to produce food for The Valley. Taking a sheepskin rug from his pack, he presented it to t'Hura.

"It is my pleasure to be able to present this to the Watcher of Earth."

Balack nodded his head a few times. He appreciated the respect Vem was showing for t'Hura who accepted the rug without comment. Neja, sitting next to her, ran her hands over the rug, delighting in its softness and warmth.

"Next!"

Dec spoke of his love of wood, telling of the buildings he had made in The Valley and then produced a wooden toy to place on the table.

Balack took it in his hands, enjoying the smoothness of the wood and the detail of the work.

"What creature is this?"

"It is a horse. Tober and Vem use them for farm work."

"How can something so small be used for work?"

Dec explained a real horse was many times bigger, using his hand to indicate how tall it would be.

Balack decided he was tired.

"Meeting all these beings has been trying and tiring. They will spend tonight here in this chamber and the meeting will continue in the morning."

Kalend stood and reminded Balack that he had asked to be entertained and now would be a good time for the Months to show their musical skill.

"What is musical?"

Balack, as Kalend suspected, had never experienced music before.

Kalend said it would be easier to show him than try to explain in words.

The musicians had talked as they walked about the pieces they would play. Gust remembered with great clarity the first time he had gone to a concert and heard 'Morning from Peer Gynt by Grieg'. It had brought tears to his eyes, and it was because of this piece he had purchased his first flute and learned to play. Tober and June were happy with his choice, saying they would accompany him.

Taking his flute from his pack he began. The acoustics in the chamber were excellent, filling it with sounds that had never been heard there before. Tober joined in with his violin and June with her cello. All, except Hiemal, were held in thrall by it. There was silence when they finished, and the Months were uncertain if the music had pleased or not. Kalend prompted Ari and February and they played 'Dueling Banjos'. Several Watchers found their feet moved in time to the music and they smiled, this 'music' was wonderful.

A nervous Ember stepped forward and began to sing, accompanied by Tober on his violin.

'Summertime, and the livin' is easy.

Fish are jumpin' and the cotton is high.

Your daddy's rich and your mamma's good lookin'

So hush little baby, don't you cry.'

Stolesc could not remain seated. He had no idea the voice he used for talking could be used in this way. Ember's voice trembled with emotion as she finished. Stolesc threw back his head and produced several whistles of appreciation. The sound caused alarm among the Months, but Kalend moved beside them explaining this was applause on the world of Stolesc.

When Gust began to play 'Stranger on the shore' on his clarinet, May clasped Ari's arm and whispered.

"Look at Thades, he's glowing!

Kalend who had remained beside them whispered.

"This happens to Hernians in moments of extreme pleasure."

Thades was indeed experiencing such pleasure and knew he didn't want a future without this 'music'. The Months applauded when he had finished and Balack looked at his hands before bringing them together as he had seen them do, clapping faster and faster. He looked very pleased with himself.

"I like this music better than cake."

When the recital was over, the Watchers were quick to speak to the Months. Only Hiemal never moved from his seat. Most Watchers wanted to hold the instruments and tried to produce the sounds they had heard. Dynak asked Gust to tell her what the first music maker was called.

"This one is a flute and the other a clarinet."

He showed her how to hold the flute and blow into the mouthpiece, but when she was unable to produce a sound, she laughed and said she obviously had no ability. Gust reassured her that it had taken him many years to learn how to play it, but he would be happy to teach her. Balack wanted to play the violin and told Tober to show him how, but the screeching sounds he made caused everyone to cover their ears and he threw it back at a laughing Tober.

"It has been a long day and this meeting is over. Watchers will leave the Chamber and have no contact with the Months until I return in the morning. Is that clear to everyone?"

t'Hura spoke.

"Balack, it would be a kindness to the Months if they were able to bathe before the meeting tomorrow. Perhaps, in the morning, the ladies could come to my dwelling and the men to Stolesc's dwelling, but only after you have returned to the Chamber and given permission."

"Yes, I can see that bathing would be a good idea, but no one enters the Chamber until I arrive."

February had hoped to speak to Kalend before he left but, still angry with him for his outburst, Kalend left without speaking. With his chilling silence echoing in his ears, February watched the Chamber empty until only the Months remained. Balack took the remaining cake and Tober's cheese with him.

t'Hura hadn't known if she wanted to help the Months, all she had considered was what was best for her. She had been surprised to find herself liking them, except for July and February who had done nothing to endear themselves to her, or anyone. Unlike the other Watchers she was familiar with music from her visits to Earth but had enjoyed the concert. She was curious about most of them, particularly liking Ember and May; they might have been friends if things had been different.

"Your idea is the only hope they have"

Kalend, Verna, Neja, t'Hura and Stolesc gathered in Dynak's house with Verna and Stolesc going to help Dynak prepare a meal. t'Hura told him Neja had a plan to help convince Hiemal to vote in favour of the amendment.

Neja began.

"Hiemal's black crystal showed his hatred for the Months. Even if he's offered Earth, he may still refuse to approve the amendment."

She told of her plan to have a Quest with the amendment as the prize. If the Months were successful, they would remain in their Valley. If they failed, they would be subject to the law of the Charter. Dynak added her support.

"Hiemal believes the Months are flawed beings who will almost certainly fail. t'Hura would still swap worlds with Hiemal, in return for his agreement to the Quest."

Kalend wasn't convinced.

"Hiemal has the right to insist the Charter is enforced. We all saw him reach for the Earth sphere at the Allocation of Worlds ceremony. Exchanging Earth for the lives of the Months is a good offer. This Quest could still mean the Months are destroyed if they fail."

Stolesc, returning to place food on the table was confused.

"Hiemal may have wanted the blue planet, but when he bonded with his own, those feelings would have disappeared."

Kalend sighed.

"Hiemal didn't touch his sphere, so no bond was made."

A feeling of sadness filled the room. Verna whispered.

"Poor Hiemal. To have spent all this time without the comfort and joy of his world."

t'Hura was desperate to no longer be Watcher of Earth so spoke quickly.

"The amendment must give Earth to Hiemal if the Months lose or win. Becoming Watcher of Earth and Presidion would both be guaranteed."

Neja was more convinced by her Quest than ever.

"If he refuses your amendment as it is now, they are certainly destroyed. Just because he reached for the sphere way back then doesn't mean he desires it now. The Quest gives the Months a chance. His hatred for the Months is so strong he caused a black crystal. What if that hatred is stronger than his desire for Earth?"

Kalend was silent as he considered her words. He believed Hiemal wanted Earth to restore his status on Uclair, but what if he was wrong? What if Hiemal dismissed his amendment? He would only get one chance to present it and if he got it wrong the Months would perish. He slapped the table to give his agreement to Neja's proposal.

Neja reached into her bag and pulled out a rolled parchment, but Kalend stopped her.

"Wait, this Balack is different from the Balack we thought we knew. He is no fool, and if he suspects we have all plotted together he could refuse to allow your proposal. It is better if you tell us nothing of this."

"But I need your help, or at the very least your approval for my idea. What if it's too difficult and they have no chance of winning?"

"The survival of the Months is out of our hands. Your Quest is the only hope they have. Now I need a good sleep and suggest you should all do the same. Tomorrow is going to be a difficult day."

Neja approached t'Hura as she left.

"I wish to apologise for my words yesterday. You were correct in reminding us Balack is deserving of our respect, no matter who he is. I was impressed with the manner in which Balack dealt with Hiemal and Thades and am sure he couldn't have done so without your help. Will you please forgive me?"

t'Hura smiled sadly.

"Of course I forgive you and I too apologise. I believe nothing will be quite the same after this matter is decided and I am responsible for it all. Hiemal as Presidion and Watcher of Earth is abhorrent to me, but I can't blame anyone but myself, Goodnight Neja."

Neja felt sorry for her but couldn't help but agree this problem was all t'Hura's fault. She would have felt much better if the Quest she'd written had the support and approval of the others. She went home, but sleep didn't come easily.

"She saw a glimpse of the girl she had been before she came to The Valley"

There was silence in the Chamber after the Watchers had gone. No one knew what to say. February had admitted his behaviour had been premeditated and could not now claim he had acted on a sudden overpowering desire. Sitting on the floor away from the others, he held his head in his hands just as Kalend had done earlier. Even Gust could not find it in his heart to speak to him.

Still smarting from the humiliation, she had suffered at Balack's hands, July went to lie on his chair while she tried to think of tomorrow. Hiemal had insisted she must step forward and speak out, but Balack had swatted her aside like an irritating fly. Jan had been sitting quietly but now stood up calling for them to listen.

"I think I can prove Hiemal has been lying to July about Kalend. Did you see the looks on the faces of the Watchers when you played for them? They were enthralled and then speaking to us all afterwards, smiling and laughing with us. It was Kalend who suggested we bring our instruments and the only one not to join in or show any support for us was Hiemal. If he is trying to help us, he has a funny way of showing it."

The Months nodded, Neja had made a reasonable attempt to play Ari's banjo and been very complimentary to both him and February. Thades had spoken to Gust about his clarinet, handling it like it was a precious possession. Stolesc had shyly approached Ember asking how she changed her voice to make the sounds he had heard. She'd told him it was singing and anyone could do it.

Gust had found Dynak to be gentle and kind. There was much agreement with Jan.

"If Kalend is against us, as July is saying, he would never have done any of this."

This sounded convincing even to July, but she still defended Hiemal.

"If he was quiet tonight, it was because he was thinking how best to help us."

Jan shook his head in disbelief – how could anyone be so blinded to the truth? Tired and dispirited, the Months settled for the night.

Even though he had been travelling all day, and without a drink from the flask of Thades, sleep eluded February. No one had spoken to him since the meeting ended and he felt more alone than ever. He tossed and turned, replaying the last two days events over in his mind, but finding no one to blame but himself. It had been his selfish idea to stay on Earth and now there was no way to undo the great wrong he had done. It came as a shock to realise how much he cared for the other Months. He had always thought of himself as a loner, but his life was inextricably linked to every Month in the chamber.

As he tried to marshal his thoughts and plan his defence for the next day, he felt some of the old anger return. It wasn't his fault he had been denied equality. He was the victim of a miscarriage of natural justice. A miscarriage he had repeatedly asked to have remedied, but he had been ignored. It wasn't fair. February fell into a fitful sleep with great surges of resentment once again filling his mind.

Sometime before dawn July woke. What if Jan was right and

Hiemal was against them? She had informed him of February's escape plan, and he might use it against them rather than in support of them. Enough light came through the glass roof to let her see sleeping bodies in chairs and on the floor, with the only sound Gust's snoring. She crept past Ari who lay with arms flung above his head and moved around the edges of the Chamber to the doorway and stepped outside.

Upon reaching the boulder she fell to her knees and felt for the crevice which was in shadow. No slip of paper was to be found. Frantically searching she found nothing. She knelt where she was, trying to calm herself. She knew Hiemal must have her note and feared Jan was right about him. She'd been a fool and now she was as much to blame for their fate as February. She made her way back to the Chamber finding Ember standing in the doorway.

"Where have you been? You know we're not supposed to leave the Chamber."

"Unfortunately, the toilet facilities are somewhat lacking inside."

This was true and the reason Ember had woken. July pointed to the boulder which could just be seen in the moonlight and told her there was a sheltered spot behind it.

July had gone into self-defense mode. No one knew she had drawn a picture of the tunnel door and the rock holding it open for Hiemal, and perhaps some animal or bird had taken it. There was no evidence she had done anything wrong and perhaps Hiemal was on their side. July lay down again, but sleep would not come, and she was still staring at the ceiling when the sky lightened.

t'Hura and Stolesc stood outside the Chamber to wait for Balack as neither doubted he would suspend anyone entering without his permission. He didn't keep them waiting long as he was thoroughly enjoying being in charge, spending much of the night planning today's meeting. Ember heard voices outside and woke those not already awake. They tidied themselves and the Chamber and stood, waiting.

t'Hura took May, June, July and Ember to Dynak's dwelling, where water had been heated for them to wash. Neja brought some clothes for July to replace her torn dress. July was surprised by her kindness, selecting a plain tunic and trousers made from an incredibly soft fabric. Both items fitted her beautifully. She did wonder if there was something 'magical' about these clothes to make them fit whoever wore them. She tried brushing her hair but it had become very tangled during the night. When Verna arrived with some ornate hair clips to replace the ones she had lost, she was moved by the kindness of these Watchers she had feared.

Verna brushed July's hair suggesting a softer style would suit her and used eight strands of hair to make a complicated plait which she softly draped around July's shoulder. When she looked in a mirror, she saw a glimpse of the girl she used to be but quickly dismissed her.

The others had also been given a change of clothes and accessories. May now proudly wore a very fancy pair of earrings and billowing trousers given by t'Hura, while May and June selected practical but colourful trousers and tops. Upon returning to the Chamber they found the men also dressed in clean garments. In their new attire they felt almost cheerful.

Balack called the meeting to order. The Months were asked to sit on the floor, except February who would stand. He was glad it was going to be over. Nothing could be worse than the waiting and the not knowing. Balack continued.

"February will speak in his defence before being questioned. Kalend and Hiemal will then state their position."

Before February could begin a newly confident July went to stand beside him.

"What are you doing?" February hissed, but July ignored him.

"Balack, we are creatures of Earth and in our system of justice, the defendant has someone to speak for him. I will speak for February."

'No, you will not' and 'I don't need or want you to speak for me' were spoken at the same time by Balack and February, but July would not be stopped.

"I demand this Council respects the culture and values of those on trial here today."

"You demand. You are nothing. As for treating you with respect, what respect have you shown for this Chamber or the Watchers who sit here?"

Balack was almost purple in the face with what he saw as a slight to his position, a terrible stench filling the Chamber making all put hands over their noses.

Jumping to his feet Gust tried to drag July back to her seat on the floor but kicking his shins, she pulled free from him. Seeing Kalend heading towards her, she pointed at him shouting.

"There is the man who should be on trial today. If he had carried out his duties as he should, then none of this would have happened. Instead he spent his time fishing or having cups of tea. He is not fit to be in charge, and I denounce him as the guilty one here."

Hiemal was beside himself with delight. The Months were all on their feet, talking and shouting at the same time with

Balack screaming for order which everyone ignored. Oblivious to the blows repeatedly aimed at his face and head, Gust picked up July and carried her outside the chamber. Throwing her to the ground he demanded to know just what she thought she was doing. The other Months followed them out and stood in a circle around them. July tried to calm herself before speaking.

"You fools, that was our only chance and you have destroyed it."

"Blaming Kalend, that was your great idea. Let me guess, Hiemal suggested it."

Gust kept his hands in his pockets as the urge to wrap them around July's throat was very great.

"Don't you see? February has already admitted his guilt so there is no defence he can make. Showing that Kalend failed to provide proper leadership means the blame can be shifted to him. You can't punish someone for doing something wrong if he had never been told it was wrong. If Kalend is guilty, then February is innocent."

Although Jan could see the logic in her words, he knew she was wrong.

"Do you really think this Watch will turn on one of their own to protect a Month? Kalend is our only hope here and with your baseless accusation you have turned him against us."

Inside the chamber an equally heated debate was taking place. Seeing the horror his displeasure was inflicting on everyone, Balack removed the offensive smell.

Hiemal made an impassioned speech in which he reviled the Months for daring to accuse Kalend when all knew he worked tirelessly for them, even though they didn't deserve it. He argued that no further evidence was necessary, the Months must be destroyed.

The day was saved by a declaration from Stolesc.

"July has been arrogant and disrespectful towards Judicial Watcher Balack. It was most unfair of her to try to blame this situation on Kalend. However, I can't help but admire the passion behind her words."

Dynak added her support for July, being careful to agree a Month had no right to challenge a Watcher.

Neja commiserated with the outraged Balack.

"You have shown great patience and tolerance for these inferior beings and should have been shown gratitude instead of insolence."

Hiemal could see what Kalend and the others were trying to do as Balack's outrage began to ease but could not refute them without angering Balack.

Kalend was last to speak.

"As the aggrieved party I can't find it in my heart to be angry with July. It took courage for her to act as she did when she has previously shown how she fears the Watch and Balack in particular."

These words of support made Balack feel much better, but he was no fool and knew the Month's supporters were trying to flatter him. He also knew if he ended the matter here, his term as Judicial Watcher would be over.

"I am glad you agree this attack on me was heinous in the extreme, but I must rise above such pettiness and show mercy on those lesser beings. Kalend, you will speak to the Months and when July apologises to me then the matter can be forgotten and the trial of February can continue."

Hiemal protested that no such trial was now needed, but Balack dismissed his protest.

Kalend left the Chamber in time to hear Jan's words and

called to them, his voice making them turn in fear.

"July's words have wounded me deeply, but I would never turn against you. You are to return to the Chamber where July will apologise and then sit down and be quiet."

July said she would never apologise but Vem made it clear she would not be allowed to return to the Chamber if she refused. Furious, but reasoning she couldn't speak for them from outside the Chamber, she agreed. Showing she was prepared to fight for her people could be used to her advantage.

She used her apology to make a short speech.

"Balack, I apologise for my angry words. I showed none of the respect for your world that I expected you to show for mine. It was my love and fear for my friends that made me speak in the only way I could see to help and defend them. I ask for your understanding and your forgiveness."

Ari and February thought 'love' and 'friends' were a bit of an exaggeration, glancing at each other but saying nothing. Balack wasn't prepared to let July off so easily.

"Come and kneel before me. Beg me for my forgiveness and I may give it."

July knew some of the greatest leaders in history had been prepared to humble themselves to save their people. Her anger was replaced with a sense of nobility as she spoke graciously begging the 'all powerful Balack' to have mercy on her.

Balack liked being called all powerful. Cheering up immensely, forgiveness was dispensed and the trial resumed. February stood, trying to gather his thoughts and to speak calmly but forcefully. His nervousness made his voice louder than he had intended.

"Watchers I am February, and I am guilty of breaking the contract. I did so without knowing the consequences my actions would have on others. I cannot find words to express my distress and remorse."

February had spoken all this in one breath and knew it didn't sound as if he was remorseful at all. He struggled to compose himself so he could present a true vision of who he was to the other Months as well as to the Watch.

"You are all members of this Watch, but your planets are not all the same size. Some are many times the size of others, but all have equal status. Can you imagine how you would feel if you were the only Watcher to have a lesser rank than everyone else. If you can, you may understand how I have felt since I was created. I asked for two extra days, not four or five. I have no desire to be greater than the others, all I want is to be treated as an equal."

February stopped for a moment and looked around the Chamber. Meeting Kalend's eyes he wondered how anyone could doubt he was their friend. Seeing Kalend's smile gave February the courage to continue.

"I have freely admitted my guilt, but I didn't discuss my plan with anyone because I knew they would tell me not to do it and would have taken steps to prevent it."

He made a sweeping gesture with his arm to encompass the others seated around him. "These Months are blameless in all of this – they have not and would not break the contract. Kalend is and has always been a true friend. I beg you to do with me as you see fit, but do not punish anyone else for my crime."

February had spoken truthfully, his face showing his compassion for his friends and grief for the pain he had caused. Kalend felt tears sting his eyes as February's words had moved him and could see others were moved too. The sound of three slow slaps on the table broke the silence which had fallen over the chamber. Hiemal had risen to his feet.

"I have been moved by February's plea. What a truly remarkable performance. If what he says is true, I could not have their demise on my conscience."

July felt vindicated by Hiemal's support and could not resist flashing a smug smile at Jan and Ember, but Hiemal continued.

"February, you say your friends are blameless, can you prove that?"

Unsure what Hiemal wanted, February began.

"I was angry when Kalend said I couldn't have any more days but May said there was no point in being upset about something I couldn't change. It was after that I had the idea to just stay on Earth and not return, but I told no one."

Hiemal looked steadily around the Chamber before asking.

"Having learned of the existence of this Watch are you or are you not already planning to deny us our right to carry out the sentence against you?"

February's mind was whirling, trying to work out what Hiemal knew or suspected. He was sweating and looking more uncomfortable as Hiemal's voice became louder.

"Let me make it simpler so your half-formed mind can understand. Did you place a rock in the tunnel doorway in your Valley so you can escape to Earth if things don't go the way you hope?"

February's face fell – how could Hiemal have known? He looked at Gust and Jan but there was only disbelief in their eyes too. July felt her legs go weak and if she had not been sitting, would surely have fallen.

"February, I am waiting for your answer."

"Yes," whispered February.

"Speak up so everyone can hear you."

222

"Yes I did, but not for myself, it was to be for the others."

Everyone looked at February, but Hiemal hadn't finished yet.

"Judicial Watcher Balack, with your permission, I wish to ask the other Months one question."

Balack nodded, this was a more exciting morning than he had expected. Kalend stood again, not having any idea what he was going to say. Balack again refused to let him speak. Hiemal addressed the sitting Months.

"Would anyone who knew of the plan to escape to Earth through the obligingly open door, please stand?"

No one moved for a moment as all looked to Vem for a lead. Slowly he stood nodding to the others to show they should do the same. Verna was closely watching the unfolding events. Seeing the look on July's face as she stared at Hiemal, Verna felt her fear, hurt and betrayal and knew July had told Hiemal of the escape plan.

Hiemal turned back to February in delight.

"It would appear your friends are not blameless after all – they are prepared to keep silent and join in your plan to defy us. I find all here guilty of deceit and treachery, there are no extenuating circumstances that would allow the Charter to go unenforced."

Kalend stood again and Hiemal sat down to give him the floor.

"Balack, we are not here to discuss any escape plan. This is about February breaking the contract. None of what Hiemal, or February said is relevant."

Balack didn't agree.

"February is guilty, that is not in any doubt, and he was the one who raised the issue of the others being blameless. Clearly they are just as ready to break the law as he is. Does anyone have any further questions for February?"

Several of the Watchers stood but when they began to speak on behalf of the Months, Balack stopped them.

A smiling Hiemal turned to Thades with delight but did feel a twinge of guilt when he caught a glimpse of a distraught July who stared at him. Fear, loathing and pain were written in equal measure on her face.

The Months were horrified, they were doomed and there wasn't anything they could do. They began to talk and cry and the sound in the chamber rose to a new level. Balack stood and shouted for silence.

"Silence, silence. Kalend, you may speak in support of the Months."

"I ask that you remove the months from the Chamber so that I may make a proposal."

Anything that could prolong his tenure appealed to Balack who told the Months to wait outside.

"You must return to the Chamber and tell us all…
What I am"

The Months were too distraught to do anything but obey Balack's order and stumbling and supporting each other, left the Chamber. No one knew what to say and sat on the ground in silence.

Inside, Kalend continued.

"I agree with Hiemal that the contract has been broken and the Charter should be enforced. As Presidion I exercise my right to propose an amendment to the Charter law."

Kalend had visited Balack the night before to instruct him in System law so Balack knew he could not refuse to allow him to make an amendment. Hiemal stood to object but Balack forestalled him.

"System law does allow a Presidion to amend an existing law."

Kalend continued.

"t'Hura has often told stories about the challenges faced by people on Earth to win their freedom, gain some great prize, or the love of a woman. The challenged would be given a Quest to complete. This would require them to use all their skills to succeed. My Amendment is that the Months will undertake a Quest to determine their worthiness to live. If they fail, the Charter will be enforced but if they win, they will return to The Valley unharmed. February would then face a trial after the custom on Earth with his fellow Months as judges."

Hiemal was learned in matters of politics and jumping to his feet demanded clarification.

"Kalend, as all voted in favour of the Charter, am I right in thinking all must approve your amendment?"

"You are correct, Hiemal. All must agree, but time must be given to consider my proposal fully before any vote is taken."

Balack had been intrigued by Kalend's suggestion. The idea of a Quest was appealing, not least because it would mean he would remain as Judicial Watcher for longer.

"Kalend's proposal will be discussed. What is the nature of this Quest?"

"Balack, my involvement with the Months would make anything I proposed questionable in the eyes of some. Neja has come up with the Quest, but as Judicial Watcher you must give your approval."

Balack was suspicious, Neja was well known for her dislike of Hiemal, making her support for Kalend more likely. Perhaps, despite Kalend's words, this may well be some plan of his.

"Who else has seen or helped with this… suggestion of Nejas?"

Neja held her hand across her chest so her crystal could clearly be seen.

"No one else has seen it, what I have suggested here are my thoughts alone."

The crystal shone with the silver of truth and Neja was pleased Kalend had stopped her from sharing it with them.

"Very well, I will look at it. t'Hura, as Watcher of Earth you will remain here with Neja while the other Watchers wait outside."

Hiemal was uneasy. He had been unaware Kalend could make such a proposal but all he had to do was vote against it. Kalend obviously had something more in mind.

Outside, February was first to question what had just happened.

"How did he know about the tunnel, it was our only way out and now it's gone? He must have been listening to us when we were at Dynaks."

Jan, trying to make sense of all that was happening was sure of one thing.

"No, he couldn't have been. Stolesc said all the Watchers were in the meeting chamber."

Ember had her own suspicions about how Hiemal had known but having no proof, could only ask, "July, Hiemal is your friend and according to you, our saviour. Can you explain what just happened?"

July was in a state of disbelief, feeling a fool for believing anything Hiemal had said, but a determination to protect herself still dominated her thoughts.

"I admit I was wrong about him, but there was time for him to visit our Valley before meeting us with Kalend. He could have found the stone in the tunnel. February was the last to come through so it would have to have been him who put it there."

"Perhaps," said Dec. "But how did he know we all knew about it? Someone must have told him, and you were the only one who thought he was a good guy."

Everyone was looking at her with anger and distrust, and for the first time July felt afraid of them.

"I've been with you all since February told us of his plan. There wasn't an opportunity for me to speak to Hiemal even if I'd wanted too. After the concert, he stayed by himself, or perhaps you think he just read my mind."

After much grumbling they had to agree with her, but Ember knew July had two possible opportunities.

With the Watchers joining them, Ember told Kalend how

July had gone for a walk in the garden at Dynak's house, coming back after Stolesc had come for them. Kalend confirmed Hiemal had been in the meeting and couldn't have met with her then. When told about July sneaking out of the chamber the night before, all eyes turned to look at her. She dropped her gaze, immediately raising it again. July knew she must not look guilty, or she was lost.

Watching this little scene acting out before him Hiemal considered exposing July by showing the note she had left for him. Deciding division and suspicion would suit his purpose better than any momentary satisfaction, he kept silent.

Despite her overwhelming need not to be discovered, July did feel guilty, but only for a moment. Her newborn hatred for Hiemal matched her feelings for Kalend wiping out all other emotions within her.

Despite a lack of evidence and no matter what July said, Ember knew she had betrayed them.

Inside the chamber t'Hura felt a mixture of emotions. Learning of the Month's plan to escape to Earth had angered her. To return there as immortals would be a return to the chaos removed by bringing them to The Valley. If their plan had succeeded, she would have been left with the consequences of their actions. In a fit of exasperation, she decided they didn't deserve the mercy Kalend was trying so hard to win.

In the Chamber, Balack asked t'Hura about the quests on Earth and she briefly outlined the Labours of Hercules. Balack was excited by her telling of their trials and bravery, demanding t'Hura tell him more stories after the meeting closed.

Neja explained most Quests involved a physical part and an intellectual part, often in the form of a riddle. Balack had never heard of a riddle but was delighted with the idea when Neja said it was a kind of 'trick poem'. Together they sat to read what Neja had compiled. t'Hura, even with her knowledge of Earth, was unsure of the solution. Taking a smaller parchment from her bag Neja explained.

"I have written the answer to the riddle on this sealed parchment. It is best if Balack keeps it secret until the quest is complete."

Having given his approval, Balack sent Neja to bring the Watchers back to the Chamber and ask the Months to wait. He turned to t'Hura as Watcher of Earth he was certain she would know the answer to Neja's trick poem, but she could not help him.

"I'm well acquainted with Earth but I'm not sure what the answer is."

Balack was disappointed but the Quest sounded like fun and he wanted to see it unfold.

When all Watchers had retaken their seats Hiemal could see by the look of pleasure on Balack's face that Neja's proposal had met with his approval. Now was the time for t'Hura to make her proposal to Hiemal but she kept silent.

Neja looked expectantly at t'Hura who resolutely stared at the ground, her anger at the Months still raw. Verna touched her arm and said gently.

"Are you not going to try to save them?"

t'Hura didn't answer but after a moment got to her feet. This was her chance to do the right thing for Earth, not for the Months.

"Balack, may I have your permission to make a proposal to Hiemal?"

Hiemal looked up in surprise, what could t'Hura possibly propose to him?

"As Watcher for Earth, I propose that if Hiemal will vote in

229

support of the Amendment, when the Quest is completed, and regardless of its outcome, I will surrender the blue planet to him and I will become Watcher of Pluto."

Hiemal was stunned, this must be a trick. His mind furiously thought of all this could mean. If the Months lost, they would be destroyed, if they won, they would continue to live isolated in their Valley. He would be Presidion. He would also be Watcher of the blue planet. Everything he wanted would be his, but first he needed to check something.

"Presidion, the worlds were allocated by the Senaten, is it permissible to exchange them as t'Hura suggests?"

Balack looked to Kalend indicating he should clarify the situation.

"Once the worlds have been allocated, any Watcher has the right to step down. To become Watcher of another world in the same system, all members of the system Watch must agree. If there is not agreement, then the Senaten must be approached to give their approval."

"Will all members agree to t'Hura's proposal?"

Balack asked for the signs of approval and Hiemal was stunned to find all were indeed in agreement. This had to be a trick. What was Kalend up to?

"May I have time to consider this proposal?"

Balack suggested a break for everyone would be helpful and the Chamber emptied.

Hiemal walked by the lake, he couldn't believe what had just happened. Thades had come to join him but Hiemal sent him away so he could think alone. He calmly reasoned step by step. February was guilty so he could enforce their destruction. He would become Presidion, but Earth would still be out of his reach until he found a way to remove t'Hura. His plan had been to accuse her of failure to protect Earth by allowing the Months to exist but even if he was successful, it would take time. If he approved the Quest he would have everything he wanted. As Presidion he could eradicate all mankind from Earth meaning there would be no need for the Months or their calendar. He would rename the blue planet Uclair and present it as the means to restore his status in his own House. There didn't appear to be a trick but t'Hura wouldn't give up Earth unless she had a good reason, and he had no idea what that might be.

He returned to the Chamber and Balack called the meeting to order once more.

"Hiemal do you agree to t'Hura's proposal?"

"After much thought and in recognition of the admirable qualities demonstrated by the Months, I will support the Quest. After it is over the Blue planet will be mine, whether they win or lose."

Balack was still confused by all that was going on and asked t'Hura, "Are you sure you want to do this? It's a great sacrifice you are making."

"I am quite sure. Do we need to take a vote or is the matter now agreed?"

"We will vote just to be certain. All those in favour of the fate of the Months being decided in the manner proposed in the amendment, show their approval."

Nine signs of approval were given, Stolesc pointing out that Balack didn't need to approve, but he said he wanted too, so did.

The Months were once again summoned to the Chamber and Balack asked them to sit.

Explaining that it had been suggested they undertake a Quest to decide their fate the Months looked around at one another. Vem

231

and Ember looked at Kalend who nodded to show he supported the idea. Balack nodded to Neja.

"Neja, will you please read the Quest."

Neja moved to stand beside Balack unrolling a parchment as she did so.

"It is in two parts. The first part is a journey around the lake in the centre of Tir Dhuchais. You will find a way through the mountains, travel around the far side of the lake before returning to the Chamber. You will find food as you go, and the water from the lake is perfectly safe to drink. You must complete this journey in the time allocated."

The Months listened and then began to talk among themselves. Balack called for silence, asking Neja to continue.

"The second part involves solving a riddle. You will be deemed to have succeeded if you return in the time given and can provide the correct answer. The riddle is as follows:

'What am I?

The source of all your troubles,

I have no place in Tir Dhuchais

A Wise man said 'I am an illusion'.

I am not alone and we tarry together for no one.

I am what you want the most

But you often misuse me and take me for granted.

By the 24th day of March

You must return to the Chamber and tell us all…

What I am.'

When Neja retook her seat there was dissention from both sides of the chamber. Hiemal had no idea what it meant but nonetheless said it was too easy. Kalend said it was too difficult. He added the Months had no knowledge of the plants and creatures of Tir Dhuchais and should be given some time to learn of them. Hiemal said the Quest must be difficult or there would be no point to it.

Dynak reasoned that some Months were older or had health issues which would be a burden on the others. She suggested the Months be allowed to choose who among them would undertake the challenge. Hiemal no longer cared but objected as it was expected of him. When Thades suggested February be put in charge, Hiemal could see the difficulties this would cause and gave his approval. Kalend knew Vem was the natural leader and while he may be persuaded to follow February, many of the others were still too angry with him to do so.

The Months had no idea what the riddle meant and began to ask questions and talk all at once. Balack called for silence several times before order was restored.

"February will lead the Quest and I will allow him to choose those who will accompany him. Those not chosen will return to The Valley until the challenge is completed. Do you have any questions?"

The Months had been whispering together and now Vem stepped forward to speak, but Balack ignored him.

"February, you are leader. Any communication must come from you."

Vem stepped back to let February speak but overwhelmed by the enormity of the task he had been given, hung his head while mumbling.

"Balack, I have appointed Vem as spokesperson."

Kalend was pleased. He'd seen the mutterings among the Months when February had been declared leader and knew it would make the Quest impossible. Supporting Vem had been a good move. Vem was taken aback by February's statement but nonetheless stepped forward again.

"We need time to discuss this and respectfully beg that we be allowed to ask our questions when we have done so."

Balack liked Vem. He always spoke to him with courtesy and respect. He agreed to his request and instructed the Months to go to Dynak's dwelling and then return before dark as they would spend the night in the Chamber before leaving in the morning.

Neja stood to speak.

"Forgive me Balack, It is common practice for the challenged to be given gifts to accompany them on their quest. May I organize what those gifts may be?"

Balack hadn't known about any gifts and was about to refuse when Hiemal jumped to his feet demanding to be heard. Balack couldn't help the feeling of resentment that filled him every time Hiemal tried to intimidate him. Instead of allowing Hiemal to speak, he turned to Neja and smiled.

"You may do so. Hiemal, you have something to say?"

As Balack had already ruled on the matter Hiemal scowled and retook his seat without speaking, but Thades noticed his crystal shone clear. All watchers left the Chamber while the Months considered what lay before them.

"It's going to be all right. I can feel it in my bones"

"And just when did you appoint me as spokesperson. I must have been asleep because I missed it?"

Before February could reply, Dec pushed to the front speaking angrily.

"You can't expect us to obey your orders, you caused this mess and I for one won't be doing anything you say."

Several voices echoed his words, but Ember was wiser than them all.

"This is exactly why February is in charge. They want us to fail and the surest way for that to happen is for us to quarrel among ourselves. Like it or not, this is the hand we've been dealt – how we choose to play it is up to us."

Ari slipped an arm around February's shoulders.

"Okay boss, what do you want us to do?"

February hadn't a clue and asked for a few minutes to think. July felt an acid comment make its way up her throat, but wisely swallowed it, it was best to keep a low profile for the present. February paced up and down while he got his thoughts in some kind of order.

"I don't want to be in charge, I would be useless at it. Vem and Ember should lead us."

Tober was exasperated by February's insecurity.

"We don't have time to debate this now and Balack has made it clear he expects you to be the leader." He hesitated before continuing.

"The best thing would be to announce that you have appointed Vem and Ember to be your advisors and they will speak for the group."

February thought this was a good idea and as Vem and Ember realised February was in no fit state to make decisions, they agreed. Vem started by asking.

"The first thing we have to do is decide if we accept this Quest."

All agreed they didn't have a choice.

"Second. Who will go with us?"

May was the first to speak.

"My bunions are playing up and would never stand the journey. I think it's best if I go back to The Valley and look after things until you return."

Jan also asked to go back as he was worried about his gardens. Ari grinned widely and said he wouldn't dream of missing it. June wanted to go home, saying she would look after the farm. Everyone expected July to refuse but she surprised them by saying she wanted to go. Ember looked at her suspiciously.

"Why?"

"I was fooled by Hiemal and want a chance to prove my loyalty to you all."

Ember wasn't convinced but accusing July of telling Hiemal would only make things more difficult than they were now.

Dec, Gust and Tober pledged their support too despite their feelings for February, as their varied skills may come in handy. Jan said he would escort May and June back to The Valley and together they would look after the animals and the gardens.

Ember focused everyone's attention by reminding them they needed to decide on the questions they would ask. Jan pointed out that Neja had written the Quest and no one had any idea whose side she was on, but Ari disagreed.

"Kalend put this Quest in his amendment. If he hadn't, we could all be on our way to extinction now. As he proposed this to save us, then he must believe Neja will have selected a challenge she thinks we can win."

Ari's reasoning seemed to cheer everyone a little and February was glad he was coming with them. Ember called for questions that needed to be put to the Council and a short list was drawn up.

1. How big is the Lake, and how will we know where we are to go?

2. As we know nothing of Tir Dhuchais, are there any wild animals that we need to protect ourselves against, or foods that would be poisonous to eat?

3. Can we return to The Valley first to gather anything we might need?

4. Would the watchers be involved in the challenge – either to help or to hinder?

Dec asked this last question because he feared Hiemal would interfere unless Balack forbade him to do so. If they were allowed to go to The Valley first, Vem suggested he and Tober should go. They would bring back supplies using the two shire horses from the farm. It was difficult to know what they would need when they had no idea where they were going. Blankets, rope, tools, shelter and despite Balack's assurances, something to use as weapons were suggested, with Vem stating it was better to be prepared. February had noticed that Balack seemed to like Vem and suggested he should ask the questions.

When the meeting resumed Balack was in a bad mood, he was bored with meetings and wanted to go home. February

237

stepped forward and timidly announced that Vem and Ember were his advisors and Vem would put their questions to the Council. Balack no longer cared, he just wanted the meeting to be over but was very scornful of their first question.

"Solving that is the first part of the quest. If I told you, there would be no point in going, would there?"

In response to their second question Balack assured them there was nothing to harm them. Their third question was more favourably received than anyone thought it might be.

"The Quest will begin at daylight and you can do and go wherever you want. Just remember to get back here when you're supposed to."

But it was the last question that caused the most dissention. Kalend had seen immediately why this question had been raised and made a proposal.

"I propose there is no interference with the Quest. If help is given, the Quest will be over, and the Months will be deemed to have failed. Any attempt to hinder them, means they will have won."

Hiemal was furious, not because he intended to tamper with the Quest but because his integrity was once again being called into question. He was from the House of Uclair and should be treated with greater respect. Thades once again glanced at Hiemal's ring, but his crystal was clear. How was this possible when his anger was so evident?

Now was not a good time to give the Months their gifts so Neja decided she would do it in the morning before they left.

The Months were told to sleep in the chamber, ready to begin the next morning. Vem and Tober wanted to set of that night to get a head start but May reminded them they'd had little sleep for two days. They would make better time if they rested tonight and set of early in the morning. Ari wanted to talk about the riddle, but Vem disagreed.

"We will have eighteen days to consider it. A good night's sleep is more important before facing whatever tomorrow will bring."

During the night it began to rain and the sound of it on the roof woke the Months. Each drop sounded like a pistol shot and they moved to the doorway to look out. Vem stuck out his hand and each drop hit with such force he felt the sting, and mentally added another item to their list of supplies. The rain stopped as suddenly as it had begun, and the Months drifted back to sleep.

Early next morning, Watchers and Months once again gathered. Dynak, Verna, Stolesc and Neja had all brought food and piled it on a table. Verna whispered to Ari.

"The Quest began as soon as it was morning, and you can find food where you will."

Ari told the others who all began to fill their back packs with the bread like querbana, fruits and leaf wrapped fish parcels. Pockets were also filled, much to the amusement of Thades who watched intently from the side of the chamber. Gust went to speak to him holding out his clarinet.

"I would be pleased if you would care for this for me. Play it and perhaps you will be entertaining us on our return."

Thades was too stunned to speak, taking the clarinet from Gust's hands and cradling it gently. Hiemal arrived just as Balack remembered about the gifts, asking Neja to come forward. She moved towards February, but Balack demanded that he see them first. Neja held out the first gift which had been prepared by Kalend. Balack looked in distaste at a stained cloth wrapped bundle and unfolded it to find a small piece of metal. He turned it over in his hands, but it appeared to be a small rectangular bar with no distinguishing markings.

Balack had no idea what this was for but had no intention of revealing that to anyone. Hiemal had returned to his default position of objecting to everything

"This is clearly helping and under Kalend's ruling is not allowed."

Balack really hated it when Hiemal tried to take over like this. Telling him he had already ruled on the subject of 'gifts', he asked Neja to give the bundle to February. A sudden thought came to him and his face became wreathed in smiles.

"Hiemal, you object more than anyone else, so that must qualify you to be the 'most objectionable' member of the Council."

He laughed loudly at his own joke and it was such an infectious laugh that even the Months couldn't help joining in. Neja knew to laugh at Hiemal was a very foolish thing to do and stepped forward with the second gift; Balack immediately became serious again. Opening a leather pouch, he took out a fine silken rope with many small knots tied in it. Balack yawned and said it had to be the most boring gift he had ever seen. Ember took it from him and put it in her pack.

Vem and Ember had decided the others would follow the lake shore towards the mountains and when he and Tober returned with the supplies, they would do the same. They left before anyone else and set a fast pace for The Valley.

June bade a tearful farewell to Ari while May straightened February's collar and brushed an imagined speck of dust from his shoulder. She looked into his eyes and smiled.

"It's going to be alright. I can feel it in my bones. You take care of yourself and I'll see you when you come back."

May wasn't returning with Jan and June as t'Hura had invited her to stay with her. There was no need for her to make the journey there and back when her foot was so painful.

The Watchers saw them leave with a mixture of emotions. Dynak, Verna, Neja and Stolesc liked them, wishing them well. t'Hura hoped the Quest would let them prove their worth. Thades was so entranced by the music they possessed he wanted them to succeed. Balack just wanted to remain in charge for a while longer and Hiemal was so pleased with t'Hura's offer he cared little whether the Months won or lost.

Kalend watched with a mixture of pride and concern. It wasn't an easy journey they would make but working together would surely be a good thing. Dynak rested a hand on his shoulder.

"It's in their hands now, trust them. I've been impressed by many of them. Gust is strong and I don't just mean physically. Ember is clear headed and intelligent. Ari will keep their spirits up. Vem is a just and clever man, and Dec and Tober will do whatever Vem asks of them. February is already learning humility, and no matter what July is up to, I believe they will succeed."

Dynak's reference to July echoed his own reservations about her. July had changed since learning all he had kept secret from them. Her attack on him almost certainly came from her talk with Hiemal. He would have been much happier if she had gone back to The Valley with Jan.

February felt strangely elated leaving the Chamber. He had no idea what the days ahead might bring but doing something was better than doing nothing. Being in control of your own destiny was preferable to being powerless.

The Months didn't know that the glass roof in the Chamber could be used for looking at things other than the stars. Their every step could be seen by the Watchers without leaving the comfort of their chairs. Balack invited them to join him to keep track of each day's events, but Hiemal had replied.

"I would rather watch rock gametians mate."

This was a process that took seven years to complete on Pluto. He had stormed off leaving a laughing Thades and Balack to share a bottle of Pestiar wine. Balack asked if Thades wasn't going to go after him, but he replied.

"He's better alone for the moment."

Once again, Thades had noticed Hiemal's crystal failed to show his anger and was puzzled as to how he was controlling it.

"Kalend had to take some responsibility for all they were going through"

Tober and Vem headed back along the path they had followed on their way here while the others headed towards the lake. The going was easy, but the large silver sun was hot. Where the forest came down close to the shore, Gust led them under the shade of its strange blue leaves. The ones they had used on the way to the Chamber having become flattened with use, Gust suggested they collect new ones plus one each for Tober and Vem. Dec would have liked a faster pace but Ari and February were experienced trampers knowing they would make better time if they settled for a constant, slower pace, stopping to rest less often.

During a lunch break they began to discuss what the riddle might mean as it had been in their thoughts as they walked.

"I have an idea about the riddle."

All eyes turned to February, who suddenly felt self-conscious and cleared his throat.

"The first line talks about a source. This could mean a start or even a person, but I think it's a place. You know, like the source of the Nile. The Valley is where we lived until I broke the rules so its where all this started. The second bit says 'it has no place in Tir Dhuchais' so that could be The Valley too. The Watchers do see us as a problem and The Valley was made to be our home. Look around you, The Valley is nothing like Tir Dhuchais, so it doesn't belong here."

Ari was excited by February's idea.

"Yeah, and it says the thing we have to find is an illusion.

Kalend made The Valley look like Earth, but it's not real. So, doesn't that make it an illusion?"

"What about the not being alone and not tarrying bit?"

Gust was being drawn into the debate and Ember could see that working together was a good thing, and let the discussion continue. February had to admit he hadn't worked out the next bit yet.

July had been listening with growing anger. She had her own ideas about the answer, raising her voice to make herself heard.

"Of course, February wants you to think he has the answer. The true answer is so obvious. The source of our problems is him. He broke the contract so he has no place here. What we want most is to live, but thanks to him we may all die."

February stared at her in horror, seeing at once she could be right. He was the answer. He hung his head, but Ari wasn't haven't any of it. He rounded on July forcing her to take a step backwards.

"That's rubbish and you know it, Neja wrote this to help us, not Hiemal to condemn us. You did that when you told him about the rock in the tunnel."

Everyone except February began talking or shouting at the same time. Dec raised his voice.

"That's enough, all of you. Squabbling like this is no help. We must work together. You've come up with two possible solutions in just one day, but neither meets all the clues. I'm sure we will come up with many more answers before we find the right one. Now, we've been stopped for quite long enough, time to get moving."

As they walked Ari tried to convince February that July was just being nasty to cover her own mistakes but even he could see she could be right. For the rest of the day the Months walked in an uncomfortable silence. Ari and Ember gave up trying to cheer them and it was a fractured group who settled down for the night.

On their way back to The Valley Tober and Vem made good time, eating as they walked. This part of Tir Dhuchais was relatively flat and both were used to working long days on the farm. Interspersing walking with short runs they reached The Valley by the middle of the night. A full moon showed the raft still tied to the tree stump. Vem was relieved. He planned to swim back with the horses, but the raft meant all the supplies could be ferried across in one trip. They had hoped to gather some of the things they would need that night but once across the river, tiredness overcame them and they decided to make an early start in the morning.

Tober thought he'd find it difficult to sleep with so much going through his mind but he was snoring before his head touched the pillow.

Going to Dec's workshop early next morning, Tober collected tools and two sturdy, long wooden poles. A sharp blade was attached to the end of each pole to be used for hunting, fishing or protection. Two more knives and Dec's axe were put into a leather sports bag with some of Dec's work tools before heading to the river.

He was greeted by shouts from June and Jan who had travelled for a greater part of the night and had just reached the river, but with no boat they couldn't cross. Tober sent the raft over for them. As they landed, Tober asked June to go to the homes of the Quest party to collect changes of clothes and warm blankets. Jan said he would go to his garden to collect some food and then to the meeting hall for eight of the torches, each with a new battery and a few spares just in case.

Heading back up to the farm Tober found Vem had been

busy. Four 'saddle bags' using strips of leather harness and a collection of bags and sacks hung around the necks of Amazon and Titan. Vem had already begun filling them with the things they would need. A large package drew Tober's attention, and he pointed to it.

"Oh, that! Well, do you remember those yellow waterproof poncho things Jan brought back a few years ago, the ones worn by mounted policemen, the ones we all laughed at? Yeah, those. Well after the rain in Tir Dhuchais, I thought we might be glad of them."

Vem knew Tober could ride but saw him looking anxiously at Titan and Amazon. The farm horses were as tall at the shoulder as Vem and strong. Tober had often ridden the smaller horses but these great shire horses were unused to a rider. Vem had been planning to get Tober to ride Titan as he was taller and slightly heavier but changed his mind as Amazon was older and more docile. The collars from the harness were placed around the horses' necks and the straps used for holding the shafts of carts and ploughs were shortened to form stirrups for the riders.

Vem had put two large tarpaulin on one side to be used for shelter. Two long pieces of thick rope were added to the sacks. Making reassuring noises to the horses they mounted and set off for the river.

June and Jan had loaded the raft with a pile of neatly folded blankets, clothes, two cooking pots, bags of peaches, tomatoes, apples, potatoes and a first aid kit filled with what they could find in March's cabin. The supplies from the two horses were added while Vem swam across with Amazon. Tober and Jan used the pulley to pull the heavy raft across. Tober stayed with Amazon while Vem made the return journey before swimming back with Titan.

It was early afternoon by the time Vem had changed into dry clothes and the supplies were divided evenly. Two blankets each would be used to sit on as they had no saddles. June had raided May's cottage to make food parcels for them with bread, tomatoes, cheese, cake and two bottles of water. June suggested they share a meal before leaving, but Vem said they would eat on the way.

The first problem came at the cliffs. The horses didn't want to walk through the narrow gorge and had to be coaxed with apples. Even so, it was late afternoon before both horses were through. Vem wasn't worried about finding the others. He knew they had to follow the lake shore and even if it took two days, they would catch up with them eventually. He just hoped the weather would be kind until he arrived with shelter.

The Quaan who had remained in The Valley was surprised when Tober and Vem had appeared in the early morning without coming through the cave. He communicated this to Y Quaan who quickly returned with three tracker Quaan. They watched, expressionless as Tober coaxed Amazon to walk through what appeared to be solid rock. Using the cover of the forest and the waterfall they crossed onto Kalend's side of the river. They merged with the cliffs around them and made their way towards the place where Tober and Vem had disappeared. Leaving one Quaan in The Valley, Y Quaan led the others into Tir Dhuchais.

Vem and Tober walked beside the horses in silence. Tober was thinking about the trial in the chamber and while he had previously had no strong feelings about July, he believed she'd betrayed them. Much as he had always admired Kalend, he couldn't help but think that July's outburst against him had some measure of truth in it.

Vem was noticeably quiet as anger was steadily growing in

him. He thought of the fields he had cleared, the crops he had planted and the animals he had raised. What would happen to them when they were gone? Would they be allowed to send the animals through the tunnel to Earth, or would they be considered part of the problem and destroyed too? He understood that February had reason to be aggrieved about his lack of days and hadn't acted out of malice, but it was still because of him that he may lose his farm as well as his life. His thoughts turned to Kalend. On fishing trips, not once had he hinted they were somewhere other than Earth. He'd never spoken of the Watchers or the Contract between them. Vem had given Kalend a number of chances to speak truthfully but he had kept silent. His anger grew as like Tober, he came to the conclusion that July was at least partly right. Kalend had to take some responsibility for all they were going through.

"Magic was out of their comfort zone"

Ember and July were unused to constant walking and despite their best efforts, their pace was slower than the first day and two; rest stops were needed before lunch. Ari, Gust and February discussed this lack of progress while the women had a nap. February wanted to go ahead with Ari to spy out the surroundings but Gust was against it.

"If we split up you may get lost or hurt and what will we do then? Ember and July can ride when Vem and Tober return with the horses."

Ari had been constantly scanning his surroundings for any signs of wildlife but saw none. By late evening they stopped to make camp for the night. Ari suggested they light a fire as it may help Vem and Tober to find them, although he didn't expect them until the next day. February, agreeing a warming fire would raise spirits went with him to collect firewood.

Ember went down to the lake to fill the water bottles and heard a soft lapping sound just offshore. Something was moving on the water but in the dim light it was difficult to see what it was. She hurried back to camp where Gust hurried to accompany her to look. Straining to see in the darkness they heard a splashing noise to their right. They were amazed to see a creature come out of the water and stop to look at them. It reminded Ember of an otter sitting up on its hind legs, but this had a beak, was covered in feathers, and walked upright. It had talons for hands and was holding a large, wriggling fish. It made a strange chirruping sound. Smiling, Ember knelt in front of it.

"Hello there, I don't suppose you would like to share your fish with us?"

To her surprise, Rogue, for that was who this creature was, came closer and threw the fish towards her. She laughed in surprise and the creature chirruped again before returning to the water and disappearing into the darkness. Gust looked at Ember in surprise and delight before hurrying back to the others to tell of their strange but friendly benefactor. Ember wrapped the fish in some leaves and cooked it on hot stones from the fire. It was delicious and everyone felt in better spirits after a hot meal.

Dec had been thinking about the riddle.

"I can't see what use the gifts are unless they are to help solve the riddle."

Despite having studied it intently the previous night, February took the bundle out of his bag and held it close to the fire to see it better while the others gathered around. A rag and a metal bar, what help could they be?

Ember looked at Gust and back to February and shrugged.

She took the cloth in her hands and looked at it carefully, it had several coloured stains on it, yet it didn't look used or worn. If this was not some cleaning cloth, then the stains could mean something, they could be the secret. She told the others and looking at it with different eyes, July leaned forward and spoke.

"What if they aren't stains? Do you remember the cloth Kalend brought to us in Rome, the one that turned into a map of The Valley? These dyes are the same colour as the landscape here. See this yellow bit that covers the middle part of the cloth, well I think it may be the lake and the blue stains here and here could be whispering forests. If that's right, then that purplish bit over there could be the mountains we have to get to."

Ari came closer and noticed a silver dot in the bottom right corner.

"What about that, what's it supposed to be?"

February was quick to guess that it had to be the Chamber, but none of this really helped.

While the others were talking Ari picked up the piece of metal. He turned it this way and that and leaned closer to the fire. He noticed what appeared to be a lighter dot at one end and looked at the cloth again. It was surely too much of a coincidence for both metal and cloth to have a silvery dot. He pointed this out to the others and February took the cloth, spreading it out on a flat stone. He placed the metal bar so the two dots were touching, but nothing happened. After several minutes of staring at it, Ari spoke.

"Well, it's not doing anything. Put it next to the fire where the flames are."

February turned the cloth so the metal was closest to the fire. It began so slowly and gently that at first the Months weren't sure it was happening. The yellow stain seemed to be moving like ripples on a pond. The blue stains fluttered as if a breeze came from under the cloth, rising up to become the whispering forests. The breeze that moved the blue sails caressed the faces of the silent, and nervous Months. Further along the lakeshore a dark line on the cloth became a barrier surrounding an area upon which the word 'Forbidden' gleamed in brilliant green. The purple mountains were last to appear, growing out of the forest and reaching higher and higher until they stood almost as tall as Gust's knee. Only when the cloth was still did the metal bar move, beginning to flow like a river. It followed the lake shore until it came to the barrier where it flowed around one long and one short side before turning towards the mountains and beginning to climb. The mountains had several valleys leading into them, but the river of metal never faltered. Taking one turn after another it continued climbing until it turned and descended, until it flowed around the far side of lake to the Chamber.

The secret of the bundle wasn't quite over yet; small flames appeared along the route the metal had outlined. Dec got quite excited.

"They must be campfires. We can use these to work out exactly where we have to go and how long it should take to get there."

Gust counted the flames, eight to the mountains, three through the mountains and another seven to get back around the other side of the lake to the Chamber. Eighteen days, and they had left the Chamber on the sixth day of March. That left no room for any problems they might encounter. The fires died, the metal flowing back to become the dull, grey, small bar once more and the cloth returning to being just a cloth. February carefully wrapped the metal in the cloth and put them into his pack.

No one was quite sure what to say. Magic was out of their comfort zone, even magic that was obviously on their side. Ari asked Ember to get the silken rope out to see if it did anything clever, but it just looked as it had done when Neja had given it to them. Ember had counted the knots in the Chamber before leaving and knew there were eighteen in all, one for each day. She thought she should untie two now to mark the end of the first and second day but the knots were tied so tightly she couldn't undo them. Ari offered to cut them off, but his knife made no impression on the cord. Ember counted the knots again and exclaimed that two were missing, leaving only sixteen.

"It does it all by itself. It will tell us exactly how many days we have left; we can't make a mistake or forget to undo one."

Filled with wonder and a little fear, they once again settled for the night.

Ember was first to wake and went looking for food, finding bushes covered with yellow and white spotted fruit about the size of blueberries along the shore. Picking one she sniffed it. On Earth red was usually the colour associated with danger, but this wasn't Earth. Even though Balack had said there were no poisonous foods here, that didn't mean these couldn't make her unwell. She knew it would be foolhardy to taste one, if she were taken ill it could prove disastrous. Realizing how foolish she had been to wander off on her own, she resolved not to do it again.

A chirruping sound made her turn to see the same strange creature who had given her the fish the night before. They stood looking at each other for a long moment before Ember spoke.

"I don't suppose you'd like to tell me if these are safe to eat?"

Rogue waddled over to the bush. Picking a berry he held it out to her, chirruping excitedly. Ember tentatively took a small bite. It didn't taste of anything much, but it was juicy. She shrugged, taking off her jacket and tying the sleeves together to make a basic basket which she filled with fruit. She was closely watched by Rogue who then waddled beside her chirruping constantly as they walked back to the camp.

Gust was relieved to see her as they had been worried, and Ember apologized for her foolishness before introducing her little friend.

"I'm going to call him 'Gossip' as he hasn't stopped talking since he found me."

The others came closer to look but July pointed to his talons and said she'd keep her distance. Ember showed them the berries she had collected and they crowded around to look and taste. Ari thought they tasted like strawberries but the others agreed they were tasteless; still, it was all they had.

With no one paying him any attention, Rogue wandered around the camp plucking articles from bags and making little tutting noises. When Ari spied him pulling a shiny buckle off Dec's pack, he shouted at him and shooed him away.

With breakfast over Gust said no one should leave the camp without telling the others where they were going. July wanted to wait for Vem and Tober but Ari said they should move on. The path was still along the lake shore, and it had been agreed they would follow it until Vem and Tober found them.

"We can leave a marker if you are worried."

No sooner said than done, Gust collected stones from the edge of the lake and formed them into an arrow pointing in the direction they would take.

As soon as they were out of sight, Rogue reappeared. He looked at the stones, shaking his head and making loud, clucking noises, obviously in disapproval. Carefully picking up each stone he replaced them all in their exact positions on the lake shore. He then removed any sign of the campfire, covering the blackened spot from their fire with fresh soil and leaves. With all traces of their presence removed, he seemed satisfied and returned to the lake where he paddled off in the direction the Months had taken.

"With so much time lost they broke camp and headed into the darkness"

Vem and Tober woke early hoping to catch up with the others, but the time taken in The Valley had put them several hours behind where they had hoped to be. They'd estimated how far the others were likely to have travelled the day before and were disappointed to see no sign of them. They passed the spot where the others had camped but thanks to Rogue, no marker remained. They stopped, walking alongside the horses and scouting the ground for some sign, but the grass was thick and no sign was visible.

As she walked, Ember thought of how strange her life had become. Tir Dhuchais, Watchers, and her newfound friend Gossip, but most of all she thought of the consequences if they failed. 'It has no place in Tir Dhuchais' could mean anything, and how would they know? Almost everything here was strange, tall blue trees, yellow water and even though Gossip seemed friendly and helpful, he did have a sharp beak and talons.

As morning wore on there was still no sign of Vem and Tober. The horses could easily cover twice, or even three times the ground they could. Unaware of the delays at the river or the amount of supplies they carried, Ember feared some mishap may have befallen them. Even though Hiemal was forbidden to interfere with their quest, Ember didn't trust him and worried he may have set some trap.

With only berries for food everyone was hungry and tired, but February wanted to continue until they reached the spot marked by the campfire on the map. With morale low Gust felt it would be better if they rested and waited for the others who would bring shelter, clothing, tools and hopefully food.

Jules had the sharpest eyesight and saw something moving in the distance. Everyone was cheered when Vem and Tober arrived bringing food with them. Gust looked at the bags but with eight of them to feed, knew it wouldn't last long. They would have to find more substantial food than berries and once leaving the lake fish would no longer be an option. Ari hurried the group to resume their journey as he wanted to reach the spot on the map for the third campfire before nightfall. After a quick rest they set off again, heading for the 'barrier' which grew taller as they neared it.

As soon as they made camp, Gossip appeared with another fish but upon seeing two more beings he sauntered off, returning a short time later with a second fish.

"Who's your little friend?" laughed Vem, and Ember told them of Gossips valuable contributions. Sitting around the fire eating fish, baked potatoes and tomatoes, Dec showed them the secrets of the cloth and the knotted rope. Vem and Tober stared in amazement as the land grew and the river of metal flowed. Like the others they were grateful for the assistance the map gave, but in awe of the magic.

Tober told how they'd found no marker or sign from them along the way and Gust protested strongly, telling of the stone arrow left beside the remains of their camp beside the lake. Vem confirmed that there had been no marker anywhere and they could find no explanation.

"We'll finish what food you brought in a few days, and we can't live on fish and berries," complained July, and Vem was forced to confront two difficult problems, lack of food and July.

The rest of the group were still angry about her behaviour in the Chamber and barely spoke to her. Vem knew some way to heal the breach must be found or the Quest would fall apart.

Talking about food, Ember remembered a 'purple grapefruit' tree by the lake edge. She said the tree was very tall and reaching the fruit would be difficult. Vem suggested using the horses as a platform and held Titan's head while Gust stood on his back. Using the improvised spear, he managed to cut one of the fruits from the lowest branch. Ari and February held a blanket to catch it, but when Jan reached for it, a sharp thorn bit deeply into his hand. Ember used some of the potions brought in the first aid kit to clean and then bandage it.

Three more fruits were all Gust could reach before jumping down, muttering that they had better be worth it after all that effort. Because of the thorns, each fruit was carefully held upside down over a pot while its soft, velvety skin was pierced allowing the juice to flow. Ari dipped a finger in it and licked it tentatively.

"Wow, this stuff is beautiful."

If Rogue had been there, his strong reaction would have made the Months think twice about eating them, but he was sound asleep in a burrow. The Months consumed all four fruits. February was concerned they were falling behind and wanted to discuss their progress, but everyone was so tired he decided to leave it until morning. The next day dawned bright and clear, but no one stirred in the Month's camp. Rogue arrived and finding some Arkolin juice in the bottom of the pot, finished it and hurried away. The sun rose higher in the sky and still the Months slept. By late afternoon a wandering family of Neutsche found their camp. Meeting no resistance, they used their tusks to rip open backpacks and saddle bags looking for food leaving the camp in a total mess. Ripped blankets and clothes were trampled and belongings scattered or broken. The apples, tomatoes and peaches were all eaten, leaving the potatoes trampled into the ground. One Neutsche left the camp with the precious map cloth skewered on his tusk.

Back in the Chamber Hiemal howled with laughter and admitted he had been mistaken in thinking the Quest would be boring. Kalend and Dynak exchanged worried glances. With the limited number of days available to them, the Months could ill afford to lose time like this. Arkolin would cause them to sleep deeply, but no one knew how long they would remain under its effects, and it was impossible to tell if there would be any other reactions to the Arkolin fruit. Kalend asked if he could go to the camp while they slept to recover the precious Arkolin seeds that had been discarded, but Balack refused.

With no sign of the Months waking, the horses wandered away.

February was the first to wake and rubbed his eyes several times before seeing the wreckage of the camp. Jumping to his feet and shouting to the others, he was alarmed when no one answered. Fearing they were injured or dead, he hurried from one to another only to find each sleeping deeply. No amount of shaking or shouting could wake them, so he hurried to the lake, filling a cooking pot with water which he threw over Gust and Vem. Even this did not wake them fully, but they stirred enough to allay February's fears. He could tell by the position of the sun that it was early afternoon and couldn't believe they could have slept so long, or so deeply that an attack on the camp had failed to disturb them. He scouted the area around the camp and discovered one set of footprints in a small patch of soft earth. It was a cloven hoof, like that of a pig, but could find no other signs. It took several hours before everyone was awake, feeling totally refreshed and well. There was much concern about what had happened and July was quick to blame Gossip.

"I told you we should avoid those talons of his; see where he has torn my clothes and bag."

Ember tried to defend him, but even when February told of the hoof prints he had found, July would not be shaken from her belief. Much as Gossip's contribution had been valued the others agreed he did seem to be the most likely culprit. It was agreed – a rare event – that the purple fruit was responsible for their long sleep as nothing else had been eaten that would account for it. Each Month tried to salvage what they could of their belongings and the effects of the Arkolin juice soon restored good humour. Jan was amazed to find the wound made by the sharp thorn had not only healed, but there was no trace of it. February became angry at everyone's time wasting and eventually shouted at them.

"I'm so glad you all slept well, but we've lost another day. Each day we spend on the journey puts the quest in jeopardy."

February's anger had a sobering effect on everyone, and Gust was quick to agree that they would have to pick up the pace the next day. Vem and October set off to find the horses. Thankfully, they hadn't gone far and were brought back to the camp.

Just when February thought things couldn't get any worse, he discovered the cloth bundle was missing from his torn pack. He told Vem and a search of the camp and immediate surroundings was made, but only the metal bar could be found. It was Ari who suggested they make a copy of the map while the memory of it was fresh in their minds and asked July if they could use her diary.

"Who said I had a diary; have you been going through my belongings?"

"Why do you always have to think the worst of people? It was lying on the ground beside your ripped bag."

Ember was intrigued to learn July kept a diary, having paper opened up possibilities about how Hiemal had learned February's secret.

July reluctantly agreed and turning to an empty page, began to draw. The route was simple, along the lake to the barrier, around one long and one short side, then through the forest to the mountains. It was here the problems began. February clearly remembered there were four passes through the mountains but said they were to take the first one. Ari was equally sure they took the second one and then the left fork from that. No one was certain and with no way of finding out, they would have to wait until they got there and hope that the terrain might give a clue.

After so much sleep no one was tired and Gust suggested they use the torches and keep going for at least part of the night. February wanted to wait for daylight so they could have a proper search of the area to see if the cloth could be found, but it was Ember who settled the matter. While packing her bag she had been relieved to find her knotted cord had not been lost in the attack, but she noticed it seemed to have fewer knots than expected. She counted them three times, but each time the answer was the same. There were only thirteen knots remaining. They had slept for four days.

Stunned silence settled over the camp as the Months gathered around the knotted cord in Ember's hand. Gust suggested that perhaps the cord was faulty or unreliable, but when Ember asked if he really believed that, he shook his head.

"But how could we sleep for so long, it doesn't make sense."

Vem was a practical man and didn't believe in all this 'magic maps and cord stuff' but knew his horses wouldn't have wandered off if they had only been asleep for less than one day. With so much time lost February agreed they couldn't wait for morning, and they broke camp and headed into the darkness. Ari stayed behind as he insisted on tidying the camp, burying food scraps and other rubbish. Upon finding the seeds from the purple fruit, he dug small holes and planted them, placing the thorny cage upside down over them to give some protection to the emerging shoots. Clearing up complete, Ari set off at a run to catch the others.

"The first tendril lovingly caressed his neck"

Those watching in the Chamber were relieved when the Months began to wake. So much time having been lost, Kalend feared it would not be possible for them to return in the allotted time. When the loss of the map was discovered, Neja asked anxiously.

"Without the map to guide them, how will they find their way?"

"If your riddle had given them a few more days it might be possible. Without the map and with the lost days there is no hope for them."

Kalend left the Chamber unable to watch any longer. Neja was upset by Kalend's suggestion that she was somehow responsible for what was happening. Hurrying after him with eyes blazing, she grabbed his arm.

"I asked you to look at what I had written. You refused so if anyone is to blame it is you."

She stormed off leaving an anxious and distressed Kalend looking at her retreating back. Standing completely still as his mind hurled accusations at itself Kalend returned to the Chamber. Not watching was harder to bear than watching.

Most of the Months couldn't help but feel cheerful, and progress was quick despite the darkness. Even though they didn't know it, each was healthier than they had ever been. July's blisters had completely healed and her feet were covered in a new, strong layer of skin. Even the fit and healthy February had increased stamina that would benefit him over the coming days. February and July glanced at each other several times as they walked, and eventually July came to walk beside him. With no greeting she came straight to the point.

"Did Thades give you anything to drink when we were on our way to the Meeting Chamber?"

If February hadn't been thinking along the same lines, he would have resented her question and her tone, instead answering truthfully.

"Yes, he did, and I slept much better than I expected. Did Hiemal give you a drink?"

"Yes, it had a faint, but similar taste to those purple fruit."

February had thought there was something familiar about the fruit but hadn't made the link to the drink he had been given on their way to the Chamber.

"If a diluted drink helped us to sleep soundly for one night, then having consumed a larger quantity could explain what happened to us."

July wasn't entirely convinced, but February asked her to look around at the others. They were all walking faster and more easily than on previous days. He pointed out that with four days lost, they would need all the help they could get. It was then July remembered January's hand.

"January said his hand had healed and there wasn't even a mark where the cut had been. If the fruit made us sleep well, do you think it could have healed his hand too?"

February was excited by this prospect and told July they should talk to Vem and Ember before telling anyone else.

As the sun hinted at its appearance, Gust could see some of the berry laden bushes growing alongside the barrier which they had reached during the night, and suggested they have breakfast and a few hours rest before travelling any further. Vem was surprised to see February and July approach him as soon as they stopped, listening in amazement to their story. While Vem had to agree, there may be some truth in what they said about the purple fruit he cautioned any further experimenting with it. Ember joined them, saying how well she felt even though they had been walking for hours without a break. As daylight flooded their surroundings Tober, Ari, Gust and Dec also realised there was something unusual about how they were feeling. Vem asked them to sit down and told them what July and February had said. Ari became very excited.

"Wow, just think how much faster and stronger we would be if we found more of this stuff."

Vem pointed out that sleeping for most of the time would be a drawback and the others laughed. As no more of these trees could be seen, the question about its use was irrelevant.

The barrier they'd seen on the map was a wooden fence taller than Gust. Hoisting Ari onto his shoulders he asked what he could see as he peered over the fence.

"It's some kind of park, or garden. It's got some weird looking things growing here."

He looked back over his shoulder at the others while speaking. Turning back, he screamed in fright and fell to the ground. Ember rushed to him asking if he was alright, but he sat up and grinned sheepishly.

"Yeah, I'm fine. There was this big flower, and it was looking at me."

As he was speaking, he knew it sounded even more stupid than he thought it would. February couldn't quite keep the smile out of his voice as he asked

"A big flower looked at you, and it frightened you so much you fell?"

Ari scrambled to his feet, wiping the dust from his clothes.

"I know how it sounds. It wasn't there a minute ago and when I looked back it was just a few inches from my face. It would have scared anyone."

Everyone turned to look at the fence, but there was no sign of any 'big flower'. Gust suggested July should have a look as she was the lightest, but Ari was determined to redeem himself.

Once again, he balanced on Gust's shoulders and slowly peered over the fence. No flowers were in sight and he visibly relaxed. He could see a path that stretched away from the fence as far as he could see but couldn't see the other side.

"There's no sign of animals or anything dangerous, just some really neat plants."

The Months ate berries while they discussed their options. July wanted to go around the fence as shown on the map. Concerned about the lost days Vem said as there was nothing sinister in the garden, they could save three days if they cut across it. He pointed out that the map had FORBIDDEN written on the garden, probably because the owners didn't want people trampling through it. Gust agreed this was a valid point, but Dec thought they had been given the map as a guide and should follow it. Ember turned to February and asked what he thought they should do. He considered for a moment before replying.

"We don't know for sure there is nothing dangerous in the garden, and there must be a good reason for going the long way around. I would say we should go around but we can't ignore the fact that we've lost four days. If we can save three by cutting across the garden, then we must do it. Providing we are careful to stay on the path and not touch or eat anything in there, we should be fine. If we don't make up some time, we won't make it back before the deadline."

Gust nodded in agreement, but July was hungry.

"We have no more food and can't go for a whole day without some. I suggest we spread out to see what we can find. If after walking for an hour we find nothing, we can still return and go around the fence in the hope we find food there."

Ember suggested that perhaps the reason for going around the fence was because there was a plentiful food supply there and Vem could see this made sense.

Gust said he would go with February. Vem and Dec set off for some trees they could see in the distance. Ember said she and Tober would head back to the lake and try to catch some fish. This left Ari to pair up with July, but there was no easing of their mutual dislike and Ari asked Gust to swap with him. Gust wanted some time to talk to February and told Ari to make the best of it. Ari and July wanted to go in different directions and argued loudly until Gust bellowed at them. His uncharacteristic show of anger subdued them sufficiently to let them agree to head toward a rocky outcrop on their right.

Gust was pleased to see February had adopted a more practical attitude toward things and told him he was glad he had started to think positively about the quest. He didn't expect the reaction his kindly words caused.

"What do you know about what I think? This is all pointless, just a delaying of the inevitable. I don't know where I'm going, how to get there or what I'm looking for. I've lost the map, lost time, we've no food and I've just agreed to embark on a path we've been told is forbidden. None of this would be happening if I hadn't spent an extra day on Earth. No matter what way I look at it, this is all my fault, and I can't save any of you. So why don't you do us both a favour, kill me now and put me out of my misery? Perhaps Hiemal would let you stay if he had a sacrificial lamb to gloat over."

Gust's distress at these words was evident on his face but February wasn't looking at him. He stormed off but Gust quickly caught up with him and picking him up with one hand, held him against the fence.

"You think this is about you? Well, it isn't, this is about all of us. I don't have to be here, neither do the others. We came because we're fighting for our survival. People have birthdays and anniversaries on specific days of the year. They may talk about 9/11, but Christmas is still December 25th, Halloween October 31st and Saint Valentine's Day February 14th. We are important to Earth, so we must survive. The reason Hiemal wanted you in charge is because he thinks you can't do it. I for one know he's wrong. Now you can either stop feeling sorry for yourself and start thinking how we can do this, or you can sit down here and wait for us to do your job for you."

He let go of February who slipped to the ground. Gust turned his back on him and held his face in his hands. Perhaps February was right and this was all a waste of time, but this time was all they had. His anger left as quickly as it had come, and he admitted to himself that he was afraid. Everything he knew was about to be taken away from him and he felt helpless. He'd always thought he was the strongest of them, but his strength wouldn't help them in a land of strange beings, magic maps and cords.

"Gust." February's voice was barely a whisper and Gust turned to face him. "Did you mean what you said about Hiemal being wrong? Do you believe in me?"

His desperate need for Gust's faith was painfully evident on his young face and Gust smiled gently.

"Yes, I meant it. I'm sorry if I hurt you, but you're not the only one who is afraid."

"You, afraid? I can't imagine you being afraid of anything."

"Well now you know, but I'd appreciate it if you kept that to yourself, no point in scaring the women eh?"

February nodded and Gust slipped an arm around his shoulders.

"Well, young Feb, let's go and find some food."

For the first time February didn't mind being called Feb, in fact he quite liked it.

Ari and July weren't getting along; they walked in silence with Ari setting a pace he felt July would not be able to match, but she gritted her teeth, determined he would not outdistance her. Reaching the outcrop, they began to climb. In crevices among the rocks Ari saw plants that looked a bit like artichokes and called to July. Ari squatted beside one, gently poking it but it didn't seem to mind. He tugged one of the outside leaves and it came away quite easily. It was thick and fleshy at the base and smelled of garlic. He took a small bite, pleased when the thick skin was easily broken revealing a soft and creamy inside that tasted of, surprisingly, garlic.

"Hey this is good, try some."

He held the leaf out to July who immediately suspected it tasted horrible and that Ari was trying to fool her. She sniffed it, then squeezed it until the filling oozed over her finger. A tiny lick satisfied her that it was indeed good.

"Don't eat any more of it, it may be potent like the fruit. Pick as many as we can carry and take them back to the others."

Ari was about to ask her who put her in charge, but the memory of Gust's outburst was fresh and he started gathering the plants.

Vem and Dec were the first to get back. They'd found nothing to eat but had encountered a group of green, pig-like creatures whose footprints were the same as those found at their wrecked campsite. Vem told how these pigs had no fear of them and had followed them, sniffing their packs and their pockets.

"I bet you anything you like it was these pigs that raided our camp and not Gossip."

Vem had liked the little chap and was pleased to have found a way to clear his name, but July was still not convinced.

Tober and Ember had caught ten fish and were cooking them over a low fire. The ones they didn't eat now were wrapped in leaves to eat the next day. She was delighted when Ari produced the 'Garlichokes' as he'd named them and put some of the creamy filling inside the fish. The smell was wonderful and wafted on the breeze to Gust and February who were returning with two sacks full of Querbana that they'd found further along the fence.

After they'd eaten, Dec and Gust looked for the gate they knew had to be where Ari said the path ended. They found it quite easily but when Dec went to open it, Ari stopped him saying, "Best not let the garden know we are coming before we are ready."

Dec looked at him strangely but said nothing. The food was distributed among their backpacks and sacks which were hung from the straps on the horses. The camp site was tidied as per Ari's instructions before moving to the gate. Ari reminded them not to leave the path or to touch anything inside, and to be as quiet as possible as they had no way of knowing what they would find. Ember felt uneasy about how Ari was behaving, but he laughingly assured her he was fine. Dec used his axe to cut the stout leather straps and a gate swung open revealing the garden before them.

Ari had said there were some 'neat plants' but that

description was woefully inadequate. The colour, shapes and sizes of the plants were beyond anything they could have imagined. Tall trees with multicoloured leaves bordered the path for a short way. Jan could not help reaching out a hand to touch one of the leaves that was changing from a brilliant blue to turquoise as he passed. The tree shivered at his touch and seemed to pull back from him, but then emitted a perfume so sweet and strong it was overpowering. When a suspicious February asked what had happened, Jan remained silent.

July could not help a shriek of alarm when a small succulent uprooted suddenly and ran across the path in front of her. They all stopped to look and the 'offender' stopped too. It squatted on the path for a moment and then hurried off again. Its bottom row of leaves turned down rather than up and it used these like legs to move. Tiny roots hung below it and when it stopped on the grass, these burrowed into the ground before uprooting and moving again. Tober thought it was cute and wanted to pick it up but Jan was quick to stop him.

"I wouldn't do that; you never know what it will do."

They moved on through the morning marveling at the rare and mainly lovely plants around them. One plant had reddish leaves that swelled up like cushions and then opened to emit a gust of foul air that made the Months cover their noses and hurry past.

Feeling in good spirits they ate cold fish and Querbana for lunch while continuing to walk. Ari heard music and asked the others about it, but they heard nothing. Ari heard it again and again, each time getting louder and more beautiful. He looked at Vem and Jan who were just beside him, but it was obvious they weren't hearing it. When it became really loud, he couldn't help himself.

"You must have heard that, it's loud now?"

July told him to stop wasting time with practical jokes and he pulled a face behind her back, but he was confused. How could he hear the music so clearly and yet no one else could?

As they rounded a bend they came to a clearing on the right side of the path. In the centre stood one black tree. Ember voiced her disappointment that all that space had been given to such an uninteresting specimen, but Vem warned it may have been placed there for a reason. Ari stared at them in amazement but decided it was pointless trying to tell them this tree was making the music. He held back as the others moved on, but Jan told him to hurry up. He knelt as if to tie his shoelace then stood and stepped off the path towards the tree. Its dull, drab leaves began to shine as if lights had been switched on inside them. Different leaves lighting up when certain notes were played. Ari walked closer and the tree began to lift its drooping branches towards him.

"Ari, what are you doing? Get back on the path." Either Ari didn't hear Ember, or he ignored her because he kept walking towards the now fully extended branches. February and Vem began to run and the music became loud and angry. They could both hear it the moment they stepped off the path and they too could see the dancing lights, but they were concerned only with rescuing Ari. Vem's outstretched hand grabbed Ari's pack as the first tendril lovingly caressed his neck before Vem jerked him back. Ari struggled violently as February grabbed his other arm and together pulled him free. The tree shrieked and the dancing lights that had so entranced Ari became dark and flashing. As soon as Ari was back on the path, he stopped fighting and moaned softly, reaching out towards his beautiful tree before collapsing. Ember examined him and found a wound on his neck where the tree had touched him. Before she could do anything about it, Gust picked him up and threw him over his shoulder, shouting.

"Let's get out of this place before anything else happens."

No longer showing any interest in the plants that bordered their way they ran as if Death itself was on their heels. Dec, bringing up the rear, became aware of a sound on his right, getting louder as it got closer. Without breaking his stride, he looked around only managing to stifle a scream as something was moving parallel to them among the plant life.

There was no mistaking what it was – a stem about the thickness of his arm was racing after them. At its head was a blossom; he knew it was the 'big flower' Ari had spoken of. Without warning it veered away from them, disappearing from Dec's sight.

By dusk there was still no sign of the fence and Gust worried the path was another trap. What if it wound round and round and never went anywhere? Gust forced the thought from his mind. They switched on two of the torches, one in front and one at the rear and kept going. When the path began to turn to the right, Dec knew the 'big flower' lay in wait for them.

Jan offered to carry Ari for a while but Gust refused to let anyone else take him. Gust shouted that he could see the fence in front of them and they rushed forward. Dec pulled the axe he carried in his belt and with a loud shout dashed from the path as the stem became visible once more. He swung two mighty blows, chopping the stem in two. Even at this distance the Months could hear the shriek of rage from the black tree as it was finally denied its prey. Dec quickly regained the path and caught up with the others. Vem gave him a quick pat on the back as neither had enough breath to speak. The gate wouldn't open and Gust, in his fear and frustration, raised his foot and gave it an enormous kick, breaking it from its hinges and the Months fled into the darkness, trampling a dead flower that lay across their path.

"The thoughts of each returning to Ari and Vem"

t'Hura asked if May could join them in the Chamber to watch her friends, but Hiemal, who now watched enthusiastically despite his earlier comments, refused. t'Hura was glad May was not there to see this day's events unfolding. As the Months reached the barrier, Stolesc and t'Hura glanced anxiously at each other as Ari peered over the fence at his 'big flower'. Kalend, seeing their concern asked why they were so worried. They had chosen to write 'Forbidden' on the map only to protect the plants in the garden, hadn't they?

Stolesc glanced at t'Hura before answering.

"On a strange world on the far side of the universe we found two small symbiotic plants. The flower of one attaches itself to the roots of the other and grows underground before appearing above ground some distance away from its partner. The flower breathes a fine mist over any living thing that crosses its path, a mist so light its presence goes unnoticed by its victim. Slowly it alters the nervous system and causes the victim to see and hear things that an unaffected creature would not. Helpless to resist, they are drawn to the partner plant where they are captured by its branches and slowly squeezed until all life is ended. The sustenance from the victim passes into the roots allowing the flower a share of the spoils."

Dynak rose to her feet, her normally calm face showing anger and revulsion at Stolesc' story.

"How could you bring such plants here and not tell us of the danger? It was totally irresponsible, and I'm horrified you have

273

done such a thing."

t'Hura too had risen but to speak in their defence.

"Dynak, on its own world the 'tree' you saw was so small it fitted easily into the palm of my hand. The climate here obviously caused the transformation to their current size. They grew so quickly that by the time we realized the danger, it was impossible to easily move them. We built the fence to contain them and protect animal life. As there is little food for them, we hoped they would soon die and we could be rid of them. We didn't tell you not to visit the garden because we are immune to the effects of the flower and not in any danger. I asked Kalend to write forbidden on his map to ensure the Months would not enter."

Neja jumped to her feet to face the others.

"We have to stop them. If the Months go in the garden, it could mean death for Ari. We cannot allow it."

Kalend, trapped by his own plan to protect the Months from interference by Hiemal said sadly.

"We can't do that, Neja. To help them is to ensure the failure of the Quest and they will all die. We must hope there is safety in numbers – Ari will not be alone." Hiemal couldn't help his broad smile and obvious glee as Neja's concern for the Months showed in her heightened colour and the high pitch to her voice.

"I cannot believe you are proposing to sit here and let this happen. The rule of non-interference was never meant to cover situations like this."

Kalend voiced his agreement, but Hiemal was adamant.

"My dear Kalend, you cannot keep making a law and then changing it when it suits you. The Months must follow their own course and accept the consequences."

No amount of persuasion was able to convince him to change his mind and it was a sad and worried group who watched helplessly.

Almost immediately after entering the garden, Stolesc could see a change in Ari – the way he cocked his head as if he were listening to something. The tree, recognising Ari's love of music used this to entice him. When he left the path and was touched by the black tree Verna wept. When the Months fled into the darkness the Watchers sat in silence. Hiemal wisely deciding now was not the time to show his pleasure, opted to spend some time on Earth, soon to be his world.

"Gust, stop! We have to rest." February placed a restraining hand on Gust's arm and pleaded with him. "We have to tend to Ari, see what's wrong. Please, put him down."

February's words pierced the blanket of fear that enveloped Gust since Ari was struck down in the garden. He'd started to run to help Ari, but as soon as he stepped of the path he could see and hear the tree. Its black flashing lights and shrieks of anger terrified him as nothing had ever done. There was no man or beast he would fear to face, but magical trees were another matter. He'd stepped back onto the path but it was too late, he could still hear and see as the tree howled in rage when Ari was pulled free. Ari was moaning and writhing in pain as Gust snatched him and began to run. All he wanted was to go home, but that life was gone forever.

Tober added his pleas to February's.

"Gust, give him to me – Ember must see how badly he is hurt."

Gust handed Ari's limp form to Tober and walked away. Vem and Dec made a rough shelter out of some low branches and the tarpaulin and were now looking for wood to make a fire. July spread a blue sail under the shelter, Tober tenderly lying Ari on it then stood back to let Ember see her patient. By torch light she pulled Ari's jacket away from his neck and her anguished cry brought the others running to her side. The small scratch on his neck was swelling along its length. It was dark, almost black in colour and when Ember gently pressed it, Ari moaned in pain. The swelling was hard and felt like a knotted cord and all thoughts returned to the black tree.

Ember and July tried to pour some water down Ari's throat, but he coughed and choked after just a few drops and they had to stop. Ember looked at where the others were sitting around the fire – silent and defeated. She wished March was with them. She would have known what to do. A banging sound could be heard in the distance and it took a few minutes to realise Gust was not in the camp. He had gone back to repair the gate and keep the garden within its boundaries.

Despite her dislike for him, July was concerned for Ari and volunteered to sit with him while the others tried to sleep but some hours before daylight, her shout of alarm woke them. Ember came running to find the tendril that had pierced the skin around Ari's throat was growing and was now several inches long. His face was cold and clammy and small moans escaped his lips. Ember touched the swelling and made a decision.

"We can't wait. He will have to be taken back to the Chamber where the Watchers will have something to help him. If he stays here the tree will strangle him."

February, desperately worried for his friend, agreed with her, but Vem issued a word of caution.

"We were assured there was nothing in Tir Dhuchais that would harm us, perhaps this tree is harmless to them and they will have no defense against it."

Ember knew she must stop this negative thinking.

"The assurance there was nothing to harm us assumed we

would not enter the garden. We must take Ari back to the Chamber. They will surely have a remedy for this tree. If someone rode one of the horses and carried Ari, they could make it back in two days."

Jan remembering how his hand had been healed had a suggestion.

"If you make it back to the lake, try getting another purple fruit. It healed my hand, it may help Ari."

The others agreed this was a good idea, but Ember urged caution.

"You cannot spend too much time trying to get one. You could take a more direct route through the trees to reach the Chamber. I feel Kalend may be the best help for Ari."

February sat beside Ari, holding his hand as his fear increased. Ari was moaning softly in obvious pain and February's feelings of guilt and responsibility grew. Suddenly Ari opened his eyes, grabbing the front of February's shirt and crying.

"It's time, it's time."

"Don't talk like that Ari. You mustn't give up. Once you are back at the Chamber Kalend will be able to help you."

His words fell on deaf ears as Ari had fallen unconscious. February wept.

Vem, used to working with the horses was the only one capable of managing Titan and a helpless Ari. Despite his protests he finally agreed he would go.

Gust cut up one tarpaulin making a kind of hammock with ropes to pass behind Vem's back. Ari would be placed in the hammock allowing Vem to hold him and tend to his needs as they travelled. Some food and two bottles of water were attached to the collar on Titan. Vem mounted and the hammock was placed around him. Gust gently lifted the unconscious Ari, placing him in front of Vem with a blanket to cover him. Farewells were short. Ember feared Ari would not survive the journey, but told no one except Vem, who promised to ride as swiftly as he could. He hoped to be able to rejoin the Quest once Ari was safe, promising he would try to meet up with them when they came through the mountains on the other side of the lake.

The day and nights events had been so traumatic no one realised that despite all they had gone through, including running for several hours without stopping, energy levels were still quite high and no one thought of sleeping. The Arkolin juice was still exerting some influence over them, especially February who was thinking more clearly that any of the others. He took the blankets, tools and personal items from the packs on Amazon, distributing them among the four men. July and Ember climbed on Amazon with the remaining items and they set off at a brisk pace for the mountains. Their mood was subdued with the thoughts of each returning to Ari and Vem.

The Chamber was silent. Verna and Balack weeping silently as Ari became unconscious. There was silence for a long time before Kalend turned to face Stolesc, anger flashing in his eyes.

"Do you have a cure for what has happened to Ari? Will he recover fully?"

Stolesc was as shaken as the others, admitting he didn't know. He had never seen anyone, particularly someone part human, attacked in this way before. He did have a potion he was working on to destroy the tree but thought he could modify it to help Ari.

Despite the feelings for the Months that she tried to deny, t'Hura was moved by Ari's plight, her voice was husky with emotion as she spoke.

"Now that Vem and Ari have left the Quest we must help

them."

With Hiemal absent the others murmured their agreement and Stolesc said he would go at once, with Kalend saying he would go too, but Balack objected.

"You are too closely involved with them. You must stay here. Is there anyone else who will go with Stolesc?"

Thades stood. "I will go."

It was a silent and concerned group that made their way home with Kalend, nodding to Thades to show his appreciation.

"Stolesc picked up Ari in his arms and started towards the Chamber"

Vem urged Titan to run and the big horse happily stretched out. Vem decided to follow Ember's suggestion and only follow the fence until he reached the forest at the far corner. From there he would cut a path to the Chamber. He wished there were some way to let Kalend know of their plight. All he could do was get help as quickly as possible.

Ari was making small moaning noises, so Vem slowed Titan to a walk trying to pour some water down Ari's throat. Unable to swallow, the water dribbled out of his mouth and down his tunic. Unseen under the blanket, the tendril was making its way slowly around Ari's neck as his head rested on November's shoulder. A small piece grew away from the rest, moving closer to the surface of Ari's skin, becoming finer and finer as it grew. It broke the surface and stretched into the space between Ari's head and November's shoulder. Rising up it struck November's neck, making its way inside before breaking off from the original piece. The tendril was so fine November barely felt it, but after only a few minutes he began to feel unwell and reached up to touch his neck. At once he knew he too was infected and fear rose in him, threatening to render him incapable of functioning. He knew he must resist and urged Titan to run.

At Stolesc' dwelling, Stolesc and Thades were preparing the elixir Stolesc had spoken off. In a locked box, he kept a few dried pieces of twig from the black tree and he carefully took one and poured a blue liquid over it. It began to writhe and shriek and Thades hastily moved back.

"Don't worry, we appear to be immune to it. The broken-down twig will become diluted in this potion, which should be strong enough to overpower the piece in Ari's neck and render it inactive so it can be removed."

"How much will we need? Vem is on his way here, but how much time does he have?"

Stolesc didn't reply, just sighed and continued working, taking another piece of twig from the box and repeating the process. He knew so little of what was happening to Ari and felt a great responsibility for it, fearing Thades' response if he told him he really didn't know what he was doing.

Elixir complete, Stolesc placed it in a bottle in a box with a narrow glass tube, a small sharp knife, a fine pincer type instrument and a roll of soft fabric to bandage the wound if they were successful.

Asking Balack if he could use his Presidion's crystal to tell Thades and Stolesc what was happening, Kalend informed them Vem had reached the second corner of the fence and was moving slowly and seemed unstable on the horses' back. Balack was happy to agree.

Travelling by thought Stolesc and Thades quickly reached the fence and saw the horse grazing. November and Ari were both lying on the ground, neither was moving.

Despite the effects of the purple fruit, February could see Tober, Dec and Gust were tiring and called a halt to rest. The mountains were much closer now, but the fine day was changing. Dark clouds were forming above the mountains and a cold wind was beginning to blow. Gust suggested they should put on the waterproof ponchos and hats he'd brought as the rain could come suddenly and with great force. Tober was concerned for Amazon. Heavy rain could hurt him, causing him to bolt with all their food and belongings. February made a decision.

"If we distribute the food evenly between the backpacks and we each carry our own, the remaining tarpaulin could be used to cover most of Amazon. Several blankets could be fixed around his head and neck to protect him, and with Gust and Tober to hold him, he should be fine."

Tober disagreed. Amazon was strong and if frightened it would be impossible to hold him. He advised setting him free now and sending him back towards the fence where he might find shelter under the trees. Much as they hated to lose the big horse, it was unlikely he would make the difficult journey through the mountains and would soon have to be freed anyway. Aware Tober knew the horse better than anyone February agreed and after deciding what was essential to take with them, let Amazon go with a sharp slap on his rump.

Ember said that when the rain started, they should all sit down, with knees drawn up and the poncho spread out to cover knees and legs. Hopefully the rain would be as short lived as it had been the night they spent in the chamber.

Preparations made, they continued towards the mountains which were much closer now and with some luck, they should reach them before dark. But luck was not on their side. The wind increased and the rain came. Sitting in a circle they huddled together to protect themselves from the savage drops. The rain was so heavy Gust couldn't help but cry out as savage raindrops sliced his hands when he reached out to rearrange his poncho which was insufficient to cover him completely. This was no quick shower like they had experienced nine days previously, this rain fell until darkness came and continued for most of the night. July and Ember huddled together and Ember could hear July's sobs as there was no letup in the storm.

Thades and Stolesc were fortunate the storm didn't reach them as they worked, but they could see the heavy rain clouds over the mountains and exchanged worried looks. Stolesc had been distraught when he saw the tree was in Vem's neck too and quickly instructed Thades to lay each man flat on the ground. He opened his box and took out the knife and the pincers.

"We will treat Vem first…"

Thades interrupted him.

"Why don't we take them back to the Chamber? If that storm reaches us, we will be unable to help either man. If we stay here, should we not treat Ari first as he is obviously in greater need."

"I don't know if I will have enough elixir for both men. If I use most of it on Ari and there is not enough for Vem, then both may die. Vem has the greater chance of survival but only if I treat him now. It may already be too late for Ari."

Thades saw the wisdom of his words.

"What do you need me to do?"

Stolesc turned Vem on his side so the infected part of his neck was visible.

"I will make a cut a short way from the end, and you must quickly use the pincers to grab the invading tendril. Hold it tightly and do not let go. I will then cut the skin to reveal the end and place the elixir in it. It will take a little time to work but you mustn't let go until I tell you."

As soon as Stolesc cut the skin, the tendril began to wriggle and move further into Vem's neck.

"Quick, quick, grab it, now!"

Thades did as instructed, struggling as the tendril twisted and wriggled deeper. Stolesc pushed the tube into the exposed end and then used the narrow glass tube to suck up the elixir to blow it into Vem's neck. Vem began to scream, sounding like the tree when Ari had been pulled away from it. Vem thrashed about so violently Stolesc had to sit on him to stop him wriggling free. It seemed like an eternity, but in fact was only a few minutes before they could see a change. The tendril shriveled before becoming still and limp.

"Pull it out, gently."

Stolesc had another small box which he opened and held for Thades to drop the removed piece into, quickly closing the lid before wrapping it with a cord to keep it sealed.

Stolesc returned to Vem and inspected the wound. He was relieved that the removal appeared to have been successful, but there was no way of knowing what effects it may have had on him.

"I think we got it all."

Both men relaxed for a moment as Stolesc placed some of the clean fabric over the wound before turning to Ari. His infection was by now three quarters of the way around his neck and his face had a bluish tinge as he struggled to breathe.

"This piece is much longer so we will make one cut in the middle. It has been in his system for longer and is much stronger so you will have a harder job to hold this one. I will put the elixir in from one end first and then move to the other. I will have to move Ari to do this, and you must not let go. If you do, it will burrow deeper into his body and we will lose him."

Thades was fearful of the task Stolesc had placed on him.

"When I have hold of it, can I pull it out a bit so I can get a better grip on it with my hands?"

"I don't think that is wise. Even though we are immune to

its effects, it may still try to pierce your hand and that will make my task more difficult."

Thades nodded hiding his alarm at Stolesc' words. Cleaning the pincers which had become coated with slime from the twig, he was ready. Ari was rolled onto his stomach. Before Stolesc even touched the skin, the branch began to writhe as if it knew what had happened to the part in Vem. Stolesc moved to sit across Ari's body and told Thades to sit at his head. Stolesc worked quickly to slit the skin, but the branch almost immediately began to expand to cover over the wound.

"Now, quickly grab it."

Thades just managed to get the pincers around it and squeezed with all his might. Ari bucked and squirmed almost throwing Stolesc of him. It was difficult to get the glass in position and Stolesc made several abortive attempts before finally managing it. The elixir was placed in it, but some of it was squeezed out again as the branch contracted and twisted in Stolesc' grasp.

"Damn. We can't afford to waste one drop of this."

Stolesc tried again and to Thades it seemed there was less resistance to it than previously.

"Now I will roll him slightly to expose the other end. Hold tight."

The other end, aware of what was happening, was already burrowing into Ari's shoulder and Stolesc had to reach for it, twisting it so the end was once again to the surface. He forced the tube into it while trying to hold Ari still. Thades was struggling to keep hold, his fingers were cramping and he didn't know how much longer he could do this.

When Stolesc had no elixir left he could only pray it had been enough. Seeing Thades' struggles he held out his hand.

"Give the pincers to me, carefully, but I think the worst is over."

Thades was only too pleased to relinquish the pincers and sank back onto the grass. Ari was totally still with Thades fearing he was dead. A small moaning noise followed by a deep breath made both Stolesc and Thades sigh in relief.

"Get the other box," said Stolesc.

The tendril was still too strong to pull out and they had to wait. Finally, with a prolonged effort it began to slide out of the wound. Even now, it still managed to writhe and twist as Thades trapped it in the box and slammed the lid in place. Stolesc asked Thades to bind the box while he bandaged the wounds in Ari's neck.

The clouds which had covered the mountains were moving steadily closer to them and Stolesc told Thades to mount the horse and moved to place Ari in front of him, but Thades had never been on a horse. Titan, sensing his inexperience, danced and tossed his head causing Thades to slip to one side and fall to the ground. The storm was closer now and there was little time to get the two injured men back to the chamber. Vem was now sitting up.

"Thades, if you get on Titan and Stolesc puts me in front of you, Titan will know my voice and let us both stay mounted. Stolesc, you will have to carry Ari."

Working quickly, they started towards the Chamber.

Balack had been watching events unfold. Seeing the extent of Ari's infection and Vem's plight, he gave permission to Kalend to help. Travelling to meet them he arrived just as they were setting off. Kalend had often ridden the horses in The Valley and suggested he ride Titan with Ari, as it was clear Vem was recovering and could walk with help. Stolesc and Thades walked either side of him, supporting him.

"Is Ari going to be alright?" Kalend asked.

"I don't know. The tree had a lot of time to infiltrate his body. I have no way of knowing what, if any, permanent effects it may have on him. We will have to wait. We cannot risk giving him Arkolin as the tree may have altered his body, making it possible the tree may benefit from it rather than Ari."

Kalend was disturbed by Stolesc's answer but there was nothing to be gained by apportioning blame now. They reached the Chamber as the first heavy drops of rain began to fall. Inside, Dynak had prepared two beds for the injured men and food to help restore them.

"There is strength and goodness in them, I have seen it"

When Neja had seen Amazon running free, she travelled by thought to intercept him. The big horse reared up in fright when she suddenly appeared, but she had a gift with the animals on her home world. Making soothing sounds and gentle movements to calm him, she mounted and headed through the forest, reaching the Chamber before Kalend and the others. Balack was entranced by the horse, reaching out tentatively to touch his nose. When Amazon blew through his nostrils onto Balack's fingers, he fell hopelessly in love with the animal.

"I declare this creature, Amazon, is to be kept here in Tir Dhuchais. He will be mine."

"Balack, this animal belongs to the Months, you have no right to claim him as your own." Neja felt if anyone were to keep him, it should be her.

"Regardless of the outcome of the Quest, the Months will leave this place. Amazon will not, he will stay with me."

When Ari and Vem arrived at the chamber, despite his weakness Vem was confused and angry to see Amazon there. Neja explained.

"Tober, set him free as he feared the hailing would cause him harm and pain. I went to him and brought him here."

Vem would happily have collapsed into one of the beds, but concern for Ari kept him on his feet. Ari was unresponsive and Kalend said rest was the best medicine for now.

Neja, concerned by Ari's ashen face and labored breathing,

asked why he wasn't being given Arkolin juice to heal him, but Stolesc repeated his fears that the tree could benefit from the Arkolin and not their patient.

Vem's fear and anger were rising and he turned to Kalend.

"We were told nothing here would harm us but that was blatantly untrue. The tree in the garden almost killed me and may still kill Ari, and if the 'hailing' as you call it is the same rain we experienced when in this chamber, it would only have lasted a few minutes. Tober would never have let Amazon go."

Neja exchanged nervous glances with t'Hura before saying,

"The hailing you experienced on the night in the Chamber was what is normal, but only once in our time in Tir Dhuchais have we seen such a storm as this. Your friends have covered themselves in strange garments, but Amazon would have been badly hurt. Tober made the right decision to set him free."

"How do you know what is happening to them, are you spying on us?"

Kalend began.

"Vem, the ceiling of this chamber allows us to monitor what is happening, but …"

Vem could control himself no longer, punching Kalend, he knocked him to the floor.

"Another secret kept from us."

"Vem, stop immediately."

Dynak knelt beside him, but Kalend brushed her aside and stood to face a still furious Vem.

"I deserved that, but a hailing like this has not been seen in Tir Dhuchais since before you were brought here. It's an extremely rare event and one that could not have been foretold. As to the garden, you were told it was forbidden to enter. Only Stolesc and t'Hura knew about the tree and both were distraught

289

to see what happened to Ari and to you."

At the mention of Ari, Vem turned to the beds Verna had prepared. Kneeling beside Ari he asked, "Is he going to be alright?"

Stolesc knew he must not give false hope and answered as honestly as he could.

"The infestation has been removed from both your necks. His longer exposure to it will make recovery more difficult, if at all. I will continue to care for him and will keep you informed of his progress."

"No, you won't. I will be with him all the time. He needs to be among friends, not strangers who plan to kill him if he recovers. Perhaps it would be better for him if he didn't."

The last words were spoken in a whisper before Vem sank to the floor. Stolesc and Thades lifted him onto the other bed and exchanged saddened glances. Stolesc spoke.

"What he said is true. The lost days, what happened in the garden and now the hailing make it unlikely they will return in time."

Neja heard their words and looked helplessly at t'Hura who placed a comforting arm around her.

"This is not your fault; all you did was to try to save them."

Neja would not be consoled, turning to Kalend in her distress.

"If you had allowed me to show you the quest you could have prevented this."

"And then what? Send them off to be destroyed? All I have done was to protect them. They are willful and disobedient and when it all goes wrong, I am to blame."

Kalend strode from the chamber and returned to his cabin by the river. He moved between feelings of anger and sorrow, as a sense of helplessness overcame him. Perhaps he should go to the Senaten and confess all that had happened. A plea for mercy was unlikely to be granted, but they couldn't be in a worse state than they were now. He stood for some time looking out towards the distant mountains, wondering where and how the Months were. He knew Verna or Dynak would follow him, turning when he heard the door, but it was Thades who stood before him.

"Kalend, all we can do is to wait until this is over. There is nothing we can do to help them. I wish the outcome would be different, but the rules have been set and the game must be played. There is strength and goodness in them. I have seen it, and there is still a chance they may succeed."

Without waiting for Kalend to reply, Thades left as silently as he had come.

Kalend sighed. He couldn't go to the Senaten as he had appointed Balack to be in charge. Even if he could, he wouldn't make such a decision without the consent of the Watch. He remained in his cabin for several days before returning to find a slightly improved Ari. Vem apologised for punching him, but his anger was still evident.

"None of this changes what is happening here"

The rain stopped just as suddenly as it started. The incessant thundering on the waterproof hats was stilled, but no one moved until Gust bellowed.

"Are you going to sit there all day or is someone going to speak?"

Spurred into movement, February and Dec stood, immediately feeling pain in their knees from prolonged sitting in a hunched position. Tober was relieved to find no sign of Amazon and hoped he was safe. It was still dark, but February said they should use the torches and get on their way and try to get to the mountains as soon as possible. They made slow progress over the sodden ground so when dawn came, they were surprised to find the mountains closer than they had hoped. They ate the remaining querbana, berries, and fish, and were faced with the problem of where they would find food in the mountains.

Gust saw movement ahead of them as a group of the green pigs came towards them; he took the pole with the blade attached and when one creature came too close, he hurled it into its body, kneeling by its side to slit its throat. The other creatures squealed in fright and fled back towards the forest. Ember and July were surprised by the suddenness of Gust's attack but could see how necessary it was.

Tober butchered the animal while Dec and February looked for wood they could use to light a fire but everything was wet. Eventually they used the wooden handles on some of the tools and a few pages torn with great reluctance from July's diary. With the fire going, wet wood was placed beside it to dry. A rough frame was made, and the creature was roasted over the flames. The flesh had a slightly green tinge but the smell was mouth-watering. Dec removed the tusks saying they could be tied to some of the drying wood to make digging tools but nothing else on the animal was useful.

While eating, they surveyed the mountains ahead. Sheer cliffs faced them with no obvious sign of the valleys shown on the map. They hoped a closer inspection would provide a way in. July suggested there might be one of those curtain things like the one from The Valley into Tir Dhuchais but Dec dismissed her idea.

"That curtain was put in place to prevent an accidental discovery of Tir Dhuchais, but we're already here and we are to travel through the mountains, so a curtain makes no sense."

February hoped he was right. What was left of the roasted animal was wrapped in leaves, put into July's pack and the journey resumed.

The going was a little harder as the foothills became progressively steeper. Ember was pleased when they stopped for a rest midafternoon. A dark line on the cliff face had become larger the closer they got and it was apparent this was a valley – but was it the right one?

February argued they could spend days looking for another entrance, but without the map they would be guessing, and it was best to just go and see. As no one had a better idea they shouldered their packs and went in, beginning to climb steadily upwards.

The ground, though steep was relatively smooth, and they made good progress until they came to a left fork. Dec thought they should take it, but February remembered Ari being certain it was the second fork they should follow and the next left from that. A heated discussion began until Gust shouted for quiet and in the silence, they could all hear it – a low rumbling sound coming from further up the valley.

"What's that noise?" asked Ember anxiously. No one spoke for a moment, then Gust shouted.

"It's water and it's coming very fast, run!"

The decision about which way to go had been made in an instant as all turned to run into the left fork. The roar of water was close behind them but the fork only went a short distance before a solid wall of rock faced them. Gust yelled at them to climb. They were barely two metres above the ground when the water came – most pouring down the way they had come, but enough rushed into their fork for the level below them to rise. No one needed to be told to climb higher or to hurry. Gust was in the lead as his height allowed him to grip handholds higher up than the others. February was an experienced climber and shouted to Ember and July to follow his movements. Dec was bringing up the rear and helped July with a firm push to her bottom when she struggled to reach the next hold. Her fear of water was so great she never flinched at the unexpected touching of her person. Gust was well above the others and found a narrow ledge which widened as he turned a corner. He stopped and shouted.

"There is a ledge here, wide enough for all of us, hurry."

February was next to reach the ledge followed by Tober who reached down to grab Ember's hand and pull her up. Still climbing, Dec moved to one side as July was directly above him and the water was still rising around his feet. Looking across at her, he saw her slip becoming stuck between the mountain and a projection rising from the valley floor. Her backpack was squashed tight behind her while the waist belt and buckle were now firmly lodged between her and the rock in front. Her scream of terror alerted Gust and February. Gust went to go back but February stopped him.

"I'll go. Get the rope and tie one end around me while you provide the anchor up here. I'll send Dec back up to help you as I'm the lightest and you, Tober and Dec will have to pull us both up once she's free."

Gust didn't argue, lowering February down. Dec was trying to pull July free, but she became more tightly stuck. When February shouted to make himself heard above the roar of the water, Dec climbed up to help Gust. July's fear was so strong she couldn't listen to February and when he produced a knife, she screamed again. As he began to cut the shoulder straps, she realised what he was doing and became a little calmer. With both straps cut February hoped to be able to pull her free but it was no use. Water was now swirling around July's legs and the pressure was pulling her further down. February used the now slightly blunt knife to hack his way through the strap around July's waist which was now below water. With just a few strands to go, February told her to get a firm hold on the rope.

"Be ready for the pull from above."

Ember was watching closely and could see July's terrified face as she grabbed the rope, shouting to Gust.

"You need to pull as soon as you feel the tug on the rope. The water is above their waists and still rising. You will have to hurry."

Strap cut, February tugged July free from the backpack and felt Gust, Dec and Tober begin to raise them. At the last moment, February grabbed the broken pack before the water could snatch it from them, all too aware it held the last of their food.

Ember was in place to grab July as soon as she reached the

ledge and both collapsed beside the exhausted men.

In the growing darkness, February could see the ledge was wide enough for them all but with a sharp fall, a short distance from where they stood. The sound of the water seemed even louder from here and Gust grabbed a torch and shone it over the edge. In its light he could see water rushing several metres below them. They may have escaped one flood but another raged through a valley beside them.

July and February were wrapped in blankets while their clothes were laid out to dry. Two torches lit their refuge and they sat in silence. July looked directly at Gust.

"Why did you save me? At the raft, you said a good drowning would do me good so why save me now?"

Gust spoke in exasperation.

"You have been a colossal pain in the backside, but you're our pain. You're one of us, so of course we saved you."

"If you knew what I've done you would have left me, and I wouldn't have blamed you. I was the one who told Hiemal about the rock in the tunnel. You are all here because of me."

Tober almost laughed.

"We all knew it was you, we may have had no proof, but we all knew."

"Then why save me?"

Ember spoke softly.

"What we want to know is why you did it?"

There was silence for a long time and February was just about to suggest they try and get some sleep when July answered.

"I loved a man called Paulinus. He was killed fighting in one of Caesar's many wars. I thought I couldn't go on without him, but then discovered I was going to have his child."

A child. Stunned disbelief filled each of the listeners as the ache they all experienced for the absence of children was felt.

"Kalend told me we would all be safe in his Valley, but a few days after arriving I started to bleed. I went to March who tried to help, but it was no use. My baby died and the pain I felt for that loss was greater even than the death of his father. I blamed myself, believing that if I'd stayed in Rome my baby would have lived. My guilt consumed me, turning me into the July I am now."

July took a few deep breaths before continuing.

"When Kalend spoke of the curtain in the tunnel to stop us from having children, two thousand years of self-loathing turned to rage and hatred for him. Hiemal told me lies about Kalend and I believed him, agreeing to his ridiculous plan and betraying you. I do not ask for your forgiveness, just your understanding."

Ember was first to move, hugging July and weeping softly.

"July darlin 'ta bron orm.' I'm sorry for all you have endured. I wish I had been a better friend and of course I forgive you."

One by one each came to wrap their arms around July and express their sorrow.

Slowly at first, July began to sob, then her body became wracked in great waves of grief, but the others held her until she was able to stop.

Dec spoke in a voice husky with emotion.

"Well, I think we should try and get some sleep. Tomorrow is going to be a busy day."

"Wait," said February. "I have something to say."

"As long as you don't make me cry again, speak up."

Gust was not a man given to showing emotion, but like the others, he had been greatly moved by July's words. February cleared his throat.

"It's the 'Feb' thing. I know I always make a fuss if you call me Feb, but I actually like it, so would you all call me Feb in future."

Gust gave Feb a playful punch.

297

"At last, he sees reason, now can we sleep?"

"Not yet, please."

July felt a new chapter in her life was beginning.

"You have all adopted names that reflect who you are. I would like a new name too, but July is short already. Do you have any ideas?"

Ember suggested, "How about Jules?

Gust gave no time for debate.

"I think it suits you."

"Yes, yes, we all love Jules and now if no one else wants to talk, can I go to sleep?"

In the Chamber silence and sorrow reached out filling every space, the weight of it threatening to overcome them. Dynak was glad Kalend hadn't been there to hear. He hadn't come to watch any of the Quest since the night Vem and Ari returned. Stolesc spoke.

"What have we done? With the best of intentions we condemned July to unending grief and then judged her without considering why she acted as she did."

Thades was also deeply affected by what he had just heard but spoke a word of caution.

"None of this changes what is happening here. The Quest must be completed and won if they are to survive. We cannot interfere with a process we agreed to. Hiemal may have his victory. Dynak, I think Kalend should be told, do you want me to do it or will you?"

Dynak's face paled as she realised what this would do to Kalend. He was already devastated by what had happened to Ari, but this would break his heart.

"I will tell him, thank you Thades."

"Surrender was easier than fighting and she felt her face turn once again into the water"

Kalend closed the door softly after Dynak left him. She had offered to stay but he had declined her kindness saying he needed time to be alone. He did ask her not to say anything to Vem, May or Ari as they already had so much to deal with. Sitting, he made a mental list of all his crimes against the Months. Repeated deceit, lying, pretending to be their friend when a true friend would never have acted as he had done. And now he could add murder to his list – the murder of a helpless, unborn child which had effectively destroyed the life July should have had. He berated himself for his smugness, for enjoying life in The Valley, believing he was somehow a father to them. Hiemal was right, he was unfit to be Presidion of this or any other Watch. He made a vow to leave Tir Dhuchais when this matter was over – after he'd watched the destruction of those he considered friends. In a sudden fit of temper, he swiped everything from the table in front of him and let his despair overwhelm him.

The Months stirred into wakefulness, the memory of the night before forefront in their minds.

"Morning Jules, did you manage to get some sleep?"

Gust's greeting took Jules by surprise and it took a few moments for her to remember all she had revealed.

"Yes, thank you Gust. A softer bed and a warm blanket would have been nice but being alive was all I required."

Feb, looking over their ledge could see the river had dropped during the night, but it was still rushing at a great speed, tossing tree stumps and boulders along its way.

"I don't think this is the way we were to come. There is no way to cross this torrent. We must go back and try further up the other valley."

Feb's suggestion was welcomed by the others. Feb went ahead to find the safest route but stopped in horror as the deluge from the day before had washed away part of the valley side leaving a steep and dangerous scree which was unpassable. Tober had followed him.

"Now what? We can't go back so it looks like we'll have to go up the side of the river but I don't fancy our chances that way either."

Tober was a quiet, home loving man, working with animals and providing for them all. This dangerous journey was becoming too much of a challenge for him. Feb mentally agreed with his comments but kept his opinion to himself.

"Let's go back to the ledge and have a proper look, it may be better than we think."

The ledge quickly narrowed, so single file was all that was possible. The rough track began to drop closer to the river and the speed of the torrent became more evident as the day progressed. When they stopped for food Ember was horrified to find the cooked meat they had packed so carefully in Jules' bag was completely rotten. It may have been the soaking in the river, or perhaps this meat didn't keep for more than a day. Whatever the reason it was only fit for throwing away. With nothing else to eat, they had no choice but to continue, hoping they would find some berries along the way.

Dec was leading again and as they turned a curve in the riverbank his heart sank. The track here was either washed away or submerged below a swirling cauldron of dirty water which swept in from the river and washed around and around before rushing out again. Twenty metres separated them from the next part of the track which was clearly visible leading away from the river. It was higher above the water than this side making it impossible to know how deep the whirlpool was in the centre. To add the final affront, one of those purple grapefruit trees was growing on the other side of the track. Its special properties could have saved them but it was out of reach.

Even Ember couldn't find anything hopeful to say to boost their spirits.

With no way to cross, the Months sat in silence, despair filling their minds. With growling stomachs reminding them that in addition to their present hopeless situation, they had no food it was a dispirited and hungry group who settled for the night.

Waking before the others, Feb stood at the end of the track and watched the river continue its relentless path, praying for a miracle. He turned his gaze away from the river to the rock face and felt a slight glimmer of an idea.

Moving closer to the rock face he could see some possible handholds to cross the lost portion of track. Gust, who had come to join him saw his gaze and was horrified.

"No Feb, you can't."

"If you have a better idea Gust, let me have it. If not, it's the only way. I have to try."

Tober, July, Ember and Dec joined them. Looking at the missing part of the path and the raging torrent below the cliff face, they agreed with Gust. Ember had been silent as the others begged Feb not to go, but now spoke.

"Feb is right. We can't go back and we can't stay here. I know you have to try Feb, but if you can't make it, come back and we will find another way. Just be careful, please."

"I have no more desire to fall into that whirlpool than you have. I intend to be careful."

Feb turned the knot on the rope around so it was behind him, letting him get closer to the rockface and began his climb. The first part was relatively easy with both hand and foot holds within reach but then he reached a section where it looked like a slice of the rockface had been washed away. The remaining surface was smooth as glass. He had no choice but to climb higher. With the trailing rope becoming heavier, it threatened to pull him down making a difficult climb impossible.

"Gust, hold the rope up of the ground. It's dragging me down."

Gust, Dec and Tober rushed to help, holding the rope above their heads and feeding it out as he climbed. Feb was now well above the water but the rockface was wet and slippery. Both feet slipped from crumbling projections, leaving him dangling by his fingertips, metres above the swirling water. With no food for over a day he was exhausted, fearing he would fall. The shouted encouragement of the others could no longer sustain him, his strength was gone. All this for an extra day. If he fell the Quest would fail and their destruction was assured. Desperately trying to lift himself just a little higher, his searching feet found only air. His fingers began to slip.

Gust called out to him.

"You're more than halfway there, you can do it."

As he struggled February felt something take hold of him below his arms and raise him so the pressure on his fingers was eased. He looked up in terror, only seeing bare rock. He couldn't stop crying out in fear as he felt his left leg being held and moved to a solid foothold, a foothold he was sure hadn't been there before.

Y Quaan had watched Feb begin his climb and ordered the Quaan to move onto the cliff and down towards him. Their colour and texture made them invisible from below. The thinness of their fingers and toes enabled them to cling securely to the slightest crevice. Reaching the dangerously placed Feb, one took hold of him below his arms and held him. Two others moved below Feb, holding and moving his feet. They formed their hands into fists which they used as footholds for Feb's feet as they slowly moved him across the rock. When the rock became less slippery with foot and hand holds more plentiful, the Quaan climbed unseen back up the rock and disappeared into the mountain. They would follow the progress of the Months until this trial was over and the memories of February could be harvested.

February was aware when his hands and feet were able to move of their own volition and sobbed in relief. Looking up and down the cliff he almost thought he saw a piece of it move, but when he blinked it was solid once more. He climbed down until he could jump safely onto the ground below.

Back in the Chamber and unaware of Feb's helpers, the Watchers were spellbound as Feb made his perilous way one small step at a time. They could not resist a cheer as Feb reached solid ground. Stolesc spoke.

"This doesn't seem like the timid boy/man who stood in this chamber a short time ago. He is proving to be a strong leader after all."

Neja refused to leave the Chamber, even at night she feared to miss something of their journey– a perilous journey she was responsible for.

Stolesc was staying in Balack's home as Vem and Ari had taken over his dwelling. Vem was there now with Stolesc, sitting beside Ari's bed. Hearing Kalend enter the room and greet Stolesc, Vem turned to look, quickly turning away again. Kalend addressed Vem.

"Stolesc said Ari was having difficulty sleeping and we both felt a little diluted Arkolin would help him now he is a little stronger."

Vem was too tired to remain angry but his words clearly showed his fear.

"He cries and screams still, and his hands reach out for his beloved tree. He will not recover without help."

Kalend silently held out the flask to Stolesc and left. After a few moments, Vem hurried after him.

"Kalend."

When Kalend stopped and turned, Vem was surprised by the person before him. Kalend had always been straight and strong with a smile on his face. This man looked many years older, his bowed head reflecting the strain clearly written on his face.

Vem stood for a long moment without speaking and Kalend turned to leave again but Vem caught up with him and turned him around. Kalend flinched, expecting another blow but Vem put his arms around him and held him. Tears did not come easily to either man, but they came now.

Stolesc watched out the window as the two men walked away together. Kalend didn't hold back anything. From the day t'Hura told him about the Months, the debate in the Chamber, Hiemal's Charter, everything including the truth about July. Stopping when the lake came into view, they sat in silence, a comfortable silence such as that between friends of long standing. Vem was first to move.

"I must get back to Ari, see if that juice is doing any good. Kalend, I regret my anger and ask your forgiveness."

Kalend didn't speak, holding out his hand in the gesture of friendship used on Earth and Vem grasped it firmly.

Upon entering the room at Stolesc's home, Vem was struck by the quiet. Ari was sleeping soundly with no sign of the bad dreams which had been haunting him. Stolesc didn't ask Vem about his conversation with Kalend for he could see the anger had left him and was pleased for them both. Stolesc left to go to the Chamber and Vem sat down next to Ari. A rough shake some time later woke him.

"Wake up, Vem. Where are we and where is everyone else?"

Ari was sitting on the edge of the bed and his eyes were clear and bright, no hint of the darkness that had been there for days.

"Ari are you okay? Lie back down, you have been terribly ill and need to rest."

Ari was in no mood for resting, he said he felt fine and demanded to know what had happened as he couldn't remember anything after standing on Gust's shoulders to look over the fence. Insisting he lay down, Vem told Ari all about the 'big flower' and the black tree. Even telling of Ari's fear that he was dying when he'd shouted out 'it's time."

Ari sat up. "I didn't think I was dying, I had solved the riddle and wanted Feb to know."

"You solved the riddle? What are you talking about?"

"First line – the source of all our problem – remember this was written by a Watcher. The creation of a calendar is a problem to them as they don't seem to have time here. They have days without names and I suppose they have seasons, but no months or anything like the measures we have on Earth."

'I am an illusion' – dividing the passage of time into manageable pieces is an illusion. People on Earth get up when an alarm goes off, not when it's daylight. Time and tide wait for no

305

man – everybody knows that. How often have you said I wish I had more time? If you waste time, there is a piece of your life you never get back. It's simple."

Vem sat for a moment. Now Ari explained it, it was simple, but no one on the Quest had seen it yet. Ari interrupted his thoughts to demand food and to see Kalend. Seeing it would do no good to try to persuade him otherwise, Vem agreed on the condition that he walk slowly and came back soon to rest.

Vem knew he was forbidden to enter the Chamber without permission, but this was an exceptional circumstance. They entered the chamber unnoticed as all eyes were fixed on the ceiling and February as he made his climb.

Cheers and shouts came from Months and Watchers as Feb jumped to the ground and managed a weak wave. He took several minutes to sit and regain some of his strength before undoing the rope from around his waist and tying it securely around the tree. The tree was about ten metres from the water's edge so Feb tied it as high as he could reach and waved to Gust to tie the other end around the boulder.

Feb was sure something or someone had come to him on the climb but other than a brief glimpse of a moving rock, had seen nothing. Perhaps his exhaustion and hunger had caused him to hallucinate, but he was sure he had been saved by some other means. He looked over every inch of the rock but it was just rock, nothing more.

Feb knew his relationship with the others had changed. They were no longer angry with him, respecting his decisions and treating him as a leader. If he told them about the rock, they would think he was going mad and he could lose all the respect he had gained. He resolved to stay silent.

With nothing to do while Feb made his treacherous climb, Gust organized the backpacks so that Tober would carry Ember's pack as well as his own and Dec would take Jules'. Gust's pack was the heaviest and he would take it on his crossing. It was sensible for Tober to go first as everyone could see how exhausted Feb was after his climb and help might be needed for the rest to cross. Tober crossed without any difficulty, pulling the back packs after him and waving to the others as he stood next to Feb. Ember was next, and while it took her a bit longer than Tober, her crossing was uneventful. Dec followed, leaving Jules to come before Gust who would bring up the rear. As Dec was crossing Jules turned to Gust.

"You must go next and I will be last. Don't argue with me. This is the only rope we have, and we may well need it again. If you go last it will have to remain here. If you go next, then I will untie it and fasten it around my waist. I will be relying on you to pull me across and out of the water as fast as you can."

"Don't be ridiculous Jules, you are terrified of water. This is madness."

"No, it's not! We are on a mountain and may need a rope to climb up or down or lower things, you know it makes sense. There is a shallow bit of water just below where we are standing now. I will step into the water and wave to you to start pulling. If I do this it may make amends for the wrongs I have done. Please Gust, don't deny me this chance to prove my worthiness to be part of this Quest."

Across the whirlpool Dec and the others could see Jules and Gust arguing and believed it was Jules' fear of water that was the problem. When Gust mounted the rope and made his way across, they feared Jules was not going to come with them. Safely across Gust said what was planned. They agreed it was madness, but Jules had already tied the rope around her waist and made her way to the water's edge. She stopped, being this close to the water she could see and hear its desire for her. She was terrified as she looked across at Gust, who held up the rope to show Dec, Tober and Feb all holding it behind him.

What made her decision easy was the realization that in just a few minutes she would either have conquered her fear and been reunited with the others, or she would be dead and with Paulinus and her child. She didn't mind which one on these would eventuate, either was acceptable. She wrapped her right arm around the rope and got a tight grip before stepping into the water's edge, even here she could feel its power reaching for her. Raising her left arm, she felt a massive pull on the rope. Gust had told her to lie on her back but she had fallen face down and it was impossible to turn. It was catching her foot on a submerged rock which spun her over and she gasped for air. Despite the combined strength of the four men on the rope, the whirlpool was dragging her closer.

"We've got to get her away from that whirlpool," screamed Ember and the men, who, instead of pulling straight back, moved to an angle which seemed to work. Jules felt her strength draining and she stopped struggling, thinking of the Elysian Fields Paulinus had told her about. Surrender was easier than fighting and she felt her face turn once again into the water.

In the Chamber there were gasps and exclamations of dismay upon seeing Jules float face down. Gust and the others redoubled their efforts, dragging her limp body to the water's edge. Gust grabbed her and laid her on the track while they tried to revive her.

Jules didn't expect death to be so painful as repeated pressure on her chest caused the water she'd swallowed to surge back up her throat and spill onto the ground. She could hear a voice calling her name, but it wasn't Paulinus' voice. With another compression up came some more water and she gasped for air.

"She's alive," declared an ecstatic Ember, and wrapped a blanket around the now sitting Jules. Dec was busy lighting a fire to warm her as Gust untied the rope from around her waist. Feb knelt beside her, exclaiming as he hugged her tightly.

"That was the most stupid and the bravest thing I've ever seen."

A movement and a cheer from Ari made Kalend turn to face them.

"Ari, what are you doing out of bed? Vem how could you allow him to come here when he is just beginning to recover?"

Vem explained that Ari had made up his mind and nothing would deter him, adding that Ari had something important to tell him. Dynak, Neja, Verna and Thades all gathered around to express their delight at seeing Ari looking so much better. Vem had been captivated by the picture he had seen on the ceiling and spoke to Stolesc and Thades about the heroic action of July.

Going outside with Ari, Kalend listened as he spoke of the riddle, Ari arguing that he had solved it while still with the others so should be allowed to speak when they returned. Kalend said he would talk to Balack but was not hopeful his request would be allowed. Balack was sympathetic but insisted Ari was no longer part of the Quest and therefore not allowed to contribute anything. He also warned Kalend that if anyone tried to communicate with the Months the Quest would be over and their lives forfeited.

Balack was delighted to have the answer to the riddle, managing to drop this into a conversation with Neja who was impressed he had solved it.

"All happened as Thades suspected"

With some daylight left, Tober said the two most important things were to get Jules warm and to get that one purple grapefruit hanging in the tree. All agreed the reason it was the only fruit left was because it was at the very top of the tree and with no horse to stand on getting it wouldn't be easy.

Jules sat back and watched as the men talked and argued about the best way to reach it. She shivered as the cold of the water still chilled her. She couldn't quite believe what she'd done but at least now no one would be able to say she wasn't a valued part of the group.

She thought back to the night on the ledge when she had wept such bitter tears. They may have washed away her grief but feelings of anger and hate for Kalend still raged within her. Ember came to sit beside her, laughing at the antics of the men.

"They are really just boys at heart even if they are over two thousand years old. Give them a problem to solve and they're happy." She looked at Jules and asked, "How are…" but got no further.

"Please don't ask me how I am because I don't know. It was one thing to change my name to Jules, but that doesn't change the angry, bitter July I have been for so long."

"When you first came to The Valley, you were a young, beautiful, happy woman – I remember her. You are still that person if you want to be."

"I lost her a long time ago and even if I could find her again, how could she forgive me for destroying who she was?"

Ember stood up.

"You will never know unless you find and ask her."

As Ember went to join the men, Jules sat alone with her thoughts. She didn't have to find the young July; she knew exactly where she was. She was walled up in a faraway place deep within her. If she broke down those walls would there be anything left of who she used to be or would she have slowly diminished until there was nothing of substance remaining?

A shout from Feb distracted her and she looked up to find Gust bracing himself at the foot of the tree, while Tober stood on his shoulders. Feb was balancing on Tober's shoulders and was cutting the purple fruit free from the branches using the long-bladed pole. Shouting for a blanket to catch it he made the final cut. Jules went to help Ember hold the blanket out ready for the fruit to drop.

"Bombs away!" The fruit hit the blanket with such force it almost tore it from Ember's hands.

Jules ran to get the pot and a knife, hunger gnawing at her insides.

Dec had been busy too. He wasn't needed for the purple fruit capture and wandered a little way up the path where some vegetation could be seen. He tried some 'lettuce looking' leaves but they were too bitter to eat. Using one of the digging tools he'd made from the pig's tusk, he dug up a strange looking root. It was bulbous, twice the size of his fist and had a thick, knobbly skin. He washed the soil from it and cut it in half. The inside was white with speckles through it. Mindful of the 'lettuce', he scooped out a small piece to taste. It was slightly chewy but filled his mouth with a warmth and sweetness that was too wonderful to describe. Searching until he found four more, he took these back just in

311

time to see the juice from the purple fruit drain into a pot held by Jules.

He held out the' knobbly', as he called it, and gave a piece to everyone. All agreed it was wonderful and wanted more but Feb urged caution.

"We don't know what effects it may have, better to just have a little and see how we feel in the morning."

Feb gave instructions for everyone to fill the water bottles.

"We must dilute the juice enough so it won't make us sleep like before but will give us the stamina we need to keep going."

Each filled bottle was given just a teaspoon of juice and then shaken to mix. Feb and Jules tasting to ensure it was the same as the drink they had been given on the way to the Chamber. The remaining juice was secured in a bottle from March's first aid kit to be used on subsequent days.

Ember suggested they each have just one mouthful of the diluted drink now to ensure a good night's sleep and the rest could be drunk throughout the next day if no more food were to be found.

Back at the Chamber, Kalend persuaded Ari to go back to bed as the drink he'd been given would only be effective for a short time and rest would still be needed. He and Vem made a brief visit to May before returning to Stolesc's home. May was delighted to see Ari, hugging him to her ample bosom and stroking his hair.

In the Chamber, Neja turned to the others.

"I think May, Vem and Ari should be allowed to watch the progress of their friends. It's cruel to keep them in the dark."

"Hiemal will never agree to it, he's made that very clear."

But Thades was not as sure as Stolesc.

"He has shown no interest in the Quest for some time and

never comes to watch, so it may be possible."

Thades omitted to say he had his own reasons for believing this. He'd not seen Hiemal for several days and was certain he had gone to visit Earth, even though it was still t'Hura's world and she hadn't been asked for permission. He also believed Hiemal had done something to the crystal in his ring, preventing it from disclosing his emotions. If he were correct, a call to attend a Watch meeting may not be received and the meeting could go ahead without him.

Neja asked Balack if he would be willing to call a meeting. As Balack wanted the horse Amazon to be his, he thought the Months were more likely to agree if he was nice to them so gave his approval.

All happened as Thades suspected – the call was sent to Hiemal, but he didn't reply or come to the meeting. Neja put her proposal to the Assembly and was unanimously supported. The Months were delighted and determined not to miss a single moment.

"Well, I'm glad I made it, as I don't have another heroic feat left in me!"

No one suffered any aftereffects from the 'knobbly' so next morning, everyone hungrily ate half each of the remaining ones. Dec carefully described the small orange leaves forming a halo above ground which indicated the presence of the knobbly and asked everyone to keep an eye out for anymore.

"Purple juice may keep us going but doesn't satisfy grumbling stomachs."

Feb and Tober were leading the way and Feb said quietly.

"You know we have to cross this river at some point, don't you?"

"The level may have dropped but the speed makes it impossible."

"The further we head in this direction the further we will have to go back once we are across and the days are running out."

They walked for the rest of the morning in silence as there was nothing to say which would help. The track led slightly away from the river although it could still be clearly heard but the going was easy until Jules gave a sudden shout

"The bridge! I'm sure there was a bridge on the map and there it is."

She pointed ahead to a narrow point in the river crossed by a natural stone arch. The river pouring furiously through the narrowed gap was even more powerful here. Luckily the bridge was a few metres above it.

Feb could see where Jules was pointing but there was a

problem. To get to the bridge they would have to climb up a steep slope of what looked like the very loose shale type rock which had blocked their way after the night on the ledge.

Gust suggested they should make a shallow zig-zag course to the top thus reducing the risk of a slip. Dec said if they roped together, it would be safer for everyone in case someone fell on the way up.

More discussion followed about the safest way to go until Ember saw some of the orange 'halos' Dec had spoken of and helped him to dig up another eight of the knobblies. Sharing one between two, the remaining Knobblies were carefully packed for tomorrow. The discussion returned to planning the ascent.

Gust suggested the lightest person, Jules, should lead as she was less likely to dislodge the rock but Feb was concerned she would be unable to assist anyone heavier if they fell. Tober agreed Feb should go with the rope, find something to anchor it to and that way each succeeding person would have the rope to help them. After Feb, Jules should come next followed by Ember, Dec, Tober and finally Gust.

It was a slow process with Feb causing a number of small slips on his way to the top. From there Feb leaned over to inspect the bridge supports. The one on this side was undamaged, but the other had been weakened by constant bombardment from the rocks and trees being washed downstream. When Jules clambered over the edge of the bridge, Feb pointed out the danger.

"You must cross now so at least one of us is able to make it back and get help if we need it."

"You can't be serious. I would never make it alone. I'm not going without everyone else."

"If the bridge collapses, we will all be trapped here. Go

315

Jules. The others will follow as soon as they get up here. I promise."

A reluctant Jules did as Feb asked, feeling the bridge shudder as a huge boulder hit the far support. Feb shouted down to Gust.

"We can't wait for one at a time. Send Ember and when she is part of the way up, get Dec to start."

The others followed more quickly, joining a happy Jules on the other side of the bridge. When it was Gust's turn, he yelled out to Feb.

"You go across now. I will follow as soon as I can. You must be with the others."

Feb didn't want to leave him but a glance upstream horrified him. A huge tree was hurtling towards the bridge. As he watched, its branches became entangled with trees on the bank, halting its progress for now.

"Gust, hurry. You only have minutes. I'll cross now."

Feb felt close to tears as he ran to join the others. From their position they couldn't see the tree so Feb stepped back onto the bridge, his gaze swinging from the tree to the point where Gust should appear. He almost sobbed in relief when he saw Gust's head reach the top.

"Gust, run."

Gust had untied the rope when Feb's cry of alarm stopped him. Feb was pointing upstream where the tree had pulled free and was once again careering towards them. Gust grabbed his pack and dragging the rope behind him began to run.

By now the others knew what was happening and moved onto the bridge to watch. Feb shouted.

"Get back. If it hits this side of the bridge, we could all be swept into the water."

Despite the dangerous situation, Ari became tired, needing

to rest. Thades volunteered to take him back to Stolesc's place. On the way Ari talked about his friends, his admiration and respect evident in his recounting events he had shared with them in happier times. Thades asked questions about each of the Quest members and was particularly interested in Feb. The circumstances surrounding Feb's arrival in The Valley caused Thades to quicken his interest. Back at Stolesc's dwelling Ari collapsed on the bed, sleeping deeply. For several days Thades considered everything Ari had told him about the Months and The Valley. There was a slight possibility a solution to the problem facing the Months could be found. He considered speaking directly to Kalend, but his loyalty to Hiemal stopped him. If he were to act on this information, it must be done by him and him alone. First, he needed to search Kalend's dwelling.

In the chamber Vem and May watched every move. May had beamed with pride when Feb made decisions which the bigger and older men appeared happy to follow. Now, as they saw the tree approaching the bridge support they cried out, May covering her face with her hands, unable to watch.

Gust was halfway across the bridge when the massive tree stump crashed into the crumbling pillar ahead of him. It weakened it enough for a portion of the bridge to collapse leaving Gust on the wrong side of the breach.

Ember screamed as Gust slipped over one side of the remaining span, his feet just inches above the torrent. Tober was about to try to jump across the gap when Gust heaved himself back onto the bridge. Holding up a hand to indicate he was okay, he told them to move back so he could throw the rope and pack across before trying to make the leap. He swung his heavy backpack three times before giving it a mighty throw which almost knocked Feb to the ground as he had foolishly stepped out to watch. Gust backed up almost halfway across the remaining bridge and took several deep breaths before starting his run. Tober and Dec stood on either side of the broken pillar to help if they could. Gust was powerful but speed and agility were not his strong points. He ran, taking one massive leap, arms and legs flailing in the air as he stretched out for the other side. He almost made it and if Tober hadn't been there to grab his arm, he would have fallen into the rushing water below. Dec and Feb ran to help pulling him to safety. He smiled weakly.

"Well, I'm glad I made it. I don't have another heroic feat left in me!"

The others couldn't help but smile, but Feb hoped the flood had no more surprises in store.

It was a weary group that made their way along the track before finding a flat place to rest. More knobbly and juice were once again their fare with Gust commenting that long jump had never been his strongest sport and believed the juice had helped him make the leap. There was still some daylight left, but the track sloped down steeply, and Feb didn't want to risk any more dangers in the dark, so they made camp. With a fire going and believing they were now on the right path, everyone's spirits lifted until Feb asked Ember how many days they had left. Ember was reluctant to tell as she had been keeping count. Her knotted cord showed only four days until they had to be in the Chamber. All knew the map had shown at least six campfires on the return journey. Feb reminded them of the restorative power of the juice and said they could still make it, especially if Vem was waiting for them at the lake with at least one of the horses.

Talk of Vem raised thoughts of how Ari may be doing, Feb insisting he was sure Kalend wouldn't let anything bad happen to him. Jules couldn't help her anger and bitterness.

"You mean apart from letting us all die when this is over."

To try to change the now gloomy mood, Dec asked if anyone had any more thoughts about the riddle. Tober had an interesting suggestion.

"Perhaps we're wrong to think the answer is about us and our situation. Maybe the answer is something like… the wind, or snow or beauty, you know something not physical."

Dec had another idea.

"I think the answer is the tunnel, you know, the temporal bridge or whatever it's called."

Each line was considered in light of this suggestion with Dec explaining his reasoning.

"The source of all our problems. From a Watchers point of view the tunnel was what allowed us to come to The Valley. 'I have no place in the Tir Dhuchais.' The tunnel is in The Valley, not Tir Dhuchais and perhaps it means the tunnel should never have been built."

Ember contributed the tunnel was an illusion for the Months, not a part of Earth as they had believed. 'I am not alone and together we tarry for no-one.' provoked a lot of discussion with no obvious answer found.

Gust was exhausted and closed any further discussion.

"It's getting late, and tomorrow will be a fast and furious day. Time for bed."

Just as Ember was falling asleep a thought hovered at the edge of her mind, something someone had said but no matter how she tried she couldn't quite catch it.

Hiemal surprised everyone by returning to the Chamber the next day to face a demanding Balack.

"Why did you ignore the summons to return for a meeting?"

319

Hiemal bowed before replying, taking a moment to think of his answer.

"Forgive us Judicial Watcher Balack, but an urgent family matter required our presence in Uclair. We are confident this Watch made correct decisions without our presence."

"Yes, we did. We voted to allow the Months to view the Quest as their concern for their friends is real and to deny them would be cruel."

Hiemal was angry, but his time spent on Earth was more important than anything to do with the excessively irritating Months. When Vem, May and Ari entered the Chamber he immediately rose and took his leave. He already thought of Earth as Uclair and was planning how he would use its beauty and resources to prosper his House. He would simply ignore the Watcher Oath which stated a policy of non-interference.

Hiemal expected to see Thades, but he was nowhere to be found. Returning the next day looking tired and frustrated, Thades refused to tell Hiemal where he'd been or what he'd been doing. His search of Kalend's dwelling had been fruitless, every cupboard, drawer and shelf had been carefully searched and then replaced to hide his presence. Perhaps what he sought no longer existed.

"I understand how you feel Ari, but we cannot help them now"

The morning after the bridge crossing Feb woke the others just before daylight, each having a drink of juice before starting to make the descent to the lake below. The track had many steep and treacherous parts but helping each other they made good progress. Just as they were thinking about a brief rest stop the lake came into view and even Gust felt like weeping. Although still some way below, it was apparent the lake was now many times the size it had been when the quest began. Its edges brushed the feet of a Whispering forest that had been at least one days walk from its previous boundary. There was no way they could get around it in time.

They sat in silence until Gust spoke.

"We could use some of those trees to make a raft and cross the lake instead of going around it. I don't see how the Watch could hold us to the Quest when the rain and flooding have changed the whole layout of Tir Dhuchais."

Dec and Tober became quite enthusiastic about the idea, but Feb urged caution.

"I think it's a great idea and the only way we can hope to be back when we should. I fear some Watchers may try to enforce the wording which made it clear we were to go around the lake and not across it."

Everyone knew he meant Hiemal and possibly Thades. Ember, as usual could see the practical side of their situation.

"If we make it back, we can argue our case, if we don't then rights or wrongs won't matter."

A solemn group once again faced a possible end to their hopes of survival.

With the decision made, the journey down the mountain continued taking another day and a half to reach the lake's edge. No one spoke of the non-appearance of Vem, each choosing to believe the size of the lake was the reason he wasn't there.

Dec took his axe and began to cut down the biggest of the trees with Gust and Tober dragging them to a dry spot to begin building. Feb used the pig's tusk to hack the thin 'whip-like' cord from the end of each great leaf. He said they would use these to tie the trunks together.

Gust said they would need to make the raft double thickness to help support their weight with the huge leaves placed between the two layers to increase buoyancy and keep it as dry as possible. The rope was cut and used to secure the two ends of the raft as the thin whip-like cords used for the poles wouldn't be strong enough to hold the whole structure together. Once again Jules' courage in saving the rope was proving to be a blessing.

While the raft was being made, Ember and Jules searched for food, finding querbana and berries. Ember hoped to find fish but the ground, now under water, was thick mud and no fish were to be found.

Ember suggested the two pot lids could be used as paddles if some way could be found to attach them to a handle and Dec took on this task. The two spades they'd brought could also be used. When they sat around a fire late that evening Tober insisted they needed to make the raft bigger otherwise they couldn't fit everything on.

"We don't need everything," said Feb. "We just take what food we have. There is only one day to do this so we can't take more time building. If we don't make it back, the things we leave behind aren't going to matter."

At first light, a pile of discarded items was left on the lake shore as the Months made one last effort to save themselves. Gust walked behind the raft, pushing it out into deeper water before climbing on. He used one trunk as a rudder with Jules standing at the front as she had the sharpest eyesight. She desperately sought a familiar landmark to guide them across. After a light lunch she shouted that she could see a tall tree on the far side and believed it to be the purple grapefruit tree they'd harvested on the night Vem and Tober caught up with them. If it was and they steered slightly to the right they should reach a spot closest to the Chamber.

It was Gust who noticed the change first – the raft was being slowly swept away to the right, much further than they needed to go.

"There is a current pulling us away. It must be the force of the water coming over the falls. We must paddle against it, or we may end up back on this side of the lake."

No matter how hard each worked, they couldn't fight the current and Feb shouted in his tiredness and frustration.

"It's not fair, we've done all and more than was asked of us and still fate conspires against us."

Ember heard a chirruping sound as onto the raft jumped Gossip. She knelt before him with tears in her eyes.

"My little friend, if you could help us now, please do so or we are lost."

Gossip cocked his head on one side and chirruped before returning to the water.

"What, did you really think he could understand you, or help if he could?"

The bitterness had returned to Jules' voice as she sank to the floor of the raft. All heart seemed to have gone out of them. Gossip returned, but he was not alone. A large group of the creatures swam to the raft and then dived underneath it.

"Start paddling," shouted Feb. "Perhaps there is help for us after all."

The change to their course was so slight at first that Gust wasn't sure it was happening, but Jules, still looking ahead shouted.

"It's working, we're turning."

The Flughs worked in shifts, some jumping onto the raft to rest while others kept swimming below. Ember was amazed at the diversity of them. Obviously the same species, but some were tall with a white crest like Gossip, and others while shorter, were more muscular with a dark blue crest. The biggest of them looked quite fearsome and only Ember spoke or moved close to them. It was almost dark when Gust shouted.

"We're out of the current, all we have to do now is keep going."

Gossip climbed back onto the raft and Ember bent to kiss the top of his head.

"Thank you, thank you, my little friend. You are my hero."

Gossip turned and in the fading light, pointed ahead where Ember could see a large rock in the water. She recognised it as the Sentinel rock they had passed on their way to the Chamber. Gossip and the other Flughs swam away and Gust jumped into the water to see if he could feel the bottom, but not yet. He kicked out with his feet, pushing the raft ahead of him as he could see the others were exhausted. He was greatly relieved when his feet felt purchase on the bottom, and he pushed the raft until it ran aground.

As the Quest crossed the lake, Jan and June returned to the Chamber. They cheered, laughed and cried with Vem, Ari and May to see their friends such a short distance away and wanted to go to help them. Balack was sympathetic but firm.

"If you go to help then the Quest will have failed. They have tonight to rest and all day tomorrow to reach here. I will give them as much time as I can. You have my word."

Ari hugged Stolesc and a surprised Thades before turning to Kalend.

"I am so proud of them, surely the courage and leadership of Feb must count for something."

"Completing the Quest and solving the riddle is all that can save them."

Ari turned to Vem. "They still don't know the answer, do they?"

Vem answered sadly. "They are still trying to work it out, but they have until tomorrow."

"We can't leave it; I could sneak to meet them, tell them and…"

"You must do nothing! You heard Balack, if you interfere, the Quest is lost. Promise me you will remain here." The urgency in Vem's voice and on his face convinced Ari and he promised to do as Balack said. Kalend told Vem he must make sure Ari did not leave his side.

June went to stay with May in the home of t'Hura. Vem and Jan were in Stolesc's house with Ari who insisted that as he had solved the riddle before leaving the Quest he should be allowed to give the answer. Vem having spent time with the Watchers knew they would be bound by the strict wording of the Quest, Hiemal would see to that.

In the middle of the night Ari slipped out of bed and tiptoed towards the door. Vem's voice spoke out of the darkness.

"Where do you think you're going? You heard Balack and Kalend. Do you think Hiemal is fool enough not to keep watch to make sure there is no contact between us and the Quest party? I understand how you feel Ari, but we cannot help them now, the matter is in their hands. Now go back to bed!"

The remaining juice in their drink bottles ensured they slept well, although the strenuous work of the day would have contributed to that. Before dawn, Tober was awake and went to the water's edge. Standing on their now beached raft he could see fish in the water and used a spear tool to catch three before heading back to camp and lighting a fire. The smell of cooking fish was enough to rouse the others and with Querbana in plentiful supply they enjoyed a satisfying breakfast before Feb cleared his throat.

"We have to make a decision. Has anyone had any more thoughts about the riddle?"

Tober had thought of little else as he was fishing.

"Any of our suggestions could be true for some of the clues but none are true for all of them."

Jules spoke.

"It says 'I am what you want the most, but you misuse me and take me for granted'. What we want most is to live, so could life be the answer?"

Tober became quite excited.

"Our existence, our life is the problem, and they don't want us in Tir Dhuchais. Immortal beings from Earth could be considered an illusion. Not sure about the not being alone and tarrying together bit, but if we lose our lives, we can't use them anymore."

Ember was still grasping at something just on the edge of her mind.

"I don't believe any of our answers is the right one."

Dec agreed. Gust looked dejectedly at the five faces around him.

"We have to have something when we enter that Chamber, we have to make a decision."

Feb stood.

"Not now we don't. It should take us until late afternoon to get there so there is still time to think of something."

As the group set off, once again Ember had the feeling the answer was just there if she could only see it.

"This is my decision and it is final"

Hiemal was delighted to see the Months so close to the Chamber. All he had hoped for would soon be his. These beings would be gone forever. He still hadn't spoken to Thades and wondered where he could be. Surely he would want to watch the final chapters of this Quest.

By mid-morning, a dejected Thades returned, and all Watchers and non-quest Months gathered in the Chamber.

Balack stood and called for silence before addressing the Months.

"I wish to make it clear how the meeting will be conducted when the Quest party returns. If any Month here tries to speak or communicate in any way with them, I will rule the Quest has failed. You will stand to one side of the chamber and not move until the proceedings are completed. Is that understood?"

Following Vem's lead, all nodded in agreement.

Hiemal stood and asked to have some clarification about the riddle. He asked that Judicial Watcher Balack should write the answer on a piece of parchment and seal it. Only when the Months had given their answer would the parchment be unrolled for all to see. Hiemal was certain Balack didn't have the answer and wanted to embarrass him as punishment for his rulings against him. He was surprised when a smiling Balack held up a small parchment.

"The answer to the riddle is already written on this sealed parchment. You need have no concerns about the correct answer being given."

Midday passed and there was still some way to go. Feb told them to pick up the pace as they must enter the Chamber before darkness fell. Various suggestions had been shouted out as they walked, but none fitted the clues. When the Chamber neared Feb stopped, turning to face them.

"Well, what do you want me to do? I will give whatever answer you think best."

Ember looked at each face and could see no easy solution. Gust, placing his hands on Feb's shoulders spoke from his heart.

"You are leader of this merry band, not because some Watcher chose you but because we all trust you. We will support whatever answer you give and not attribute blame."

Feb looked at the others and could see agreement and approval on their faces. Unable to speak in the face of such undeserved loyalty, he could only nod before turning to lead the way inside.

They were greeted with applause and shouts of 'Well done' and 'Good work'.

The six who stood in the centre of the Chamber were different from the ones who had left. Beside the loss of weight and evident tiredness, there was strength, resilience, courage and a sense of togetherness that was apparent to all. Feb turned his head to look for the others and seeing Ari cried out.

"Ari, you made it and Vem too."

Balack roared.

"Silence, there will be no communication between you and the others until this matter is completed."

"Balack, please forgive my outburst, but we have not known for all this time if Ari was alive. My delight at seeing him was too great to keep silent."

Black beamed at him.

"We too are delighted to see both Ari and Vem survive the attack on their persons, but you will have to wait to hear their story. As to the Quest, you have returned in the allotted time so now you must answer the riddle."

Hiemal stood but Balack waved him away and scowling, he retook his seat.

"February, Neja will read the riddle again, not for your benefit, but to refresh the minds of others."

He nodded to Neja who stood and spoke clearly.

'What am I?
The source of all your troubles,
I have no place in Tir Dhuchais.
A Wise man said, 'I am an illusion'
But I am not alone and together we tarry for no one
I am what you want the most
But you misuse me and take me for granted.
If you lose me I cannot be found.
By the 24th day of March
You must return to the Chamber and tell us all…
What I am.'

Now was the moment to seal their fate. Feb stood, unable to choose which answer he would give. Balack was about to speak when Feb raised his head.

"The answer is…"

"It's time, the answer is time."

The shout had come from Ember who grabbed Feb's arm and looked beseechingly into his eyes. "The answer is time, Feb."

Feb turned to look directly at Ari as his words on the night outside the garden came flooding back to him. Ari was nodding furiously until Vem gave him a shake.

"February, you are leader, the answer must be given by you."

"My answer is Time."

Balack, grinning from ear to ear opened the parchment and turned it to show the assembled watchers and months. It said one word – TIME.

The quest Months yelled, laughing and hugging each other while jumping up and down. The other Months rushed to join them.

It took some minutes and a lot of shouting from Balack to bring order to the Chamber.

"February, Quest members, you have correctly solved the riddle and you have successfully …"

"Balack, the Quest has failed, surely you can see that?"

Hiemal was on his feet again, demanding to be heard. Balack, knowing he could not deny him, gave him permission to speak.

"Is it possible for Neja to read out the exact wording of the Quest for we are somewhat confused by events?"

Balack nodded to Neja who unrolled the Quest document. Feb knew what was coming but could do nothing about it.

"The Quest is in two parts. First, you will go on a journey around the lake in the centre of Tir Dhuchais. This will involve finding your way through the mountains, before returning around the far side of the lake. You will have to find food as you go, but the water from the lake is perfectly safe for you to drink. You must complete this journey in the time allocated."

"Thank you, Neja. This states quite clearly the Months were to go around the lake, yet you all watched as they built a structure and crossed it. This is clearly one failure to comply with the instructions and as such the Quest has failed."

Hiemal glared around the Chamber, daring anyone to contradict him.

"Another clear breech is the rule they insisted upon. If any hindrance was given, the Quest would succeed or if any aid or help was given to them, it would mean the failure of the Quest. On more than one occasion, Kalend's little 'pet' gave them fish and on the lake he and his friends saved the structure from being drawn back to the wrong side. February, if the Flughs hadn't helped you, would you be standing here now?"

Feb looked at the others but before he could speak, every Watcher in the Chamber stood asking to be heard.

Balack sighed, sadness etched on his face.

"February, you will answer Hiemal's question and then t'Hura, as Watcher for Earth you may speak for the Months."

Feb turned to face Hiemal and spoke just a single word.

"No."

Hiemal smiled in triumph and happily gave the floor to t'Hura who looked around with great sadness.

"When Neja wrote the Quest, she had no idea of the hailing that was to come. As a result of that, the lake flooded to almost twice its normal size. No member of the Quest party knew the original boundaries of the lake, therefore, knowing it had changed, they took the only decision open to them. They crossed it and I do not believe they should be penalized for it."

Shouts of approval and agreement could be heard from almost every throat. Balack eventually regained control and asked t'Hura to continue.

"As to the giving of help, as Hiemal knows, this rule was to ensure no help or hindrance would be given by anyone from this Chamber. Rogue is a wild creature and not subject to its laws. I say the Months completed the Quest and solved the riddle and should be allowed to return to their Valley."

Hiemal looked at Balack, intimidating him without

speaking. Hiemal had visited him the night before and chatted about how different things would be when he was Presidion. Balack understood the implied threat and despising himself for his weakness, knew he would not be strong enough to stand against him.

Hiemal stood again. Glad of even a temporary respite, Balack nodded permission. Hiemal had given up any pretense of respect for Balack, not even addressing him by name.

"It cannot be denied that Rogue helped because of his association with Kalend, therefore it is incorrect to call him wild. Any one of us can approach him and pat his head. I say again, the help he gave broke the rule specifically asked for by one of these Months and therefore the Quest has failed. Surely this Watch will finally honour my willingness to allow the Quest to happen. You can no longer refuse the enforcing of the Charter which should have happened twenty-four days ago."

Feb asked to speak, as did Vem, Stolesc, Dynak, Verna and Neja, making an angry Balack call for order. He wished he was not to be the one who would seal their fate but had no choice.

"When February broke the contract, the idea of a Quest was proposed to save them. All agreed to undertake the Quest and to abide by its rules. They have failed and I have no choice but to agree with Hiemal that there are no more barriers to enforcing the Charter. This is my decision, and it is final. February, you will all return to your Valley and spend one day and night there to prepare and say farewells. This Watch will come to the cave at sunset on the next day for your departure. I am truly sorry it has come to this."

The crystals in every ring shone orange expressing their sorrow, all except one.

"He glared his hatred at Thades who had committed this final act of betrayal"

A silence filled the Chamber as the full implications of Balack's words hit home. Kalend and Dynak moved towards the now stunned Months but Feb held up a hand to stop them.

"There is nothing you can say to change things so would you please leave us on our own to come to terms with what lies ahead."

In silence, the Chamber emptied. Passing the disconsolate group of Months huddling together, Hiemal could not resist a smirk. Gust would have struck him had Tober not reached for his arm to prevent it.

Feb knew what he wanted to do and spoke first.

"I don't want to stay here tonight; I couldn't bear to face the Watchers again in the morning. I want to go home. Anyone want to come with me?"

There was much nodding of heads but Dec suggested they should wait until dark to avoid any chance meetings and so it was agreed. Ari asked Feb if he could go to speak to someone as he had unfinished business. Feb said yes without asking who, surprised that Ari would defer to him.

Thades was pacing up and down in his dwelling. He looked at the clarinet on his table and resolved to return it in the morning. Even if he learned to play it, the memories of this day would forever sully its magic. When there was a knock on the door the last person he expected was Ari, but delighted he had come he invited him in.

"I won't stay long, I have just one question for you. When we walked and talked together was it some kind of game you were playing? Did you always want us to be destroyed?"

Thades had enjoyed his time with Ari more than he could have imagined and looked at him with sadness and truth in his eyes.

"It was no game and I never wanted to have it end like this. My species are solitary, forming just one friendship in a lifetime but I made an exception for you. I came to think of you as a friend."

Ari didn't reply, just nodded and left as quickly as he had come. Thades hung his head, he was missing something, but could not find it.

The Months left as soon as Ari returned and used the two moonlights to make their way until clouds made the use of torches necessary. Vem had collected the horses and May and Ari rode Amazon while June and July rode Titan with Vem leading him. Little was spoken, arms were linked or placed around shoulders and waists to give comfort to one another.

Kalend had gone to Earth to tell March to return to The Valley in two days' time to be with her friends when they returned, grateful when she acted with a calmness and dignity he could not master.

Next morning Verna met Dynak as she was on her way to the Chamber with a basket full of food, for breakfast and for the journey. Neither could find the words to express how they were feeling. They entered the Chamber to find it empty. The backpacks Neja had recovered from the far side of the lake were gone, the clothes the watchers had given neatly folded in a pile on the table with t'Hura's earrings on top.

"Where do you think they have gone, they can't get back to

Earth and there is nowhere to hide in Tir Dhuchais or The Valley."

Kalend arrived and answered her question in a voice heavy with emotion.

"They aren't hiding, they have gone home. They do not want or need our company now, just each other. We must respect their wishes in this matter."

t'Hura gave a gasp of dismay when she too saw the empty Chamber.

"I can't believe May would have gone without saying goodbye. We have become such good friends."

Kalend sat down wearily.

"There are no friendships between us now. They are Months and we are Watchers who have called for their destruction, nothing more."

Thades too was distressed when he arrived with the clarinet in hand. Just when they thought things couldn't get worse, Hiemal entered and gave a great shout of joy.

"They are gone from here and soon they will be gone forever."

In a moment of unheard of anger, Thades turned to Hiemal.

"Our friendship is ended. Never in the history of my species has a friendship been broken but you are my friend no longer."

Thades whose dark skin now blazed a fiery red strode out of the Chamber leaving Kalend, Dynak and a shocked Hiemal. Anger such as this was unknown among Hernians and Thades was ashamed of his exchange with Hiemal in front of others.

Hiemal returned to his dwelling. He had considered Thades his loyal and true friend but now he would have no one. He was alarmed at the prospect of being alone, and angry at his failure to recognise how much Thades' friendship meant to him.

Thades calmed his anger and then traveled to Kalend's

dwelling. Kalend assumed he wanted to talk about Hiemal.

"I am distressed to see a Hernian friendship broken, perhaps there is a way to repair it."

"I have not come to talk about Hiemal. Ari told me he brought February to The Valley and told him of the rules. Is that correct?"

Kalend was irritated by Thades' tone but replied.

"Yes, but it doesn't change anything. Feb admitted he knew the rules and willingly broke them."

Thades' impatience was yet another surprise to Kalend as Hernians were renowned for maintaining a calm and unemotional demeanour.

"I know that. All the Months had to sign a contract before entering The Valley. Did February do this?"

Kalend objected to being questioned in this way but seeing Thades was desperately seeking some way to help the Months, cast his mind back.

"I was attending the longest Senaten meeting in history. February couldn't sign before coming but I feel I would have asked him to sign on my return."

Kalend suddenly remembered the Quaan and how he had been distracted by them but was unwilling to tell Thades of them.

He looked with hope directly into Thades' eyes.

"It is possible February didn't sign."

"We must take the contract and save them. I have searched your dwelling and have not been able to find it. Where is it?"

Kalend looked in disbelief.

"You have searched my dwelling?"

"You can exact any punishment you see fit after we save them. Where is the contract?"

Kalend was sure he would have kept it in the Watch archive,

but Thades was equally sure it wasn't. Kalend insisted they look again. The search took all day and part of the night with no contract being found.

'If it is not here, would you have kept it in your dwelling in The Valley?"

Kalend thought this most unlikely but was prepared to look. Both were tired and Thades suggested they rest and go in the morning. It would take the Months at least two days to make it back and nothing would happen until then.

Thades had never been to The Valley and stood open mouthed and glowing at its beauty.

With no time to spare, the search began. Every cupboard, shelf and drawer were emptied but no contract was found. Thades was distraught that a means to save the music he loved so deeply was slipping away from him.

"Is there anything that would help us to find it."

"When I went to meet the Months, I wrapped it in a cloth map I was taking with me. I put both in a leather tube with a strap to put across my body. I do not recall seeing it since I returned with them so long ago. The air in The Valley causes most materials to decompose over time. It is possible the Contract no longer exists. I'm sorry Thades. It breaks my heart to think we cannot save them. Without the contract Hiemal would never accept our word that February did not sign."

At that moment the Months emerged from the cliff. Emotions held in check throughout the journey could no longer be contained. As they saw their homes they cried openly. Kalend wanted to speak to them, but their outpouring of grief told him he would not be welcome. Thades returned to Tir Dhuchais but Kalend remained.

He had to ensure the Quaan could not gather the memories

of February as they would contain information on Tir Dhuchais and the Watchers. Y Quaan had implied he could have passed through the curtain of protection around Kalend's house if he had wished to do so. A similar curtain around Feb's cabin may not protect him.

May said she would prepare some food, pleased when Jules and Ember offered to help. Vem and Tober went to check on the animals and Jan sat down on the hillside beside his gardens. He didn't know what to do. June came to be with him as they had grown close during the time of the Quest, and they wept together.

March returned in the afternoon, and they all gathered around to tell her what had happened. She was pleased to learn February had at last become Feb but was surprised by the confident young man who stood before her. Jules visited March later, telling her all that had happened after she had gone to Earth. The two friends stayed together that night, comforting each other as best they could. March couldn't believe all they had endured, only to have Hiemal deny them mercy.

After dark Kalend stood outside the cabin of Feb. Ten Quaan arrived with Y Quaan to collect his memories from his time on Earth and his time in Tir Dhuchais. Kalend spoke from the darkness.

"February is unwell, and you cannot gather his memories tonight. I will stand guard until daybreak."

Y Quaan threw his head back and made a strange jerking hissing sound. Kalend realised he was laughing.

"Do you fear February will tell us about the Watch, the Quest and Tir Dhuchais that you tried so hard to hide from us? Who do you think helped February when he was falling on the rock face? It was Quaan who held and helped him to safety."

Kalend was stunned, he had no idea the Quaan had been to

Tir Dhuchais. He quickly gathered his thoughts, struggling to work out what the consequences could be.

"What will you do with the knowledge you gained?"

Y Quaan moved so quickly Kalend stepped back in alarm. Y Quaan's face was just inches from his own, anger evident in his slitted eyes.

"Unlike your Senaten, we do not use what we gather for financial or political gain."

He moved back as suddenly as he had moved forward, and his voice became quiet once more.

"We just like to know things."

Stunned to hear Y Quaan speak of the Senaten, Kalend wearily moved aside to let the Quaan enter Feb's cabin.

"Thank you Kalend, Watcher of Months. You have my word no Watcher will be visited by us."

Kalend returned to Tir Dhuchais. Dynak tried to persuade him to return to The Valley, insisting the Months would need him even if they didn't know it. He had been their friend for over two thousand of their years and nothing could wipe out that much caring and sharing. Neja and Stolesc added their voices in support but to no avail. Kalend went for a walk beside the lake keen to have a sleep after his night's exertions.

Verna found him sitting under the same tree Balack and t'Hura had sat under just a short time ago. She didn't speak, laying her head on his shoulder and wrapping her arms around him. Kalend wanted to refuse her comfort but his need for it was great. She could feel his weariness and sense of failure. Kalend felt rather than saw the trees and plants reach out to enfold them both. His sorrow was deep, but Verna sat until her comfort was no longer required. His weariness left him as peace and contentment replaced it. He tried to find words to express his admiration and gratitude, but Verna smiled.

"No words are necessary after a shared time of renewal."

The tree lifted its branches and silently Verna got up and walked away.

Kalend made a decision. He would return to his cabin in The Valley, for it was home to him. He would stand outside where the Months could see him and if they wanted to speak to him, they would know he was there.

When Kalend told Thades he was going back to The Valley, Thades felt a surge of emotions unknown to him. His anger at Hiemal would fade but his concern was for Kalend who had aged and diminished as the stress of these events overwhelmed him. Thades thought Kalend may continue to live in The Valley for it was the place that was home to him.

After his walk by the lake Thades returned home to find Hiemal sitting outside his door.

"We thought a Hernian friendship could not be broken except by death. We regret the thoughtless words we spoke. Your friendship is important to us and we would like you to reconsider your decision."

Without waiting for a reply Hiemal got up and left. In that moment Thades knew he could forgive him and Hiemal would become his friend once more.

In The Valley, Jules returned to her cabin opening a drawer she had kept closed since first coming here. A carefully wrapped parcel lay in it but she could not open it, not yet.

No one slept much that night. They gathered for breakfast to discuss what they would do about Kalend who had returned to his cabin the evening before. Vem spoke first.

"Kalend told me how all things came to be and I believe he has always acted in our best interests."

Jules was not ready to think good of Kalend.

"If he had trusted us and told us the truth from the beginning none of this would have happened. He is responsible!"

Vem declared he would go to speak to Kalend but wanted others to have the freedom to do so too.

"I have explained the way the Charter was set up. Kalend wasn't allowed to tell us. That was Hiemal's doing. Kalend is over there now, desperately wanting to spend some of this last time with us. If we don't want him here that's fine but anyone who wants to speak to him should do so."

"What about you Feb?" said Tober. "Do you think he should come over to us?"

Feb spoke as honestly as he could.

"I think I want to go to my end with a clear conscience and no regrets. Forgiveness is a great healer, and it would be nice if we could all have the peace that comes with it. I will go to him if you don't want him here."

"Some of us have more to forgive than others," spat Jules.

"The more forgiveness the greater the peace," said Gust softly.

"Bring him here or not, but I won't see him."

Jules left the meeting with a concerned March following her but she would not be comforted.

With the agreement of those remaining, Feb went outside. He looked over the river to Kalend, beckoning him to come down.

Some spoke to Kalend in small groups, others alone, but there was healing for all who did.

Jules was in her cabin when Kalend knocked on her open door. She looked up, her face hardening but she said nothing. Kalend looked at the opened package on the table in front of her and saw a number of beautifully made small garments – baby clothes for her lost child. His face crumpled and unchecked sobs filled his chest as he sank to the floor. This was too much; he could not bear it. Struggling to his feet he searched for the words he needed to speak.

"I understand your anger and pain and accept that forgiveness is not possible, but there has been nothing in my life that I regret more than this."

Jules looked at this man she had hated with such force since he had revealed the secrets he kept. Inside her a wall began to crumble and a young July cried out.

"I am here, I have always been here. I do not blame or condemn anyone. We are one and we will die as one. Kalend is a good man who made a mistake, nothing more."

Jules felt a wave of emotion wash over her and lifted her head.

"There is need for forgiveness on both sides. All the time I lived here I refused to acknowledge the great gift you gave to us in this place. I allowed my sorrow to taint my thinking. I called you responsible for what would befall us, joining with Hiemal who wished your destruction as much as ours. Will you forgive my hard-heartedness?"

Kalend reached out a hand to her, but she moved away.

"Time would be needed for us to touch again and time is what we do not have. I forgive you and you forgive me, that is all either of us can expect."

It was already well past midday and time was running out. Once again Thades searched every cupboard, drawer and shelf in Kalend's dwelling. As the sun was beginning to set, he could see Kalend and Feb walking together towards the cave. Turning to leave, Thades caught a glimpse of something in a corner. It was hidden by a curtain but a small piece of thin leather could just be seen. In a last act of desperation, he pulled the fabric aside revealing a leather tube, opening it just enough to see it was what he was looking for.

The last of the Months and Watchers had now entered the cave and Kalend and Feb were a few steps behind. Thades followed by thought and entered the cave just as Vem placed torches in the hollowed wall sconces for the final time. An emotional Balack cleared his throat, unsure of what to say, grateful when Thades stepped into the space between Months and Watchers.

"Balack, it is important we ensure all protocols and regulations are followed in case this matter is reviewed at a future date. I have here the contract between Kalend and the Months and I would like to call out each name so the Months can line up ready to depart. Do I have your permission to proceed?"

Balack was too emotional to speak, just nodding his permission. A bittersweet smell, easily recognised as sorrow filled the cave.

Thades took out the parchment and carefully unrolled it. Kalend looked intensely at Thades, hope the dominant expression on his face.

"As I call your name, please form a line to pass through the door when all are ready. November, April, October, May, December, January, June, March, August, September, July."

As each name was called the Month moved to stand by the door. Thades began to roll up the paper.

"Wait! What about me, I'm the guilty one but you haven't called my name."

Kalend shouted with relief.

"That's because you didn't sign the contract. I was on

important business and asked Ari to bring you here. He told you the rules, but I was preoccupied with another matter on my return and forgot to ask you to sign it."

Vem stepped back into the middle of the cave.

"If he didn't sign the contract then he can't have broken it. He's innocent of any crime."

Hiemal was incensed.

"Ari told him the rules and February has admitted his guilt. Signing or not is irrelevant."

Balack, realizing this was his opportunity to be a hero, called for silence.

"February was on trial for breaking the contract between Kalend and the Months. If he didn't put his name on the contract, he is not bound by it. I declare February to be innocent of all charges. Nobody has to die today. You can all go home."

Hiemal exploded in wrath, calling Watch and the Months guilty of deception and dishonour. He glared his hatred at Thades who had committed this final act of betrayal.

The Months stood in silence, not sure if Balack had spoken as he had – were they truly saved? Ari moved first, rushing to throw his arms around Thades.

"Thank you, my friend. I'm sorry I doubted you."

Balack sighed as Ari claimed the friendship of Thades, but he knew he had the friendship of t'Hura, Stolesc and Kalend. Tears of relief and a group hug were all the Months could manage. March as usual was practical.

"I still have four days of my time remaining. I will go back to Earth and return on the thirty-first as usual."

May stopped her.

"March, if you return on the thirtieth then all twelve Months would be together for the first shared meal in our history. We could celebrate our survival."

Ari thought this was a great idea.

"A party to end all parties."

May, without consulting the others, faced Balack.

"Balack, we would be happy for the Watchers to join us, if it pleases you."

Balack, beaming from ear to ear, clapped his hands delightedly in front of him.

"We will be delighted to come. What is a par tee?"

"Smiling, he took his leave"

The Watchers were a happy, but tired group as they made their way to their dwellings, but Kalend could not rest yet. His first visit was to Balack.

"I need to thank you for the manner in which you conducted the issue of the Months. You have earned the respect of us all. Your name will long be remembered in the records of this Watch. I owe you a personal debt of gratitude."

Balack protested.

"You do not need to thank me. I owe you thanks for trusting me to be Judicial Watcher which was more exciting and exhausting than I could have dreamed. Tomorrow you will retake your rightful place in the Presidion's chair."

Kalend had considered telling Balack that the Judicial Watcher position was a fiction but Balack's beaming face and new-found confidence were too precious to destroy.

Despite his growing weariness, Kalend visited Thades, kneeling before an astonished and flustered Thades.

"You saved the Months when I failed to do so. I am forever in your debt."

Thades, embarrassed by this show of humility from a man he held in high esteem, urged him to stand.

After a glass of Pestiar wine the two men talked at length. Kalend had a request to make and Thades was at first horrified, then refused, but Kalend was a man of great persuasion. At last Thades agreed. As Kalend made to leave, Thades mentioned the strange state of Hiemal's crystal, unsure of what he was doing to prevent it reflecting his obvious emotion. Kalend had also noticed the apparent failing of Hiemal's ring and knew his last act as Presidion must be to discover his secret. Relieved to find Hiemal's dwelling empty he entered, searching for any clue as to what Hiemal had done to his ring. Lying on a corner of a table was something that did not belong there. Smiling, he took his leave.

Learning Hiemal's secret meant Kalend had to change his plan. He no longer felt he had to leave the Watch, but things in the future would be very different. He went to see Verna. She embraced him, feeling keenly his tiredness and something that had elements of sorrow and finality. The peace he had found before had been short lived as his feelings of having failed the Months once more overcame him.

"Kalend, you are troubled. Tell me what purpose you have for me."

Kalend felt sadness as he gazed at Verna, she was too gentle for what he would ask of her.

"A Watcher among us has betrayed the values we all swore to uphold and will face a trial in the morning."

"I assume this Watcher is Hiemal. Is this trial to do with his actions against me? Is that why you are here?"

'It is Hiemal, but it is not about you. It is his betrayal of the vows we all swore as Watchers. As Presidion, I can make a judgement myself, but my own actions will no doubt be called into question and rightly so. I do not wish to give Hiemal an opportunity to escape justice because of my failure, but fear the Watch may propose an incorrect punishment. Your gentle and compassionate nature make you the only one to decide what his punishment should be."

Verna was stunned to be chosen for this difficult task.

"Is this betrayal serious enough to mean his removal from Tir Dhuchais?"

"It is, and that is what I want to avoid. If he is removed the Senaten will allocate another Watcher to take his place. This Watcher will have no loyalty to us or to the Months. If he or she informs the Senaten of the Month's existence their destruction may be ordered and all they have endured will be for nothing."

Kalend hesitated before adding.

"If Hiemal tells the Senaten of the Months, all Watchers may be at risk for allowing them to come here."

"What do you want me to do?"

Kalend sighed.

"I do not want you to do anything you do not wish to do. Whatever decision you make I will accept, including his removal. If you do not wish to pronounce judgement, then I will do it. I came to you because you are the only one to have shown kindness or compassion for Hiemal."

"I will decide on the punishment but need time to consider what that will be."

"He would have his revenge"

Kalend returned to the Chamber, habit leading his steps to the Presidion's Seat where he sat, comfortably fitting the chair he had called his own for so long. He did not intend to sit in this chair again after the meeting.

Balack was first to arrive. He had been moved by Kalend's words the night before and for the first time, was confident with his position as Watcher. Smiling at Kalend, he bowed before taking his seat.

When Thades arrived, Kalend took him aside to tell of a change to the meeting's events. He had just retaken his chair when Hiemal strode in, clad in his blue cloak. He stood, waiting to take his place as Presidion.

"I call this extraordinary meeting of this Watch to order. We have many matters to discuss and then I will step down."

"Kalend, you appear to have forgotten that I am Presidion now."

There was anger, arrogance and authority in Hiemal's voice. Kalend kept his voice calm.

Kalend, knowing Hiemal would not be quietened gave his permission to let him speak. Hiemal strode to a position where he could face all the Watchers, his carefully rehearsed words clear in his mind.

"When we learned of the Months, we expressed our strong and legitimate belief they could not be allowed to exist. Against our better judgement we agreed to a Charter with five clear parts. All in this Chamber agreed to these parts - ALL."

Hiemal looked around the Chamber, meeting everyone's eyes.

"One part stated that if a Month broke the contract, Kalend would step down and I would become Presidion. A Month did not return as he should and someone must be held responsible. February may not have signed the contract, but it was Kalend's failure as Watcher of the Months that allowed this to happen. He must step down in my favour."

Hiemal looked around the Chamber and could see anger and disbelief on every face but he didn't care, he would be Presidion. His voice rose as he said, "My claim to be Presidion is valid and I insist it is honoured."

All eyes were fixed on Kalend, a game was being played here, and only Kalend appeared to know the rules. Kalend remained seated, his authority still evident to all.

"Hiemal, we know how you like to have the wording of every agreement correct. It was the wording of the Quest that ensured its failure, so let me read what your Charter said.

a) If the contract was broken by one Month then all Months would be removed from the valley and destroyed immediately.

b) No Month was to be told the consequences of breaking the contract.

c) The Watcher for the Months would be responsible for their removal.

d) As the Watcher responsible for the Months, if such a breach arose Kalend would be stripped of his position as Presidion and Hiemal would be his successor."

Kalend rolled up the document and gazed steadily at Hiemal.

"It is clear my removal would be the direct result of the contract being broken and I would stand down if such a breach occurred. I have obviously failed in my duties and will take full responsibility for my actions. However, it has been made plain that a breaking of the contract by a Month has not occurred, therefore my position remains."

Hiemal was furious his own words were being used against him. As Presidion, he could have dismissed the charge of the black crystal but now that danger was real once again. He saw only hostility from each face around him and knew he could not win nor could he remain standing. He took his seat, anger and hatred exploding in every part of his being.

Kalend let the silence continue for a time then spoke.

"No one is to interrupt until I have finished speaking when any questions will be answered."

A silence filled the Chamber with every Watcher's eyes fixed on Kalend. Not even Verna knew what he was about to say.

"As we all know, on the first day of the month of March we believed a crime had been committed and a series of events began based on that belief. We now know that belief was incorrect. Everything that happened as a result is therefore invalid and must be erased from the records of this Watch. The black crystal caused by Hiemal which would have resulted in a serious disciplinary hearing is erased. No action against Hiemal will be taken in this regard."

Hiemal felt a rush of relief quickly followed by anger that he may be indebted to Kalend. He refocused on what Kalend was saying.

"Any deals or agreements reached as a direct result of the alleged crime are also erased. t'Hura, you will remain Watcher of Earth and Hiemal Watcher of Pluto."

T'Hura felt a stab of fear. Her relief at no longer being responsible for Earth was erased. Hiemal exploded with wrath, again.

"This is insufferable. We entered into an agreement with t'Hura and we see no reason to suspend it."

Kalend faced Hiemal explaining with great patience.

"Earth is now your world if you wish to proceed in this way, but either all events are erased, or none are. If you insist on the agreement with t'Hura being upheld, then you will face a disciplinary hearing for causing a black crystal. This is likely to lead to your expulsion from this Watch and a return to your home world."

Hiemal was trapped. Fearing he could be sent home and from there to the prison world of Hatrion, he glanced around the Chamber, seeing no one would support him. His fury was like an icy core to his being and his voice reflected that.

"Very well, but we want it to be known that we consider the actions of this Watch and its Presidion to be unfair, unjustified and self-serving."

Hiemal was so angry he could not remain in the Chamber, but he would have his revenge. He would report the existence of the Months to the Senaten and hope his reward would be a pardon for all his previous crimes. He went to leave, but Thades barred his way.

Kalend continued.

"There is another matter before this Watch. One crystal ring, given to ensure truth and honour would prevail in this Chamber, has been tampered with. Hiemal will you please remove your ring and give it to me."

Thades was the only one not looking in horror at Hiemal who turned, furious the failure of his ring had been discovered. He hesitated. Stolesc moved towards him.

"If you are having difficulty removing your ring, allow me to assist you."

Hiemal removed his ring, hurling it at Kalend, who very deftly caught it.

He turned the ring over and at first could not see the substance he knew had to be there. A rush of doubt filled him, but a small reflection of light caught his eye. Pulling a thin, clear paper-like substance from the back of the ring, he held it up for the others to see.

"This substance was taken from the Months. It has properties which prevented the crystal from reading Hiemal's emotions, allowing him to speak untruths and display anger and hate without fear of disclosure, until now."

Kalend crossed the Chamber, placing the restored ring in Hiemal's hand.

"Replace your ring and answer these questions."

Hiemal was no longer angry, he was beaten. If he refused, he knew Kalend would inform the Senaten. The misuse of the ring was a crime that would not be tolerated. He could do nothing other than answer truthfully and accept the consequences.

"Have you used this substance to conceal your travel to Earth without permission from its Watcher?"

"Yes."

"When asked to explain your absence from a Watch meeting did you lie?"

"Yes."

"If you had not used this substance would your hate and lies have caused other black crystals?"

Hiemal hesitated, but seeing his ring turn red with his anger answered the question which could seal his fate.

"Yes."

While other Watchers were horrified by Hiemal's deception, Thades was sorrowful. His friend had dishonoured not only himself, but this Watch. Hiemal was desperate to leave the Chamber but first needed to know the answer to one question.

"Will you remove us from this Watch?"

Kalend looked around the assembled Watchers.

"I have decided your punishment will be decided by Verna."

Many were dismayed by Kalend's suggestion. Verna was gentle and kind. The proper punishment should be Hiemal's removal, but Verna was unlikely to do that.

Hiemal knew his past offences on his home world may be pardoned in exchange for the information of the Months, but his crimes here would not. He knelt before Verna.

"You more than any other know we do not deserve your compassion but ask that you would consider some other punishment than our removal from this Watch."

There was just a faint hint of yellow in his ring showing fear and Verna knew she would never be afraid of him again.

Verna asked Hiemal to stand in the centre of the Chamber facing her.

"I have decided that removal from here is not in your best interests. The punishment for your crimes is a change in the status of your world, Pluto. It will be known as a dwarf planet for a period of fifty of its orbits around our Sun. As Watcher of a dwarf planet, you may contribute to debates within this Chamber but only vote on matters relating to your world. After fifty orbits the matter will be reviewed by this Watch. Do you accept this is a fair punishment?"

A deflated Hiemal stood in silence. Kalend prompted a reply.

"Hiemal you must speak for the record. Do you accept?"

"If I do, will my crimes here be removed from the record as other matters have been?"

Kalend was first to recognise Hiemal said I and not we. A

man with nothing left to lose was a dangerous man. He glanced at Verna who moved her hands slightly.

"No record of any crime here will be recorded."

Taking a small grey sphere from his pocket, Kalend held it up for all to see. Tossing it in the air it floated towards Hiemal filling with a soft glow. As Hiemal caught it the bond was made and all desire for the blue planet left him. Unfastening his blue cloak of Uclair, it fell behind him onto the floor. Hiemal left the Chamber and this time no one tried to stop him.

The meeting was expected to end there but Kalend had one more surprise. He walked to stand in the same place Hiemal had stood before.

"February did not commit a crime, but Hiemal was correct when he said I failed in my duty to make sure the contract was signed. This is a serious matter and must be dealt with appropriately. I will no longer be Watcher for the Months and I am stepping down permanently as Presidion of this Watch. I nominate in my place, someone who has shown integrity, compassion, intelligence and fairness in the past times. Thades, will you accept the position?"

Gasps of surprise and shouts that it was not necessary for Kalend to act in this way filled the Chamber, but Kalend called for silence.

"It would be unjust if a price were not paid for all I have made the Months endure and everything this Watch has faced. That price must be paid by me. Thades, will you accept the role of Presidion?"

Thades moved to stand before the Presidion's chair but did not sit.

"I will accept if Kalend reconsiders his position with the Months. No one knows them as he does. Hurts and guilt will need careful handling by someone who cares deeply for them. Will this

Watch show their approval for Kalend to continue in this role?"

Unanimous approval was given and Kalend sighed before replying.

"I will return to The Valley where I will ask the Months if they wish me to continue. If they do, I will accept the role, if not I respectfully ask if someone else is willing to be appointed."

Balack made a move to stand, but Stolesc kicked him under the table and he sat again. As Thades sat down every Watcher stood and bowed in recognition of his appointment.

Returning to his dwelling Hiemal saw it as others did, an ostentatious monstrosity filled with stolen items from the home of his parents. He was no longer an Uclairian or a member of his family. Being careful to remain unseen he took back to his former home what he had stolen, until only his basic needs remained. He began the dismantling of the excessive building leaving an adequate but humble home. Thades and Balack both called to see him, but he removed himself until they left. A surprise visitor was Verna who left him a message and a package. He left both unopened until curiosity overcame him.

When you left the Chamber, it was clear you no longer felt a part of Uclair.

The bonding with Pluto gives you a chance to begin a new chapter in your life.

You may choose to remain as you are or become Hiemal, founder of the House of Pluto.

I leave you a gift, use it or discard it as you will.

Verna

He opened the parcel to find his cloak, no longer blue but a silvery grey that immediately reminded him of Pluto. Putting it on he stood a little straighter as he felt a stirring of pride. Founder of the House of Pluto was something he could aspire to.

"Vem told him he would happily supply something called sausages"

Kalend had been given almost unanimous approval to continue to live in The Valley and asked Thades if he would come to speak to him there on a matter of grave importance. After a tour of The Valley where he was warmly welcomed by all, Kalend took him back to his cabin to tell him about the Quaan.

Thades was horrified. He had never heard of such creatures but Kalend assured him they caused no harm to the Months and had no interest in the Watchers. Thades asked how long he had known about them.

"Do you remember me saying I was preoccupied on my return from the longest Senaten meeting ever and that was why I forgot to get Feb to sign the contract? I saw the Quaan for the first time on my return from that meeting. I was consumed with finding out who they were and what they were doing here."

"That was a very long time ago. How can you be sure these Quaan will not discover us?"

"They know of our existence already. They followed the months into Tir Dhuchais. It was their presence that saved February from falling into the whirlpool. They collect the memories of the Months, keeping them in an archive under the mountains but have no interest in the memories of Watchers. If you feel you must inform the Senaten of the Quaan, the existence of the Months would be revealed and everything they have gone through would be for nothing."

"You are asking me to keep this secret from the Watch, the Months as well as the Senaten. This is a great burden to carry. I will need to consider what I will do. If I agree then at least it is a burden we can share."

Thades went back to his dwelling. Sitting on the table was the clarinet of Gust. He had tried returning it, but Gust insisted it was a gift and gave Thades his first lesson. Picking it up now he placed his fingers as Gust had shown him. He blew softly and a single clear note filled the room. Thades closed his eyes and shivered with pleasure. As he cradled it in his hands he knew he would keep Kalend's secret.

On the thirtieth day of March, Ember asked all the Months to come to a meeting.

"Before we left for Tir Dhuchais I said Feb would have to face the consequences of his actions if we returned. Now is the time to decide what those consequences will be."

Gust was first to speak.

"We would not be here now if Feb hadn't risked his life crossing the cliff by the whirlpool. He made good decisions and has earned his place among us."

Other Quest members agreed Feb should be forgiven for his mistake. Jules stood.

"I do not believe he should be let off so lightly. I agree he was a good leader, but I will not forgive him unless he agrees to my condition."

Feb was relieved by Gust's words but feared what Jules would ask of him.

"Feb, you must swear that you will never again wear lycra shorts in The Valley."

There was much laughter and applause as Feb turned to give

Jules a hug … and his promise.

The night of the party was a cause for much excitement. There was much cooking and baking, a barbecue was planned with of course music and dancing. The meeting hall was festooned with paper lanterns and ribbons.

The Watchers were meeting at the Chamber before travelling to the party together. Eight waited but Hiemal did not appear. Thades used his ring to remind him that he too was invited and his company would be appreciated. Hiemal did not reply. At Ember's request, Rogue was also included in the invitation.

The party was a great success. The food was wonderful. Stolesc was intrigued by the structure called a barbeque. He determined to build his own when he returned to his dwelling, Vem telling him he would happily supply something called sausages.

Rogue was an instant admirer of the dark beer. Stolesc discovered him under a table with a supply of bottles. He removed them and gave him a glass of lemonade instead.

The dancing began and produced much hilarity as both Balack and Neja appeared to have two left feet. Balack however, surprised everyone with his ability as a drummer. Jules joined with Ember to sing a song called 'Danny Boy', their voices blending perfectly together and Stolesc was once again enraptured.

Thades and Kalend stood watching with their backs towards the door to the hall which was open as the night was warm.

Dynak came over to ask them to join her on the dance floor but they both declined. Dynak laughed.

"There will be other times for I hope we can have more such events now there are no more secrets between us."

She returned to the dance floor where Gust was quick to take her hand and show her the steps to take.

Due to the noise of music, laughter and dancing Thades leaned closer to Kalend saying loudly.

"If they discover the secret we are keeping, this merry gathering could be the one and only with both Watchers and Months removed."

Kalend winced at Thades' words, neither of them aware that a figure had come in through the open door just in time to hear their conversation.

A last secret – one that could remove them all. He smiled as visions of the power he would wield filled his mind.

"We will discover this secret. With fifty orbits to fill, Hiemal of Uclair will have his revenge."

The End

Appendix 1

The one thing that separates man from all other creatures on Earth is his desire to control and organize his future. Not content with the seasons to divide the year, the Greeks created time portions based on the phases of the moon, called months, to further divide time to enable them to plan ahead - especially for the planting and harvesting of crops.

First there were ten months, each with thirty or thirty-one days, with the remaining days simply called winter.

When the Romans became the dominant power in the world, they adopted the Greek calendar, but renamed the months after their Gods, or numbers. As Mars was their chief god, the first month of their year was called March with the last four called **Sept**ember, **Oct**ober, **Nov**ember and **Dec**ember after the numbers seven, eight, nine and ten. Later another month was added at the end of the year; named January after their two-headed god Janus, the god of beginnings and endings.

Some 600 years exact number of days to orbit the Sun had been calculated by Nicholas Copernicus. The remaining days were gathered together to make the final month, with twenty-eight days for 3 years and a fourth year with twenty-nine days. This month was called February, so called because of a februar – a leather thong used to beat infertile women through the streets on a feast day during this month.

When Mars fell out of favour, January and February were placed at the start of the year and in 1752 the Julian calendar was replaced by the Gregorian calendar, making the calendar we know today. The word Calendar comes from the Roman word Calends meaning the first day of the month.

This story is based upon the problems caused by the creation of the months – especially the last one …Feb.